THE BILLIONAIRE'S BLISS

Three Romances to steal your heart

LORANA HOOPES

LORANA HOOPES

The BILLIONAIRE'S *Secret*

A CLEAN BILLIONAIRE ROMANCE

DEDICATION

To my family who lets me write the stories in my head.

To all the single parents out there - especially single fathers - You are doing a great job!

NOTE FROM THE AUTHOR

Thank you so much for picking up this book. I hope you enjoy the story and the characters as they are dear to my heart. If you do, please leave a review at your retailer. It really does make a difference because it lets people make an informed decision about books.

Sign up for Lorana Hoopes's newsletter and get her book, The Billionaire's Impromptu Bet, as a welcome gift. Get Started Now!

Maxwell Banks smiled at the buxom blond across from him. Her name had escaped his memory, but she would make a suitable companion for the night. The image of her long blond hair splayed like gold across his pillow filled his mind, sending his pulse into overdrive. Her yoga instructor body was just calling out for his attention if the tight shirt she was sporting was any indication.

Discreetly, he turned his wrist to check his watch. Fifteen minutes since they finished dinner. Surely that was a long enough segment of small talk. "You want to finish this somewhere more comfortable?" He reached across the table to stroke her hand as he said the words. A little flattery went a long way. He had mastered that art in the last few years.

Her tongue darted out and swiped across her lips, and her teeth bit the bottom one, causing the blood to flow to it and tint it a shade darker. "Um, sure, I guess that would be okay."

Her words were hesitant, and Maxwell knew he would have to turn up his charm. He didn't usually have to work hard to get women to come home with him. With his dark hair, blue eyes, broad shoulders, and chiseled chest his looks alone attracted many. The fact that he came from money attracted the rest. Those were the harder ones to get rid of, the ones after his money. They tended to show up uninvited and blow his phone up all hours of the day.

But this one wasn't looking for a sugar daddy. This one he picked up in yoga class. Yoga was not usually his thing; he preferred lifting and running, but his friend Justin had dared him to try the class, and as the instructor was hot, Maxwell had taken the chance.

He could tell when he entered the large room that she found him attractive as her eyes followed him as he crossed the room to grab a mat. His blue cut-off t-shirt had showed off his muscular arms and brought out his eyes, and his playing dumb had kept her by his side most of the class. Asking for her number had been easy after that. He had simply put on his puppy dog face and emphasized the need for private lessons if he was ever going to improve. She had fallen for it; hook, line, and sinker. Now it was time to seal the deal.

"Great." He whipped out his wallet and placed four twenties on the table. It was more than enough money as she only had salad and water–another perk to taking out weight conscious women. Then he stretched out his hand to her.

"Don't you need to wait for the change?" she asked, glancing around for the waiter.

"No, I believe in big tips." He flashed his best smile, hoping it would soothe some of the hesitation in her voice.

She shook her head in disbelief, but accepted his outstretched hand. He gave it a squeeze for good measure and then led her out of the restaurant and back to his black BMW Z4.

"What about my car? Shouldn't I just follow you?" She glanced around for her car in the full parking lot.

"Don't worry about it. I'll bring you back to your car later." Her smile relaxed as he opened the car door for her, and she slid into the grey leather seat.

After shutting her door, Max walked to the driver's side, folded himself into the driver's seat and turned on the engine. As the air had cooled considerably, he pressed the button for the heated seats before pulling out of the restaurant parking lot.

The girl—he really should remember her name—

pulled on her skirt to stretch it back down. It had crept up her leg revealing her smooth, toned thighs underneath.

"Can I turn on some music?"

Max mentally kicked himself. He'd been so distracted with her thighs that he hadn't realized they were driving in silence. Silence was never good. It let them think. "Of course, whatever you'd like."

She punched the buttons on the dial a few times before landing on some newer pop music. Inwardly, he cringed–he was more of a hard rock fan himself, but he knew the payout would be worth it.

Fifteen minutes later, he heard the sharp intake of her breath as he pulled into the driveway of his house. While not a mansion, the 4000-foot ranch home was impressive. The craftsman style boasted three slanted roofs, two chimneys, a grey-brick exterior, and a white wraparound front porch. A small working fountain sat in the middle of the circular drive.

"You live here?" The awe was plain in her voice.

He smiled inside. The deal was almost sealed now. "Yeah, it's a little big for one person, but I hope one day to fill it with a family."

When she turned back to him, he could almost see the stars in her eyes.

He pulled into the three-car garage and parked next to his Harley Davidson. The third bay contained no vehicle. At least not yet. The garage was neat as Max

detested messes, and the few tools he owned meticu-
lously lined the shelves along the wall.

Her heels clicked across the cement floor as he led
her to the door into the house. It opened onto a large
laundry room with a washer, dryer, and table to fold
clothes on. The door from the laundry room led into the
hallway. To the left was the kitchen, dining room, and
family room. To the right were the bedrooms. Max
turned left, leading her to where he had a bottle of wine
waiting on the counter. It was yet another tactic he had
learned would loosen women up and lower their inhi-
bitions.

The large kitchen was half the size of the first floor
of most houses. Stainless steel appliances filled the
room, and a marble topped island in a crème color with
brown and gold flecks sat predominantly in the middle of
the room. A large silver light fixture hung above the
island, and a deep sink took up a portion of the space
under the light. The island hosted a bottle of red wine
and two glasses, and across from the sink four plush
barstools covered in black leather lined the island. The
cabinets that circled the room were a deep brown, and a
large walk-in pantry covered most of the back wall, but it
was the wine Max focused on.

"Drink?" he asked as he uncorked the bottle and
began pouring the glasses.

"Oh, I don't know if I should. I can't stay too long. I

teach an early class tomorrow." The hesitation was creeping back into her voice, and her eyes darted around as if she might bolt. It was time to turn up the charm.

Max pushed his lower lip out in a slight pout. "You wouldn't make me drink alone, would you? Besides, what will one glass hurt?" The glass he extended to her was half full, and he focused his steely blue eyes on her. Many women had told him that his eyes were what drew them in, and Max knew how to use them to his advantage.

Her eyes flickered back and forth, but returned to his gaze, and he knew he had her. "Okay, maybe just one." Her arm rose and accepted the glass.

"To a wonderful night with a beautiful woman," he said, clinking her glass ever so slightly. A blush spread across her face, and she dropped her eyes to the murky red liquid as she took a sip. Max was about to suggest they retire to the living room, where his leather couch would be more inviting and conducive to his seduction, when the doorbell rang.

A glance at his watch revealed it was nearly ten p.m. No one he knew should be ringing his bell, and it was too late for solicitors. "Make yourself comfortable," he said to her, "I'll be right back."

As his shoes echoed on the hardwood flooring, he cursed the timing of whoever stood on the other side of the door. He had worked hard to get this woman here, and she had proven more skittish than many before her. If he lost her because of this interruption, there would be retribution.

Max was fully prepared to lash into the unfortunate soul on the other side of the door, but when he swung it open, his heart stopped, and his words failed him. The anger sizzled as if doused like a campfire, and he blinked not believing his eyes.

"**S**arah?"

Though much paler and thinner than the last time he had seen her, Max was almost certain that the woman before him was the only woman he ever loved, the woman he lost three years ago without a word of explanation. Though he had been promiscuous before, it was her disappearance that had sent him into the philandering tailspin he'd been in for the last three years.

"Hi Max, can we come in?"

We? His eyes dropped lower to take in the small child clutching Sarah's hand in a death grip. She had dark brown hair and large blue eyes. Her daughter? But she didn't have a daughter when he was seeing her so that meant the girl must have come after she left. Not much longer though. Max was a terrible judge of age, but the child couldn't be younger than two.

Though every fiber in his body screamed for him to say no, shut the door, and return to his busty blond—who must be getting bored by now—he found himself opening the door wider. "Of course, come on in." He never could deny Sarah. In fact, though he never told her, he probably would have married her if she hadn't just up and left him.

Sarah and the little girl crossed over the threshold and stood, staring at him. "Can we go somewhere more comfortable so we can talk?" Sarah asked, tilting her head at him.

"Right, of course." He shut the front door and led them into the living room, completely forgetting the blond until she stood as they entered.

Her eyes shifted from him to Sarah and the child and back again. "What is this, Maxwell?"

"Uh, this is my friend Sarah, Sarah this is…"

The blonde's eyes widened as she realized he didn't know her name. "Seriously? You don't remember my name?"

Max cringed and shrugged. He should care; he didn't like getting caught, but Sarah had taken his attention. "Brigitte? Heather? Selena?"

The woman's face flamed red as her hands curled into fists and jammed into her slim hips. "Those aren't even close. It's Margo. I can't believe you." She pulled her purse strap tighter on her shoulder and shoved past Max, pausing to turn at the doorway. "Don't bother walking me out; I can find my own way home." The angry clomp of her heels echoed on the floor as she stomped to the front door.

Sarah turned her hazel eyes on Max. Her left eyebrow arched on her face. "I see some things haven't changed."

"What can I say?" he said, shrugging again. "Women find me irresistible, and there are too many to remember all their names."

Sarah shook her head back and forth. "I'm not sure this was a good idea."

"No, wait." Max's demeanor straightened as he reached out to stay Sarah. "Tell me why you're here."

"Sweetie, why don't you go in the living room and play while I talk to Max?" The little girl responded with wide eyes and a silent head shake. "Go on, you have your tablet. I'll be right in here." Reluctantly, the little girl let go of Sarah's hand and trudged into the living room. A tattered backpack hung from her thin shoulders.

As Sarah sat in one of the barstools, Max noticed the dark circles under her eyes and the hollowness of her cheeks. What had happened to her? He eased himself onto the stool next to her and waited for her to speak.

Sarah's frail shoulders rose with her inhaled breath,

and she forced her eyes to Max's. "I guess there's no easy way to say this, but I'm dying. I have anaplastic carcinoma. There's a cancer hospital in New York that specializes in treatment for my condition, but I'll be too weak to watch Peyton. You know I have no other family, and"—she looked into the living room where the girl was curled on one of the couches playing a tablet before turning her attention back to Max — "Peyton is your daughter, so I'm hoping you'll take her in."

Her words hit him like a truck, shaking any response from his mind. She was dying? He had a daughter? When he could finally wrap his mind around it, the words came out small and quiet. "Why didn't you tell me about Peyton before?"

She tilted her head at him as if she couldn't understand why he would even ask that. "Maxwell, you always told me you weren't one for settling down, and the day I was going to tell you, you told me about your friend Justin being trapped into a relationship with a pregnancy and that he was going to push the woman to have an abortion."

Maxwell's eyes dropped. He remembered the conversation. Justin was as much of a philanderer as he was, maybe even more so. Justin had taught him a few trade secrets, and it was true that the few times he had ended up getting a woman pregnant, he forked over the five hundred dollars for the abortion rather than being sucked into a relationship or fatherhood. But Maxwell wouldn't have pressured Sarah into that, would he have?

"I couldn't take the chance you would do the same, as I wasn't strong enough to fight back because I loved you so much. I probably would have agreed just to keep you, and then I would have hated us both, so I left."

"Does she know?" Max asked, shrugging towards the little girl in the other room. He was still having trouble grasping the gravity of Sarah's words.

When Sarah smirked, he saw a glimpse of her old playful nature. "That I'm dying or that you're her father?" Then her face grew serious. "Yes, she knows both. She isn't excited to be left behind, but she understands I have little choice. It's either you or foster care, and she is more inclined to try you than a total stranger not related to her."

"But, Sarah, I'm no role model for a little girl."

"So I see, but I took that into consideration." She reached into her purse and pulled out a card. "This is my best friend's number. She has known Peyton since she was a baby, and she can help you out if you need anything."

"Then why doesn't she just take her?" Maxwell didn't mean for the words to come out as catty as they did, but the thought of being left alone with the little girl —even if she was his—terrified him.

Sarah's brow furrowed. "Because she is still going to

school and can't afford a full-time nanny. You can. And because you're her father. I've never asked you for anything, but I'm asking you now." She reached across and clasped Maxwell's hand. "Be a dad. For once in your life, stop thinking about yourself or your next easy woman and think of someone else for a change. Peyton needs you. I need you."

The words cut him to the quick. Her directness and unwillingness to put up with his crap were two things he loved about Sarah. "You should have told me about her sooner," he said and found that he meant it.

"You're right. I should have. We both made some mistakes, but none of those mistakes are Peyton's fault. She's a good girl, Max. She's a lot like you when you aren't trying to be suave and debonair."

"I thought you liked my suavity and debonairness," he said with a crooked, sexy smile.

"No, I hated those two traits. I liked you for the man you are when you take off the masks, and one day, if you can keep those masks off, you'll find another woman who will feel just as I did."

Her words sobered him and wiped the smile off his face. "Do you have a chance?"

A small, sad smile played across her lips. "There is always a chance, but it doesn't look good. The cancer spreads quickly, and we may not have caught it in time.

I'm going to give the doctor's a chance, but at this point, I think it would take a miracle from God."

God? She hadn't been religious in the past, and he wondered if her cancer had made her seek solace in fairy tales.

"Here," she reached into her bag, pulled out a notebook, and handed it over to him. "I've written down Peyton's schedule, her bedtime routine, her fears, and what calms her down. I hope it's all you'll need, but again Alyssa can help. She's expecting your call whenever you might need to make it."

As she pushed herself up from the barstool, his heart tightened. "Wait, you're going now?"

"I have to; I have a plane to catch. I have a few more bags for her in the car. I'll set them on the front step before I leave." Sarah looked past Max and called, "Peyton, come here please."

The little girl appeared by her mother's side, so quiet it was almost stealthy. Sarah knelt until she was face to face with the girl. "Peyton, Max is going to take care of you, but he might need some help. Be patient with him and help him out."

Peyton's big blue eyes filled with tears, and she wrapped her arms around Sarah's neck. "I don't want you to go, Mommy."

"I know, Baby, and I don't want to go, but it's Mommy's last chance to get better."

As the two hugged, Max felt a stirring in his soul that he'd never felt before, but too soon, Sarah was standing again, and the little girl was crying big hitching sobs as tears streamed down her cheeks.

"I love you, Peyton," Sarah said, and then she was gone, and Max was left staring at the small girl. What was he going to do now?

❧ 3 ❧

As the sunlight streamed in the bedroom window, Max opened his eyes, hoping the previous night had been a bad dream, but as he rolled to his left side, he saw the little girl curled up with her pink bear clutched tightly in her arms. Her long lashes fanned out on her cheeks, and she looked peaceful as her little chest rose and fell, but he knew that wouldn't last long.

Last night after Sarah left, the little girl had been almost inconsolable. She had cried for an hour straight while Max awkwardly hugged her and tried to offer her books or movies–he had no toys, and she hadn't brought many with her. He had finally decided to lay her down, but she hadn't wanted to stay in his guest room either, so he had nestled her in his own bed and laid with her until she had fallen asleep.

As quietly as possible, Max edged out of bed and headed into the kitchen for coffee. It had been a long night, and he had the feeling today would be a long day too. As he passed the front door, he remembered Sarah saying something about putting more bags on the front porch. He had forgotten all about them last night, but thankfully they were still there when he opened the door. After bringing them inside and locking the door once again, he continued his trek to the kitchen. His cell phone rang just as the coffee started percolating.

"Hey, man, we still on for tonight?" Justin's voice carried through the phone.

Max sighed. He had forgotten all about their plans for the evening. "I don't know. Something happened last night, and I have to take care of some stuff."

"Stuff? What are you talking about? This party is going to be epic."

Max grabbed a mug from the cabinet and filled it with coffee. "Sarah showed up last night."

"Sarah? The girl from four years ago? What did she want?"

"She wanted to introduce me to my daughter."

Justin let out a long, low whistle. "Daughter? Are you sure? Did you ask for a paternity test? I know you liked her, but she could just be trying to trap you, man, get some money, you know?"

Max hadn't considered asking for a paternity test, partly because it was Sarah, and he couldn't believe she would come back for money, but also because the girl looked like him. She had his nose and his blue eyes. He had no doubt she was his.

"It's not like that. She's dying, and she needs to get treatment, so she left Peyton with me until she either gets better or..." He trailed off. If Sarah didn't get better, that would mean Peyton would be his responsibility forever. What had he agreed to?

"That's heavy, man, what are you going to do?"

Max took a sip of the hot coffee and shook his head though he knew Justin couldn't see the motion. "She left me the number of her friend. I'm going to call her today and see if she can take care of this."

"Maybe her friend will be hot, and it will be worth it."

Max rolled his eyes. Justin should know better than to mix business with pleasure. "Yeah, maybe. I'll let you know." Max hung up the phone before Justin could add more. He took another sip of his coffee and almost dropped the mug when he saw Peyton. Again, he had not heard a sound.

"Hi, Peyton, you hungry?" he asked, pasting on what he hoped was a smile. "I think I have cereal or we could go get breakfast." What did three-year-olds even eat?

"I want my mommy."

"I know you do," he said, kneeling to her level as Sarah had last night, "but Mommy had to go away for a while."

"I want her back." She stepped to him and threw her arms around his neck. Last night, she had barely let him touch her, so the force of her hug threw him off guard and off balance.

She smelled sweet and innocent. It was such a different smell from what he was used to that he wasn't sure he could explain it if he had to. Without thinking, his arms wrapped around her, and his hands began to pat the soft brown curls of her hair. It was an awkward and unfamiliar gesture. He didn't even like to console the women he dated, and he could feel his shoulder getting wet from her tears.

"Peyton, I know you miss her, and I am a lousy replacement, but I'm going to need your help, so can you try to be a big girl and stop crying?" His words did not have the desired effect as a loud screeching noise began to accompany the sobs.

Crap. What do I do now? He remembered the card with Sarah's friend's name on it and untangled himself from the child to search for it. The counter. Sarah had laid it on the counter. Thankfully, he was a neat freak and his counter was clutter free. The white card called like an SOS beacon from the same spot Sarah placed it last night.

Scooping it up, he perused the information. Alyssa 434-555-1347. The screeching had gotten louder and shriller from Peyton, and he nearly dropped his phone in his haste to extricate it from his pocket the first time.

Please be home. Please be home. The mantra ran through his head as he input the digits. Though it felt wrong to leave Peyton alone, he headed down the hall and away from the kitchen, so when Alyssa hopefully picked up, he would be able to hear her.

"Hello?" The voice was soft and feminine—music to his ears—but not for the usual reasons.

"Is this Alyssa?" His own voice sounded strange in his ears—desperate and high pitched.

"It is, to whom am I speaking?"

The properness in her return gave him pause, and he blinked trying to re-form the words he had seconds ago. "My name is Maxwell. Sarah gave me your number and said you could help with Peyton. She's crying—well, screaming is more like it—and I can't make her stop. Is there a trick? Can you help?"

A small chuckle met his ears. "There is no magic pill you can give her. She's lost her mom. You have to learn how to console her. Hug her and let her know you are there for you."

"I tried that," he said, the desperation now clawing at his throat. "It only made her cry louder."

"You have to give it time," she said, "but give me your address, and I'll swing by. It sounds like you are out of your element here, and I'd like to make sure Peyton is taken care of."

4

Alyssa hung up the phone and grabbed her keys. Sarah had told her to expect a call from Maxwell, and while she hadn't expected it so soon, she was curious to see what this man was like. The stories she had heard from Sarah had her intrigued to say the least.

Half an hour later, she pulled up in the grand driveway, and her eyes widened. Sarah had said he was wealthy, but the appearance of this house made *wealthy* an understatement. Alyssa was sure she was going to feel underdressed in her jeans and "I love Paris" t-shirt.

Not bothering to lock her car door—she had nothing worth stealing compared to this house—she dropped her keys in her purse and approached the massive front door, which was actually two large wooden doors with an ornate gold trim. She pressed the bell, curious as to what the inside would hold.

Alyssa was surprised when, a moment later, the doors opened and Max himself stood on the other side. At least she assumed it was Max. He wore no uniform, just a pair of cargo shorts and a t-shirt. His dark hair was tousled as if he had just woken up, but it was his piercing blue eyes that convinced her. Sarah had spoken of these blue eyes often, but even her description held no candle to the effect they had in person.

"Maxwell?" Alyssa asked, tilting her head and holding out her hand.

"You must be Alyssa," he said, shaking her hand. It was strong, but not rough. He must not work with them much. Sarah had never mentioned his job, but looking at Maxwell, Alyssa could see why. His physical appearance dominated her brain.

"Yes, sorry, I was just expecting someone else to answer the door. The house is so large; you must have some help." Her eyes scanned the foyer behind him. It was clean and minimalist, decorated in browns and creams.

"I don't keep full-time help," he said, dropping her hand. "I like my privacy."

Though Alyssa nodded, she couldn't imagine one wouldn't still have privacy in a place this big even with full-time help. "Where is Peyton? May I see her?"

Maxwell stepped back, scooting boxes aside with his foot, and motioned her inside. "She's in the living room. It took forever to get her calmed down enough to eat, but a frozen waffle and some cartoons seemed to have helped."

Maxwell led the way through the ornate foyer and down a hall into the living room. Alyssa tried to keep up, but her attention was drawn to the left and the right as they meandered through the house. She wasn't sure if his artwork was genuine, but the sheer amount of famous paintings hanging on his walls was enough to awe her.

A large television screen hung on the living room wall, displayed an episode of Sophia the First. Peyton was curled into one corner, her bear snuggled tightly to her chest. She looked smaller than her three years on the large leather couch.

"Hey, Peyton, how are you?" Alyssa asked, as she sat down beside her.

Peyton turned big blue eyes up at her. They weren't quite the same blue as Maxwell's, but it was clear the gene came from him. "Hi, Aunt Lyssa. I miss my mom."

"I know, sweetie, but your mom is going to get treatment to see if she can get better. Has Maxwell been taking care of you?" Alyssa could feel Maxwell staring at her back, but she kept her eyes focused on Peyton, who shrugged.

"I guess. He didn't want to read to me last night, or pray, or sing, though."

"I don't sing," Max chimed in.

Alyssa shot him a silencing look. "Well, Peyton, Max isn't used to having a little girl in the house, and he doesn't know the routines, but I bet you could help him."

"Okay, I'll try."

As her attention turned back to the screen, Alyssa rose from the couch and motioned Max to follow her to the kitchen where they could speak privately.

"You have to try to follow her routine," she said as she placed her hands on her hips. "She just lost all stability in the world. Those routines are the only thing grounding her."

Max crossed his arms, and Alyssa's eyes were drawn to the well-toned appendages. "Maybe you should take her. I don't know how to be what she needs."

"I would if I could, but I have to finish school. Besides, you're her father. If Sarah doesn't get better, you'll be her custodian legally. Show me her room."

"Her room?" Max blinked at her as if her words were not computing in his brain.

"Yes, her room. Where she will be sleeping."

"She just got here last night, and she didn't want to stay by herself, so she ended up in my room."

"She can't stay in your room. She needs a proper

room. Show me your guest rooms then, and we'll work on fixing one up for her, so she feels comfortable."

"What do you mean fixing one up?" There was a hint of panic in his voice, which Alyssa couldn't decide if she found annoying or charming.

"I mean paint, a kid's bed, toys." As his eyes widened in alarm, she pointed her finger at him. "Unless you want to be sharing your bed with a three-year-old for the foreseeable future."

Max took a step back and shook his head. "Fine, you can decorate a room. Follow me."

He led the way back down the hallway toward the foyer.

"What are these boxes? Are they Peyton's?" she asked as he passed them again as if they weren't there.

He shrugged. "Yeah, Sarah left them last night."

"Why haven't you opened them?"

"To be honest, I forgot about them until this morning."

"Well, you should un-forget, and when we get her room figured out, we should unpack them for her. That would help. She needs familiar things to help her get through this."

Max rolled his eyes but nodded. "Fine, we'll unpack them later. Do you want to see the rooms or not?"

Alyssa swallowed her agitation and motioned for him to continue showing the way. They crossed through the foyer and down another hallway. Three doors lined the hallway on the left and right plus a door sat at the end.

Grasping the handle, Max swung the first door on the right open. A spacious bedroom lay on the other side with a queen bed and a large dresser. Nothing else was in the room, not even a book or a lamp.

"Don't use this one much, huh?" Alyssa asked, surprised by the sterility of the room.

"Don't use any of them much. It's just me, remember?" He opened the next room which was very similar to the first. The third door was the first-floor bathroom.

"Well, I can see why she didn't want to stay in either of those rooms. They are impersonal at best and probably scary to a small child. We need to go get some paint, a smaller bed, and toys. Are you free now? I have some time."

"Yeah, I guess," he said shrugging. He closed the doors, and they returned to the living room to grab Peyton.

As they entered the garage, Alyssa looked around. Her brow furrowed as she turned to Max. "Where is your car?"

"What do you mean? It's right there," he said pointing to the BMW.

"You can't take Peyton in that. There's no backseat. Where would you even put a car seat in there?"

He blinked at her. "A what?"

Alyssa rolled her eyes. Had this guy been living under a rock? "A car seat. Kids have to use them until they are old enough or tall enough to sit in a booster seat, which also wouldn't fit in your car. Children can't sit up front because of the airbags. Your car is a deathtrap."

Max's face turned to stone and his arms crossed. "My car is a work of art. It goes zero to sixty in less than six seconds."

A short burst of irritated breath flew out of Alyssa's mouth. "A three-year-old doesn't care how fast your car goes. She cares about being safe in your car. Never mind," she said, shaking her head, "we'll take mine."

"You have a car seat in yours?" The comment was snide and meant to get under her skin, but Alyssa chose to ignore it and closed her eyes for a moment before answering.

"No, I don't have a car seat in my car, but at least it has a back seat. Didn't Sarah leave Peyton's car seat?"

"Not unless it's in one of those boxes by the front door," he said.

"No, it would be bigger than those boxes. She must have forgotten. Well, we can strap Peyton in my back-seat, and I will drive very carefully to a store where we can get a car seat for her." Alyssa looked down at Peyton who had been quiet during the exchange. Her eyes turned expectantly to Max as if she had been following them like an unseen tennis match.

"Fine, we'll take your car, but I'm not getting rid of my BMW." He hit the garage door button, and the bay began to lift, allowing them access to her car in the driveway.

"With your money, you could just buy another car," Alyssa said under her breath as she grabbed Peyton's hand and followed him. She couldn't believe the nerve of this man nor could she understand how Sarah was ever attracted to him. Sure, he was good looking, with his dark hair and tempting blue eyes, and he obviously took care of his body as his shorts hugged his frame just right and his arms displayed the lines of finely toned muscles, but he was just as self-absorbed as he was handsome, and that was a trait she could not stand.

Max stopped short at the sight of her blue Ford Escort. "You want me to ride in that?" he asked as his head dropped forward in disbelief.

Alyssa pulled her shoulders back. Her car might not be a convertible sports car like his, but it was reliable and hers. Through dedication, she had managed to pay it off while going to school. "There's nothing wrong with *that*," she said pointedly. "My car is safe and reliable."

"And boring," he said in a sing-song lilt.

Letting the comment go, Alyssa opened the back door for Peyton and strapped her in. "I promise I'll drive safely, Peyton."

Still grumbling under his breath, Max climbed into

the passenger seat, and after strapping herself in the driver's seat, Alyssa started the car and pointed it in the direction of the nearest Wal-Mart.

"I cannot shop here," Maxwell said as she pulled into the discount store parking lot.

Exasperated, she rolled her eyes at him. "You can, and you will. They have everything we need here, and I don't know where the nearest hoity-toity store is that would have what we need."

The look on his face led her to believe that no one had ever talked to him that way, and it gave her a small amount of masochistic pleasure to see him put in his place.

After rescuing Peyton from the back of the car, she placed her in the front section of the shopping cart and fastened the strap.

"Is that really necessary?" he said over her shoulder, pointing to the strap.

"Every time." She said the words, slow and pointedly, hoping they would sink in his thick skull. "I've heard stories of kids standing up and falling out of the carts while their parents' backs were turned. If you keep them buckled that never happens."

Max shrugged. "If you watch them close enough, it also never happens."

"Yeah, and I'm sure that would be your specialty if she were twenty-three instead of three."

His eyes narrowed into a glare at her, but he said nothing as they made their way into the store.

Alyssa walked the store as if she owned it, steering the cart directly to the baby aisle where she began perusing the options of car seats. Max stared at the variety as if the sheer amount of options had never occurred to him. "That one," she said pointing to a red and grey Graco convertible seat.

"Why that one?"

"Because she can use it up to one hundred pounds, which means it should last you a few years."

"Years? How long do kids have to ride in car seats?" He hefted the box and slid it onto the bottom of the cart.

"Until they're old enough or weigh enough not to. You should look up the rules now that you'll have her full time." Her lips pursed as she tapped a finger to the side of her mouth. "Next, baby monitor."

Max's forehead furrowed. "Baby monitor? What for? She's three."

"And if you lived in a normal house where you could hear her, I'd say maybe you're right, but you live in the flipping Taj Mahal, which means you wouldn't hear her cry out if you were on the other end of the house, so you need a monitor."

"Fine. Lead the way." The words were tight and forced through clenched teeth. His jugular bulged out on the right side and put another little smile on Alyssa's face.

After the monitor, they picked out a bed. Even though it was broken down and in a box, there was no room in her car to carry the bed, so they arranged to have it delivered. Then she wheeled him through the clothes, picking up a few more things for Peyton. She knew Sarah hadn't packed all her clothes; she also knew Sarah hadn't had much money for clothes recently.

The toy aisle was next, and while she didn't want to overwhelm Peyton, the girl deserved a few toys, puzzles, and of course bubbles. Every time Alyssa visited, Peyton wanted to drag her outside and blow bubbles. The last stop was the hardware section for some paint and brushes.

By the time they wheeled up to the checkout line, the cart was overflowing. Alyssa almost felt bad for the amount of money Max was about to spend, but then she remembered his house and how he treated Sarah, and she decided he could afford it.

5

As they pulled up to his house, Max glanced over at Alyssa. As much as she annoyed him, he had to admit she had been helpful as well. Not only had she helped him figure out which car seat to buy, but she had also picked out the bed, some clothes, and a cart full of toys. He was not much of a shopper himself, unless it was for cars, but she seemed to have been right in her element. Had she helped Sarah do all of this when Sarah first found out she was pregnant?

If he was honest, it also intrigued him that she stood up to him. He couldn't remember the last time a woman had since Sarah, and he found it interesting. Not that he would ever consider dating her; she was far too uptight, though she was gorgeous with her long dark hair and her bright green eyes, but she would be too much work. Still, he had learned a lot watching her with Peyton today.

"Peyton and I will take the clothes and toys in and unpack her room," Alyssa said, forcing his attention back to the present. "Why don't you try to fit her car seat in your BMW?" A sly smile played across her face as she said it, like she knew it wouldn't fit, but Max was determined to prove her wrong.

"Fine," he said. After fumbling with the strap but finally unhooking Peyton from the contraption, he placed her down on the ground and reached in for the handles he knew Alyssa clipped to something. Though he could feel the bulky plastic, he couldn't seem to get it unfastened.

"Here," Alyssa said, leaning in from the other side of the car. She placed her hand on his and guided it to the release button. Though he heard the click, his focus was on her hand, which still laid across his own. It was smooth and pale, like fine porcelain, and was causing a warmth to spread across his hand.

His eyes found hers, and there was a spark, a connection that wasn't there before. She pulled her hand back as if the warmth he felt were a fire to her, and the moment was broken. Shaking his head, he unhooked the other side of the car seat and finagled it out of the car.

Alyssa stood, several bags hanging from her arms. She glanced at Max before heading into the open garage, Peyton trailing behind her. Max watched her go, wondering what that connection had been. He couldn't be developing feelings for her. It would be too complicated.

When Alyssa and Peyton were safely inside the house, he carried the car seat to his car. As he opened the passenger door, he could see Alyssa was right. Not only did the car seat not fit, but there were no hook things like there were in her car for the seat to attach to. He hated the fact that she was right and even more the fact that he would have to buy a new car. He hadn't been planning to purchase a new vehicle, least of all, a family car. He'd have to see if he could get Alyssa to watch Peyton as he couldn't very well take her with him in his car. The good news was that he could hit the party while he was out, and Alyssa could stay and watch Peyton.

After placing the car seat against the wall of the garage, he headed inside to find Alyssa. He realized she was right about the monitor too as he stepped inside the quiet house and turned toward the bedrooms. If he hadn't known they were there, he would never have guessed it from the lack of noise.

He found them in the first guest bedroom. Alyssa had unpacked Peyton's small backpack and the boxes that had been sitting by the front door and was folding the clothes, placing them in the dresser while Peyton played with her bear and a new doll on the floor.

"Can you watch Peyton for a little longer?"

"Why? What's the problem?" Though she posed them as questions, he could hear the teasing inflection in her voice.

Biting his lip to keep from smiling, he crossed his arms and leaned back. "You know very well what the problem is. The car seat won't fit, and I need to go get a different car. Can you watch her while I do that? I can pay you."

"Oh, I know you can, but there's no need for that. Knowing I was right is payment enough." She smiled sweetly at him. "Though if you wanted to bring back some pizza for dinner, I wouldn't argue with that."

"Yeah, pizza," Peyton said, offering him a genuine smile.

"I don't know how long it will take, but I'll leave money for pizza on the bar."

After placing forty dollars on the counter, he climbed into his BMW and checked his watch. If he was quick at the dealership, he should still be able to hit the party before all the good women were hooked up.

The dealership was just about to close as he pulled in. Salesmen were locking the cars and driving them back to the display spaces.

"Hey," he called to one of the overweight salesmen as he parked his BMW. "Who's in charge? I need a car, and I have money to spend."

The man's tired demeanor disappeared at the word

"money," and his eyes lit up. He even tried to smooth the wrinkles out of his Hawaiian shirt to make his appearance more presentable. "Roger is in charge, but I'll be happy to help you out."

"Good. I need a sedan. I don't even really care which one as long as it's safe, and it has those hooks to fasten a car seat in."

The large man smiled widely. "Oh, a new dad, huh?"

"Yeah, something like that." Maxwell wished the man would just take him to the cars. He was in no mood for small talk and he wanted to get this done so he could get to the party.

"Okay, well our best family car is the Chevy Malibu. It comes with the Rear Seat Reminder system, so you never leave a child in the back seat accidentally. Plus, it has Apple Play for when they get older."

"That sounds perfect," Max said, though he had no idea what either of those actually were.

"Don't you want to see it first? Drive it?" the salesman asked, as he blinked at Max.

"You said it's your best family car, right?"

"Yes, but everyone has their own opinions," the man stated.

"I trust yours. Get me a blue or a black one and let's wrap this deal up."

The salesman's eyes narrowed as if he was trying to decide if Max was pulling his leg. "Alright," he said, obviously deciding Max was the real deal, "let's go meet Roger to start the paperwork, and I'll get you the best one on the lot."

Max followed the salesman into the office. Most of the other men were packing up, but one man sat at a large desk near the back. Though plump in the middle, Max could tell from his arms that he still worked out.

"Roger, this is… I'm sorry I didn't catch your name."

"Max, Maxwell Banks."

"Maxwell Banks of Banks Inc.?" the salesman asked, his eyes wide.

Max bristled. Ever since his parents tried to force their newly acquired religion on him a few years ago, he hadn't been on speaking terms with them. "Yes, that's me, well, my father, I guess, but it's my family."

"We're so glad you stopped in Mr. Banks," Roger said, rising from his desk. "I'm sure Paul here helped you out, but what can I do for you tonight?"

"Paul suggested a Chevy Malibu, so he brought me in to start the paperwork while he gets me the best one on the lot."

"Of course," Roger said, sitting back down and motioning to a chair across from him. "Please have a seat, and we'll get you taken care of."

"Thanks, Paul," Max said to the salesman as he hurried out of the office and back to the lot. "I'll need this delivered tomorrow to my house. That won't be a problem, right?"

"Not for you, Mr. Banks," Roger said. Max could see the dollar signs flashing in the man's mind.

Less than an hour later, Max had signed the paperwork and left his address and an extra five hundred dollars to have it delivered the next day. Now to hit the party.

The party was already well underway when Max stepped inside. He scanned the crowd, finding Justin snuggled up with a blond in the far-right corner. As he made his way that direction, he garnered the attention of a pretty redhead. A quick glance revealed a stunning body, and he hooked an arm around her waist, propelling her with him towards Justin.

"Hey man, I didn't think you were going to make it." Justin untangled himself enough to shake Max's hand.

"Yeah, me either, but an opportunity presented itself. Never look a gift horse in the mouth, am I right?"

"Well, pull up a chair and we'll get more drinks." Justin pointed to the open chair across the table.

Max looked around for a second chair, but the place was packed. Deciding they could share the chair, he sat down and pulled the red-head onto his lap. She took no time in leaning forward and claiming his lips.

"My name is Liza," she whispered seductively in his ear, after tracing her lips across his cheek.

"Pretty." He made no attempt to remember her name. He wouldn't be seeing her after tonight, but for now he enjoyed the feel of her against him.

"So, how's the friend?" Justin asked, when Liza let Max come up for air.

"A handful, but serving a purpose." Max winked at Justin, hoping he would get the meaning.

Justin smiled and nodded.

"Let's take this back to your place," Liza whispered in Max's ear.

"I can't," he said, running his hand through her hair. "My place is being renovated. How about your place?"

She shook her head. "Roommates."

"Hotel?" He didn't normally shell out extra money, but extenuating circumstances called for extraordinary measures.

Liza stood and held out her hand. It was all the invitation Max needed.

"See you next week." Max flicked a mock salute at Justin and then led Liza to his car.

"Where have you been?" The anger in Alyssa's voice was unmistakable, though it was punctuated by her crossed arms and narrowed eyes.

"Getting a new car, remember?" Max hung his keys on the hook and turned to face her.

"Uh huh, do all new cars come with lipstick?" Her eyes flashed with each word.

Lipstick? He knew he wiped his mouth, but his hand touched his lips just to be sure.

"Not there," she said, advancing on him. "There." She ran her finger across his neck and held it up. A slight red smudge was smeared across it.

Dang it. He forgot to check his neck.

"I can't believe you would go out on a date with your daughter here all alone."

"She wasn't alone. She had you."

"You barely know me." She threw her hands up in exasperation. "What if I were some serial killer or baby snatcher?"

Max shrugged. "Sarah trusted you, and she is an excellent judge of character."

"Evidently not, since she hooked up with you." Alyssa's eyes widened, and her hand clapped over her mouth. "I'm sorry, Max, I didn't mean it."

"No, you did, but it's okay. You're right." He shook his head and plopped down onto a barstool. "I don't know how to be a dad. I only know the single life. You should take Peyton before I make some colossal mistake and screw her up forever. I can pay for a nanny for her."

"Max, we've been through this. I can't take Peyton right now, and like it or not, you are her father, so you have to learn to take some responsibility. Look, I'll help out all I can, but you can't treat me like your babysitter and dump her on me while you go fulfill your"–her nose turned up in disgust as she uttered the last word–"urges."

"Fair enough," Max agreed. "I won't do it to you again."

She eyed him as if debating with herself if he would keep his promise. "Fine. I'll be over to pick up Peyton in the morning for church. Try to have her ready by 10:15."

"Church? I don't go to church."

"But Peyton does. Routines remember? And you don't have to come. You can stay here and do"–she waved her hand in the air–"whatever you do all day. When I get back, I'll teach you how to put Peyton down for a nap and we'll talk about the nanny situation."

"You mean I can't just take her with me?" He meant it as a joke to lighten the mood, but Alyssa merely crossed her arms again and raised an eyebrow at him. "Okay, okay. I'll call a nanny service tomorrow."

"You can't just get any nanny though. You have to get someone who will jibe with Peyton." She sighed. "Look, I don't have a final on Monday. Call and set up interviews for Monday, and I'll help you screen them. You can take a day off work, can't you?"

"I guess I'll have to. You know you're pretty cute when you're all riled up." He smirked at her, knowing the words would ruffle her feathers.

Sure enough, she stiffened and glared at him. "Don't even think about it. Some other woman's lipstick is still fresh on your neck, remember? Peyton's in bed. I'll show you how to do that tomorrow too, but for now I'm going to go study."

She whirled around and marched off, her shoulders pulled back and her head held high.

Max smiled at her retreating figure. It might take some time, but he was pretty sure he could win her over one day.

6

Alyssa made her exit before he could say another word. She didn't want to chance him seeing the effect he had on her.

When she was safely in her car, she laid her head on the steering wheel. What was this feeling? Was this jealousy? She couldn't develop feelings for this man. Forget the part that he was her best friend's ex-lover, but he was also a complete player.

She had thought maybe Sarah had been exaggerating about his less than desirable qualities when she had met the man this morning. Though obviously clueless, he had seemed willing to do what it took to make sure his daughter was taken care of. It was almost… sweet. But then he had left her to go make out with some unknown woman. Worse yet, she was jealous. Jealous! She should not be feeling jealousy. She should not be feeling anything for this man. He was a walking danger sign, neon lights and all.

Get ahold of yourself, Lyssa, you can't fall for this guy. The mantra played over and over in her head, but it couldn't seem to push the image of his arresting blue eyes out of her mind.

She was still trying to convince herself when she entered the apartment fifteen minutes later.

"How did it go?" Roxy asked. Roxy had been her roommate for the last few years and while the girls didn't see eye to eye on religion, they had enough other things in common that they became friends.

"Oh, um, fine, I guess."

"You guess, huh?" Roxy crooked an eyebrow and scrutinized Alyssa's face. "Let me guess, the man is handsome."

"What? Why would you say that?" Even as she protested, Alyssa could feel the heat burgeoning on her face.

"Your reaction for one. Plus, you came in all moony. I haven't seen you look like that in a long time."

There was truth to that. After a few bad relationships, Alyssa had pretty much sworn off men and focused completely on school. She couldn't even remember the last time she found a man attractive, until now. "Yeah," she sighed, "He's handsome, but he's also irritating and completely wrong for me."

"Sounds like you have it all figured out then," Roxy teased, as she turned her attention back to the television.

Alyssa had nothing figured out, but saying the words out loud had convinced her, at least a little. She headed to her room to spend some time in prayer and give the issue to God.

The next morning, she found herself waffling over what to wear for the first time in ages. It wasn't that she didn't normally take pride in her appearance, but today Maxwell would be seeing her, and she felt the need to dress even nicer.

Finally deciding on a hunter green shirt with a lace detail on the back and a black skirt, she dressed quickly. The green in the shirt brought out her eyes, causing the tiny gold flecks in them to sparkle. After a small dab of lip gloss for a little sheen, she headed out the door, Bible in hand.

Her heart began ramping up its acceleration as she pulled into Max's driveway, and her hands suddenly felt slicker than usual. What was going on with her? Why was she letting him affect her this way? She took several deep breaths on her way to the front door to try and calm her speeding heartbeat.

The door swung open just a minute after the doorbell chime had ended and Max stood on the other side in a pair of sweats and a white t-shirt that stretched across his well-formed chest.

"Good morning, you look beautiful," he said, swinging the door wider for her to enter.

She would take that as a compliment, but with his track record, he probably said that to every woman, even if they showed up in sweats. Still the look in his eyes sent a heat searing across her face as she stepped inside. "Thank you. You do as well."

His eyebrow raised at her as he glanced down at his casual dress, and her face flamed.

"I mean thank you." The smile on his face annoyed her. He was taking too much enjoyment in her discomfort. "Is Peyton ready?"

"Yes, she's in the kitchen finishing breakfast."

As Max led the way, Alyssa forced herself to focus on anything other than his physique. She didn't like him knowing he affected her.

Peyton sat at the table dressed in a pretty pink summery dress, but her hair was a mess. Tangles caused it to bunch together on one side, and on the other side, strands stuck out willy-nilly.

"Did you comb her hair at all?" Alyssa asked as she took in the disheveled appearance.

Max shrugged. "I wasn't sure how, and she didn't seem to want me to…" he trailed off.

"You can't let her make the rules. She's three. Come on Peyton." Grabbing the tiny hand, Alyssa propelled her down the hallway and to the bathroom. Once there, she grabbed the brush off the counter and slowly brought it through Peyton's thick hair.

"Ouch." Peyton's hand covered her head in an attempt to thwart Alyssa.

"Hold still. You can't go out looking like a ragamuffin. Your mother would beat me if I let you do that."

The mention of her mother calmed her down, and Peyton dropped her hands. Alyssa smiled up at Maxwell as she continued brushing. "See? That is how you win."

"I have a lot to learn," he said, shaking his head.

Max smiled as he watched Alyssa finish cleaning Peyton up. She was cute when aggravated and even cuter when embarrassed. What was he thinking? He couldn't think about her like that. For one thing, she was a total Bible thumper, which would never work with his lifestyle, but he also needed her to help with Peyton, which meant he needed her to stay around, and he never let women stay more than one night. They got too clingy.

"Okay, I think we're ready," she said as she exited the bathroom.

Max smelled something sweet as she passed, some perfume that flooded his senses and sent his heart thumping. "Have fun." He meant it as a joke as he couldn't imagine church being fun, but she turned and smiled at him.

"We will."

Then they were gone, and the house was quiet. Max headed to the bathroom to take a shower before curling up on the couch to watch some sports. Football was over for the year, but he found a baseball game and settled back.

It didn't hold his interest though and after flipping the channels for a few minutes, he turned off the TV and wandered into the kitchen. He wasn't really hungry, but he made himself a couple of eggs, toast, and coffee to kill some time.

When the food was gone, he washed the plate and checked his watch. 11:15. He had no idea how long church services lasted. How weird that the house felt different without Peyton in it now. Normally, he would relish the solace of a quiet Sunday morning. Of course, he would usually be finishing a late breakfast with a date and then kissing her goodbye at the door right about now.

He moseyed down the hallway to Peyton's room and pushed open the door. Her few toys were scattered around, and he picked them up, placing them in the toy bin they had purchased. As he surveyed the room, he remembered the paint they had picked up. He could paint the walls while they're at church and have a surprise for Peyton when she returned. Plus, it would show Alyssa that he was trying.

After muscling the furniture to the center of the room, he grabbed the paint and rollers from the garage and headed back to the room.

The pink Alyssa picked wasn't too bright, and though he never thought he'd be painting his walls pink, he found he didn't mind it too much.

The doorbell rang before the job was finished. Placing the brush on the open can, he headed to the front door, checking his watch as he walked. 12:30, good to know.

"We're back," Alyssa said as he opened the door. "I see you've been busy."

"What?" He looked down and noticed paint splotches on his shirt. Good thing it wasn't one of his favorites. "Oh yeah, I thought I'd make myself useful while you guys were out. I didn't quite finish though."

"Hi, Max," Peyton said as she entered the house. "We went to church."

"Yeah, I know. Did you have fun?"

"Uh-huh."

"Did you manage to get any on the walls?" Alyssa's laugh was sweet, and the teasing glint in her eyes made her even more beautiful.

"I think I have done a good job so far." He crossed his arms and stuck out his chest. So what if he had a little paint on his shirt? He hadn't painted in years.

"Would you like some help?"

Max eyed her skirt and dress shirt. "You aren't really dressed to help."

"Well, I'm sure you have another old shirt and some sweats I could borrow, right?"

He had never let women wear his clothes, but the thought of Alyssa in them sent his heart racing. "Yeah, I can probably find something."

"Good. Is it okay if I lay Peyton down in your room since we're painting hers? She's already had lunch, and she was dozing off in the car."

Max quickly ran through a mental memory of his room. Was there anything out he wouldn't want Alyssa to see? Since he liked it clean and simple and was generally good at putting things away, he was almost positive it would be fine. "Sure, come on."

He led the way, trying to brush away the image of

Alyssa in his room for other reasons. As she laid Peyton in his king-sized bed, he grabbed a t-shirt and a pair of sweats from a drawer for her. "I'll let you get changed, and I'll go find another brush."

After scrounging in the garage for a few minutes, Max returned to Peyton's room, another brush in hand. Alyssa stood there, his clothes hanging off her lean frame but looking sexy nonetheless. "Here." He shoved the brush in her hand and turned back to the wall he was painting, trying to get the image of her out of his mind.

If she were any other woman, he doubted they would be getting much painting done, but Peyton was asleep in his bed, and there was something about decorating a kid's room that dampened the desire. Besides, Alyssa had been a help with Peyton, and he'd hate to lose that help.

The painting went much faster with her helping, and an hour later the room was done.

"You're a messy painter," she said as she smiled at him.

"What do you mean?" He looked at his side of the room. It didn't look any different than her side.

"You have paint on your face." Alyssa reached a hand out and touched his cheek, sending a tremor down his spine.

Max covered her hand with his as their eyes locked.

Kissing her would be a bad thing, but he couldn't seem to tell his body that.

"Max." Her voice was low and throaty with emotion. "I can't. I'm sorry."

Her hand slipped out from under his, leaving a cold and empty feeling where it had been.

"Aunt Lyssa?" Peyton's voice carried down the hallway and Alyssa hurried from the room to attend to her. Sighing, Max ran a hand through his dark hair in frustration before replacing the lid on the paint buckets and taking the brushes to the kitchen to wash them out.

As the water ran over them, sending swirls of pink paint down the drain, his mind returned to the previous moment when he had been alone with Alyssa. What was it with her? Why did she keep affecting him when he clearly knew how wrong they would be?

He was so lost in thought, he nearly dropped the brushes when Alyssa and Peyton entered a moment later. She had changed back into her church outfit, a sure sign she was leaving, and he couldn't help but feel disappointed.

"I have to go study, but I'll be back this evening to help put her to bed." Alyssa said. "Do you think you can manage not to screw up too badly in" –she checked her watch— "four hours?"

"Haha. I think we'll be fine."

"Good, I'll see you then." She bent down to Peyton's

eye level. "Be good for Max, and I'll see you later, okay?"

"Okay, bye Aunt Lyssa."

"Bye Peyton. Bye Max."

He flashed a wave goodbye as he took the brushes out of the sink and laid them on a towel on the counter. "I have to make a few calls, Peyton. Do you want me to put on a movie for you?"

She scrunched her face as she thought about it. "No, I'll just play in my room."

"Okay, don't touch the walls though. They're still wet." As she wandered off down the hallway, he finished patting the brushes to dry them some. *Raising a kid isn't that hard. I can do this.*

He picked his phone up off the charger and googled a nanny agency. None were open on Sundays, but thankfully one had a call service that took his message and assured him they would send nanny candidates to his doorstep the next morning. His next call was to Justin to fill him in on the plan.

"A day's fine, but don't get dragged into this 'dad' thing. You don't want to get tied down yet."

"That's not happening," Max said, but as he hung up the phone, he wondered if being tied down would be so bad. Having Alyssa around had been rather nice, even though she was kind of a pain sometimes.

With nothing left to do and time on his hands, Max

collapsed on the inviting leather sofa and flicked on the television. Golf was on, but he was not a huge fan. News and reruns didn't grab his attention either. Another click landed him on some movie channel. He left it there for lack of something better, but soon found his attention focused on it.

The movie followed a philandering man who suddenly woke up with a wife and kids and found himself a poor preacher rather than the rich business man he was at the beginning. At first the man was angry and wanted to get back to his original life, but as the movie progressed, the man found a fulfillment with his wife and kids that he never had with his job, and he wanted to stay in the new life.

The similarities were not lost on Max, and he leaned forward, engrossed in the story.

"What are you doing?"

He jumped at the sound of Peyton's voice. How had he missed her entering the room? She was like a tiny ninja. "I'm watching a movie," he said patting the couch beside him. "Do you want to finish it with me?"

Peyton pursed her little lips, but climbed up beside him. Max found himself wishing there was more left in the movie as the feeling of Peyton sitting beside him was enjoyable.

"Max, do you want to color with me?" Peyton asked, when the movie ended.

Max couldn't remember the last time he colored or the last time he thought it sounded fun, but he agreed and joined Peyton at the dining room table. She handed him a book filled with dogs, and he picked up a crayon.

As his crayon moved over the paper, he wondered if he could be happy like this. Could he get used to a life with Peyton in it full-time?

"You like coloring?" she asked.

"I like coloring with you," he said, smiling.

After they finished, she asked him to read her a book and play dolls with her. Though completely out of his comfort zone, he stretched out on the floor and held one of her dolls while she created a fantastical story about them. He caught most of it, but a few of her words were still hard to understand.

At six on the button, the doorbell chimed. Alyssa stood on the other side, holding bags of grocery food. "I looked in your fridge last night and noticed you didn't have a lot of fresh ingredients. I thought I could bring some over and cook dinner."

Max had never let a woman use his kitchen, but he stepped back, allowing Alyssa to enter. She handed him a few bags and, after shutting the door, he followed her into the kitchen.

"Aunt Lyssa. We're playing dolls, wanna play?"

"Dolls, huh?" She raised an eyebrow at Max as she set the bags on the counter. He shrugged. "I would, sweetie, but I'm going to make us some dinner. How does spaghetti sound?"

"Yay, pasgetti." Peyton ran off with her doll, leaving the two of them alone in the kitchen.

"Do you know how to make it?" she asked Max. "It's a kid staple, so you should learn if not."

"I think I can handle boiling some water," he said as he grabbed the large pot from the bottom cabinet. He filled it with water and placed it on the stove.

"Good, though there's a little more to it than that." She began pulling out groceries and putting them away in his fridge and his pantry.

He watched her, unsure of what else to do. Part of him wanted to tell her to stop, that this was his kitchen, but the other part of him enjoyed watching her shuffle ingredients around, as if she'd cooked here a million times.

When the water began to boil, she handed him the spaghetti strands and then began opening up cupboards.

"What are you looking for?"

"A skillet to brown the meat."

He reached into the bottom cupboard and pulled one out. Their gazes locked as he handed it to her. The moment drug out until she shook her head as if mentally breaking the connection.

"Thank you. Can you get me the hamburger meat?" She pointed to a package of ground beef on the counter.

He handed it to her and watched as she began browning the meat.

"Why don't you finish the salad?"

Max followed her finger to a large bowl filled with greens. A tomato sat on a cutting board next to it. Grabbing the knife, he made short work of the tomato and added the chunks to the salad.

"Where are your paper plates?" Alyssa asked a few minutes later, poking her head out of the pantry. "I wanted to use them for the salads."

"I don't have any. The plates are in the cupboard closest to the sink." He pointed in the direction as he grabbed parmesan cheese from the fridge.

Alyssa shook her head, but grabbed the plates and set them down on the counter. Max loaded each up with a scoop of spaghetti and salad, and the two carried the plates to the table.

"Peyton? Dinner's ready."

At Alyssa's words, Peyton scurried into the living room and climbed up in her chair.

As he sat down, Max noticed Peyton's hands folded together. Alyssa struck a similar pose, and Max was left staring at his plate uncomfortably as the two prayed over theirs.

"You don't pray?" Alyssa asked as she finished her prayer.

"No, I don't believe in God, so, why would I?"

"You'll still take me to church though, won't you, Max?" Peyton's voice was small and pulled on Max's heart.

He opened his mouth to speak, but before he could, Alyssa jumped in. "I'll come get you Peyton, okay?"

Peyton nodded and took a bite of her spaghetti. Max looked from one to the other, deciding this was a perfect arrangement. He could stay out late on Saturdays and Alyssa could take Peyton to church while he slept in the next morning. Now, he just needed to find someone who could watch her on Saturday nights.

After dinner, Alyssa helped him clear the table and put away the leftover spaghetti. "I'm going to put Peyton down. Do you want to come watch how it should be done?"

There was no condescension in her words this time. Only sincerity. "Sure, why not?"

Alyssa frowned at his flippant attitude, but turned to Peyton. "Peyton, honey, it's time for bed. Grab your bear."

Without a word of protest, Peyton grabbed her bear and headed down the hall to the room they had fixed up for her. As Alyssa grabbed pajamas for Peyton and helped her change, Max touched the walls. The paint had dried, so he scooted the toddler bed back to the wall, smoothing out the pink Minnie Mouse bedspread before retreating to the doorway to watch. As there was no chair in the room, Peyton and Alyssa sat on the bed and Alyssa read one of the books they had picked up yesterday. Alyssa's voice was soft and soothing as she read, and Max crossed his arms. He couldn't imagine doing this routine himself.

When the book was finished, Peyton crawled under the covers and Alyssa sat on the floor beside her. "Lord, thank you for Max and for the blessings you have bestowed upon him that allow him to watch Peyton. Please heal Sarah and bring her back to us and help Peyton get adjusted to this new life until that happens. Help us keep our eyes on you. In your name, amen."

The mention of his name in the prayer surprised him.

"Amen," Peyton echoed. "Thank you, Aunt Lyssa. Thank you, Max." Peyton's voice was heavy with sleep as she pulled her bear closer to her. Alyssa leaned down and placed a kiss on her forehead before standing.

Max stepped out of the way as Alyssa approached the doorframe and pulled the door closed behind her. "Thank you for coming here today and helping me with Peyton." His gaze locked on hers. She was beautiful, and though he knew it would never work, that knowledge didn't stop his desire.

"You're welcome," she said, clearing her throat and looking away. "I promised Sarah I would help."

Right, Sarah. Alyssa was only here because of Sarah. He should remember that, and he should be thinking more about Sarah. After all, he needed her to get better or else he'd be watching Peyton forever, but Alyssa kept appearing in his mind.

"Did you call the nanny agency?" Her eyes were still averted as she asked the question.

"Yes, they said they'd send the candidates starting at ten a.m."

"Great, I'll see you then."

7

Alyssa checked her outfit in the mirror one more time before grabbing her keys. She shouldn't care what she was wearing, but there was some unknown need to make a good impression on Max. The image of their locked gaze and the texture of his cheek against her hand had played through her mind the previous night. She had wanted him to kiss her. Why had she said no?

Yes, there was Sarah to consider, but Sarah had told her she was over Max. If Alyssa was honest, it had more to do with his lack of faith and his lifestyle.

Her freshman year of college, a junior had approached her. He was popular and appeared nice, but it turned out he only went after freshmen to score. When she refused to sleep with him, he had dropped her like a hot potato. Though she knew it was nothing she had done, it still stung, and it had affected her trust of men in the next few relationships.

With Max's past, she knew getting tangled up with him would probably lead to heartbreak, but her heart didn't seem to want to take her brain's advice.

Her traitorous heart began its steady ascent as she pulled into Max's driveway and parked the car. Why did he affect her this way? She took a deep breath on her way to the door in hopes of calming the erratic beating of her heart before pressing the doorbell.

A minute later, Max opened the door wearing cargo shorts and a blue button-down shirt that highlighted the matching color in his eyes. With the top two buttons undone, a hint of his muscular chest appeared. Heat seared across Alyssa's cheeks as she forced her gaze up to his face, but not fast enough. A playful smirk crossed Max's lips.

"Come on in. We have half an hour. Would you like coffee?"

"Tea." Her voice was raspy as it fought to escape past the emotions lodged in her throat. She cleared it and tried again. "Do you have any tea?"

He flicked his head in a "follow me" gesture and led the way into the kitchen. *Get ahold of yourself Alyssa. You're acting like a school girl.*

Peyton sat coloring at the table as they entered, and

hoping to regain her composure, Alyssa joined her while Max set the kettle on the stove and rummaged in the pantry for tea.

When the kettle whistled moments later, he placed a steaming mug in front of her before pulling out a chair and sitting, a similar cup of coffee in his hand.

"You color?" Alyssa couldn't hide the surprise in her voice as he reached for a crayon.

"Yeah, Peyton and I colored last night before you came back. Evidently, I'm a natural." He turned the book around for her to see the image, and the attention to detail was amazing. He had used shading and high-lighting to bring the images to life.

"Did you study art?"

"Well, I am in advertising, so I've learned a few things along the way." The crooked smile he flashed sent her heart dancing again, and she dropped her eyes to her mug to hide the effect.

The doorbell rang as Alyssa took her last sip of tea. "Here we go," she said, pushing back from the table.

"Why don't you and Peyton sit in the living room, and I'll bring in the first one?" Max was heading down the hallway as he finished the question.

Alyssa took Peyton's hand and led her to the plush couch. "Okay, Miss Peyton, we will interview women to watch you while Max is at work. You be sure and tell us the ones you like and the ones you don't, okay?"

"Okay." Peyton's eyes displayed a smidgen of fear, but she hugged her bear and nodded.

Max returned a moment later with a blond woman trailing behind him. A tight bun topped her hair, and a flawlessly pressed skirt and shirt hugged her curves. A string of pearls hung around her neck. She appeared dressed more for a date than interviewing for a nanny position.

"Alyssa, Peyton, this is Claire. She has nannied for several families in the area."

As Claire glanced Alyssa's direction, it was obvious that she found her competition and was sizing her up. Alyssa shifted in her seat as she tried to keep an open mind. She wasn't dating Max after all.

"Yes, my last family was the Mayor's family. Their children outgrew the need for a nanny which is why I am even available. I have an impeccable list of references."

Max waved the two crisp white sheets of paper as evidence and nodded at Alyssa to take the lead.

"Claire, describe a typical day with Peyton under your charge."

Like a machine, Claire recited the passé statements. "I'll feed her, play with her, read to her, etc.," but the words rang hollow to Alyssa's ears. While she had no doubt the woman *could* watch Peyton, she couldn't see any bond of trust forming.

"Thank you, we'll be in touch."

Claire blinked at Alyssa before turning to Max for confirmation. She must have thought her references alone would get her hired on the spot, but Max took Alyssa's lead and walked the woman out.

"What was wrong with her?" he asked when he returned.

Alyssa smiled and turned to Peyton. "You want to tell him?"

"Too stiff," Peyton said, shaking her head.

A chuckle bubbled out of Max's lips. "Yeah, I guess she was, wasn't she?"

The following three women were like Claire, and Peyton negated each one with the same two words, but she brightened when Max returned with the next candidate, an older woman with more silver than brown left in her hair. She wore a pair of glasses that slid down her nose, causing her to keep pushing them up, and she was plump like a teddy bear but nicely dressed. Alyssa wondered if Peyton's attraction to her stemmed from the fact she had no grandmother, at least not on Sarah's side.

"Well, aren't you a dearie?" The woman's voice held the hint of an old English accent as she smiled at Peyton.

"This is Helen. Helen, this is Alyssa and Peyton." After making the introduction, Max sat beside Alyssa on the couch. She flashed him a quick glance. It was the first time he had sat next to her. For the other interviews, he had perched on the other couch, but she wasn't complaining.

"Now, I know I'm a bit older than the other women you've interviewed, but don't let my age fool you. I'm a grandmum to six babes and I can keep up with them."

"I have no doubt," Alyssa said with a laugh. "Well, why don't you tell us how Peyton would spend her day."

"I believe in starting with a healthy breakfast and quiet time where we will either read or do crafts. Then I prefer to go outdoors. Fresh air is good for children, you know. Lunch will follow and a nap if she still takes one. If the weather is nice, we will read and go outside again. Art projects are my passion, so we'll do many of them, and I'd teach her how to cook and sew. It is important that children learn to do things on their own."

Alyssa sneaked a peek at Peyton, but even those words didn't strike the smile from her face. With a slight nudge, she motioned Max to look at Peyton who was still staring at Helen with bright eyes and an open expression.

"Peyton is pleased, so I guess I am too." He glanced at Alyssa who nodded back.

"Can I say you two make the cutest couple? The love is abundant in this house." Helen smiled at Max and Alyssa.

"Oh, no, we're not a couple…" Alyssa began.

"We're not together…" Max said at the same time.

Peyton giggled, and Helen winked at her. "My mistake. You appear so in sync."

A blush spread across Alyssa's face as Max cleared his throat. "Yes, Alyssa has been a great help, and I feel you'd be wonderful for Peyton. Can you start tomorrow?"

"I can. Seven o'clock?"

"That will be fine." Max rose from the couch and shook her hand.

Alyssa stood beside him and shook Helen's hand next, trying not to smile as Helen winked at her. If Helen saw something between the two of them, could there be something there?

"I like her," Peyton said as Max walked Helen out.

"Me too." Alyssa glanced at her watch, but it was barely noon. Should she stay or should she go?

"Well, I don't know about you, but I'm hungry," Max said as he re-entered the room. "What do you say we grab lunch to celebrate?"

"Yes, lunch." Peyton clapped her hands.

"Did you get a bigger car yet or should we take mine?" Alyssa asked.

"No, they delivered the Malibu yesterday, and I have the car seat in the back, though you should make sure I got it in right."

Alyssa tilted her head at him, surprised. "Okay, let's go then."

After a quick check of the car seat, she nodded her approval and helped strap Peyton in before climbing in the passenger side. "It's nice," she said, feeling the leather sets.

"Hmm, yeah, it's not bad."

She turned shocked eyes on him. "Do you mean you didn't test drive it when you bought it?"

He shrugged. "Nope, I told the salesman to get me the safest car with those hook thingies."

Alyssa shook her head as he started the engine. Their lives were so different.

A few minutes later, they arrived in the parking lot of an upscale restaurant. Images of Peyton fussing or crying and annoying the wait staff filled her mind. "You want to take Peyton in here?" Alyssa couldn't keep the incredulity out of her voice. "It is near her naptime."

"And?" The subtlety of her hint was lost on him.

"Sometimes even well-behaved children have a hard time being quiet when they are hungry and tired."

"I'm sure it will be fine."

The edge in his tone told her he hadn't taken her advice the way she meant it. Alyssa shrugged, not wanting to argue with him, and opened her door. After he rescued Peyton from the backseat, they headed into the restaurant.

A woman in a starched white shirt and spotless black pants greeted them. "Welcome. How many?"

"Three," Max said, taking charge.

"Will you need a high chair?" the woman asked, nodding at Peyton.

"Yes." Alyssa jumped in before Max could say no. He hadn't been out to eat with Peyton yet, but she knew if the girl wasn't locked down, a bumpy meal was ahead.

"Okay, I guess yes."

"Perfect, it will be about fifteen minutes. Can I get a name?"

Max left his name as Peyton tugged on his pant leg.

"Fifteen minutes? But I'm hungry now."

Alyssa pressed her lips together and raised her eyebrows at him. This was what she had feared. Peyton's voice was dripping with whine.

"Don't worry, Peyton, it rarely takes as long as they say."

His luck held this time as the hostess called his name just a few minutes later. As she led them to the table, Alyssa noticed an extra sway in her hips and the meaningful look she flashed at Max as she seated them. Did women everywhere come onto him all the time?

Max, to his credit, either didn't notice or ignored the gesture as he picked Peyton up and deposited her in the high chair.

"Don't forget to strap it."

He looked at Alyssa as if she had spoken in a foreign language.

"The high chair strap. Trust me, you want to fasten it."

"Is she Houdini or something?" he asked, snapping the strap together before taking his seat.

Alyssa laughed. "You don't understand. Once, she stood up in the high chair before we could catch her and she snagged the arm of a waiter passing by with a tray full of food. Burgers and fries went flying everywhere."

Max's eyes widened in alarm, and he checked the strap one more time. "That can't happen here. We could never return."

"You'll learn that with little kids, these places may need to wait for dates or special occasions." Alyssa's face flamed as the mention of dates. Would he think she was asking him out or hinting for him to ask her out?

"What about you?" he asked.

"What about me what?"

"Do you want kids one day?"

Alyssa glanced at Peyton who was coloring on the paper the hostess had provided. "Yes, I'd like a family with at least three kids."

"I never thought I wanted kids, but Peyton is cool, and there's something about her that warms my heart."

The tone in his voice as he spoke of Peyton and the look in his eyes as he glanced at her coloring warmed Alyssa's heart, but she couldn't say those thoughts out loud. "It's not all unicorns and rainbows though." Alyssa didn't want to scare him, but she would be remiss if she didn't prepare him for the other side. "There will be tantrums and sicknesses and you can't just leave the house on a whim."

"I'm hungry," Peyton said, interrupting their conversation. Her voice was an octave louder than necessary. She complemented her whine with banging her small hands on the table and throwing the crayons.

"Peyton, stop!" Max's voice was quiet and terse, and he glanced around at the other patrons.

"It's okay, Max. She's just hungry," Alyssa said. "For these times, I always bring something with me." She dug in her purse for a moment before pulling out a small square cube.

"What's that?" Max asked as she handed it to Peyton.

"It's a fidget cube. The buttons push in and out. It's smart to always have something on you to keep Peyton entertained."

Max tilted his head at her. "How did you learn all this?"

"From watching Sarah. She is an amazing mother."

Peyton looked up from the dice. "I miss mommy."

"I know, baby, but she's trying to get better."

The waitress returned then, placing a tray of bread in the middle of the table. Max grabbed a piece, but he didn't eat it. Instead, he rolled it in his hand as if something was on his mind. "How long have you known Sarah?"

"About three years, I guess. I met her after Peyton was born. I offered to rent a place with her, but she was determined to do it all on her own. Since we hit it off though, she let me come around and help with Peyton."

"I'm sorry I missed those days." His soft voice pulled at Alyssa's heart.

She tore a piece of bread for herself, debating if she should ask the question rattling around in her head. "What happened with you and Sarah? I mean, I know how it ended, but why?"

Max took a bite of his bread and glanced at Peyton before answering. "I think I wasn't prepared. I wasn't ready to be with just one woman, but I loved Sarah. I would have done anything for her, and I'd like to think I would have settled down if I'd known about Peyton."

Their heavy discussion was broken when the waitress returned again to take their order. The rest of the lunch conversation was lighter, but Alyssa couldn't help looking at Max a little differently. Sarah must not have known how he felt about her because she rarely spoke of him, and when she did, it was always about his philandering. Alyssa was now seeing a different side of him, and it was one she could learn to like.

※ 8 ※

When the alarm went off the next morning, Max hit the buzzer and replayed the previous day in his mind.

After lunch, Alyssa had excused herself to go study. Max had been left with Peyton again, and after an hour blowing bubbles and another coloring, she had become cranky and whiny. Max had sat her in front of the television and suffered through cartoons with her until bedtime.

Then, he hadn't done her bedtime routine correctly, and she had teared up, crying for Sarah. Needless to say, after a good morning, his day had quickly deteriorated, leaving him wondering if he could raise Peyton on his own.

With a sigh, he pushed himself out of bed and into

his bathroom. After a quick shower, he donned a blue chambray shirt and khaki slacks. The hall was silent as he made his way to the kitchen, but he checked Peyton's room just to be sure.

She was still sleeping, her hair fanning out around her. He smiled as he shut the door quietly behind him and continued down the hallway. As hard as last night was, she looked like an angel when she slept.

Once in the kitchen, he readied the coffee pot and pressed the button to start it percolating. Then he began preparing his protein waffle for breakfast. He had just finished the last bite and was rinsing the plate in the sink when the doorbell rang.

Hoping it wouldn't wake Peyton, he hurried to open it. Helen stood on the other side, her arms laden with bags.

"What is all this?" he asked as he grabbed a few bags from her, freeing her arms.

"Crafts and games for Peyton. I hope you'll forgive me, but I didn't see many when I was here yesterday. I had a ton sitting around my house."

"That's fine, just try not to make a huge mess." In his mind, he could see paint and markers all over his floors and walls. So far, Peyton had kept the house clean and most of the mess in her room, but he feared with all these crafts that it would trickle into his space. He set the bags down on the dining table as they entered the kitchen area.

"I always clean up whatever mess I might make, Mr. Banks."

She had pulled her shoulders back, and he knew he had ruffled her feathers, but he didn't have much time to apologize. He was running late for work.

"Glad to hear it," he said, grabbing his coffee mug and his satchel. "I'll be home after work."

"Mr. Banks," she called after him, but he didn't turn around. He felt a little bad when he realized he had forgotten to show her around and she was probably just asking for directions, but she seemed like a smart lady, and he was sure she would figure it out.

He slid into the BMW, the leather seat fitting like an old, comfortable glove, perfectly molded to his shape. *Ah, this is so much better*. The Malibu drove well, but it just didn't hold a candle to his BMW.

"Welcome back, man," Justin said as Max entered the office. He held up his hand for a high five, and Max slapped it back. It was good to be back at work where he felt like a grownup again.

"I've only been gone one day." He picked up the messages on his desk left by his assistant from the previous day and rifled through them.

"Yeah, but Maxwell Banks never misses work. What's going on with you man?"

Max shook his head. "I'm trying to get used to having a toddler in my house. I thought it would be easy, and sometimes it is, but then she cries and I don't know how to handle it."

"Dude, I know Sarah didn't have a family, but are you sure you want to keep this kid? Couldn't you put her in foster care?"

Max glanced up at Justin. Though the thought had crossed his mind a few times, he would never say it out loud. "I'm not going to do that. It's not the way I would have wanted it, but I'm going to take responsibility for my actions."

"Sure man, that's admirable, but it's really going to cramp your style."

Max knew that as well, but he was nearing thirty, so maybe changing his style wouldn't be such a bad thing. "I better get to returning these calls." He waved the stack at Justin for emphasis.

"Sure, man, lunch though?"

"Yeah, lunch sounds good."

Shaking his head, Max picked up the first message and the phone.

"Hey, man, you ready for lunch?"

Max glanced up at Justin and down at his watch. Four hours had passed already? "Yeah, give me one second. Where are you thinking?"

"We haven't been to Hooters in a while."

Max nodded. Though he'd never drink while at work, taking in the view of the wait staff would be a welcome relief.

Twenty minutes later, the two were at a table admiring the tight tops and short shorts as the women bustled back and forth.

"We should go out after work," Justin suggested, his eyes following a busty blond. "Today is busy, and I could sure use a drink. You have someone to watch the kid, right?"

"Yeah, I have a nanny now. I never knew the cost to raise a kid, but my wallet has certainly taken a hit since Friday night." Max took a sip of his tea as he checked out a passing brunette. *Pretty, but not as pretty as Alyssa.* He coughed on his tea a little as he realized he was comparing these women to the one woman he should stay away from.

"You all right?" Justin asked.

"Yeah." Max wondered if he really was though. He couldn't remember the last time a woman kept appearing in his head like Alyssa did.

The waitress appeared a few moments later, and after taking their order, she laid a napkin down in front of Max and winked at him. "For later," she said before sashaying away.

Max picked up the napkin to see a name and number

scrawled across it.

"What is it?" Justin asked, leaning across the table to try to catch a glance.

"Her number," Max said. He folded the napkin and shoved it in his pocket though he wasn't sure he had any intention of using it.

"You sly dog. Well, I guess you have your weekend planned now." Justin winked at him as he picked up his glass and took another swig.

Max nodded, but suddenly he couldn't wait to get out of the restaurant.

"Hey, we're heading out to Charlie's for a drink. You coming?" Justin stood in Max's office doorway tapping the face of his watch.

"Yeah, let me call the nanny." Max picked up his work phone and dialed his home number. He had given Helen the green light to answer phone calls while he was at work, so he hoped she followed through.

"Hello?"

"Helen, It's Max. Can you stay with Peyton a little longer tonight? I uh need to catch up on some work." He had no idea why the lie tumbled out instead of the truth, but there was not much he could do about it now.

"Sure, do you have a time estimate or should I plan

on putting her to bed?" Though Helen's words were friendly, he could hear something in her tone.

"Um, I'm not sure. It should only be a few hours."

"Okay, then. I'll let her know."

The phone clicked without a goodbye, and Max sighed. He would have to do something nice for her. He couldn't afford to lose a nanny Peyton liked.

"All right, let's go."

"Awesome. I'll meet you there."

Charlie's was just getting busy when they arrived. After scanning the room, Justin waved to a few other people from work and the two headed that direction.

"Maxwell, we didn't expect to see you. Justin told us about your kid issue," Jake, one of their sales reps said, from the back of the booth.

"It's not really an issue," Max said, sliding in beside Rhea, one of their receptionists. "Peyton is pretty cool."

The others nodded, but their faces registered their disbelief. He couldn't blame them. He would have had the same expression a few days ago.

"Two beers please," Justin said when the waitress stopped by, and a few minutes later, the pale amber liquid was set in front of Max.

He took a swig as he listened to the conversation of

the surrounding group. As the liquid worked its magic, he found himself thinking less of Peyton and Alyssa and more of nights out like this. That was, until his phone rang.

Grabbing it from his pocket and shooting apologetic looks at the rest of the crowd, he stood up as he punched the answer button and headed for the outside door where it was quieter.

"Hello?" He had to jam a finger in his opposite ear until he reached the front entrance in order to hear the voice on the other end.

"Maxwell? Where are you?"

The voice threw him for a moment as the last time he heard his name used with such vitriol was when he was in trouble with his mother.

"Alyssa?"

"Yes, it's Alyssa. Care to guess where I'm at? I'll tell you. I'm at your house, consoling your daughter because she thought yet another person was abandoning her when you didn't come home today."

"I told Helen I had to work late," Max said, the lie spilling from his lips before he could stop it.

"Yes, and that would have been fine except you aren't at work. Helen tried your office before calling me. You forgot to give her your cell phone number, but thankfully you left mine up on the fridge."

"Is Peyton okay?" Max glanced at his watch. He had

only been out an extra two hours, but that must seem a lifetime to a three-year-old.

"She is now that I'm here, but Max you can't do this to her." Her voice softened, "She just lost her mother. She can't afford to lose you too."

"I'll be right there." Max hung up the phone and stepped back into the noisy restaurant. It wouldn't be right to leave without at least telling Justin what had happened.

"What's up, Max?" Justin asked as he approached the table. "Where did you go?"

"Sorry, that was Alyssa. Evidently Peyton had a scare. I have to go." He reached into his wallet and pulled out a twenty. "This should cover my drinks. I'll see you tomorrow." Without waiting for the protest he knew would come, he turned and walked out of the bar.

Though the drive only took him fifteen minutes, he felt even worse when he arrived home and saw Peyton curled up on Alyssa's lap in the living room.

Alyssa held a finger to her lips, telling him to be quiet. With a small sigh, he sat beside her on the couch.

"I messed up big time, didn't I?" he whispered to her.

Her eyes stared into his. "It's a big change, having a kid in your life, but you have to think about her now and not so much about yourself."

"I'm trying, but I guess I still have a lot to learn. Thank you for coming though."

"Of course. I'll always be here for Peyton."

Her words struck his heart. She would be there for Peyton, but would she ever be there for him? Probably not, if he kept messing up.

"Shall we lay her down?" Max whispered.

Alyssa nodded and shifted Peyton slightly in her arms, so Max could reach down and scoop Peyton up. Her head flopped onto his chest, but her eyes remained closed as he carried her down the hallway, Alyssa a step behind.

Peyton mumbled softly in her sleep as Max laid her in the bed. He touched her forehead and smoothed her hair back. He hated that he hurt her even though he hadn't meant to.

Alyssa stood just outside the room as he closed the door.

"Thank you for coming. Again, I'm so sorry."

"You're welcome, but I have to get back to studying now."

"What are you studying?"

"Psychology. I want to be a therapist or a counselor. I think."

A light chuckle crossed her lips as she said the last two words, and he wondered why. She would make an excellent counselor; he found himself wanting to talk to her about anything and everything, something very unusual for him. Usually, he said just what he had to do to get the woman home with him and in his bed and then he let his body do the rest of the talking. While he couldn't deny he wouldn't love to share his bed with Alyssa, he was also interested in her mind.

"I think you would make an excellent counselor. I know you've really helped me." He reached out and grabbed her hand.

"Max, I... I'll come check on Peyton later in the week." She extricated her hand and turned to leave.

"Wait, when is your last final?" he asked, stopping her.

"Thursday, why?"

"Can I take you to lunch on Friday? As a thank you and to celebrate the end of your finals," he added hastily, hoping it would feel less like a date to her that way and she would say yes.

Her eyes stared into his. They were a deep emerald like pine trees, and he could get lost in them easily.

"Just lunch?" she asked.

"Just lunch, and you can tell me more things I need to know to keep Peyton happy. I'll be a sponge soaking up all your advice. Promise."

A tiny smile flicked across her mouth at his analogy. "Okay, just lunch. Shall I meet you at your office at noon?"

"That would be wonderful," Max said and pulled a business card out of his wallet for her. He almost couldn't believe he had agreed to her coming to his office; he would never have done that in the past, but Alyssa was different.

She took the card, nodding at him as she left. It was not the reaction he had been hoping for, but she had agreed and that meant the door was at least open a crack. He would find a way to show her he was changing.

9

Peyton was still sleeping when Helen arrived the next morning. Though tempted to be late to work to talk to her, Max still had a lot on his plate to catch up on after taking Monday off.

"I owe you an apology, Helen," Max said as she entered the kitchen. "I wasn't working late last night. I went out with friends. I'm not sure why I didn't tell you the truth, but I promise I will in the future."

Helen tilted her head, regarding him with her experienced eyes. "I can tell you are trying, Max, but it is important that I can reach you at all times."

He nodded. "I've written down my cell number for you." He slid the paper across the counter to her. "I'll be home no later than 6:30 tonight, I promise."

"Max, you're back." Peyton's voice broke into the conversation. She had entered the kitchen silently again.

"I was home last night, Peyton, and I'm sorry I worried you. I'm not going anywhere." He leaned down and hugged her.

"Okay. Look what Helen and I did." Her excitement was barely contained as she bounced up and down on her toes. Any hurt from yesterday appeared to have been forgiven and forgotten. Grabbing his hand, she pulled him into the dining room. "We painted my high fives."

On a white canvas board were two perfect hand prints in pink and purple. Peyton's name was spelled out across the top and the year was at the bottom. Those small hand prints tugged on Maxwell's heart. Suddenly, he realized all the time he missed with Peyton—time when her hands were even smaller—and it hurt. He had never gotten to hold her as a baby or watch her take her first steps. He had no idea what her first word was. Though this realization rocked him, he pasted a smile on his face to mask his emotions.

"It's beautiful, Peyton. We must hang it somewhere special."

"There will be more years in the future," Helen said, coming up beside him. "You may have missed the beginning, but you'll have plenty more if you are paying attention."

Max stared at her with wide eyes. How had she read his mind?

"Besides, I believe there will be more children in your future."

The words were so quiet, he wasn't sure he even heard her right, and before he could ask her to repeat them, she had scooted away and was rummaging in her bag.

"What happened last night?" Justin asked, plopping down in the seat across from Maxwell.

"I scared Peyton." Max said, turning on his computer for the day. "She is still adjusting to not having Sarah, and she feared I was abandoning her."

"Dude, are you sure you want to keep doing this?"

"I'm not shipping her off to foster care. I'll figure it out."

Justin held his hands in a defensive posture as he stood. "Hey man, I'm just trying to look out for you."

Max sighed as Justin left the office. He doubted Justin would ever fully understand.

At six pm, Max turned off his computer and headed home. He still had work to catch up on, but he had promised Helen he would come straight home.

Peyton greeted him at the door. "Max, I drew a picture." She tugged his hand, pulling him down the hallway. Max smiled at her exuberance. There was something contagious about her positive attitude.

"I drew us." She pointed proudly to a white picture with four colorful blobs. "There's me and there's you. There's Aunt Lyssa and there's Helen."

Max noticed she hadn't drawn Sarah, but he didn't point it out to her in fear of making her cry again. "That's beautiful, Peyton. Shall we hang it on the fridge?" He glanced over at his stainless-steel fridge. It had always been completely bare, just the way he liked it. Alyssa's card was the only thing on it, and it was small enough not to grab much attention, but he wanted Peyton to understand he was proud of her. Swallowing his fear of clutter, he grabbed a piece of tape to post it in the middle of the fridge.

"You'll be glad you did." Helen patted him on the shoulder, and Max wondered again how she seemed to always know his thoughts. "I'll see you tomorrow. There's dinner in the oven which should be ready"—she held up her finger and a timer dinged — "now!"

As Helen said goodbye to Peyton, Max grabbed plates and set the table. Helen had prepared a cheesy casserole which he scooped onto each plate. He added left-over salad and helped Peyton up into her chair.

"Aren't you going to pray?" she asked as he picked up his fork.

"Why don't you do it?"

She bowed her head and closed her eyes. "Dear God, thank you for food and Max and Helen and Aunt Lyssa. Help Mommy get better. Amen."

It was a sweet prayer, and though Max wasn't the praying kind, the words resonated with him. What must that kind of faith be like?

After dinner, Peyton watched television while he cleaned up. Then he joined her in the living room.

"Can I sit on your lap?" she asked as he plopped down on the couch.

Max hesitated. He had never been one to show too much affection; he rarely cuddled with women, but the angelic look on her face caused him to nod. She climbed up in his lap and curled against his chest.

Her hair smelled sweet like strawberries, and though it was an added weight, he didn't mind and curled his arms around her.

"Okay, bedtime," he said when the show ended.

"Do I have to?" she whined.

"Yes, you have to. Come on."

Begrudgingly, she followed him to her room, her

bare feet plopping on the hardwood floor with her exaggerated steps. Max pulled out jammies and helped her change before helping her into bed.

"Read this one," she said, handing him a book with Elmo on the cover.

Max opened the book and read. When he finished, Peyton's eyes started to close, but before he could get away, she opened them and focused on him.

"Will you pray with me?"

The question caught him off guard as he tucked her into her bed. "Um, I'm not sure how, Peyton."

"It's easy. Just close your eyes and thank God. You can ask him for things too, but not too many."

Max smiled at her innocence. "Okay, I'll try." He closed his eyes and cleared his throat. "God? I don't know if you recognize me, but I'm praying for Peyton. Thank you for letting me meet her and help her to be happy and sleep well. Um, amen?"

Peyton giggled. "See, was that so hard?"

"No, I guess not," Max said, enjoying the smile on her face. "Now get some sleep. You have another fun day tomorrow."

"Okay, night Max."

"Good night, Peyton."

He touched her forehead lightly before standing and exiting the room.

As he undressed for bed that night, he pondered his

life. He had thought he was happy, spending his weeks alone and his weekends with beautiful women, but in the last few days, something had shifted. He wondered if his weekend flings were because he was looking for something more but not finding it.

"Hey, man, we're going out again tonight. You coming?" Justin stood in his office doorway, looking hopeful.

"No, not tonight. Peyton and I have a movie date planned."

Justin entered the office and sat in one of the open chairs. "What's going on with you, man? You seem different."

After taking a deep breath, Max replied. "I think I am different. Peyton is amazing, and I'm enjoying being a dad, and then there's Alyssa."

"Wait, who's Alyssa?"

"Sarah's friend, the one helping me with Peyton. She's beautiful and smart and spirited." A smile stretched across his face as he spoke about her.

"Dude, are you falling for her?" Justin's head dropped forward as his left eyebrow went up.

"Maybe." Max glanced at Justin before returning his attention to the computer. He had to finish one more report before he would feel comfortable leaving for the day. "I mean I'm looking forward to seeing her again. We're having lunch tomorrow."

Justin let out a low whistle. "She better be something special if she's taking Maxwell Banks off the market."

Off the market? Was she taking him off the market? He certainly didn't have the same desire to date other women he used to, but was he ready to be a one-woman man?

"Peyton was wonderful today," Helen said, greeting him at the door. "Tomorrow is your lunch with Alyssa, right?"

Max didn't know what it was about Helen. He had only known her a week but was comfortable sharing his life with her. "Yes, she's meeting me at the office tomorrow and going to lunch. Can I ask you something? It's about Alyssa. You said you saw something between us, right?"

Helen smiled. "I did and I do. It is clear you both have feelings for each other."

Max blinked. He didn't think it was clear Alyssa had feelings for him. In fact, she seemed determined to avoid contact with him. "I like Alyssa, really like her, but she knows about my past. I guess you could say I was never into relationships. Now that Peyton's here, I am starting to look at things differently, but I'm not sure Alyssa sees that. How can I get her to give me a chance?"

There was no shock on Helen's face at his words, which made him wonder if he exuded the aura of a playboy. "I don't think you will win her with words. You must show her you've changed."

"I could barely get her to agree to lunch tomorrow after Tuesday night."

"Alyssa is looking for something more. She's looking for an equal. You will have to try things she is interested in." Helen looked at him matter-of-factly. "You'll have to go to church, and not just go, but give it a real effort."

Church. The word used to send shivers through his body, but if that's what it would take to show Alyssa he was changing, then he could do it. What's the worst that could happen? Losing a few hours on Sunday morning didn't sound that bad.

He nodded. "Church. Okay, I'll give it a shot."

"Good. I'll be praying for you both."

The words should surprise him, but they didn't. Helen seemed to embody the same peace and love that Alyssa had, and Max wondered if there was something to their beliefs.

As Helen left, Peyton filled him in on the rest of her day.

"We read this book about trains, and we blew bubbles outside. She's really fun."

Max smiled at her sweet voice and made a promise to himself that whatever happened with Sarah, he would be in Peyton's life from now on.

Alyssa woke with butterflies in her stomach on Friday. She hadn't spoken to Max since Tuesday night, but that hadn't stopped her from thinking about him. Even though she knew he was not the kind of man she should fall for, she couldn't help thinking about the "what ifs." What if he could change? What if she could convince him to attend church with her? What if he became a believer? Though there was much about him not to like, she had seen those glimpses of the man he could be.

It was just lunch today though. She needed to put the "what ifs" aside and focus on this just being lunch. She needed to keep her head on her shoulders and listen to it rather than her heart.

After a shower, Alyssa dried off and stood in her closet, surveying the offerings. What did one wear to "just a lunch?" Were shorts too casual? Was a dress too dressy? She had no idea where they were going for lunch; she should have asked him.

Deciding a longer summer dress would fit wherever they went, she pulled one over her head and put on a little makeup. Her skin was so fair and pure that she didn't need much, but decided a little powder to highlight her eyes and a touch of gloss on her lips wouldn't be too much.

With her make up done, she headed to the kitchen to make breakfast and do her devotional. It was her favorite time of day because Roxy usually slept late and she had the table to herself. Since she had no final today, she could take her time and really get into the word.

As she sipped her tea, she opened the Bible to the book of Psalm she had been reading. Psalm 34:4 jumped out at her. "I prayed to the Lord, and he answered me. He freed me from all my fears." Perhaps she needed to spend even more time in prayer to hear the Lord's answer.

When she entered Max's office building a few hours later, she was greeted by two receptionists behind a large white desk. The building was bright and open with lots of natural light coming in.

"Can I help you?"

One receptionist was on the phone, chatting through the headset covering her right ear. The other, an attractive brunette, was the one who had addressed Alyssa.

"Yes, I'm here to see Maxwell Banks. Alyssa Miller."

The woman's eyes widened as she appraised Alyssa. "Just one moment. Is he expecting you?"

Alyssa nodded as the woman clicked a button on her phone handset. "Mr. Banks, there's an Alyssa here to see you." She paused, and her eyes flicked to Alyssa again. "Yes, sir, right away." She clicked the button to hang up the call and raised her eyebrow at Alyssa. "He'll see you now. Take the elevator to the third floor. His office is 307."

"Thank you." Alyssa wondered if the woman's odd reaction was because Maxwell often had women come in and she didn't fit the model or if it was because he rarely had women come in.

As the elevator opened onto the third floor, Alyssa found herself staring into the face of a man with sandy brown hair. His green eyes locked on hers and then traveled down her body, sending a thread of disgust down Alyssa's spine.

"Well, hello, I haven't seen you here before. Who can I help you find?" His voice was rich, but it didn't erase the creepy feeling he gave Alyssa.

"I'm here to see Maxwell Banks."

Surprise alighted the man's face. "Maxwell is my best friend. I'm Justin. I'll take you to him."

He stuck out his hand, but Alyssa didn't want to touch it. However, her upbringing had always taught her it was rude not to return a shake, so she swallowed her unease and took his offered hand.

"You don't have to do that. Weren't you waiting for the elevator?"

"Oh, it's no big deal. I can catch it again in a minute."

Alyssa pasted a smile on her face and followed him through the open room that housed cubicles. A few employees looked up as they passed, but no one spoke to them.

Justin deposited her in front of office 307 but not before knocking at the door jamb and announcing her to Max.

"Your lunch date is here."

Alyssa looked to Maxwell. He must have told Justin because she sure hadn't.

"Thanks, Justin."

Justin hung just a moment longer before leaving when Maxwell said nothing more to him.

"Sorry about that," Maxwell said when they were alone. "He means well, but Justin…" He didn't finish the statement, just shrugged. "Anyway, are you ready?"

"Sure."

They garnered even more looks as they walked back through the office and to Maxwell's car.

"So, I have to ask," she said as he opened the car

door for her, "do you have a lot of women visit you at work or am I the only one?"

His head tilted to the side as a lopsided smile pulled at his mouth. "Why do you ask?"

"Because I received rather strange, disbelieving looks from the moment I stepped into your building." She stretched the belt across her chest and snapped it into the clasp.

Maxwell stared at her as if deciding how much to tell her. "You are the first woman I have let come to my work," he said finally. "In the past, I never wanted to see the women again, so I didn't want them showing up at my job."

A tiny flicker of something burgeoned in Alyssa's heart. "So, I'm special then."

She meant it as a joke, but his face was serious as he answered her. "Yes, you're special." He flashed her a smile before turning the key and backing the car out of the space.

Alyssa's eyes dropped to her lap as a faint blush crawled across her face. That she was the first woman to attend his work gave her a fuzzy feeling.

The restaurant he pulled into was a small deli. They must have beat the lunch rush as there weren't many people inside. He led her to a small booth at the back. A brown fabric covered the seats, and a simple decor adorned the walls. Alyssa was a little surprised at the restaurant choice.

"The food is good," he said, catching her reaction. "Plus, you said this wasn't a date. I promise if you'll let me take you on a real date that the restaurant will be of higher caliber."

"Oh, I didn't," Alyssa started.

"Yes, you did, but it's okay." His lopsided smile displayed a dimple in his cheek. "I don't always dine at five-star restaurants, and I know a lot of good dives."

"Really?" She couldn't help teasing him. "Maxwell Banks crashes dives?"

Her teasing set the tone for lunch, and by the time it ended, her cheeks hurt from smiling so much.

"Thank you so much for joining me for lunch," Max said as he laid money on the table to cover the meal. "I'd love to see you again, and I've been thinking. Can I come to church with you this Sunday? I want to see what's so important to you and Peyton."

Alyssa blinked at him. "You want to come to church?"

"If you'll let me." He flashed that smile again, and Alyssa couldn't say no.

10

Alyssa smoothed her flowered dress as she stood in front of Maxwell's door, waiting for him to open it. Her breath caught as the door swung open, and an audible gasp escaped.

"This will do then?" He smiled and gestured to his dark blue shirt and black slacks. "I wasn't sure. I don't know that I've been in a church as an adult other than for a wedding or a funeral."

Alyssa couldn't imagine never attending a church service, but then she and Maxwell had lived very different lives.

"It will do nicely. The blue really brings out your eyes." The intensity in his gaze caused her to drop her eyes. "Is Peyton ready?"

"Uh, mostly, I think." He opened the door, and she followed him to the kitchen.

She was expecting another repeat of last week but was surprised to see Peyton not only dressed but with her hair combed as well.

"You did well, Max."

He grinned and grabbed Peyton's hand. "Ready?"

"Let's go," she said, pumping her other hand in the air.

Alyssa laughed as they headed out to the garage and climbed into the Malibu. Though Maxwell drove, Alyssa directed him through each turn, and minutes later, they pulled into the parking lot of a single story white church.

"Huh, I thought it would be bigger."

"There are other churches that are, but this is the one Sarah and I went to. It's the perfect size for us. People know you so you don't feel lost."

The inside was larger than the outside seemed with a large sanctuary directly in front of them and a hallway that led to offices and meeting rooms to the right. A nursery and toddler area were to the left. Two women stood behind a brown desk at the front of the right hallway.

"Hi, can I check in Peyton Moore?"

The women's smiles faded at Alyssa's voice. "Is she...?"

"Sarah is in New York. We'll be praying for the

best." Alyssa's tone was forceful but kind. She had known these questions would come, but that didn't make them any easier to answer over and over.

One of the women handed over a white sticker, and Alyssa led the way down the hallway. After placing the sticker on Peyton's back, she hugged her and sent her into a small classroom.

"What's the sticker for?" Max asked as they headed back toward the sanctuary.

"It's a safety thing. If she needs something, they will flash this number on a little box at the front of the sanctuary, and I know to go get her. I also have to show this tag to pick her up, so they don't send her off with a stranger."

"I guess that makes sense."

Alyssa led the way into the sanctuary, and Max sat beside her. His head slowly turned as he took in the surroundings. The sanctuary was large, but not overly decorated. A white screen hung at the back of the room to display the words to the songs, and a piano, drum set, and a few guitars sat on the slightly raised stage at the front.

"Hi, Alyssa, we're praying for you and Sarah." Though said in different variations, that seemed to be the mantra of the day as people she knew came up to her. She introduced Max to each one, and though most were courteous and pleased to meet him, she saw a few vainly trying to hide their contempt for the man. Unfortunately, even church goers were human and often struggled with the same sins.

The worship team took the stage a few minutes later, and Alyssa lost herself in the songs. Though Max didn't sing beside her, she caught him watching her a few times, and it created an odd sensation in her heart. She could see herself with him here each Sunday, if he could open up his heart to the possibility of God, but then there was Sarah. If she got better, wouldn't she want to get back together with Max? And if she didn't make it, would Alyssa feel guilty for being with him when Sarah couldn't?

Pastor Brown spoke on love as he took the stage, and Alyssa couldn't have asked for a more perfect message. She had been hoping it would be a nicer one that would allow Max to see the good side of God and not just the "rules part" that a lot of people got hung up on.

"What did you think?" she asked Max when the service ended.

"It was interesting."

It was hard to tell from his voice if he was being serious or dismissive, but the expression on his face suggested the former. Alyssa sent up another prayer for him as she led the way back down the hallway to get Peyton.

"Aunt Lyssa, look, we made bracelets." Peyton

shoved her tiny arm in front of Alyssa's face to show off the shiny beads on the story bracelet.

"I remember these. I made one when I was a kid too."

"What does it mean?" Max touched the beads, as Peyton shoved the bracelet in his face.

Alyssa smiled as she remembered the lesson from years ago. "The black represents sin, showing that we all have sinned. The red represents Jesus's blood shed on the cross for us. Blue is for faith because sometimes you can't see with your eyes. The yellow represents eternal life, the kind we receive when we let Jesus into our hearts. Do you know what the white is Peyton?"

Her eyes closed, and her face scrunched as she tried to remember. "Uh, white is for no more sins."

"Close," Alyssa smiled, "it's for the forgiveness of our sins. I never can remember what the green is though."

"It's for growth in God's love," a woman with blond hair said as she approached the entrance. "Hi, I'm Kim. I'm Peyton's Sunday School teacher."

"Max," he said, sticking his hand out to take hers.

Alyssa watched the exchange and was surprised to feel a tiny pang of jealousy sprout in her heart. "Thanks, Kim, we'll see you next week." As she grabbed Peyton's hand, she noticed the tiny flicker of shock in Kim's eyes and the look of amusement in Max's.

"Was that jealousy?" he whispered as she marched them down the hall and toward the entrance.

"No," she hissed back, "I'm hungry. I thought we could get some lunch." The words were not convincing, even to her, and the chuckle that escaped from Max's perfect lips told her he wasn't buying it either.

"Can we go to McDonalds?"

Max and Alyssa both looked down at Peyton at the same time. She could see on his face that he didn't want to go there either.

"How about an upscale version of McDonalds?" he offered.

"Does it come with a toy?"

"No, but it comes with ice cream."

Peyton shrugged her small shoulders. "Okay then."

"Wow, I was hoping for a bigger reaction."

"Hey, you take what you can get when they're three," Alyssa said with a chuckle.

He smiled back at her and held her gaze a little longer than necessary, sending another tremor through her body.

When they reached the car, he opened the passenger door for her before helping Peyton into the car seat. Though he fumbled a little, it was clear he had been practicing strapping Peyton in.

Max was quiet as they drove, and Alyssa used the time to sneak furtive glances his direction. Perhaps this was the man Sarah fell in love with. She could see the possibility in his strong cheekbones and the tender side she had seen show itself today. *What am I thinking? I can't be equating love with this man.* But as hard as she tried to deny it, the feelings still crept in.

Max pulled into a casual bar-b-que restaurant. Although it had tables to sit at, it was definitely more fast food.

"Learned your lesson last time, huh?" Alyssa said, a teasing glint flashing in her eye.

"Yeah. I'll save the nicer restaurants for kid-free time, but this place has great food."

"I know. It's one of my favorites."

As they drove back from lunch, Max sneaked glances at Alyssa. He had enjoyed the day. Her church had been different from what he expected, but in a good way. The pastor had spoken on God's love, which was something he hadn't heard much in the past. If that trend continued, he might find himself tolerating church.

Lunch had even gone well. There had been a few harrowing moments when Peyton nearly upturned her plate, and he'd had to apologize profusely for the mess she left on the table, but all in all, he considered it a success. Now, if he could just get Alyssa to go out with him again.

His eyes slid to her as the thought seared through his brain. She hadn't given him any new indications that she was interested other than her teasing interactions, but he had caught her looking his way a few times. Her face was turned out the window currently, watching the scenery pass by, and he wondered what was going on in her head. He hadn't been this curious about a woman since Sarah. Ah, but there was the rub. What if Sarah got better? Shouldn't he try to make it work with her since he knew about Peyton now? He had no business developing feelings for Alyssa. There was just too much muck in the middle.

She flashed him a small smile as they pulled into his garage. The desire to ask her to stay pounded in his head. They could have some alone time after Peyton went down for a nap, but fear of her answer kept his mouth shut. He was afraid she would say no, which would crush him, but even more afraid she would say yes, showing she felt something for him too. How awkward this felt. Maxwell Banks had never second guessed himself when it came to women, yet here he was waffling like a school boy.

Peyton was nearly half asleep as he unstrapped her from the car seat. She felt like a ton of bricks as he carried her inside.

As he laid her in the bed, her eyes fluttered open. "Will you keep me?"

The question caught him off guard as he tucked Peyton into bed. "What do you mean?"

"I mean if my mom dies. Will you keep me or will you send me to foster care?"

His heart broke a little that such a tiny creature was worried about such big issues. "Peyton, I didn't think I wanted kids, but I honestly can't imagine my life without you in it now."

"Thanks, Max."

Max, it was like a slap in the face. He shouldn't expect her to call him Dad or Daddy; it had only been a week but hearing her call him Max didn't sit well either. He leaned in and kissed her forehead before exiting her room and returning to the living room.

"What's the matter?" Alyssa asked as he entered.

Max shook his head. He almost didn't want to say the statement aloud, but Alyssa's face softened his resolve, and the words began to spill out. "She called me Max. I know it's still early, but... I don't know, is it crazy that I want her to call me Dad?" His hand ran across his forehead as he said the word, a gesture he hadn't done in ages.

"No, I don't think it's crazy. Knowing you have a child—your own flesh and bone—does crazy things to you, but," she laid her hand on his arm, "she doesn't see that yet. She needs to know that you'll take care of her and protect her before she'll feel safe enough to open up her heart."

His eyes dropped from her emerald gaze to the pale hand on his arm. Could she feel the heat that was radiating up his arm at her touch? As his eyes moved back up, they stopped on her perfect lips. Full and pink, he longed to know what they would feel like pressed against his. Her lips parted slightly as she noticed his focus. That would normally be his cue, but he wanted to be sure. He flicked his eyes back to hers and a jumble of emotions poured out of them. He could sense her desire, but also her confusion and trepidation.

Suddenly, the warmth receded from his arm. She had pulled her hand away. "Well, I guess I should be going."

"Are you leaving already?" His heart constricted at the thought.

"Do I have a reason to stay?"

Her words opened the door for him to make his move, but suddenly his throat was dry. He never lost his cool around women, so why was he finding himself tongue tied now? He took a step toward her. His hands wanted to reach out to touch her, but an invisible barrier kept them glued to his side. Still, the closeness caused her to take a breath.

"I'd like you to stay." His voice was low and throaty. He cleared his throat as he took another small step toward her. The unseen heat building between them billowed over him.

"Max, I... "

The hesitation was evident in her eyes, and it killed him.

"I know you know about my reputation, but having Peyton and meeting you... I feel different."

Her head shook slowly, but not as if she was saying no, more like as if she was trying to convince herself.

"Will you give me a chance to show you at least?" This time his hand did reach out and cup her face. She leaned into his hand, and he couldn't fight the feelings any longer. He pulled her close and touched her lips ever so slightly with his own. It was more breath and expectation than actual kiss, but it was enough to send a shock through his lips and a tremor through Alyssa's body.

Her eyes snapped open, and she pulled back. "Max, I don't know if I can do this."

"Alyssa, if you can promise to at least give me a shot, I'll do my best to show you a different Max."

Her lip pulled into her mouth as her teeth bit down on it. It was the cutest gesture he had ever seen, but his heart thudded in his chest as he waited for her answer.

"The nanny, Helen, she sees it. There's something here, Alyssa."

"I... I will think about it, Max. I'll call you later."

As Alyssa hurried out of his house again, Max sighed

and leaned his head back. He'd have to come up with some way to win her over.

Alyssa didn't stop moving until she was at her car, but as she fumbled for her keys, she nearly dropped them; her hands were shaking so badly. Once inside, she grasped the steering wheel to try to calm herself before driving. Why had she run again? She had wanted him to kiss her; she had liked him kissing her. Was that the problem? Was it that she liked it too much?

When her heart had slowed its rhythm down, she inserted the keys and started the engine. Though music played on the radio, she could hardly hear it, her thoughts were spinning a mile a minute. Was it possible he could have changed that quickly? He did seem different, but was it different enough?

"Lord, I need your guidance here. I know I'm developing feelings, but are they misplaced? He isn't a believer yet, but I feel like his heart was opening today. Please guide me in your will." Saying the words out loud was like putting aloe on a burn—it soothed and calmed her nerves, and while she didn't get an immediate answer, she knew that God would answer in his own time. She just had to try to listen.

11

"You missed another great party, man." Justin leaned against the door to Max's office, his arms crossed over his chest. "It was phenomenal."

"That's great, Justin, but I just don't see parties in my future right now." *Or ever again.* "I had a good weekend too. I spent the time with Peyton and Alyssa." He smiled as he remembered their first kiss. He wished it had lasted longer, but her response to it at least gave him hope that she felt something too.

"Yeah, Alyssa. She's hot, man. I can see why you dig her, but do you really want to get tied down right now? I mean you are in the prime of your life!" Justin sauntered in and plopped down in the chair across from Max's desk, stretching out his long legs and folding his arms behind his head. "There were so many beauties there on Saturday."

"There's something nice about seeing the same woman more than once though," Max replied. He shouldn't have to, but he felt the need to defend his actions. He and Justin traveled the same circles together, but now a distance was growing between them.

"I don't know about that, but I'd like to see what this woman offers that has you so intrigued. How about a double date on Friday? I'm sure I can scrounge up someone."

The proposition would have been one he jumped on a few weeks ago, but now the thought sent a feeling of dread through Maxwell. "I don't know if that's a good idea. We aren't even dating yet." *Though I'm trying.* "Just more like getting to know each other."

"That will be perfect then because I won't be dating the woman I bring either. Come on, just a dinner or a movie or something."

"I'll ask her," Max said, "but I can't promise anything."

He contemplated the call to Alyssa the rest of the day but could never seem to find the right words. However, as he pulled into his driveway, he was surprised to find her car parked in front of his house.

He pulled out his phone, but there had been no missed calls. *What is she doing here?*

The sound of laughter greeted him as he entered the house, and as he placed his mug on the bar, he spied Helen, Alyssa, and Peyton in the living room. Alyssa was tickling Peyton on the floor and all three were giggling.

Peyton noticed him first and struggled to her feet. "Max." A smile of sheer delight lit up her face and she ran to him. He bent down to hug her, enjoying the sensation of her happiness to see him. "Aunt Lyssa is here. She's playing tickle monster." Peyton wiggled her fingers at Max to demonstrate.

"I see that," he said, laughing. "You guys look like you're having fun." His eyes caught Alyssa's gaze before she dropped her eyes to the floor.

"Can she stay for dinner, please?"

Max could think of nothing he would like more. "It's up to Alyssa. It's perfectly fine with me. Helen, you are welcome to stay too." Though he hoped she would say no, it would have been rude not to invite her.

"Oh no, dearie. I have my grandbabies coming over tonight. I best be getting home to them, but I put a Shepherd's pie in the oven. It ought to be enough to feed three." She winked at Max as she gathered her things.

"See you tomorrow, Peyton. Thanks for the visit, Alyssa."

"You're welcome," Alyssa said, rising from the floor.

"Well, would you like to stay for dinner?" Max asked again.

Alyssa opened her mouth, but before she could utter a word, Peyton grabbed her hand. "Please, Aunt Lyssa?"

"How do you say no to that?" she asked, laughing. "Okay, I'll stay."

"Good. Why don't you grab some plates and I'll get the pie out of the oven?" Max asked. He grabbed two pot holders and opened the oven. The smell of meat, vegetables, and potatoes wafted out. Reaching in with the potholders, he grabbed the sides of the casserole dish and pulled it out. White wisps of steam rose into the air as he carried it to the table and set it in the middle.

Alyssa had already placed three plates on the table and filled glasses–milk for Peyton and iced tea for Max and herself. She helped push Peyton in before taking her own seat. Max sat last.

"Will you join us for prayer this time?" Alyssa asked.

"Sure." Max was surprised when, instead of clasping her hands together as before, she reached out and took ahold of his hand. He smiled at her before following suit and taking Peyton's hand. It still felt odd to close his eyes, but he enjoyed the warmth of Alyssa's hand as the darkness took over.

"Lord, thank you for this food and for the many blessings that you have given us. Help us to keep our eyes on you in everything we do. Amen."

Peyton echoed the amen, and Max scooped Shepherd's Pie onto everyone's plate.

After dinner, Peyton tugged his arm, dragging him into the living room.

"Can we watch a movie, Max, please?"

Max looked to Alyssa who shrugged as if to say she had nowhere to be. She took one edge of the couch and Peyton crawled up beside her, leaving the other end free for Max. He flicked on Moana, Peyton's current favorite movie of the hour, and claimed his seat.

Though Peyton sat in between them, Max could feel Alyssa's presence just a foot away. Her perfume drifted in the air, igniting his senses. He longed to reach over and clasp her hand again, but he had no idea what Alyssa would do and there was Peyton to consider.

By the time the movie ended, Peyton was almost asleep on Alyssa's lap.

"Come on, Peyton. Let's get you into bed," Max said as he scooped her up. "Can you stay a moment?" he asked Alyssa. "There is something I want to ask you."

"Uh, sure," she answered, her voice filled with curiosity.

"Great, I'll be right back." He carried Peyton to her bedroom, changing her quickly into pajamas and laying her in bed. As she was almost asleep, he decided to skip the story and the prayer, but placed a kiss on her head and smoothed her hair back before leaving the room.

Alyssa was still on the couch when he returned though she rose as he entered.

"So, what's up?"

"My friend Justin, the one you met at the office, he wants to get together, kind of like a double date this Friday."

Alyssa sucked in her breath and looked away. "I don't know if that's a good idea."

"I know he's not your cup of tea, but he's been my friend for years, and he's trying. He said he wants to get to know you better. Just one night, please?" Max took a step toward her as he finished the plea.

"I..." Alyssa bit her bottom lip as she thought. "Okay, one night, but if it's awful, we never do it again, agreed?"

"Agreed," Max said with a laugh.

Alyssa smiled, and silence descended. Her eyes stared into Max's and, heart racing, he took another step toward her. When she didn't move, he took that as a sign and cupped her face. Her chest moved ever so slightly with her breath and he leaned down, placing his lips on hers.

Her arms wrapped around his neck, and the kiss

deepened, but as he pulled her closer, she pushed him away, breaking the contact.

"I have to go. Thank you for a wonderful night, and I'll see you Friday."

As she dashed away again, Max wondered if she would ever stop running from their attraction.

12

Max grabbed the flowers from his passenger seat after parking the car at Alyssa's apartment. Even though Alyssa had agreed to this date, he wondered if this double date idea was a good one.

He had found himself drifting further away from Justin, and he worried that Justin would remind Alyssa of his past. Max had been working hard to show Alyssa how much he had changed, but it was too late to change his mind now and cancel the date.

After a quick knock on the door, it swung open, but it was not Alyssa's face on the other side. A pretty blond with a nose ring greeted him.

"You must be Max. I'm Roxy, Alyssa's roommate."

Max shook the proffered hand as he wondered why

Alyssa had never mentioned a roommate. "Nice to meet you, Roxy."

Her eyes traveled up and down his body, and she raised an eyebrow at him. The very gesture made Max feel more like an item being appraised than like a man, and he vowed never again to perform it on a woman.

"Thank you, Roxy," Alyssa said as she appeared behind the blond. She was dressed in a dark green top and slacks which brought out the natural green in her eyes and made her skin appear paler than it was. The effect was almost mystical.

"You look beautiful." The words slipped out before Max could reel them back in, and Alyssa blushed.

"Thanks, you look good too."

"Ah, aren't you guys cute?"

Roxy's obnoxious intrusion broke the spell of their locked gazes, and Max pasted a smile on his face to hide his annoyance. "Here, these are for you." He handed Alyssa the bouquet of red and white carnations he had picked up on his way.

"Thank you," she said, accepting them. "Roxy, will you put these in some water for me?" She handed the flowers off and pulled the door shut behind her. "I'm sorry about her. She's a little abrasive sometimes."

"Don't worry, Justin is the same way."

"Yeah, I remember meeting him. I have to say, I'm a little nervous about a double date with him."

Max stopped and took her hands. "Can I be honest? I am too. Justin has been my friend for years, but he represents a lot of the old Max. I've felt us separating as I've tried to put that guy behind me, but it would be rude to stand them up."

"I guess you're right," Alyssa said, shrugging. "Besides, what is the worst that could happen?"

An hour later, Alyssa found herself wishing she had never made that statement. Max had been trying his best to keep Justin in check, but he kept trying to bring up escapades from their past. Even worse, he didn't appear to be interested in the woman beside him as his eyes followed every woman who walked past them.

"Hey remember that time when—"

"You know, I think we'll skip dessert," Max said, interrupting him. "In fact, Alyssa has a final tomorrow, so I should get her home." He removed his wallet and placed a hundred-dollar bill on the table. "That should cover our part of the bill. You ready?"

Alyssa smiled at him. Though she didn't approve of the lie, she was immensely relieved to be leaving Justin's company.

"It was nice to meet you," she said to Justin's date, "and nice to see you again." The last five words she had to force out as she'd rather watch paint dry than go out with Justin again.

Max grabbed her hand as they exited the restaurant, and she squeezed it. She might still have some concerns about his past, but his present was showing definite promise.

"I really do want dessert," he said as they stepped into the warm summer air. "Care to accompany me to a local bakery?"

"Of course," she said, adopting his formal vocabulary. "I would be delighted."

He placed her hand on the crook of his arm and escorted her up the sidewalk and over a few blocks to a small pastry shop housed in between a clothing store and a used book shop. The Sweeter Side was stenciled in white on the glass door, and a small pink awning hung above the doorway. As he opened the door, a small bell jingled, announcing their arrival.

Delicate glass tables with white chairs dotted the inside of the shop, which was painted a pastel pink. A glass showcase spanned the wall just in front of them, ending at the cash register.

"How did you ever find this place?" Somehow, she couldn't picture the old Maxwell Banks ever stepping foot in this pretty shop.

"Actually, I know the owner."

Images of a woman from Maxwell's past flooded

Alyssa's mind, but she was not prepared for the plump, mousy brunette that appeared behind the counter. The woman was pretty, but not the type of woman she could ever see Maxwell with.

"Maxwell Banks? Is that you?" The woman's eyes lit up and she pushed her thick glasses up her nose.

"Hey, Marcy. I heard from a friend that you had opened a place here and figured it was time I tried it."

"Well, I'll be darned. I never thought I'd see the likes of you in my little 'ol shop. Maxwell and I went to high school together," she said to Alyssa, "though I don't think he knew I was alive."

"Oh, I knew," Maxwell said. "At least I did the day you baked us those brownies after our Homecoming win."

"That's right. I almost forgot about that. I suppose I should have warned the team about the nuts. Was your friend, what was his name, Doug? Was he alright?"

Max laughed and nodded his head. "He spent the night scratching a rash, but he was fine."

Alyssa smiled at this playful side of Max. Had he been more easy going in high school? If so, what had happened to him to make him change?

"Well, what can I do for you tonight?" Marcy placed her hands akimbo on her hips, reminding Alyssa of a Mrs. Butterworth's syrup bottle.

"We had to leave dinner without dessert, so we need something sweet." Max tossed a wink at Alyssa.

Marcy pursed her lips a moment and then held up a pudgy finger. "I have just the thing. Do you two like chocolate?"

Max raised his eyebrow at Alyssa, who smiled in return. "I love chocolate."

"Perfect. You two pick a table and I'll bring you something special."

As Marcy scurried out of the room, Maxwell gestured to an empty table. Marcy returned moments later with two small white plates. A petite fudgy brownie sat on each, drizzled with a white sauce and a raspberry on top.

"This is gorgeous," Alyssa said. Though it had no smell, her mouth began watering at the gooeyness she could see oozing from the chocolate.

"Thank you," Marcy said, executing a small curtsy. "This is my triple chocolate ooey gooey brownie. It may spike your blood sugar, but my customers love it. I'll leave you to try it."

She disappeared back into the kitchen area, leaving Max and Alyssa alone.

"Well, shall we?" Alyssa picked up her dainty silver fork and raised it almost like a toast.

Max smiled as he clinked her fork. "I thought you'd never ask."

As the first bite touched Alyssa's tongue, her eyes rolled back. "Oh my goodness. This is delicious." When she refocused, she realized Max wasn't eating, but watching her, and her face flamed. "Sorry, it's just so good." She dropped her eyes in embarrassment, but Max only laughed.

"Don't be sorry. You are gorgeous when you eat. I could watch you all day."

Though the conversation stalled after that, it was a comfortable silence. Alyssa enjoyed the way Max made her feel—she couldn't remember the last time a man did that—but she wondered if Max was being genuine or if this was all part of his act.

When their plates were clean, Max paid the bill and led her back outside. His hand found hers as they walked back to the car, and she didn't pull away. There was something comforting in his touch.

As they pulled into her apartment complex, she found herself wishing she lived alone so she could invite him in. It wasn't that she couldn't invite him in with Roxy there, but she never knew what Roxy would do, and it didn't invite the atmosphere she was hoping for.

He opened her door after parking the car and offered a hand to help her up, but he didn't move away once she stood. Instead he laced his fingers through her other hand so that both hands were intertwined.

"Alyssa, I really enjoyed spending time with you. I'd like to see you again."

His eyes were hypnotizing as she stared into them. She found the last pieces of her resolve that they shouldn't be together melting away. "I'd like that too."

The corners of his lips curled into a smile as he leaned down. When his lips touched hers, she didn't pull away but enjoyed the warmth of them against her own. It wasn't a long kiss, but it was enough to curl her toes and leave her breathless when he pulled away.

"Will you come tomorrow and hang out with Peyton and me? I was thinking of taking her to the park."

Alyssa nodded, her voice lost in the emotions running rampant through her body. Max smiled and took a step back. He dropped one of her hands, so they could walk side by side to the door. Once there, he gave it another squeeze and planted another soft kiss on her mouth before dropping her hand and walking away.

She stood rooted to the spot as she watched him go, wondering just what she had gotten herself into.

13

Max whistled as he entered the house after dropping Alyssa off. The evening hadn't started off well, but it had certainly ended much nicer. His lips were still tingling from the kiss with Alyssa, and though he knew he hadn't won her over completely yet, it felt like he was certainly making headway.

The sound of crying broke his daydream and he quickened his pace as he headed into the living room. Peyton was curled up on Helen's lap, her face buried in the older woman's shoulder. Her small frame rose and fell with her sobs.

"It's alright, dearie. It will all be okay."

Max rushed to Peyton. "What's the matter?"

"We were watching a movie, and she said it reminded her of her mum."

"I miss my mommy."

"Oh, Peyton. We all do," he said, reaching out to stroke her back. "I'll take her," he whispered to Helen. "You can take off."

"Are you sure? I don't mind staying and helping."

Max smiled at her. "No, I'm sure. I've got this. I won't always have you or Alyssa around, so I need to figure out ways to help her myself."

Helen's lips pulled into a smile and she took Max's hand. "You will be a good daddy, no matter what. I can see it in your eyes. Here, Peyton, go to Max."

Max reached down and grasped Peyton's arms with one arm while he slid the other under her knees. With an effortless curl, he removed her from Helen's chest and flipped her over onto his.

"Don't ever leave me, Daddy."

The word cut like a knife through his heart. He loved that she called him Daddy but hated that it was due to the tragedy she was feeling in missing Sarah.

"You see? She feels it too." Helen stood and patted Max's shoulder. "Call me if you need anything. I'll see you Monday, Peyton."

Max mouthed "thank you" to her as she left the room. Then he took the place Helen had just vacated on the couch.

Though he had no magic words to make everything better, he continued to pat Peyton's back and murmur, "It's alright."

When her body stilled, he looked down to see her asleep against his chest. Her little hand was curled into a fist near her chin and wet trails glistened on her cheeks. *How much harder will this be if Sarah doesn't get better?*

"She called me Daddy last night," Max said to Alyssa the next day as they sat on the bench watching Peyton play.

"Max, that's wonderful."

He sighed. "It is, but I think it's because she misses Sarah so much. She was in tears when I got home last night, and she cried herself to sleep."

"Oh, no. I'll call the treatment center and see if she's feels up to a phone call. That would help, wouldn't it?"

"Honestly, I have no idea what would help. I'm sort of going along by trial and error here."

Alyssa placed her hand on his knee. "I think you are doing a good job, especially for just a few weeks."

He glanced down at her hand before returning his gaze to Peyton, who was climbing the small ladder and sliding down the accompanying slide. "I'm just worried about what will happen if Sarah doesn't make it, you know?"

"That you have to give to God. It's in his hands now. There is nothing we can do on this end, except pray and be there for Peyton."

"Where does your faith in God come from?" he asked. "I mean, what started it all?"

Alyssa leaned back in the bench and tilted her face to the sky. "I grew up hearing all about him. My mom and my Aunt Sandra both became strong Christians before I was born, so God was always a part of my life. I didn't really develop a relationship with him though until my mom got sick. I was only a teenager the first time, and it rocked my world.

"I couldn't understand why God would let my mom get sick because she had changed her life around and become a crusader for him. My dad withdrew. I don't think he had a relationship with Jesus like my mom did, so the only one I could really talk to was Jesus and my Aunt Sandra. She taught me how to really pray and how to listen for God's voice.

"When my mom passed away a few years ago, I blamed God, but my aunt showed me all the extra time he gave me with my mom because she went into remission twice. Slowly, I started to see that God has a plan that we can't always see, and that sometimes, he answers our prayers in ways we don't expect.

"When I look back at my life, I can see that he's always been there for me." She turned her face back to

Maxwell. "I know you don't believe in him, but he's there for you too. He's just waiting for you to invite him in."

"I don't think your God would want me. You know a little of my past, but there's more." He adjusted his position to find Peyton, who had moved on from the slide and was now playing in the small house.

"That's what my Aunt Sandra thought after she got pregnant and had an abortion, but when she finally gave her life to God, he used her to save other women and their babies. God doesn't want you to wait until you're perfect because we never will be. Instead, he wants to meet you where you are and help you along the way."

"I'll think about it, and I'll keep taking Peyton to church. In fact, can we come with you again tomorrow?"

"Of course."

Alyssa's words continued to parade through Max's head as they watched Peyton play. He had never thought he needed God in his life, but he felt the need for some guidance, and if something happened to Sarah, he would definitely need some strength. He also never thought he'd like kids, but so far that had been a good change, and maybe letting God in his life would be the same.

14

"You look beautiful," Max said to Alyssa as he opened the door. In his hand was a bouquet of wild flowers, which he handed to her.

After their park date and church the next day, Max convinced Alyssa to join them for dinner. It hadn't been a hard sell as she enjoyed spending time with him though she still worried she was developing feelings for a man she shouldn't be.

"Come on in. We'll put them in some water for now and you can talk to Peyton."

As she followed him into the kitchen area, she couldn't help but notice his appearance. Though it wasn't what she was looking for long term, it always managed to grab her attention when she first saw him. His shoulders filled out his dark blue shirt and tapered into a narrow waist. His black slacks sat nicely on his lower half. She averted her eyes as the warmth started to spread across her face.

"Aunt Lyssa."

Peyton's voice grabbed her attention, and Alyssa leaned down to hug her. "Hey, Peyton, how are you doing?"

"Good, do you like your flowers? I helped Daddy pick them."

"They are beautiful, thank you."

"Hello, Alyssa. Nice to see you again."

Alyssa looked up to see Helen. "Hello, Helen. It's nice to see you too." Her voice held just a hint of curiosity as she thought the dinner was going to be the three of them.

"Helen's going to watch Peyton, so we can enjoy a nice dinner without distractions." Max smiled at her as he took the flowers and placed them in a crystal vase he pulled down from a cabinet while she was talking to Peyton.

"Oh, well, that's wonderful." Inside her heart had started a steady increase at the thought. Alone with Max at a nice restaurant? She could see two outcomes to this—firecrackers or disaster.

"Don't hurry home," Helen said, smiling at them. "I can hold the fort down here."

"Why do I feel like she knows something I don't know?" Alyssa asked in a lowered voice as she and Max headed back outside.

Max laughed. "Right? I always feel like that around Helen too."

The smile that lit up his handsome face caused a flutter in Alyssa's heart. He reached for her hand as they stepped outside the house and she squeezed his back. Though she still wasn't sure how she felt about his past, she couldn't deny that he appeared to be changing in front of her. Besides, the feeling of warmth that crept up her arms at his touch was too nice to let go of for now.

Opening the door, he helped her into the seat. Only then did he let go of her hand, and immediately she missed the warmth.

"Where are we going?" she asked as he slid into the driver's seat. They were in his BMW, and she could see why he didn't want to get rid of the car. The leather on the seats molded itself to her body, and she felt like she was sitting on foam.

"Do you like Italian?" He glanced at her with a sly smile.

Did she like Italian? Her mother, while not Italian, used to cook her own pasta at home, so Alyssa grew up eating Italian. In fact, one of the things she missed the most was her mother's cooking.

"Love it," she answered and couldn't tame the smile spreading across her own lips.

When they arrived at the restaurant, he hurried to open her door and took her hand once again. This time his fingers laced through hers and fit like a glove.

The inside of the restaurant was dark, lit only by dim overhead lights and candles at each table. A woman in a black dress with a white belt greeted them from behind a podium.

"Welcome to Il Piacere. Do you have a reservation?" Her voice was laced with just the slightest Italian accent.

"Yes, it's under Maxwell Banks."

Her eyes scanned a list in front of her. "Ah, yes, here you are Mr. Banks. Right this way."

She led the way to a back-corner table just big enough for two. A white table cloth draped the table top and white china plates sat at each side. Bright silverware lay on black cloth napkins that lined the right side of the plate. Two crystal glasses resided in front of each plate.

"Would you like some wine? Our house specialty is a red merlot tonight."

"Yes, that would be lovely, thank you." Max nodded at the hostess and then held the chair out for Alyssa to sit before taking his own seat. "I hope that was okay. I forgot to ask if you drink wine."

"I don't drink much, but as this is a special occasion, I'll partake."

"I hope it will be the first of many special occasions." He reached across the table and grabbed her hand as he smiled at her.

"Well, I was talking about passing my finals," she said with a shy smile, "but this is pretty good too."

"You passed your finals? That's fantastic, Alyssa." He squeezed her hand, sending another shot of warmth up her arm.

The waitress appeared then with a bottle of wine and a plate of bread. The plate she placed in between them, smiling at their joined hands. The wine she poured into Max's glass. "Try a taste, sir? Make sure it is to your liking?"

Max lifted the glass with his right hand, swirled it around, sniffed it, and finally took a sip. He had obviously done this before. "It is wonderful, thank you."

The waitress nodded and then filled his glass and Alyssa's. "Here is the menu for you." She handed over a single white sheet with about nine items on it. "Our special tonight is four-cheese tortellini. I'll give you a minute to look over the menu."

With a quick nod, she turned and walked away. Her brown hair was pulled into a loose bun and a few tendrils curled at the nape of her neck.

Alyssa scanned the offerings, her eyes widening at the prices. Though she assumed this was a date, she would hate to presume he was paying only to find out she must cover a fifty-dollar meal.

"Order what you want. Don't worry about the prices." His voice was soft and non-judgmental.

"Am I that obvious?" A faint heat stole across her cheeks.

"No, but when you have money like I do, sometimes you forget not everyone does. Tonight is on me, and I want you to choose what you want."

She nodded and returned her focus to the menu. There were two types of salad, four entrees, and three desserts listed. Though they all looked good, she decided on the special. After all, it was probably the special for a reason.

After the order was placed, Max squeezed her hand. "Tell me a little more about you."

"Hmm, well, I'm an only child. My parents always wanted more but couldn't get pregnant after me. I left Mesquite, where I'm from, when I was eighteen to go to school here. What else do you want to know?"

"How did you and Sarah meet?"

Alyssa smiled as she remembered the meeting. "At church, actually. She came in wanting help with an unplanned pregnancy. Said she thought the father would push her to have an abortion, so she left without telling him, but she had no family and needed some help. Would you have?"

Max blinked at her, clearly taken off guard. "Would I have what?"

"Would you have pushed her to have an abortion?"

After taking a deep breath, Max leaned back and ran a hand through his hair. "I'd like to say no. I mean Sarah meant more to me than anyone I had dated. I hope I would have said I'd stay with her, but I can't know for sure. As you know, I was not ready to settle down then, and I hate to think I might have pushed her to get rid of Peyton, but..."

He couldn't finish the sentence, and Alyssa was almost sorry she asked. "Do you think you're ready to settle down now?"

His hand rubbed across his chin as he considered her. "I didn't think I'd ever be ready to settle down, but then Peyton came into my life and I met you. I think I could be ready to settle down with the right person."

"Hah, don't listen to him honey."

Surprised, Alyssa glanced up to see a chesty blond in a tight shirt standing at the end of their table.

"That's nearly the same line he used on me before he 'lost my number.'" The woman made air quotes as she said the last three words before placing her hands on her hips. "How ya doing, Max?"

The color drained from Max's face as he looked from the blond to Alyssa. "I'm doing all right, and I'm sorry I didn't call."

"No, you're not. You're just sorry I ran into you and am ruining your date, along with your chance to score tonight. I bet you can't even remember my name, can you?"

Max opened his mouth as if he was going to say her name, but then he closed it and shook his head. His eyes dropped to the table momentarily before flicking back up to the woman. "No, I can't, and I'm sorry."

The woman turned to Alyssa. "Get out now while you can honey." Then she turned her furious eyes on Max and spat out two words, "It's Iris," before stomping away and leaving a stunned Alyssa staring at Max.

"You didn't even remember their names?" Her voice was barely more than a whisper.

Max hung his head. "To be honest, I didn't even know their names to begin with most of the time."

"How many have there been?"

Max's eyes slid to the side, avoiding the questions. "More than I'd like to tell you, but there wasn't a woman every weekend. It was just a different woman every time."

Alyssa sucked in her breath, disgusted and shocked. All the walls that had been crumbling the past week began rebuilding rapidly.

"But I'm not like that anymore," Max hurried on. He reached for her hand, but Alyssa pulled it back and folded it in her lap. "I don't want that life anymore. Peyton changed me. You changed me."

"Stop," she said, holding up her hand. Though her heart wanted to believe him, every other sensible part of her body was screaming at her to run, that he would be just like the guy in college. "I don't know what to think right now, and I need a little time to process."

Her heart ached when she saw Max's face fall, but she must protect herself. The food arrived a few minutes after, but the mood was broken. They finished their food in silence and opted for no dessert. This was not the night she had been hoping for. Would going out with Max be like this all the time? Even if he had changed, would the endless parade of his past never cease?

Max stared at Alyssa across the table and let out a small sigh. This was not the night he had been hoping for. He had wanted to show her the new Max, but Iris showing up had just reminded her of his past, and he couldn't blame her.

The look on Iris's face had been one of anger but also guilt. He had never thought about how the women must feel the next day when he didn't call them back or return their calls, but as he looked at Alyssa's face, he could see a sadness there that he imagined the other women must have felt, especially because he hadn't been honest about his intentions.

The rest of the meal passed in silence, torturing him. He wanted to try to explain himself, but she had made it clear that she needed space, and if he was going to prove he'd changed, then he would have to honor her wishes.

He didn't try to hold her hand as they walked back to the car, but he did still open the door for her. She flashed him a tight smile, but even that small gesture encouraged him. He might have to work harder, but the fact that she was looking at him at all, was a start.

The ride back to his house was also mute, but as he pulled into the driveway, he tried one more time. "Alyssa, I'm really sorry. This isn't how I wanted the night to go. I know I have a past, but I am trying to change."

"I believe you are." Her voice was quiet, but at least she was looking at him. "I just need some time to think things over. Will you tell Peyton good night for me?"

"Wait, don't you want to take your flowers?"

A look of indecision crossed her face, but after a sigh, she agreed and followed him into the house.

"Aunt Lyssa. You're back."

"We sure are, sweetie. Did you have fun with Helen?"

It floored Max how she could turn on her happy

voice that quickly when she had been reserved with him for the last hour.

"Uh huh." Peyton nodded her head up and down enthusiastically.

"We made dinner and then we colored," Helen said, rising from the table. She looked from Alyssa to Max but said nothing though Max could see the questions in her eyes.

"That's great. Well, I have an early day tomorrow, so I'm going to get my flowers and call it a night. I'll see you soon, Peyton." With a quick nod at Max, Alyssa turned and walked out of the kitchen.

"Peyton, why don't you go play with your doll for a minute while I chat with Max?" Though it was meant as a question, it came out more like a statement from Helen's mouth, and Peyton agreed without arguing. "I take it the night didn't go as planned."

Max sighed and ran his hand across his forehead. "No, it started off well, but then a woman from my past showed up and told Alyssa not to trust me. It was awful, Helen. I finally felt like I was making progress, but now I feel like I'm back at square one."

Helen motioned for him to sit at the bar and then crossed to the stove and set the kettle to boiling. As if she owned the place, she rummaged around in the pantry for tea and pulled out two mugs. Max watched her, waiting for words of wisdom, but she said nothing as she waited for the kettle to boil. When it started to whistle, she flicked the knob to off and poured steaming water into both mugs before joining him at the bar.

"Back in England, we believe that tea can help your mind think more clearly. Drink up." She lifted her own mug to her lips and Max followed suit though he wasn't usually a tea drinker. "Your past is not something you can change, but you can change your future."

"What's the point of changing my future if my past is always going to rear its ugly head?" Max took another sip of the warm liquid, surprised to find that he liked it.

"Perhaps it is because you are trying to change superficially?"

"What do you mean?"

"I mean you are trying to change your actions, but you're trying to do it all alone. We are all imperfect creatures, and as hard as we try, we will all make mistakes, but those of us who have Jesus in our lives get the extra help of the Holy Spirit inside us. He helps us make better decisions and people can often see a physical change from having him inside."

"I've been going to church, but I'm not sure I'm ready to make a decision like that."

Helen smiled as she sipped her tea. "Then are you sure you're ready to seriously date a woman who is?"

Her words rattled around in his head as he pondered

them. Was his lack of faith keeping them apart? Would that be enough to convince her he had really changed?

"What's up with you?" Roxy asked as Alyssa entered the door of their shared apartment.

"It's Max. We had dinner tonight, and it was going great, but then one of his one-night stands recognized him and came over. She told me not to trust him, and now I don't know what to think." Alyssa collapsed on the couch, dropping her head into her hands.

Roxy shut the book she was reading to give her full attention to Alyssa. "I know I met him, but all I saw was his hotness. How old is he?"

"I don't know. Late twenties, I guess." Alyssa's voice was muffled by her hands.

"I know you don't want to hear this, but not everyone grew up in faith like you. For those of us who didn't, sleeping with people isn't unheard of. In fact, most of us do it a lot."

"I know that, but he is—or was—I don't know, a serial one-night stander. What if he just wants one night with me? What if he's like Tyson?"

"Who's Tyson?"

Alyssa dropped her hands and looked up at Roxy. "You know Tyson, the guy from my Freshman year who only wanted to sleep with me and dumped me when I wouldn't?"

"Ah." Roxy nodded, her blond hair skimming her shoulders with the motion. Roxy wasn't around when Tyson happened, but Alyssa had filled her in during one of their late-night conversations about why she was waiting for marriage to be intimate. "Well, you said Max was trying to change, right?"

Alyssa nodded as she grabbed the pillow next to her and hugged it to her chest.

"Okay, then you have to understand he can't change his past. It's always going to be there. You have to decide if you are okay with it or not."

Though the words made perfect sense in her head, that was the problem. She wasn't sure if she could find a way to be okay with it or not.

❊ 15 ❊

Max picked up his phone and punched the button again. The welcome screen flashed the time, but no new messages. He hadn't heard from Alyssa since she left Tuesday night, and it was now Friday. He wanted to give her time, but now he wondered if he should call her and try pleading his case again.

"Hey man," Justin said poking his head in the door.

Max dropped the phone, sending it clattering across the desk.

"Still no word, huh?"

"No, do you think I should call her?"

"I think," Justin said, crossing the floor to sit in the chair opposite Max's desk, "that you should come out with me tonight. Everyone is going to be there, and it will get your mind off this woman for a bit. Maybe it will clear your thinking, and you'll know what you want to do tomorrow."

"I don't know." Max's words came out in a large sigh. "I don't feel like partying much anymore and you remember what happened last time."

"You don't have to party. Just come and have a few drinks with us." Justin leaned in, placing his hands on the desk. "Everyone has been asking about you man, and it's my birthday. Just come say 'hi,' at least."

Max pressed the button on the phone one more time even though he knew she hadn't called or texted as he would have heard it. The screen was indeed blank of any contact. Just the time of 5:55 on his screen. "Okay," he sighed, "let me call Helen and ask if she can stay a little later with Peyton."

Justin smiled and pumped his fist near his chest. "Awesome, it will be great to have you back. Billionaire Banks rides again."

Max wasn't back as he was only going because it was Justin's birthday. He picked up his phone and called Helen, who agreed to watch Peyton until he returned home. She didn't comment on his decision to go out, but he could hear the admonishing tone in her voice.

"All right, let's go," he said when the clock struck six. Knowing Justin, he had this party set at one of the hotspots that had a happy hour. Hopefully, Max could get in, grab a few drinks, and then find a nice way to excuse himself so he could go home and indulge in his misery. He snickered at the thought as he realized he was becoming like the women he so desperately avoided.

They decided to take two cars, so Max could leave when he wanted. Plus, Justin would probably be taking a woman home, and Max had no plan to do so.

Sure enough, they pulled into Club Z, a popular hangout for the after-work crowd in their late twenties and thirties. Max sighed as he exited the car. Club Z was always full of beautiful women looking to meet up with the newest guy, and for some reason, they seemed to be able to smell his wealth.

The bouncer was a broad man about their age with bulging biceps and brick shoulders, and he waved them through without bothering to check their IDs. He knew them both by sight; that was how often they came here.

Inside, the club was dimly lit. Couches and tables filled one end of the room for those not dancing who wanted to try to hold a conversation. An expansive dance floor took up the middle space. The DJ booth sat in the middle above it, blasting out the latest hip hop songs. Though it was early, the crowd on the dance floor was already large and the bodies were jockeying for positions. To the left was the bar. Three bartenders in white shirts manned the bar, grabbing glasses from a silver rack above it and filling them with liquid to hand either to the waitress or the patrons.

"Let's get a couch," Max yelled and pointed to the right. Justin nodded, and the two secured a large brown couch as far away from the music as possible. "Great place for conversations." The sarcasm was evident in Max's voice. Though the music was quieter here, he still was forced to raise his voice to be heard.

"We aren't here to converse." Justin flashed him an eyebrow raise and motioned the waitress over.

"Right." Max looked down at his watch, wishing he had just said 'no' and gone home to Peyton. She'd be eating dinner right now and filling him in on her day. Maybe she would have even heard from Alyssa, who still seemed to be stopping in to see Peyton even though she was avoiding Max, and could give him some Intel. He should have just swallowed his pride and called Alyssa to try to smooth things over again.

"Max, how are you buddy? Heard you got shackled with a kid." Chris Moore, another friend of Justin's, slid onto the couch next to him.

"I wouldn't call it shackled. Peyton is great. I'm glad I'm getting the chance to know her." Max tried to keep his voice light, but inside he was seething. Was this what he sounded like a few weeks ago? The thought created a wad of disgust in his throat.

"What'll you have?" The waitress, a blond woman in

tight black shorts and a tighter white shirt, stood looking at him.

"Just a coke, thanks," Max said, but Justin jumped in before the woman could leave.

"Uh-uh, man, you promised to have at least one drink."

"Fine, a rum and coke then, but just one."

The waitress raised her eyebrow as if she had heard that line before and traipsed back to the bar.

Before she returned with their drinks, three women joined them at the couch. It was clear from their glassy eyes that they had been drinking and were well on their way to being drunk.

"My name is Amber," the brunette who had decided to leach onto Max said. She was pretty with dark hair and brown eyes, though she wore more makeup than he generally preferred, but she didn't hold a candle to Alyssa.

"Max," he said and scooted just a bit away from her. She didn't take the hint though and curled up even closer to him.

"I like Max, like Mad Max, you know that old show? You kind of even look like Mel Gibson." She placed her hand on his arm and batted her eyes.

He did look a little like Mel Gibson, albeit it a younger version, but the flattery did nothing for him this time. The waitress returned with their drinks before he could respond, and Max tossed back a swig of the drink.

"Ooh, can I have a strawberry daiquiri?" the woman beside him asked. Her friends quickly chimed in with their orders as well.

The waitress raised her brow and glanced at the men. The silent question of who was claiming responsibility for these drunk girls was evident in her stare.

"Don't worry," Justin said, "We'll make sure they get home okay."

Max wanted to kick him. He didn't want to have to worry about getting these women home; he hadn't planned on staying that long.

After another long look, the waitress shrugged and walked off to fill the girls' order.

"So, what do you do?" The woman was competing for his attention again.

"I work in advertising." Another swig and his drink was half gone. He might have to order another just to get through another hour in this place. Chris and his woman had meandered to the dance floor though Max wasn't sure you could classify what they were doing as dancing.

"Do you want to dance?" Amber asked, following his gaze.

"No, I don't dance."

The waitress returned with frothy, fruity drinks for

the women and Max was granted a few minutes of blissful relief as Amber sucked her straw.

"Another?" the waitress asked, nodding her head at his nearly empty drink.

Max glanced down at the drink, then at the woman next to him. "One more," he said, though he promised himself he wouldn't.

By the time his second drink arrived, Amber had finished her first and was back to rambling on, this time about her exercise routine. Her lithe physique hadn't gone unnoticed—though he had tried his best to avoid his gaze lingering there—but he didn't need her regimen detailed either.

"I'm going to hit the bathroom. I'll be back in a minute." He hated having to announce his intentions to the woman, but it would be rude to just get up and walk away.

The bathroom was over by the bar, so he was forced to traverse the crowd on the dance floor to get there. At least twice, female hands reached out to him to entice him to dance, and he had to untangle himself from their grips.

Finally, he reached his destination and pushed open the men's room door. A few minutes later, he was navigating the gauntlet again to return to the table.

Only Amber sat there now, nursing another drink. "Where is Justin and your friend?"

She giggled and shrugged. "I think they left, if you get my meaning."

Max sighed. Just what he needed. "Okay, well how about your other friend?"

Another shrug. "Haven't seen her either."

Annoyance flared through him as his eyes rolled. "Right, well I can't leave you here alone, and I'm leaving, so I guess you're coming with me."

"I thought you'd never ask." She fell against his chest as she tried to stand.

Max wrapped an arm around her to steady her and led her to the bar to settle his tab. The bartender flashed him an eyebrow wiggle and a knowing smile which Max ignored as he signed the receipt.

Amber was nearly passed out as he got her to the door. The outside air woke her just enough to allow her to stumble to the car. Max had to hold her up more than once as they crossed the parking lot. She was in no shape to tell him where she lived.

He folded her into the passenger seat where she curled up and closed her eyes. Great, what now? He whipped out his phone to call Justin, hoping her friend had drank less and could give him directions, but the call went to voicemail.

"Justin? It's Max. You left me with Amber, and she's passed out. I have no idea where she lives. Call me as soon as you get this, so I can take her home." He could barely hide the agitation in his voice as he punched the end call button. His only option now was to take her back to his place and hope Justin called soon.

As Amber was still passed out in the car when he pulled into the garage, Max left her there for a moment while he checked to see if Peyton was asleep. Though the situation was innocent, he didn't want her seeing a woman coming into the house.

"That was an early night," Helen said, smiling at him as he entered the kitchen.

"Yeah, unfortunately it isn't over yet. Is Peyton asleep?" He glanced around for her as the words left his mouth.

"Yes, I put her down a few minutes ago. Why?" There was an edge in Helen's voice that was more than idle curiosity.

"Justin left me with a drunk girl. I couldn't leave her there when her friends left, so I was going to take her home. Unfortunately, she drank so much she passed out, and I have no idea where she lives. I was going to let her sleep it off in the other guest room and take her home when Justin calls me back or she wakes up, which ever happens sooner, but I didn't want Peyton seeing her come in."

"Are you sure that's a good idea?" Helen asked.

"No, but I don't have many other options."

"I could take her to my house," Helen offered.

"Thank you, Helen, but she doesn't know you, and I don't want to scare the girl too much."

Helen tipped her head. "All right, if you're sure." The raise of her eyebrow let Max know she didn't like this plan, but he didn't either. However, he had little choice.

"I am. Thanks, Helen, and I'll see you Monday."

After Helen gathered her purse and bid him good-night, Maxwell headed back to the car. Amber was still passed out in the passenger seat, her mouth open and a tiny line of drool tracking down the right side of her mouth.

Max unfastened her seat belt and snaked an arm behind her back. Her other arm he draped over his shoulder, holding her right hand in his. She was dead weight, but he managed to extricate her from the car this way. Then he dropped her right arm and squatted to slip his arm under her knees and pick her up. He was glad she didn't weigh much and that he worked out, but dead weight was still heavy.

Thankfully, the door to the house hadn't closed completely behind him, and he was able to push it open with his shoulder and shuffle down the hall to the other guest bedroom. That door was closed, and he was forced to drop her legs to open it. She let out a muffled grunt, but her eyes remained closed. How much had she had to drink?

After the door was open, he scooped her back up and crossed to the bed. He laid her down gently, pulling the covers out from under her and then back over her body. She looked young as her brown hair splayed across the white pillow, and he wondered how old she really was.

Shaking his head, he exited the room and headed down the hallway. A quick check on Peyton revealed her asleep in her bed, so he continued to his own room.

As he pulled his phone out of his pocket, he checked the screen, but there had been no call from Justin or Alyssa. Sighing, he plugged it into the charger and changed for bed. As his head hit the pillow, he decided he had given her enough space, and like it or not, he was going to call her tomorrow.

16

"You're up early," Roxy said as Alyssa entered the kitchen.

"I couldn't sleep. I was up all night thinking again about Max. I've been praying since the other night, and though I have no clear answer, I can't stop thinking about him, so maybe that is my answer. I'm going to go see him and apologize this morning."

"Good for you." Roxy raised her mug of coffee in a mock salute.

"After some coffee, of course." Alyssa laughed as she filled her own mug and took a sip.

With the coffee finished and her outfit on, she stood in front of the mirror. Dark circles still ringed her eyes though they were lighter after her application of foundation. She didn't think Max would care, but she still wished they weren't there. It was her own fault, however. If she had trusted Max the first time, she wouldn't have lost sleep over it the last few days.

As she pulled up to Max's house, she wondered briefly if she should have called first. Maybe he would still be sleeping, or maybe he and Peyton would have gone out to breakfast. It was still early after all. Dismissing the negative vibes, Alyssa parked the car and walked up the pathway to the front door. Her finger paused but pressed the round doorbell.

Max opened the door a moment later. A genuine smile flashed across his face before it fell, and his eyes widened. His head turned to both sides as if looking for something. He looked... nervous. Was it because she caught him still in pajama pants?

His pants hung low on his waist and a white t-shirt stretched across his chest. Alyssa's eyes were drawn to his muscular chest before she caught herself and looked away.

"Sorry, I guess I should have called, but..." her voice trailed off as she caught movement behind Max. A woman with long brown hair padded down the hallway as if she owned the house.

Max, hearing the noise, turned to the woman and then back to Alyssa. At least he had the decency to look embarrassed. "It's not what you think, Alyssa." His head shook back and forth, as he said the words, as if that added an extra reason for her to believe him.

"I think a woman spent the night in your house." Alyssa nearly spat the words at him in her anger.

"Okay, it is what you think but nothing happened. I went out with Justin last night because it was his birthday and Amber was too drunk to tell me where she lived—"

"Amber? You remember her name? Well, I guess that is an improvement from the lady at the restaurant. What was her name again? I should have listened to her. I can't believe I spent the last few days losing sleep over not believing you, and then when I come to apologize, you have another woman here." Her words were rushing out like a waterfall, but she couldn't stop them. "Was I just another notch to put in your bedside then? Were you going to seduce me and then forget my name too?"

"That's not fair," he said, firing back at her. "First off, you haven't let me explain. Second, you haven't called all week or returned my calls. I didn't know if you were ever coming back." His posture had quickly shifted from nervous to agitated, and he seemed to fill the large doorframe.

The woman appeared behind Max and laid a hand on his arm. "I heard shouting. Is everything all right, Max?"

He glared at her as he brushed off her hand.

After she looked from Max to Alyssa, the woman disappeared again.

"So, you just jumped on the next train, huh?" Alyssa hated the caustic tone in her voice, but she couldn't turn it off.

His arms crossed as he leaned back onto the frame. "I was trying to be a gentleman. I couldn't leave her at the club, and as she passed out in my car, I had no way of knowing where she lived. I didn't really have another option, Alyssa."

"There's always another option, Max." His name felt like poison on her tongue now. "Here, I'll give you one more." She narrowed her eyes at him. "See anyone you want. I'm done. I should have known you couldn't really change." She turned and headed toward the car, tears pricking her eyes and blurring her vision.

"Maybe it's a good thing," he shot back. "You talk about love and forgiveness, but all I see is a stubborn woman who thinks she never makes mistakes."

"That's not true," Alyssa said, but even as the words left her mouth, she wondered if it was. She spared one final look at him before climbing in her car. He still stood in the doorway, shaking his head at her. Her hands were shaking as she buckled the seatbelt, but blissfully the tears waited until she pulled out of the drive before tumbling down her cheeks.

"I'm such a fool. Why did I think he could change?"

She said the words aloud, hoping for a sense of peace, but silence was all she received in return. Silence and the mocking reminder that she had been too angry to believe him when he tried to explain. Could it be possible that he was just being a gentleman? The woman had been fully dressed after all, but she could have put on her clothes before exiting the bedroom. And if he was just being a gentleman why even go out in the first place?

She had no answer by the time she pulled up to her apartment, but at least the tears had stopped for now.

"Whoa, that was short," Roxy said, pausing the show she was watching on TV when Alyssa entered. "What happened?"

Alyssa rolled her eyes as she slumped down beside Roxy. "There was a woman there who spent the night. He said it was innocent, but I don't believe him. I feel so stupid." At the last word, the tears sprung anew and began another slow trickle down her cheeks.

"Hey, it's not your fault. This guy has been playing the game for a while it sounds like. The only one to blame is him. I know what will make this better. Hang on." She bounded up from her chair and into the kitchen. Roxy had been a track star in high school and her long legs were still toned and in shape as she ran three miles every day.

There was the sound of cupboards opening and porcelain clinking, followed by the drawer and then the fridge opening and closing two times. A moment later, Roxy returned with two bowls of Chocolate Monkey ice cream.

"Ice cream? It's not even lunch time."

"Hey, ice cream makes everything better. It doesn't matter what time."

Alyssa smiled as she took the bowl, but though ice cream would make her feel better for the time it took to eat it, she knew it wasn't going to fill the aching spot inside her heart.

Max sighed as Alyssa's car exited the drive. How had this gone so wrong so fast? Why hadn't she let him explain? He shut the door and trudged to the kitchen. Amber was perched on a barstool with a cup of coffee in her hand.

"I hope you don't mind that I helped myself to some coffee. I tried to ask, but you looked a little busy. Boy, this is quite the place you have here."

Her voice was too perky this early in the morning, and Max was already feeling grumpy after the argument with Alyssa. "Yeah, it's great."

"You seem angry. Is it about the woman at the door?" Her wide eyes were filled with curiosity but seemed to be lacking the knowledge of her part in his anger.

"Yes, it's about the woman at the door. She thinks I brought you home to... she thinks we…" He shook his head. "Anyway, it doesn't matter now. She left."

"Why didn't you just tell her that nothing happened?" She flicked her hand and took another sip of her mug. "I mean, I assume it didn't, since I woke up by myself and still in my clothes from the night before."

He stared at her, trying to contain his anger. "I tried telling her that, but unfortunately your poor timing didn't help matters."

Amber's head snapped back in surprise. "Well, excuse me. I had a pounding headache and needed some coffee. By the way, where's your aspirin?"

Rolling his eyes, he stepped over to the highest cabinet and pulled out a bottle of aspirin. He walked back to her and slammed it on the counter before returning to his room. He wanted this woman out of his house now, and as Peyton was still asleep, he needed Helen to come stay at the house in case she woke.

She showed up fifteen minutes later wearing what looked like a housecoat with curlers in her hair.

"You could have gotten dressed first," he said as he opened the door. A sliver of his anger fizzled at the sight of her.

"And risk your daughter seeing some strange woman in the house? I think not. You should have let me take the girl home last night." She poked him in the chest as she stepped inside the house.

"Yeah, I should have," Max sighed. "Alyssa showed up to apologize, but then she saw Amber. She's furious this time, Helen. I don't think she will ever forgive me."

Helen had the decency not to say 'I told you so,' but she did shake her head sadly. "We'll figure something out, Max. For now, get that woman home."

Max nodded and marched back to the kitchen. "Let's go, Amber."

She jumped at his forceful voice, spilling coffee on the countertop. "Go? Where are we going?"

"I'm taking you home."

"Already, but I thought we could—" She stopped as he glared at her.

"You have cost me quite enough. We aren't going to do anything. Now, come on."

After another swig of whatever was left in her coffee mug, she set it on the countertop and slid off the barstool, following him out to the garage.

"Where to?" he asked her when they were both buckled.

"3410 Buckley Street."

Unfamiliar with that location, Max plugged it into his phone and sighed when the ETA showed half an hour drive.

"So, I guess this means you won't call me?" she asked when he pulled up in front of her place.

"Out." He pointed out the door, feeling a little mean, but also relieved he would never have to see her again, and he hadn't tried to trick her. He should have just called her a taxi, but in his effort to turn over a new leaf, he had thought taking her home was more gentlemanly. Now, he just wanted to get home.

She pouted her lip as she opened the door. "Fine."

After the tedious drive home, a cup of coffee called his name. The pattering of little feet echoed down the hall as he entered the house.

"Daddy, Helen's here. You going somewhere?" Peyton asked, running up to him.

Reaching down, he swung her into the air and situated her on his hip. "Nope, I'm staying home with you all day. Helen was just watching you while I took care of some business."

"Oh, good. Can we play princess today?" Her bright blue eyes shined back at him.

"I can't think of anything I'd rather do, but can you let me get some coffee and breakfast first?"

"Okay."

After he set her on the floor, she scurried into the living room to watch her favorite cartoon. Max turned to Helen. "What does playing princess involve?"

"Well, when I play with her, it involves a tiara and a

wand, but maybe she won't make you wear the tiara."
Helen winked at him and smiled.

"Haha, very funny." Max grabbed a mug from the
cupboard and filled it with coffee. Though the warm
beverage calmed him, it did not heal the hole in his heart
from Alyssa's departure. "What am I going to do,
Helen?" he asked as he sank onto the barstool.

"First, you are going to eat breakfast." She placed a
plate of pancakes and eggs in front of him. "Then, we are
going to figure that out. Now eat up."

17

"Where are you going?" Roxy leaned against the counter, her arms crossed and her eyebrow raised, as Alyssa wheeled a suitcase behind her into the kitchen.

"I'm going home. I need to get away from here for a few days, so I'm going to see my Aunt Sandra."

Roxy's head fell forward. "Are you sure? You haven't been back there since—"

"I know," Alyssa said, cutting her off. She hadn't been back home since her mom died a few years ago from cancer, but her conflicting emotions proved too much for her. She needed some clarity and her Aunt Sandra was the one person who had always been able to give her clarity. "But I'm hoping it will help, and it's only for a few days."

"I get that." Roxy pushed herself off the counter and crossed to Alyssa, enveloping her in a hug. "Have a safe trip, and I hope you find the answer you're looking for."

"Me too."

As Alyssa pulled into Sandra's driveway, a feeling of peace enveloped her. Sandra wasn't her aunt by blood, but she had been her mother's best friend and had always been like a second mother to Alyssa. Now, Alyssa couldn't wait to see her. It had been too long, especially since Henry had passed away and all of their children were now out of the house. Sandra must be lonely, and Alyssa made a mental promise to visit more often.

Sandra opened the door before Alyssa could even knock. The smile on her face reached from ear to ear. "Alyssa, it's so good to see you."

She opened her arms and Alyssa dropped her suitcase, so she could lean down and hug the woman. "It's good to see you too, Aunt Sandra."

"Well, come in, come in. I've got chicken in the oven and a salad ready for dinner. You do still eat, don't you? You've gotten so skinny, I'm no longer sure."

"Yes, Aunt Sandra, I still eat. I've just been so busy with school that I've been going non-stop, but I finished my last final last week, so I'll have time to slow down now." Alyssa set her suitcase just inside the door as she followed Sandra to the kitchen. She must be cooking her famous garlic chicken because the scent of garlic was strong in the air.

Alyssa watched as Sandra wheeled over to the modified counter and began tossing in the few remaining ingredients needed for the salad. "How did you do?"

"I did well. I got A's and B's on all my finals."

Dropping the wooden spoon she was using to stir the salad, Sandra turned her deep brown eyes on Alyssa. "Your mother would be so proud of you—is so proud of you as I know she's looking down on us."

Tears pricked Alyssa's eyes at the mention of her mom. "Thanks, Aunt Sandra. I just wish she could help me with finding a good man."

Sandra opened her mouth to speak but was interrupted by the doorbell. "Oh, that will be my friend Callie. Will you go let her in? I invited her over because you two are about the same age and she needed a night off. She's got a little one at home."

"Sure." Alyssa blinked as she headed back to the front door. Why would she invite someone else over? Alyssa had told her she wanted to talk, right?

On the other side of the door was a beautiful woman with dark hair and green eyes. Her face lit up in a smile as she saw Alyssa. "You must be Alyssa. Sandra has told me so much about you. I'm Callie," she stuck out her hand, "and I'm so pleased to meet you."

"Uh, same," Alyssa stammered, shaking the outstretched hand, "though Aunt Sandra didn't tell me much about you."

"That's Sandra for you." Callie stepped into the living room and closed the door behind her. "I'm sure she has something planned. She always does. Called me up today and said you were coming and could use some sisters in Christ around you, so here I am." She leaned in and lowered her voice. "Plus, I needed a break."

Alyssa nodded though she had no idea what Callie was talking about. The only thing she was sure of was that her aunt had set this up, but she was not sure she'd feel comfortable telling a stranger about her issue."

"Sandra, can I help?" Callie had reached the kitchen ahead of her and was already grabbing glasses down from a cupboard.

"Just with what you're already doing. Here, Alyssa, take this to the table please." Sandra handed her the bowl of salad and Alyssa carried it to the table set for three.

"Tea or water?" Callie asked, setting a jar of sun tea on the table.

"Tea is fine," Alyssa responded watching Callie and her aunt interact. They must get together often because Callie seemed to know where everything was in the kitchen.

"Sit, sit," Sandra said, wheeling over with the baked chicken in a dish on her lap. She set it on the table and motioned for Alyssa to sit.

Callie took the other chair, and the three women scooted up to the table. Sandra grabbed Alyssa's left and Callie's right hand in hers before bowing her head. "Lord, we are so thankful that Alyssa has come to visit. Be with us in this place and fill us with your wisdom as we tackle her problem. Bless this food and this company. In your name, Amen."

"Amen," Callie and Alyssa echoed, and the passing of the food began.

Alyssa hadn't expected to feel comfortable sharing her information with Callie, but as the dinner progressed, she saw why the two were friends. Callie appeared easy to talk to, and as she shared some of her past with Alyssa, Alyssa realized she might have a good perspective on the situation.

By the time dinner was over and the women had retired to the living room with cups of tea, Callie felt like an old friend, and Alyssa found herself sharing the whole ordeal with them both.

"It sounds like you might care for him," Sandra said as Alyssa finished.

"I care for Peyton," she said taking a sip of her tea, "He is just... I don't know what he is, besides frustrating."

Callie and her aunt shared a glance, and Alyssa wondered what unsaid words passed between them.

"I know he made some mistakes, but we all have," Sandra said. "Remember, we are all broken people and God can use us even broken as we are."

"I get that Aunt Sandra, but he had a woman there. What if it means he hasn't changed and he'll just keep doing the same thing? I don't want to get mixed up in that."

"People can change. I did. Your mom did. Callie did. It just takes someone showing them the love of Jesus." Her aunt looked down into her tea cup. "Darn. Empty. You two keep talking, I'm going to get a refill."

Had she shown Max the love of Jesus? The image of their last fight flashed through her mind, and Alyssa cringed. That was definitely not Jesus' love that day.

"I don't want to contradict what Sandra says," Callie's voice brought Alyssa back into the present. "She's probably the wisest woman I know, but I was with a man who couldn't change or wouldn't change. The thing is, if you do some soul searching, you'll know. I was blind at first, but when I really looked inside, I realized Daniel would never change, or at least not for me. I think if you look inside, you'll know whether this Max is capable of change or not."

"Thanks, Callie. I'm glad Sandra invited you over tonight."

"I am too," Callie said, returning the smile.

"Why are we here?" Peyton asked, as Max unhooked her from the car seat.

"Well, Alyssa and I are in a bit of a fight. I thought it would be nice if we gave her some space, so this is Helen's church."

Max had been unsure when Helen first suggested the idea of changing churches. What if Peyton hated it? But as they approached the small white church, Max felt a sense of peace.

Helen was at the door waiting for them. "You made it." She gave Peyton a high five before turning to Max. "Come in. Let me introduce you around."

The thought sent ice water through Max's veins, but he followed her in anyway, Peyton's hand clasped in his.

"This is Pastor Bill."

Pastor Bill was an older man with grey at his temples. He wore a button-down shirt and some slacks but no tie, and he looked a little more relaxed than Max's images of typical pastors.

"Pastor Bill, this is my friend Max and his daughter Peyton." Helen made the introductions and then stepped back, smiling.

"Pleased to meet you, Max and you, Miss Peyton. I hope you enjoy the service."

"Oh, I'm sure he will," Helen jumped in before Max could speak. "I know we all do every week." She grabbed Max's arm and steered him to the right. "Let's check Peyton in, and then you can escort an older woman to her seat."

Max smiled as he looked down at her hand on his arm. It seemed that she was escorting him currently, and he knew she was quite capable of finding her seat herself, but he humored her. After dropping Peyton in the small Sunday school room, he led Helen back to the sanctuary, but she took over when he tried to snag a seat in the back row.

"Oh, no no no," she said, pulling him forward. "The best seats are toward the front."

"But I don't want to sit up front." His fear, though he'd never tell Helen, was that if he was up front, people would watch him and be able to tell that he was a faker and not a believer.

She ignored his protests and situated herself in the middle of the third aisle, patting the chair beside her. With a sigh, Max entered the row and took the seat. The music started shortly after, and Max was surprised by the upbeat music. He knew Helen was young for her age, but he hadn't expected her to like this type of music. Three guitars, a drummer, a keyboard, and a piano made up the band along with four singers out front.

When the music ended, Pastor Bill took the stage and Max found himself drawn to the message. It was all about Jesus meeting you where you are. Though Max hadn't considered religion much in his adult life, he remembered the few times his parents had taken him when he was young, and the message then was all about being perfect or going to Hell. It was one reason why he had avoided religion for so long, but here was a man saying he didn't have to be perfect to have a relationship with Jesus because a relationship with Jesus would change him. He wondered how it would change him? He already felt different just having Peyton in his life.

The sermon was still bouncing around in his head as he and Helen walked down the hall to get Peyton.

"Max, Helen, look I drew us." Peyton proudly waved a white paper with purple scribbles on it. "That's me and there's you, Helen, and there's Alyssa."

Max's heart tightened at the mention of Alyssa's name. Would she ever forgive him?

"Who is that up in the sky?" Helen pointed to the scribble near the top of the paper. "Is that Jesus?"

Peyton's face fell. "No, that's Mommy. She's on her way to see Jesus."

Max and Helen exchanged a glance before Max turned to Peyton. "Peyton, honey, your mom isn't going to see Jesus yet. She's just in New York."

"No, she's not." Peyton shook her head. "Jesus told me last night he was taking her but not to be scared."

Max wondered if Peyton was going crazy. Wouldn't he have gotten a call if Sarah had passed? He pulled out his phone, expecting nothing, but the little green phone icon had a number one floating to the upper right. He clicked on it and the voicemail loaded.

"Hello, Maxwell Banks? This is Dr. Steven Young-blood with Memorial Sloan Kettering Cancer Center in New York. You are listed as a contact for Sarah Moore, and I need you to call me right away."

Max lowered the phone before he heard the number, but he would listen to it again. Right now, his shock at Peyton's knowledge was more than he could take.

"Why don't I stop and grab some lunch and meet you at the house?" Helen suggested after seeing the look on Max's face.

"Sure, that sounds fine." He took Peyton's hand and headed to the parking lot. The walk there was silent, but as soon as she was strapped in the car, he turned to her. "How did you know, Peyton? About your mom?"

"I told you; Jesus told me. He said he had to take my mommy for now, but that he'd send me another mommy soon. He said you'd take care of me and be my daddy from now on. You will, won't you?" Her voice held no fear as she spoke about issues much bigger than herself.

"Of course I will, Peyton." The words constricted his heart though. He didn't know the first thing about being a dad permanently. He had failed miserably in his first few weeks, and without Alyssa, he didn't know how he'd get through it.

Alyssa was at lunch with Sandra and Callie's family when her phone rang. As she pulled it out and glanced at the caller ID, her heart filled with dread. With a New York area code, it was either Sarah or someone from the hospital, and she feared it was the latter as they had told her Sarah was too weak for phone calls when she had tried a few days ago.

"Hello?"

"Yes, can I speak with Alyssa Miller?"

The voice was masculine and the vice on her heart pulled tighter. "This is Alyssa."

Sandra and Callie both stopped conversing and stared at Alyssa.

"Alyssa, this is Dr. Steven Youngblood. I was treating Sarah Moore—"

"Was? Is she?" Alyssa couldn't bring herself to say the words, but she didn't have to.

"I'm sorry, Alyssa, her cancer was too advanced, and she passed away this morning."

Alyssa thought she had been prepared for this knowledge. After all, Sarah had been diagnosed nearly a year ago, and she had been at her appointment two months ago when the doctor told Sarah the cancer had progressed to a point that probably wasn't treatable. Memorial Sloan had been a last-ditch effort, but Alyssa had still held on to hope that God would perform a miracle.

She dropped her head in her hands as words failed her. Peyton! The little girl popped in her mind amid her grief. "Does Peyton know?"

"We tried to reach Maxwell Banks, but I was forced to leave a message, and he hasn't returned my call yet."

Maxwell. Of course, she would have to talk to Maxwell again. They would have to plan the funeral, and she needed to make sure Peyton was okay. His very name still dredged up feelings in her heart, but she was no longer sure if they were feelings of attraction or anger.

"Thank you, Dr. Youngblood. Is there anything else we need to do?" Her voice sounded strained to her ears, and her throat was quickly constricting with tears.

"I just need an address to send her belongings and the name of the mortuary you would like her transferred to as I'm assuming you would like her buried there."

Alyssa rattled off the information and managed to hang up the phone before the tears broke through the gates and flooded her cheeks.

"Alyssa, what's wrong?" her aunt asked, taking her hand.

With no voice, all she could do was shake her head and let the tears fall. Callie passed Hope to JD and huddled next to her, wrapping her arm around Alyssa for support.

When the tears finally tapered, Alyssa told them about Sarah.

"Oh, Alyssa, I'm so sorry," Sandra said. "First your mother and now this. I can't imagine how you must be feeling but remember that God can ease your burden. And so can talking to other believers. Don't shut this grief in."

"I have to get back. The doctor hadn't been able to reach Max. I don't even know if he knows or if he plans to keep Peyton."

"Would you like me to come with you?" Callie offered after shooting a quick glance at her husband.

Alyssa attempted a small smile. Callie had quickly become a friend in the short time she'd known her, but this was her battle. "No, I'll be fine, but thank you."

"We'll be here for you whenever you need us," Callie said, squeezing her arm.

After she was packed, Alyssa hit the road, playing over and over the words she would say when she saw Maxwell again.

19

"I don't know what I'm going to do, Helen." Max dropped his head into his hands. Peyton was napping, and Helen had stayed to listen to his fears.

"You'll do what we all do. You'll pick yourself up and become a great father. You're already getting better."

She placed a cup of tea in front of him, eliciting a small smile. He had come to enjoy these chats with her over tea.

"But what if I mess up?"

"You will, but we all do." She reached across the table and covered his hand with hers. "You apologize and you try to do better the next time. Peyton will understand, and believe me, she'd rather stay with you than be put into a house she doesn't know. Plus, you have something else on your side. You have the money to be able to take care of her and provide her with anything she might need."

Max took a sip of tea as he stared at the wise woman. If nothing else, he'd done something right to have her in his corner. "Thanks Helen, I don't know what I'd do without you."

"What about the rest of your family, Max?" Helen asked. "You never talk about them, but it might be time to introduce Peyton to them."

Max sighed. "I know. I've been thinking about that. My parents live here in the city, but we haven't spent time together in years, not since my brother moved to Scotland and they became believers. I was fresh out of college and thought I knew everything, you know?"

Helen nodded and motioned for him to continue.

"Anyway, they tried to push Jesus on me, probably hoping to save at least one of their wayward sons, but all it did was push me away. Then I met Justin and he introduced me to the party lifestyle. I thought it was filling the void in my life, but boy was I wrong. Needless to say, my lifestyle drove an even bigger wedge between us."

"You know my strength doesn't come from myself, right?" She took a sip of her tea and looked at him over the rim of the cup as if measuring his reaction. "It comes from my friends, my family, and trusting God to help me handle anything I can't."

"How long have you been a believer?" Max couldn't believe he was even asking the question, but the combination of the sermon, Peyton's dream, and Sarah's death had all been working in his head.

"Since I was ten. Of course, it was much easier then." She laughed wistfully, and her eyes glazed over as if she was remembering some fond memory. "I strayed for a time in college when I was trying to figure out my own way, but God saved me when I was at my lowest, and when I stopped fighting him and started listening, my life got simpler. Not easier, mind you. Following Jesus doesn't always mean an easy life, but simpler, and I knew he'd always be there for me."

"I'm not sure I'm ready for all that," Max said, twirling the cup around, "but could you tell me how in case I get there?"

"Of course." Helen smiled and began to lay out the simple steps to accept Jesus into his heart.

Alyssa inhaled deeply as she parked in front of the palatial house. Was she sure she wanted to do this? After all, it had only been a day since she left in anger. Somehow, she felt less angry now. The loss of Sarah had put things into perspective and whatever happened between her and Max, she needed to be around for Peyton.

She was surprised when Helen opened the door. "Hi, Helen, I wasn't expecting to see you."

"Nor I to see you." She smiled and stepped outside, closing the door slightly behind her after sneaking a glance down the hallway. "However, I am glad you're here. I needed to speak with you."

"If it's about Sarah, I already know."

"It isn't. It's about Max."

Alyssa held up her hand. "Helen, I don't—"

"No, you're going to listen to me," Helen said, cutting her off. "Then you can make up your own mind with what I have to tell you."

Shocked by Helen's firm tone, Alyssa closed her mouth and nodded for her to continue.

"Thank you. Now, I know Max has a history, but he did not sleep with that woman who was here Saturday. I was here when he brought her home Friday night. He put her up in the guest room for the night. He tried to take her to her home, but she had passed out before he got her address. He was put in a bad situation, and he tried to do the right thing."

"Do you trust him?" Alyssa asked, her voice quiet.

"I've never seen a man make such a drastic change in such a short time, but I see the way he looks at Peyton and the way he looks at you, and I do trust him. He's been a wreck since you left Tuesday and even more yesterday at the thought of losing you. He will never be perfect, but his heart is open and he's asking questions about Jesus. I'm going to keep encouraging him, and it would help if you did too, but I'll leave that up to you. He's in the living room."

With that, Helen opened the door for her and waved goodbye as Alyssa stepped in.

"Alyssa?" Max's face registered his surprise as she entered the living room. "What are you doing here?"

"I came to see if you knew about Sarah. Dr. Youngblood said he couldn't reach you and had to leave a message. Does Peyton know?"

"She does. In fact, she knew before we got the call. She had a dream," he added, as her eyes widened in confusion.

"How is she doing? Is she okay?"

"She seems all right. She's napping now." He stood and crossed to Alyssa. "I'm glad you came, though. I didn't like the way we parted last time." His hands reached out to hers, and after a moment, she accepted, taking a step closer to him.

"I didn't either. I'm sorry I didn't trust you. There's been hurt in my past, and I have to admit your past frightens me, but I know you're trying."

"I promise to keep trying if you'll let me. I don't think I can do this with Peyton all on my own."

As he took another step closer, Alyssa could feel the heat radiating off him combining with the heat building inside her. Her breath caught as his fingers intertwined with hers and he pulled her closer. Was he going to kiss her? Did she want him to?

His eyes flickered back and forth between her eyes and her mouth before closing. His face began to lean down to hers, but before their lips could touch—

"Aunt Lyssa." Peyton's voice caused them both to jump back.

Heat seared across Alyssa's face. "Hey, Peyton. How are you doing?"

"I'm okay. I'm sad about Mommy, but Daddy said he wouldn't leave me."

A small smile crossed Max's mouth as Alyssa glanced at him. "That's so good, Peyton, and I'm going to make sure and be around for you too."

"Are you going to be my new mommy then?"

"Uh," Alyssa looked to Max for help in answering the question.

A sheepish grin covered his face. "Sorry, I didn't tell you all of her dream. I guess Jesus told her he'd be sending a new Mommy to her soon."

"Oh, well, um, I'd never want to replace your mommy, but I'll always be here for you." The words stumbled out of Alyssa's mouth as she tried to find the best way to answer Peyton's question without promising something she couldn't.

"Okay." Peyton shrugged and switched the subject. "Daddy, can I have a snack?"

Alyssa smiled at the shifting thoughts of a nearly four-year-old as Max headed to the pantry to get her some goldfish.

When Peyton was distracted with her snack, Alyssa grabbed Max's arm and pulled him to the opposite side of the kitchen. "We need to discuss funeral arrangements. They're shipping Sarah's body back, but we need to get a casket and a ceremony set up."

"Right." Max's eyes shifted back and forth. This topic was clearly uncomfortable for him. "I have no idea how to go about that, but I'll cover the costs."

"Sarah left a list of what she'd like, just in case," Alyssa said, laying a hand on his arm. "We just need to get together to get it all done."

"Okay, I'll leave work early tomorrow. We should probably get it organized soon."

"Probably." Alyssa sneaked a glance at Peyton. "I know she seems okay now, but it's going to be hard for her."

"Maybe you can stay tonight and teach me how to pray for her?"

Alyssa blinked at him. She didn't think he prayed.

"I went to Helen's church this morning," he said, smiling. "I really liked the preacher and his words have been cycling through my head all day. I'd like to start small, but I figure Peyton will need someone praying with her nightly now. Real prayers and not the half-baked ones I've been saying lately."

Alyssa nodded, tears pricking her eyes, but not from sadness this time. This time, they were tears of joy that Max appeared to be opening up his heart just as Helen had said.

20

"Dude, sorry about not returning your call Friday night, but I was a little busy if you get my drift." Justin sat in the chair across from Max and wiggled his eyebrows for emphasis.

"Yeah, well, that little stunt nearly cost me something real, so I hope you enjoyed it as it's the last time I'll be going out." Max turned on his computer as he sat behind his desk. Though it appeared Alyssa had forgiven him, he was still miffed at Justin's behavior.

"Whoa, man, what do you mean? I heard you hooked up with Amber."

Max rolled his eyes. "No, I didn't hook up with Amber. I tried to take her home since you left her there, but she was so drunk that she passed out before I got her address. I ended up having to take her to my place, which is where Alyssa found her the next morning when she came to apologize. Needless to say, that didn't go well, and we'd probably still be fighting if it weren't for Sarah dying."

"Wait, what? Sarah's dead?"

"Yes, she passed away yesterday." Max bit his lip to keep the hurtful words in his mind from spilling out of his mouth. He shouldn't be judging Justin so harshly. He had been the same a few short weeks ago.

"So, what are you going to do with the girl?"

"The girl?" Max's head fell forward, his eyes wide. "You mean my daughter?" Hard as he tried, he couldn't keep the angry edge from creeping into his voice. "I'm going to raise her of course."

"Dude, that will totally put a cramp in your style."

Max shook his head sadly. "I don't think you understand that my style has changed. I don't want the playboy life anymore. I don't want a different woman every time. I want just one, and I want to be a good father to my daughter. She needs me, especially with her mom being gone now."

Justin blinked as if these concepts were completely foreign to him, and maybe they were. They had been foreign to Max before Peyton and Alyssa entered his life.

"Wow, I have no idea who you are anymore, man." Justin shook his head as his stood.

Max could try to explain, but he saw no need.

Suddenly, he had way less in common with Justin, and he didn't see their friendship lasting anyway.

With a final glance, Justin shook his head one more time and exited the office. Max sighed in relief.

The rest of the day passed uneventfully, and at two p.m., Max shut down his computer for the day. He was picking Alyssa up, so they could pick out a casket for Sarah.

"What do you think?" Alyssa asked, running her hand over a casket a dark mahogany color. "She always said she wanted simple, but I can't put her in that thing." She pointed to the bargain basement casket, which was just a step above a pine box.

Max couldn't imagine putting Sarah in there either. "Look, I have the money. Let's get a nice one. I want it to be something that doesn't scare Peyton as well."

Alyssa's eyes widened. "Oh, I hadn't even thought of that. Do you think she's old enough to go?"

"Whether she is or isn't, Sarah was her mother, and I think keeping her away would be a big mistake." Max recalled a childhood friend who lost his father in a motorcycle accident. He hadn't been allowed to attend the funeral, and he had carried a lot of hurt afterwards causing him to act out in school.

"You're right. I should have remembered that from my psychology courses."

"Hey, don't be hard on yourself. You have a lot you are dealing with right now."

Alyssa eyes filled with water. "I mean, I expected this. I thought I was prepared for this, but I'm not. Peyton needs a mother."

Max pulled her to his chest. She did not fight him but curled up under his chin. "Look, didn't you tell me that God will provide a way? That he's always there for you?"

She sniffled and looked up at him. "Yeah, but I didn't think you were listening."

He took her face in his hands. "I always listen when you speak. You are the most amazing woman I have ever known. You have this inner strength that shines through. This is hard, but God will show us what to do."

"Us?"

Max could hear the hope in the singular word. He paused for a moment as he reflected on the decision he made last night. After he had put Peyton to bed, the feeling that he needed to have Jesus in his life had pressed strongly on him, and he had sunk to his knees on the floor by his bed and prayed for Jesus to be his guide.

"Yes, us. I wanted that strength that you and Peyton and Helen have. I wanted to be the father she needs, and I knew I was going to need help, so I prayed last night."

Alyssa's eyes widened. "You prayed? Like 'accepting Christ' prayed?"

A smile pulled at the corner of his lips. "Yes, like 'accepting Christ' prayed."

"Oh, Max, I'm so happy for you." She threw her arms around his neck and enveloped him in a hug. "Oh, sorry," she said, pulling back.

"Don't be sorry. I could get used to hugs like those. In fact, I hope you are happy for us. I'm hoping that you plan to stick around with Peyton and me."

Alyssa nodded, a smile on her face, and though he wanted more than anything to kiss her, Maxwell refrained because kissing her in a room full of caskets just seemed wrong. Instead, he squeezed her hand and pointed to the deep red casket.

"I think that is the one."

"I agree."

With the casket picked and paid for, Alyssa and Max chose the flowers and then met with Pastor Brown, the pastor who would perform the service.

"Here is what Sarah wrote down that she wanted before she passed." Alyssa handed over the notebook sheet of paper, which the pastor took and scanned.

"We should be able to do this without a problem. Are

you two planning on a Friday service?" He folded his hands together and looked from Alyssa to Max.

Alyssa looked to Max who nodded. "Yes, Friday should be fine with us."

With those preparations done, Max and Alyssa headed out to his car. She held tight to his arm, drawing strength from him. "Can I spend time with you and Peyton tonight? I don't think I can handle being alone."

"Of course you can. You know you are always welcome in my house."

The ride back was quiet, and Alyssa's mind wandered as the buildings passed by. It had been hard losing her mother to cancer, but it felt even harder losing Sarah. Maybe it was because of Peyton, but she thought it was more because of Max. Her heart was torn at the contrast of her joy of his acceptance of God and the feelings she knew were developing between them and the guilt that she felt being with him when Sarah couldn't.

"What are you thinking?" he asked finally, breaking the silence.

She turned to him, a small frown on her face. "I am struggling with my feelings. I am so sad at Sarah passing, but I'm so happy for you, for us, and it feels wrong."

"I know what you mean. I'm feeling the same thing, but shouldn't we be happy that Sarah is no longer in pain?"

Alyssa shook her head. "How did you get so knowledgeable all of a sudden?"

"I had good teachers." He squeezed her hand with his free one. "It will get better."

Maxwell pulled into the garage and opened the door for Alyssa. Before stepping in the house, they both took a deep breath to try to clear their heads.

Helen, sensing their moods, hugged each of them before she left. "I'll be praying for all of you."

After the trio had dinner and Max put Peyton to bed, he joined Alyssa on the couch.

"Can you just hold me?" she asked as she scooted closer.

Max opened his arm and smiled as Alyssa scooted in. Her dark hair spilled across his chest and he couldn't keep from stroking the soft locks with his free hand. A flowery smell drifted up and tickled his nose. He wondered why he had never enjoyed this with the other women of his past. There was something comforting about having Alyssa's body curled up to his without expectation of anything else.

21

"Where are we going, Daddy?" Peyton asked as he strapped her into the car seat.

"To meet my parents, Peyton. I think it's about time you met your grandma and grandpa. Would you like that?"

Her eyes lit up as she nodded.

Max laughed and tussled her hair. "Let's hope you still feel that way after meeting them," he said under his breath as he climbed into the driver's seat.

His mind replayed the phone conversation with his mother as he drove. He had called last night, not wanting to show up unannounced and have them not let him in. Though she had been excited to hear from him, there had been a distance in her voice. He hoped it was just cautionary on her part, but as he pulled into their driveway, his stomach clenched into knots. He hadn't told her about Peyton on the phone, and he had no idea how they would handle the situation.

Their house was a modest rambler on a few acres of land. After coming to Jesus, they had sold their mansion and moved into a smaller house, another thing Max hadn't understood then, but did now.

Gathering his courage, he sighed and parked the car. After unstrapping Peyton, he held her hand and approached the front door.

His mother opened the door before the doorbell chime had finished sounding. There were a few more strands of grey in her hair, but otherwise she looked as he remembered her. "Max." Her voice was warm and her smile genuine as she opened her arms. Then her eyes took in Peyton, and her arms dropped. "Well, hello, who's this?"

"Hi, Mom," he said. "This is Peyton, my daughter."

Though her eyes widened slightly, and she shot him a look that said she expected an explanation, her demeanor remained the same with Peyton. "Hello, Peyton. I'm your grandmother. Nancy."

"Hi." Though Peyton had a death grip on his pants' leg, she released one hand and raised it in a wave.

"Well, come in, come in. Peter will be so happy to see you."

She led them down a carpeted hallway into a spacious living room. His father sat in a brown recliner, reading a newspaper. As they entered the room, he lowered it and his eyebrow rose as he saw Peyton.

"Hi Dad," Max said as his father stood. "I'd like you to meet my daughter, Peyton."

Peyton managed another small wave as Peter kneeled to her eye level.

"It is very nice to meet you, Peyton. I'm Peter, but I guess you can call me Grandpa."

"Okay, Grandpa."

Though questions remained in their eyes, his parents refrained from asking them and turned to small talk. Peyton climbed on Maxwell's lap as he took a seat on the couch. His mother perched on the other chair in the room.

After half an hour, Peyton was asleep on his lap as he had hoped.

"So, tell us how you've been," his mother said when she noticed the cadence of Peyton's chest.

Max took a deep breath. "It's been a ride, that's for sure. You know how my life was going, but a month ago, a woman from my past showed up on my door with Peyton. I hadn't known about her, but I took her in to help her mother, who was sick.

Sadly, her mother, Sarah, passed away this last weekend."

His mother gasped and covered her mouth.

"So, Peyton's mine for good. I thought you should meet her since she'll be in my life."

"Are you sure, Max? Raising a child isn't something to take on lightly," his father said, crossing his legs.

"I know, Dad, but Peyton doesn't have anyone else. Sarah's parents died in a car wreck when she was in college, and she was an only child. Besides, she's grown on me, and I can't imagine my life without her now. There's more, though."

His mother's hands bunched together as she waited for him to continue.

"I became a believer. Sarah was one and Peyton is too. So is the nanny I hired and Alyssa. Between all of them, they showed me what my life could be like, and I accepted him a few days ago."

Tears glistened in his father's eyes and streamed freely down his mother's cheeks.

"Oh, Max, we're so proud and so happy for you," she said, wiping away her tears.

"It's an answered prayer, Son. Praise the Lord, but who's Alyssa?"

Max smiled as he pictured her beautiful face. "Alyssa was Sarah's best friend. She has helped me the last month with Peyton and stolen my heart. I want you guys to meet her soon, but I wanted to see how it went with Peyton first."

"We'd be honored to meet her," his mother said. "She must be a special woman if she managed to help turn your life around."

"She is. The funeral is on Friday, but how about we plan for the following week?"

"That would be great, and I hope you'll come over more often now."

Max smiled at his mother and the hope that colored her words. "I promise, Mom, but for now, I better get this monkey home and in her own bed."

He scooped his arm under Peyton and lifted her up. His mother and father stood and wrapped their arms around him. It felt good to have his parents back in his life.

The day of the funeral dawned before Maxwell was ready. The impending ceremony put a damper on the mood he had been feeling the rest of this week.

He reached for a black shirt and slid his arms inside before buttoning it up and tucking it into his black slacks. The monochromatic look matched his somber mood. He walked into the kitchen and started the coffee pot, enjoying the rhythmic dripping. *Lord, please help this day go as well as it can and give Peyton peace.*

Her tiny feet echoed in the kitchen a moment later. "Morning, Daddy."

"Morning, Bug. Did you sleep okay?"

"Yeah, but Jesus told me it was going to be a sad day. I have to say goodbye to Mommy. I don't want to say goodbye." Her eyes glistened with unshed tears.

Her perception and connection to Jesus still threw Max. Even though he had made the decision to give his life to Christ earlier this week, he couldn't say that he'd heard Jesus speak to him. "That's right Bug, but remember what we talked about? Mommy is no longer in pain."

"I know, but I... I miss her." The tears broke through the dam and rolled down her cheeks creating shiny iridescent tracks.

"Oh, Peyton." He enfolded her in a hug and let her cry against his shoulder. His heart broke for the pain she must be feeling. He had never understood women when they talked about hurting with their children and never wanting to see them hurt, but he understood it now. He would give anything to take her pain away.

When her sobs subsided, he grabbed her shoulders and stared into her eyes. "This is going to be a hard day, but I'll be there with you and so will Alyssa and Helen, okay? And none of us are going anywhere. We will be here with you whenever you need us."

She nodded and sniffled. "Okay, Daddy, I'll try to be brave."

Though Peyton didn't have a black dress, he managed to find a dark blue one that fit her. He helped her brush her hair and then heated up a waffle for her for breakfast. She sat at the table, coloring while she ate.

When breakfast was over, and her teeth were brushed, the two headed out to his car to pick up Alyssa. Helen had offered to meet them at the church.

Peyton's pink bear was clasped tightly to her chest in one hand and her drawing in the other as Max strapped her in, and he sniffed back his own tears threatening to spill over. She looked so small and helpless, and now he had to be the one to watch out for her.

When they arrived at Alyssa's apartment, Max texted her to let her know they were waiting. He would normally ring the bell, but he didn't want to leave Peyton in the car by herself. Alyssa appeared a moment later in a simple black dress. He could tell she was putting on her fake smile and her cheerful voice as she climbed in the car and greeted Peyton, but he could see the sadness in her eyes as well.

As soon as she turned around and buckled her seat-belt, he grabbed her hand and gave it a squeeze. She flashed him a tight smile before focusing out the window. He took no offense as he knew she was fighting tears herself.

The parking lot was full as they pulled up to the church. They had opted to have the funeral at Sarah's church in hopes it would be more comfortable for Peyton and because Sarah had many friends there. Helen had also offered to continue on to the gravesite afterward to make sure everything went smoothly there as well so that Peyton wouldn't have to sit through two ceremonies or see the hole in the ground.

Hand in hand, the trio entered the church, accepting consolatory wishes from everyone they passed. Peyton managed to keep a brave face on as they entered the sanctuary and took their places at the front.

As the pastor began to speak, Peyton climbed in Max's lap and curled her face into his chest. His arms circled her, offering the only measure of comfort he could at the moment. He sent up silent prayers for her peace. Alyssa scooted over and twisted toward Max, placing one hand on his shoulder and the other on Peyton's back. He shot her a grateful look before returning his focus to the ceremony.

When it was over, he asked Peyton if she wanted to see the casket, but she shook her head. "I want to remember Mommy from my dream, but can you give her this picture?" She held out the picture she had drawn that morning, which showed Sarah sitting on a cloud next to Jesus.

"I'll take it," Alyssa said.

Max nodded and took Peyton's hand, leading her to the back of the church as Alyssa stepped up to the casket. They had opted for a closed casket ceremony in case Peyton wanted to see the casket and Max was glad. He wanted to remember the way Sarah had looked when alive as well.

They followed the crowd to the kitchen where a small reception had been set up. People came over one at a time and in small groups to give their condolences. Helen found them and knelt in front of Peyton.

"You were such a brave girl in there. I'll have something special for you on Monday, okay?"

Peyton nodded and gave Helen a hug. "Thank you," Max mouthed to her as she stood.

Helen nodded and disappeared into the crowd. Alyssa appeared a moment later. "You know, I don't know about you, but I'm tired of being sad," she said. "Your mother had one final thing on her list and that was to take you to the zoo after the funeral, so how about it?"

Peyton's eyes lit up. "I love the zoo."

"I know you do, so what do you say?"

Peyton nodded and the three slipped out of the church.

The day had started overcast, but as the trio pushed

open the front doors, a ray of sunlight broke through the clouds as if Sarah was smiling down on them. Alyssa grabbed Max's hand and smiled.

The zoo was mostly empty when they arrived. Peyton ran from one animal to the next, squealing in delight at each one.

"This was a good idea," Max said to Alyssa as they followed Peyton.

"Yeah, Sarah definitely thought ahead. She was really good at that."

"I wanted to ask if you would come have dinner with my parents next week," Max said as Peyton stopped in front of the giraffes.

Alyssa's eyes widened in mock surprise. "You have parents?"

"Haha, very funny." Max squeezed her hand and pulled her closer.

"Well, I was beginning to wonder. You never speak about them."

"We haven't had a very good relationship for a few years now, but we mended things a few days ago, and I'd like them to meet you."

"Then I would love to. I haven't been as close with my father either. After my mother died, we both processed her death differently, and he ended up remarrying."

"That's hard," Max said. "How long has your mom been gone?"

"Three years," Alyssa sighed. "Cancer took her too. I worry sometimes that it will take me as well."

"Hey now, you can't think like that. You aren't your mom or Sarah. Just because it happened to them doesn't mean it will happen to you. Besides, I'll be praying every day for your health. I need you around and Peyton does too."

Alyssa smiled and leaned into him as they watched Peyton wave at the giraffes.

22

Though Max had told her not to stress, Alyssa couldn't stop the fluttering in her stomach at meeting his parents. What would they be like? Would they like her? What if they didn't?

"Will you stop?" Roxy asked. "You're making me nervous."

"What do you mean?" Alyssa hadn't voiced those questions out loud, had she? She thought they had just been in her head.

"You have crossed and uncrossed your legs seven times in the last minute, popped your knuckles three times, and bit your lip twice. You're emitting so much nervous energy that you're making my stomach bunch into knots and I'm not meeting anyone." Roxy finished her rant with a smile, letting Alyssa know that she was kidding. Mostly.

"I'm sorry. I just haven't done this in a long time, and Max and I are still new. I mean, are we even a couple? I don't think we've said as much."

Roxy shook her head. "Alyssa, if you haven't noticed the way that man looks at you, then you are crazy. You said yourself that he's changed from the playboy you met. That ought to tell you more than words ever could."

Alyssa took a deep breath and nodded. "You're right. I need to trust God and stop worrying on this one."

As if on cue, her phone beeped with the message that Max was in the parking lot. Normally, he would knock on the door, but as he had Peyton with him, they had agreed he would just text so as not to have to get her out just to strap her back in.

"That's my cue," she said, waving the phone. "Wish me luck."

"You don't need it," Roxy replied with a smile. "Knock 'em dead."

Alyssa flashed a grateful look at her friend before heading out the door. Max's Malibu was parked in the closest spot, and she slid into the seat, turning to say hello to Peyton.

"You get to meet my grandma and grandpa, Aunt Lyssa." The pitch of Peyton's voice was so high it was almost a squeal.

"I know," Alyssa said with a smile and turned to Max. "She's not excited at all, is she?"

Max laughed. "Not one bit. Are you ready?"

Alyssa nodded, though the butterflies were still zooming in her stomach.

He squeezed her hand before pushing the gear shift to reverse and backing out of the parking spot.

Twenty minutes later, the car pulled into the driveway of a modest rambler. Alyssa blinked in surprise. Max's house was so much larger, and she had thought that at least some of his money came from his family.

"They downsized a few years ago when they became believers," Max said. "They said they didn't need to show off their money, they'd rather help people with it."

"I didn't. . ." Alyssa wondered how he knew what she had been thinking.

"Your eyes gave you away. They're expressive. Sometimes I don't think you know how much you say with them."

"I'll have to keep that in mind for the future." She should be embarrassed, but he was looking at her with such adoration that she found she didn't mind.

"Let's go," Peyton hollered from the backseat, lightening the mood and earning a chuckle from both Alyssa and Max.

"Yes ma'am," Max said, turning off the ignition and unbuckling his seatbelt.

Peyton was out a moment later and, hand in hand with Peyton in the middle, they stepped up to the front door. Max rang the bell and shot Alyssa a wink.

The door swung open a moment later, and a brunette woman with a few grey strands around her temple opened the door. She had the same piercing blue eyes as Max, and it was obvious she took care of herself from her slim figure and flawless skin.

"You must be Alyssa. I'm Nancy," she said, extending her hand.

"Yes ma'am. Nice to meet you." As Alyssa let go of Peyton's hand to shake Nancy's, Peyton broke free and rushed at Nancy.

"Grandma." She wrapped her arms around Nancy's legs and smiled up at her.

With a laugh, Nancy bent down and picked her up. "Come on in. We can get better acquainted inside."

Maxwell grasped Alyssa's hand as they stepped into the house together. She was grateful for the strength and comfort his touch gave her.

Nancy led them into a comfortable, homey kitchen. Tan cupboards lined the wall and complemented the grey and silver speckled marble counter and the stainless-steel appliances. A large dining table sat to the left surrounded by windows overlooking an immaculate backyard.

"Sit, sit." Nancy motioned to the dining table as she placed Peyton in a chair with a booster seat. "Peter, come and eat."

Peter, who Alyssa assumed was Max's father, entered the room. With the same dark hair and strong chin, she received a glimpse of what Max would look like in another twenty years.

"Hi, Dad," Max said, giving him a hug. "I'd like you to meet Alyssa."

"Ah, the girl who tamed the stallion. It's a pleasure to meet you."

He extended his hand and Alyssa shook it, blushing slightly at the title.

"It's a pleasure to meet you too, Sir."

"Please, call me Peter. Sir feels too formal."

"All right, Peter it is then." Alyssa smiled as she sat in the chair Max had pulled out for her. He squeezed her shoulder lightly after pushing her in, giving her a boost of positive energy.

Max took the chair to her right, and his father sat at the head of the table. Nancy placed a casserole dish and a salad in the middle of the table before taking her chair opposite Peter.

After a prayer, the food was passed around the table, everyone serving themselves. Alyssa enjoyed how comfortable the dinner was. It reminded her of dinners with her parents and Sandra and Henry before her mother passed.

When the dinner was finished, she offered to help Nancy clear the table. As Max, Peter, and Peyton headed into the living room, Nancy turned to Alyssa.

"I want to thank you. Even though we prayed nightly, we thought Max was going to be adrift forever. I don't know how you did it, but I can't thank you enough for bringing my son back to me."

Alyssa smiled and clasped Nancy's hand. "I didn't do anything. That was all God, but I am glad to see him changing too. He is such a different man now from the one I first met."

"I don't know how you stuck around, but I'm glad you did."

"Well, that you can thank Peyton for. I promised Sarah that I would look after her and make sure Max didn't screw up too badly. As much as he infuriated me in the beginning, I stayed for that little angel."

"She is that indeed," his mother said with a smile.

The two continued to converse as they cleared away the plates, and by the time Alyssa left that evening, she felt like she had known Nancy and Peter for years instead of hours.

"Your parents are pretty amazing," she said to Max on the drive back to his place.

"Yeah, they are. I'm glad I got to realize that." He

flashed her a quick smile before returning his gaze to the road.

"Me too." There was a completeness in Alyssa's heart as they drove back, and she found she couldn't wait to see what the future held.

Two Months Later

Max held the shiny ring in his hand and tilted it back and forth. The light glinted off the diamond, sending rainbow arcs across the wall. He couldn't believe he was thinking of purchasing this. Three months felt fast to be getting engaged, but he couldn't imagine his life without Alyssa in it and he didn't want to.

After the funeral, he and Alyssa had spent nearly every evening together. She took a job interning for a local therapist, but would drop by for dinner afterwards and stay for a few hours. They did devotionals together each night with Peyton before putting her to bed, and they made Helen's church their new home. Peyton didn't want to return to Sarah's church after the funeral, and Max liked Helen's better anyway.

Most evenings were pleasant, but Peyton still had a few days where she would cry for Sarah. Those were the hard days, but the day Alyssa brought over Sarah's belongings, including a photo album of her and Peyton and a sweater that Sarah always used to wear, Max had the idea to get a locket made for Peyton with a picture of Sarah inside. After that, whenever Peyton would get sad, she would curl up in the sweater and stare at the picture in the locket. It wasn't a perfect system, but it seemed to work for Peyton.

"What do you think?" the salesman asked as Max turned the ring one more time.

"I think it's perfect."

With the ring nestled in a black box and tucked away in his pocket, Max headed back to work. Now, he simply needed the perfect time and the perfect place.

"Do you have it all set up?" Helen asked as she gathered her items. Max had filled her in on the plan as soon as he got home.

"Yes, the dinner is Friday evening. Alyssa has already agreed to go. We'll start at six p.m., so I figure we'll be ready for dessert around seven. Will you be able to get Peyton there?"

"Of course, dearie. There is nothing in the world I would like more than to see you settled down."

Max shook his head and smiled at her good-natured ribbing, though he knew there was an element of truth there as well. Helen had been his biggest encourager from the beginning, and she would have been devastated if he had slipped back into his previous lifestyle.

"Okay, then I guess we're all set. I have to admit I'm a little nervous though. What if she says no?" Max had been wanting to ask her since just after the funeral— losing Sarah had brought home how short life could be— but it had always felt too soon. It still felt too soon, not for him, but he was afraid it would for Alyssa. Had he changed enough to thoroughly convince her he was no longer the guy looking for one good night, but instead was looking for a good lifetime?

Helen shook her head. "There's no way that woman will say no. She loves you just as much as you love her even if you two have been too stubborn to say it."

"I hope you're right." Max pulled her in for a quick hug before she left for the day and he turned all his attention on Peyton.

He hadn't told her his intentions yet because she was terrible at keeping a secret, but he didn't think she would mind having Alyssa around full time.

When Friday evening rolled around, Max logged out of his computer an hour early. In order for Peyton to participate in the dinner festivity before it got too late, he had opted for an earlier dinner. Though this meant a shorter workday, he had worked through lunch in order to not have anything hanging over his head during the weekend.

Before he could fully escape his office though, Justin popped his head in. Max hadn't seen much of him in the last month as he became more vocal about his faith and unwilling to support Justin's lifestyle.

"Hey, man, do you have a minute?" The serious tone in Justin's voice caught his attention and though he didn't really have a minute to spare, he nodded and motioned him in.

Justin closed the door, another odd thing for him, and crossed to the chair. He sat but didn't look up.

Max wanted to tell him to spit it out, but he could see that something heavy was weighing on Justin.

"You've been praying, man, right?" The words were muffled as his face was focused on the floor.

"Yeah, I've been praying." Max set down his satchel and mug and moved to the front of the desk. "What's going on?"

Justin looked up, fear and anger fighting for control

in his eyes. "I, um, just got back from the doctor's office. I've got an STD."

Max's knees gave out and he leaned against the desk. "Oh, man. I'm so sorry. Of course, I'll pray for you." As he said it, Max couldn't help but send up a grateful prayer that his life hadn't turned out the same way. He had gotten tested after Sarah's funeral partly because he was worried about not being there for Peyton and partly because he wanted to be sure he was offering Alyssa something worthy when it was finally time. "Is it the big one?"

"It's not HIV, but it's nearly as bad. I always thought pregnancy was the worst that could happen, you know?"

Max knew only too well. Though he had received the sex education talk in high school and knew all about STDs, he, like Justin, had thought he was invincible, that he was only seeing clean women, but when you didn't take the time to get to know them, it became harder to stay clean.

"I think this may be your wake-up call." Max worked to keep his tone even and non-judgmental. "Mine came when Sarah died. I realized my life had to change so I would be around for Peyton. Maybe it's time you take stock too and figure out what's really important to you."

Justin looked up but said nothing. Max took that as his cue and placed his hand on Justin's shoulder, closing his eyes and opening up his heart. "Lord, my friend

Justin is hurting. Please give him peace and insight into how to handle this problem. Forgive us our past sins and help us to follow the path you want us to be on. Amen."

"That's it?" Justin asked.

"That's it," Max said, smiling. "God knows what's in our heart, so the words aren't as important as the intention. Besides, nowhere in the Bible does it say we should pray long, flowery prayers. It just says to pray unceasingly, but this prayer isn't a cure-all. It isn't going to make your problem go away, and you'll have to decide if you want to make the life change, but if you do, you are always welcome to come to church with Alyssa, Peyton, and me. We'd love to have you with us."

"You're still with that girl?"

"Yep, in fact, I'm asking her to marry me tonight." Max pulled the black box out of his pocket and opened it up.

Justin shook his head. "Wow, I never thought I'd see the day. Maxwell Banks officially off the market for good."

"And happier than I've ever been," Maxwell said softly. "I think you could be too if you gave up this lifestyle."

Justin pulled his shoulders back and put his hands on his knees. "I'll think about it, but, uh, thanks for the prayer man."

Max's heart was heavy as he watched Justin leave.

He had hoped Justin would see the light, that a scare like this one would be enough to cause him to re-evaluate, but it looked as though Justin was more stubborn than Max thought.

Unable to do anything further now, Max gave the matter to God and gathered his things again. He'd have to take a quick shower in order to pick Alyssa up on time.

Once home, he gave Peyton a hug, promising to talk more once he was dressed. Then he jumped in the shower, letting the warm water calm his nerves.

After drying off, he picked out a blue shirt that brought out his eyes and tucked it into his black slacks. He decided to let his hair air dry to give it that tousled look. Before leaving the bedroom, he grabbed the black box from his work pants and shoved it in his left pocket.

"Wow, Daddy, you're handsome," Peyton said as he entered the kitchen.

"Thank you, Bug." He planted a kiss on her forehead. "Tonight is a special night. I'm going to ask Alyssa to marry me."

Her eyes grew wide. "You mean, she'll be my new mom?"

"If all goes well," Max said with a laugh. "And you get to help. Helen is going to bring you to dinner tonight and you are going to bring this box in,"–he pulled it out of his pocket — "and ask Alyssa to marry us. Can you try that for me?"

"What's in the box?" Her small finger reached out to touch the black velvet.

Max opened the lid and enjoyed the delighted surprise that spread across her face.

"It's so pretty."

"Yes, it is, so you have to be very careful with it. Now, do you remember what you're going to say?"

Peyton nodded, her eyes still large. "Aunt Lyssa, will you marry us?"

"Perfect," Max said, ruffling her hair. "I'm going to let Helen hold this ring until it's time, okay?"

Peyton's smile turned down into a small pout. "Daddy, I'll be careful."

"I'm sure you will, but I'll feel better if Helen has it until it's time." He looked to Helen, who nodded.

"I know exactly what to do. Don't you worry your pretty head," she said.

"Right." He handed her the box, holding it just a moment longer than necessary. His hope was that this proposal would dispel any lingering fears Alyssa might have but letting the ring out of his sight was way out of his comfort zone.

"We'll see you at seven," Helen said, tucking the box in her purse.

"What is the matter with you?" Alyssa asked as the waitress sat them. "You seem jumpy and distracted."

"Oh, just a hard day at work." It was not exactly a lie as the information Justin had shared still weighed on his mind.

"Do you want to talk about it?" The therapist in Alyssa began to show as she folded her hands together on the tabletop and regarded him.

"I do, but it's not dinner talk, so let's do it later." He reached across to grab one of her hands. "Why don't you tell me about your day?"

Alyssa narrowed her eyes at him but began to fill him in on her day. Of course, she couldn't discuss actual patients, so it was more about what she was learning by sitting in on sessions.

"Welcome to Se'bon, I'll be your waitress, Tamara. Our special tonight is—" She stopped suddenly, and Max looked up, his heart dropping into his stomach. "Maxwell? Maxwell Banks?"

Max nodded. This couldn't be happening again. Not tonight. "Hi, Tamara."

As Alyssa looked from the red-headed waitress to Max, he felt her hand tighten its grip on his.

"Well, I certainly never thought I'd see you again." Tamara's voice had lost all friendliness and now dripped with venom. "I see you got a new flavor of the month."

"It's not like that," Max protested. "I'm sorry for what I did to you, but I've changed. I've been seeing Alyssa for months."

Tamara flashed Alyssa a cursory glance. "What does she have that I didn't?"

"God," Max stated simply.

Tamara's head dropped forward, and she looked at him like he had two heads. "I'm sorry, did you say God?"

"I did. Alyssa showed me what a relationship with Jesus was about, and I realized that my behavior was because I was missing something in my life, something I thought women could satisfy, but it turns out only God can."

Tamara rolled her eyes. "Whatever. I'm not waiting on you, but I'll get you another waiter."

As she spun and walked off, Max turned to Alyssa, ready to plead his case yet again. "I'm so sorry," he began.

"Stop," she said, shaking her head. A small smile played at her mouth. "I'm proud of you. You shared your faith tonight. That's not something you would have done a few months ago."

"But the reminder…"

"The past is the past, remember?" She squeezed his

hand, filling him with assurance. "Yes, it's unfortunate that this will probably keep happening for a time, but I knew that going in, okay?"

Max swallowed the emotion in his throat. "I don't know what I ever did to deserve you, but I love you, Alyssa Miller."

"I love you too."

Max almost wished he had the ring with him to propose right then. Instead, a male waiter with dark hair appeared at their table.

"My name is Pierre. Our special tonight is coq au vin paired with seared vegetables and a pomme puree. Would you like another moment?"

"No, I think we're good," Max said after glancing at Alyssa.

"Very well then, for the mademoiselle?"

"I'll have the special," Alyssa replied.

"And for the monsieur?"

"The same and a bottle of your best red."

Pierre nodded and glided away.

"Is it another special occasion?" Alyssa asked.

Max kicked himself. He knew Alyssa only drank on special occasions. He would have to make up something quickly to ease her suspicion. "It is, but it's a work thing. I want tonight to be about us, so I'll tell you later, okay?"

"Sounds intriguing," she said with a raised eyebrow, but thankfully she didn't push the subject.

The waiter returned a moment later with their bottle of wine and salads. Max's heart beat faster with each passing moment. He stole furtive glances at his watch whenever he thought Alyssa wasn't watching.

Finally, it was time for dessert. As they ordered a chocolate mousse, Max spared one final glance at his watch. Five till seven. His throat dried, and he swallowed repeatedly before picking up his glass and taking a large swig.

"Are you sure you're alright?" Alyssa asked. "You're acting weird."

He cleared his throat. "I'm fine. Just a tickle."

"Okay, if you say... Max, what is Peyton doing here?" Her eyes had left his and were focused over his left shoulder.

He turned and sure enough Peyton was meandering through the crowd waving at the other patrons. Helen followed behind her, smiling and shaking her head.

"Peyton, is everything okay?" Alyssa asked when she reached their table.

"Oh yes, Aunt Lyssa. I just needed to ask you something." She turned to Helen. "Can I have it now? She wouldn't let me hold it, Daddy."

"It's okay, Bug," Max said, smiling.

Helen handed over the black box discreetly and Peyton covered it with both her hands before turning back to Alyssa.

"Aunt Lyssa, will you marry me? I mean us." She opened her hands and held out the black box.

A gasp escaped Alyssa's mouth as she turned to Max. "Is this the special occasion?"

Max shrugged. "It is pretty special. I mean, if you'll say yes."

"Open it," Peyton shouted.

Alyssa opened the box and her eyes widened even further. "Max, I…"

Max's heart dropped at her pause. Was it too early? Was the ring too big?

"Of course, I'll marry you."

"Yay!" Peyton's loud voice and clapping drew the attention of the other patrons who also joined in clapping.

Max rose from his chair and pulled Alyssa up, wrapping his arms around her waist and twirling her lightly in a circle. "You've made me the happiest man alive," he said as he stopped the spin and placed his lips lightly on hers.

Another cheer erupted from the surrounding patrons and Alyssa pulled back, her face red. Peyton hugged her next and, after Alyssa sat back down, climbed up in her lap.

The waiter appeared a moment later with the dessert.

"Can we get two more chairs?" Max asked. "And another one of these to share?"

"Of course, Sir. I'll be right back." He placed the mousse on the table and turned, returning moments later with two more chairs.

"Sit," Max motioned to Helen. "Join us."

Peyton had already picked up a fork and begun digging into the mousse, but no one seemed to mind. Smiles were shared across the table, and Max knew this was a night he would never forget.

❅ 24 ❅

"Do you have everything ready?" Aunt Sandra asked. She and Callie had come up a week early to help with the final preparations for the wedding.

"I think so," Alyssa said. She began to list everything on her fingers. "Catering, cake, flowers, venue, dress. Those are all done. I still need to get Peyton's flower girl dress and a dress for you, Callie, and my roommate, Roxy." She glanced down at her watch. "She should be arriving any minute."

As if she had heard Alyssa's statement, Roxy hurried over to them out of breath. "Sorry, I was helping Justin get his tux, and I lost track of time."

"Uh-huh." Alyssa smiled at her friend. Shortly after

her engagement, Justin had begun attending church with them. His conversion had been even faster than Max's, though she attributed his STD scare to that. A few weeks later, Roxy had approached Alyssa as she finished up the invitations.

"Do you have 'find Roxy a new roommate' on that list?"

Alyssa jumped at Roxy's voice and looked up. "You'll be fine. You've always been so self-sufficient, but I'll help you look for sure."

Roxy pulled out a chair and sat next to Alyssa at the table. "Actually, I'm not sure I will be. I've never said anything, but you've kind of been my moral compass. I know I don't believe like you do, but I think I've changed for the better just being around you."

Alyssa was speechless for a moment. Though she'd been praying for years to reach Roxy, she had never any sign she was making a difference. "Well, I'll still be in town and you'll be welcome at our house any time." She paused at the mention of the word 'our.' It felt odd but nice on her tongue. "You could also come to church with us. In fact, this week would be a great week to come. Max's friend Justin has just started attending too.

Roxy's brow wrinkled. "Wait, Justin, isn't he the one you said gave you the creeps?"

A laugh escaped Alyssa's lips as she nodded. "One

and the same. I guess something made him see the error of his ways, and he's thinking of changing course." She, of course, knew exactly what the something was as Max had brought it up in one of their nightly devotionals, but it was not her place to share the news, so she kept it to herself.

"So, your God has not only managed to change Max, but possibly his buddy Justin too?"

"I guess so." Alyssa had never thought about it that way, but she could see how an unbeliever might see it like that.

"Hmm, okay." Roxy shrugged, as if that answered her question.

"Okay, what?" Alyssa asked, confused.

"Okay, I'll go with you to church."

Alyssa was flabbergasted. She had never thought this day would come, and now both Justin and Roxy were planning on attending church with them. "I'll tell Max we'll meet him there this week then."

"Cool. I'm gonna go run." With that, Roxy got up from the table and grabbed her keys before heading out the door.

Alyssa stared after her. "Lord, I don't know what that was, but thank you." Her words were quiet, almost a whisper.

The attraction between Roxy and Justin had been evident from their first meeting, and while both Max and

Alyssa had worried that Justin would slip back into his old ways, he hadn't so far. Even Roxy, who, while not as active as Justin, had been with her fair share of men through her relationships over the years, had agreed to try waiting this time around.

Alyssa couldn't be prouder of her friend or happier that the two seemed to be growing together in Christ.

"Well, now that you're here, I'd like you to meet my friend Callie and my Aunt Sandra."

Roxy waved to the women. "Hi, I'm Roxy."

"Good, now that that's out of the way, let's pick your dresses. Max gave me the gold card, so money is no object today."

Alyssa smiled as she fingered the gold card in her purse. Though her mom's family had money, Raquel had tried to raise Alyssa more modestly and, after her death, Alyssa hadn't been as close to her grandparents, so she was glad not to have to ask them for money. Besides, Max had insisted on purchasing them as a wedding gift to her.

The women headed to the back of the store where the bridesmaid dresses were kept. She and Max had decided on a color scheme of pastel pink and blue, but Alyssa hadn't wanted to force the women into one particular dress, so she had opted to let them pick their dress as long as it matched the colors.

Callie and Roxy went to work flipping through

dresses while her aunt and Alyssa looked at flower girl dresses.

"I think this one is perfect," Alyssa said, holding up a pastel pink dress with rosettes across the front.

"It is beautiful," Sandra agreed.

With that task done, they turned their attention to Callie who was modeling a simple pink number in front of the three mirrors.

"What do you think?" Callie asked.

"I love it," Alyssa said, and Sandra agreed.

Roxy stepped out of the dressing room a moment later in a powder blue empire waist gown. "Will this do?"

"It looks great." Alyssa couldn't believe how easy this process had been. She had been expecting it to take hours to find the perfect dress.

"So, who is Maxwell's other groomsman?" Callie asked after changing back into her street clothes.

"His brother. I've never met him because he lives in Scotland—he's a photographer—but I guess he's flying over for the wedding."

"Should be fun," Callie said, as they headed to the checkout.

As the morning of the wedding dawned, Alyssa's stomach fluttered as if a swarm of butterflies were playing tag inside it. She had slowly been moving her items over to Max's, so all that was left were the clothes she planned to wear today and her shower items. The bed she was leaving for Roxy in case she wanted to forgo a roommate and make it a guest room.

A bittersweet feeling descended as she looked around the room she had called home for the last three years. It wasn't that she'd miss the room exactly, but she would miss the camaraderie with Roxy—the late-night ice cream binges and movie nights. Though she and Roxy planned to stay friends, she knew it would be different.

She grabbed the lone shirt still hanging in the closet and pulled it over her head. A pair of sweats were folded on the end of her bed, and she slipped into those as well. Her wedding dress was in a dress bag on the couch as she would change into it at the church after her hair appointment.

Roxy was at the table as Alyssa entered the kitchen. "You ready for your big day?"

"I think so. I'm nervous though." A pang of grief hit her as she added, "I wish my mom was here."

Pushing the sadness aside, Alyssa grabbed a plate and helped herself to the left-over eggs and bacon in the skillet. She set the plate on the table and poured herself a cup of coffee with creamer.

As she prayed over her food, she found her mind wandering to other prayers. She prayed for the day and for Stewart, Maxwell's brother. Though they had seemed happy to see each other, she could tell there was something else going on between them. She prayed for her father who was supposed to have arrived last night, but she still hadn't heard from him. They hadn't been super close since her mother died and last year he had remarried himself, which distanced them even further.

After breakfast, Alyssa packed up the last of her remaining items and took a final look around before following Roxy out to the car.

With her hair done and her makeup fixed, Alyssa entered the church behind Roxy, Callie, and Sandra. They had been given a small office on the left side of the church to change in while the men had another small room on the right side.

Shortly after hanging her dress and unzipping the bag, a knock sounded at the door and Peyton peeked her head in.

"Hi, Peyton." Alyssa opened her arms and Peyton ran into them. "You look beautiful."

Max had done a good job getting her in the dress and

keeping her clean before the ceremony, but her hair lay flat on her head.

"I'm on it," Roxy said, reading her mind and extracting the curling iron from her bag. Roxy had thought ahead and packed a curling iron, blow dryer, extra hose, and makeup in her bag just in case.

As Roxy began curling Peyton's hair, Alyssa pulled out the dress and slipped it on. She opted for something simple, so the dress was an unpretentious white shift that pooled on the floor. A delicate lace beading covered the bodice and a satin belt connected the bodice to the creamy white skirt.

Lifting up the skirt, she stepped into the Cinderella shoes she had bought. They weren't real glass slippers, but they were see-through, so they looked like them. Cinderella had been her favorite fairy tale growing up, and she and her mother had often discussed the glass slippers she would wear when she married. As her mother wasn't here to share the joy, Alyssa had made sure to have something that made her feel close to her. She blinked back tears as she remembered the many conversations with her mother.

"She's watching from Heaven," Sandra said, noticing the shine in her eyes.

"I know; it's just hard on days like this." Alyssa sniffed and pulled back her shoulders, determined not to cry out of sadness on the happiest day of her life.

Twenty minutes later, the rest of the girls were ready, and they led the way down the hallway. Helen stood outside of the sanctuary doors manning the guest book table, which also held their bouquets. She smiled at Alyssa and waved to Peyton as the girls grabbed their flowers and Alyssa handed the basket of petals to Peyton.

"Now, just like we practiced, remember? Small handfuls as you walk down the aisle."

Peyton nodded, her face focused and serious. "I have it, Aunt Lyssa."

"You look beautiful."

Alyssa turned at the voice of her father and smiled. "Hi Dad." She had been worried he wouldn't make it, but with him here, her shoulders felt lighter.

The music started, and Helen and Aunt Sandra made their way inside after one last hug.

Stewart appeared a moment later and escorted Callie in. Then Justin showed up to lead Roxy down the aisle. Peyton went next, and Alyssa smiled as she watched her through the cracked door. Peyton was not only dropping the flower petals but waving at each person she passed.

"I'm so proud of you, and I know your mother is too," Alyssa's father said as the music changed to the wedding march.

"Thanks, Dad. I'm so glad you could make it."

He squeezed her hand as she placed it on his arm. "I wouldn't have missed it for the world."

As he opened the door, Alyssa's eyes scanned the room and landed on Max. His smile was a beacon of light and like a tractor beam, she felt locked in his gaze. The connection never broke as she stepped forward.

When she reached the front, she hugged her father and handed her bouquet to Roxy before taking the final step to stand in front of Max. He grabbed her hands and a feeling of warmth and security surged down her arms.

"Dearly beloved we are gathered here today to join this man and this woman in holy matrimony."

As Pastor Bill began to speak, Alyssa's mind focused solely on Max, tuning out everything else around her.

Max couldn't believe how lucky he was as he held Alyssa's hands and stared into her beautiful eyes. His life was now so different from where it had been going a year ago, but it was better than he ever would have imagined. His faith in God had rekindled his relationship with his parents and even his brother had made the trip to see his wedding. Now, if he could just reach Stewart, but that was a thought for another day.

Before he knew it, it was time to slide the ring on

Alyssa's finger. He turned to get it from Justin and smiled at his friend. He had thought when he became a believer that their friendship wouldn't last, but instead it had inspired Justin to become a believer too and change his life as well.

"With this ring, I thee wed." The words were like lightning as he slid the ring on her finger. He felt a sense of security in his soul and knew he would never forget this feeling.

"With this ring, I thee wed," Alyssa said, sliding the gold band on his hand.

He had thought it would feel funny, like an anchor dragging him down, but it was light and liberating.

"I now pronounce you husband and wife. You may kiss the bride."

Max smiled as he leaned in and placed his lips on Alyssa's. It had been hard waiting to be intimate with her, but he knew tonight the relationship they shared would be more special than any of his other nights combined.

As the crowd cheered, he grabbed Alyssa's hand and they ran down the aisle and out of the sanctuary. The wedding planner had set up another room for them to go to directly after leaving until it was time to enter the reception and he led her there now. She was laughing as she ran beside him, one hand holding his and the other lifting the front of her skirt, so she didn't trip.

He opened the door and shut it behind them. Alyssa collapsed on one of the chairs in the room.

"That was fun, but I wish you had told me you planned on running. I did not wear my marathon shoes." She held up her feet and wiggled them, showing off the see-through Cinderella-esque heels.

"I promise I won't make you run again, at least not until you get better shoes." He pulled her to her feet and wrapped his arms around her waist. Her arms wound around his neck, bringing her body closer to his. He could almost feel her heart beating against his chest. "I am so glad I met you and that you agreed to marry me."

"Me too," she said with a smile, "though I'd have never believed it if someone had told me the first day."

He laughed as he shook his head. "I was so clueless."

"And helpless," she added.

"But we make a good team," he finished.

She nodded and parted her lips as she looked up at him. They were perfect and pink, and he needed to feel them again. Closing his eyes, he lowered his head until his lips were on hers. Though the kiss started slow, he could feel a raw need, a passion boiling inside. He knew if he didn't stop this soon they wouldn't make it to the reception.

Begrudgingly, he pulled back, breaking the connection. "We better go greet our guests."

Alyssa sighed, but nodded and followed him out of the room and down the hallway.

The church had a large room with an attached kitchen which was where Max and Alyssa had decided to have the reception, so people wouldn't have to drive to two places.

As they entered the room, a large cheer went up and the DJ announced them over the speakers. "Mr. and Mrs. Maxwell Banks."

Max blinked and shook his head. He would have never thought there would be a Mrs. Banks.

"Daddy, Mommy." Peyton ran at them, a blur of pink as her little legs pumped.

Max swung her into his arms, placing a kiss on her cheek. "You were wonderful, Peyton. You tossed those petals like a pro."

"And waved, did you see me wave?" she asked, her head bouncing up and down.

"Future Miss America right here."

"Are we a real family now?" she asked.

"Yes, Peyton. We're a real family," Alyssa said. "I'll be there every night to tuck you in and I'll be there when you wake up."

Peyton reached out her other arm, enveloping Alyssa's neck and creating a hug triangle between the three of them. Max couldn't remember a time he'd been happier.

The End!

If you liked this story, please leave a review at your retailer. Just a few words really helps!

IT'S NOT QUITE THE END!

Thank you so much for reading *The Billionaire's Secret*. The Billionaire's Secret was originally the fourth book in the Heartbeats Series title A Father's Love, but about the time I decided When Hearts Collide should be two stories, billionaires were huge. Max had already been written as rich and it was an easy switch to turn him into a billionaire and rebrand the cover.

The main story remains the same though and is one of my father's favorite books. I hope you enjoyed it as well. If you did, would you do me a favor? If you did, please leave a review at your retailer. It really helps. It doesn't have to be long - just a few words to help other readers know what they're getting.

I'd love to hear from you, not only about this story, but about the characters or stories you'd like read in the future. I'm always looking for new ideas and if I use one of your characters or stories, I'll send you a free ebook and paperback of the book with a special dedication. Write to me at loranahoopes@gmail.com. And if you'd like to see what's coming next, be sure to stop by authorloranahoopes.com

I also have a weekly newsletter that contains many wonderful things like pictures of my adorable children, chances to win awesome prizes, new releases and sales I might be holding, great books from other authors, and anything else that strikes my fancy and that I think you would enjoy. I'll even send you the first chapter of my newest (maybe not even released yet) book if you'd like to sign up.

Even better, I solemnly swear to only send out one news-letter a week (usually on Tuesday unless life gets in the way which with three kids it usually does). I will not spam you, sell your email address to solicitors or anyone else, or any of those other terrible things.

And if you're interested in meeting the rest of the billion-aires in the series, be sure to check out A Brush with a Billionaire. Turn the page for a sneak peek.

BEST-SELLING AUTHOR
LORANA HOOPES

The Billionaire's
CHRISTMAS
Miracle

A CLEAN OPPOSITES ATTRACT
BILLIONAIRE ROMANCE

NOTE FROM THE AUTHOR

Thank you so much for picking up this book. I hope you enjoy the story and the characters as they are dear to my heart. If you do, please leave a review at your retailer. It really does make a difference because it lets people make an informed decision about books.

Sign up for Lorana Hoopes's newsletter and get her book, The Billionaire's Impromptu Bet, as a welcome gift. Get Started Now!

G wen's jaw dropped as she regarded her friend. Surely, she had misheard Carrie's request. There was no way she could be serious. "You want me to do what?" Didn't Carrie understand what she was asking was one of Gwen's worst nightmares?

"Pretend to be me." Carrie flicked her fiery red hair off her shoulder and picked up the eyeshadow brush. She swiped it across her lid, nonchalantly, as if she had just been asking Gwen to hand her a shirt and not walk into a room full of strangers. Strangers!

"Just for the night. I'm so tired of these parties, and I promised Lorenzo I'd go riding with him." Lorenzo was Carrie's latest fling - a tall, dark, Italian bad boy who wore leather and drove a Harley. At least Gwen was fairly certain his name was Lorenzo. Carrie Bliss changed men like most people changed socks, and she had a hard time keeping up.

While Gwen adored Carrie, she often wondered how they were still friends. In college, it had made sense. Gwen was the studious library aide and Carrie was the sorority girl who needed help on her papers. But now? Carrie owned her own business and was steadily climbing the "Who's who in society" ladder while Gwen was an ordinary English teacher. A teacher who had nightmares every year about meeting the upcoming class of students, but they were just kids. Kids like she had been once who needed help, so she could swallow her fear of strangers and stand up in front of them, but she could not walk into a party with a bunch of wealthy adults. Carrie knew this.

"But we don't look alike," Gwen protested with a shake of her head. That wasn't exactly true. They had been mistaken for sisters more than once, but she needed an excuse. Any excuse.

Carrie set the make-up down and turned to Gwen. Her right eyebrow inched up her forehead in a stop-being-a-baby expression. "We look close enough. We both have red hair, we're about the same height-"

"You're two sizes smaller than me," Gwen finished. She wasn't overweight, but her size eight to ten frame was bigger than Carrie's perfect size six one.

Carrie flashed her manicured hand in a dismissive wave. French tips. They were so pretty. Gwen's own nails were all different lengths and not painted. She'd only had one manicure in her life. High school prom. Her foster mother had taken her to get a manicure even though she didn't have a date. "Everyone should feel pretty at least one day," she'd said. Carrie, on the other hand, had a weekly standing appointment with her nail lady, and while she'd offered to take Gwen along and pay for hers more than once, Gwen just couldn't do it. It seemed like a frivolous waste of money even if it wasn't her money.

"Just don't get too close to anyone, and no one will know. Besides, most of these people barely know me. They just know the name of Carrie Bliss Designs. The only one you'd have to watch out for is Grant." Her nose wrinkled the tiniest bit as she said his name.

Grant was Carrie's ex - a snobby stock broker who managed the portfolios of many of the wealthiest in the city. Gwen had never liked Grant nor understood why Carrie dated him, but then again, she didn't understand why Carrie dated half the men she did. "I don't know, Carrie, it's not really my thing."

"Which is exactly why you should go." Carrie turned back to the mirror and puckered her lips. "You never do anything fun. You go to work and then you come home and hang out there."

That part was true; Gwen's life was boring, but she liked it that way. At least most days. "I'm a homebody. I like staying home." Plus, it was safer there. No one would beat her or die on her if she stayed in her house. Yes, it was lonely on occasion, but still safer.

Carrie's eyes flicked up to catch Gwen's in the mirror. "But you'll never meet anyone stuck inside this house."

Which was the whole point. Gwen didn't want to meet someone. It hurt too much to love people.

"Besides, this is the perfect opportunity," Carrie continued, "you'll be wearing a mask, so you can hide behind it."

Gwen's teeth bit into her bottom lip. Wearing the mask might make it better. It wouldn't curb her anxiety about being in a room full of strangers, but it would help that they couldn't really see her. And it would be something different. "What will I wear?" Gwen couldn't believe she was even considering this. "Is it formal? Because I have nothing formal."

"Relax, I'm sure I have something in my closet that will fit you. Come on, let's go look."

She followed Carrie to her immense closet. Though they had shared an apartment for a time in college, eventually Carrie's more expensive taste and wallet had led her to purchase a penthouse in the city. Gwen, however, rented a studio in a much poorer section of town.

"Let's see." Carrie walked along the dresses hanging down, her hand touching each garment as she passed. Gwen would never get used to the size of this closet. It was nearly the size of her whole apartment. Carrie stopped and pulled out an emerald green gown. "Try this one. I remember it being slightly big on me, so it's probably just your size."

Gwen's fingers touched the satiny gown. It was more expensive than anything she would ever own. Off the shoulder and floor length, the satin rippled like waves as it fell to the floor. "What if I ruin it?" Gwen wasn't exactly a klutz, but she could just picture herself spilling a fancy drink on the beautiful gown.

Carrie smiled. "You won't, and even if you do, it's not like I'm hurting for it." She gestured to the myriad of dresses still hanging on the rods.

She was running out of excuses, and it was just one night. Perhaps it would even be fun, and she could reminisce on the evening later when the silence pressed in on her at her apartment. It wasn't like she would have another chance at something like this. "Okay, I'll see if it fits."

Carrie stepped out of the closet to give Gwen some privacy. She laid the gown across the padded bench and shook her head. Who had a bench in their closet? She didn't think she would ever get used to some of the things wealthy people seemed to waste their money on.

Her fingers trembled slightly as she removed her clothes and stepped into the dress. *This is wrong* paraded again and again in her head like a scratched record, but her hands still pulled the dress up. Her fingers still found the zipper and tugged. It was a little snug, but it fit. If she didn't eat too much.

Lifting the dress so as not to step on the hem, Gwen stepped out of the closet. Carrie clapped her hands and sighed. "Yes, you look perfect. Well, almost perfect. Hang on." She hurried back into the closet and the sound of drawers opening and closing carried out. "Ah, here we go." She re-emerged holding a feathered mask and held it out. "Now, you'll look perfect."

Gwen's fingers grasped the mask, a beautiful atrocity of purples, greens, and golds. She pulled the string and fastened it over her face before turning to the mirror. Whoa! Her lips parted at the vision in front of her, and a small gasp escaped. She looked... beautiful, and Carrie was right - no one would know it wasn't Carrie from far away. With her face covered, she appeared even more like her friend.

"See? I told you. Now let's get you some shoes, a little jewelry, and pin your hair up."

Gwen glanced down at her wrist. "Can I keep the bracelet on at least?" It was the last thing her parents had given her - a diamond tennis bracelet. And it never came off, not even to shower.

Carrie's eyes softened. She had never met Gwen's parents - they had been dead for years before Carrie entered the picture, but Gwen had told her about them one late night over popcorn and The Breakfast Club. "I'd never ask you to take your bracelet off. I was just thinking some diamond earrings would be a great match with it."

Tears filled Gwen's eyes. *This* was why she and Carrie were still friends. Though worlds apart, she was so thoughtful sometimes.

With the earrings picked and the shoes found, Gwen checked the mirror one last time. She still couldn't believe she was doing this, but she might as well make the most of it. For one night, she could pretend to be Carrie, pretend to be wanted, pretend to be wealthy and not have a care in the world. It was just one night.

Drew Devonshire adjusted his mask. He looked a little like the Phantom with his white shirt, dark pants, and cape, but the look suited him. If only he were more excited about this event, but they were all the same. He'd been attending them for years, and the results never changed. By the end of the night, he would be dying of boredom, dazed from the alcohol he'd consumed to battle said boredom, and have at least a dozen numbers in his pocket from women after his money whom he had no interest in.

It was always the same people there - the affluent and elite of society. They would gather at some elaborate venue with tiny portions of intricate food that would cost whoever was hosting the event a fortune. In this case, that was Drew, or his family rather, as his mother was hosting this masquerade ball at one of their hotels.

Occasionally, a millionaire from another town would be in attendance or sometimes a relative of one of the families would be, but even those instances were rare. His mother invited old friends and only new people she thought would attend her next benefit. Since those were priced at a thousand dollars a plate that list was small. Plus, while the food was delectable, it never filled him up, and he invariably had to have his chef make him a second meal when he returned home.

If only he could get out of this, but his mother would be there. If he didn't attend, she would be livid. As heir to the billion-dollar hotel chain, it was his duty to attend events like this. Maybe he could leave early, but what would he do even if he could? Return home to his mansion and watch television alone again? He already did that nightly.

For a time, he had filled his nights with women. One after the other, he had wined them and dined them, but none had held his interest. Soon, the very thought of dating and pretending to like them had grown old. They were all alike - cookie cutters of their mothers and their mothers before them. Tailored clothing, designer shoes, and an appetite for spending money without abandonment appeared to be all that drove these women. Drew wanted something different. He had no idea what, but something different. No, that wasn't true. He wanted someone like Marjorie had been or who he thought Marjorie had been.

A knock sounded on his door. "Come in." It had to be Pierre, his butler. Though officially the help, Pierre felt more like family. He had been Drew's butler for over a decade now and his confidante almost as long.

"Are you ready, sir? Manuel has the limo waiting." Pierre was older than Drew, gray at the temples and with more lines on his face, but still handsome. He had never wanted to marry, and as Drew paid him well, he seemed content to remain Drew's main butler, but he had a few men beneath him, so he could take time off when he needed.

Drew sighed. It wasn't as if he had much choice. "I suppose I am." He shoved his wallet in his pocket. "Pierre, is there anything else going on tonight? If I finish early?"

Pierre's brows knitted together. "Early, sir? Don't these events run on the lengthy side?"

"Yes, they do, but I was thinking about retiring

early." He hoped Pierre was catching his innuendo. "If something else were going on that sounded interesting, I mean."

Pierre nodded. "Ah, I see. I'm afraid I am not well informed on the night life around town, but Manuel usually has knowledge of such events. Although I must say, the Devonshire events are always the talk of the town, so I'm not sure what else you might be looking for."

That elicited a small smile from Drew. He clapped Pierre on the shoulder. "Me either, but thank you, my friend. I will ask Manuel."

"Very good, sir." Pierre nodded and stepped out of the way, so Drew could exit the room.

Though he lived alone, except for the help he employed, his mansion was palatial. Five bedrooms each with their own bathroom took up the second floor. A large grandiose stairway connected the two floors, and his loafers clicked against the white marble as he made his way down them.

The stairs ended in the grand foyer, a room as large as most people's living rooms with the sole purpose of connecting the front door to the living room. A single closet to hang coats in and a hat rack which held his hat and scarf were the only things in the room besides a mirror that hung on one wall.

After donning his hat and wrapping his scarf around

his neck, Drew checked his reflection in this mirror. The image reflecting back was dapper if he did say so himself. He flung open the front door to find Manuel waiting on the porch.

"Are you ready, sir?" Manuel was much younger than Pierre. Younger than Drew even, but he'd come highly recommended after Drew's last driver had run off with Marjorie. And so far, Drew had no complaints. Manuel always dressed immaculately, he drove the speed limit, and he kept the limo stocked with Drew's favorite snacks - beef jerky and Doritos.

Not the typical fare for a billionaire, but then Drew wasn't the typical billionaire. He didn't like the taste of Dom Perignon, and caviar held no appeal for him either. While the help and the limo were nice, sometimes he wished he could just go camping in the woods with some burger patties, hot dogs, and chips.

His mother hated that side of him. "We should never have allowed you to go off to a regular college," she reminded him often, but Drew was glad he'd gotten the chance to see how the other half lived. In fact, he'd wanted to do something other than inherit a billion-dollar hotel industry, but when his father died, he'd been forced to step into his shoes.

"As ready as I'll ever be, I suppose," Drew said as he followed Manuel to the long black car.

Manuel nodded as if he understood what Drew meant

though Drew knew he did not understand. People thought they wanted to be wealthy, but they had no idea the taxing monotony it carried with it. He always had to be dressed when he went outside. One poorly chosen outfit and his face would end up splashed across the tabloids within hours. Dates needed to be well planned out, and he could never say what he was thinking. Having to always be diplomatic required constant attention and control. And Drew was tired of it.

Plus, there was the prying into his private life. After Marjorie had run away with the chauffeur, he had been the talk of every tabloid. It was only after a fellow heiress had gotten herself arrested for driving intoxicated that he had faded from the public scrutiny and pity.

"Manuel, if I wanted to leave the ball early, would you know of any place that might have something of interest going on tonight?"

Manuel pursed his lips. "Do you mean of the local nightlife variety?"

Drew slid into the leather seat and nodded. "That is precisely what I mean."

"I have heard nothing other than the talk of this masquerade ball."

Drew sighed. Of course, he hadn't. Drew's mother did her best to make sure her parties conflicted with nothing and garnered all the attention. "I was afraid of that, but do me a favor, will you, Manuel? Keep your ears open in case something comes up."

Manuel nodded. "I will do my best, sir." Then he shut the door and Drew was left alone in the dimly lit interior of the limo.

G wen stepped out of the limo and looked up at the massive hotel rising against the moonlit sky. It was one of the largest in the city, and though she knew of it by name, she had never been inside. Why would she? One night's stay in this place probably cost a week's worth of her pay.

"Thank you," she said to Carrie's driver as he held the door open for her. The man blinked at her and nodded. Was he surprised? Did Carrie never thank him? Maybe she was just too used to the service or in too much of a hurry, but Gwen was neither. She was still unsure she wanted to go through with this, but a tremor of excitement flickered inside her.

The limo door closed behind her, and the sound caused her to jump. She was too skittish. Then a chill swept through the area, and Gwen pulled her shawl tighter across her shoulders. Winter was on its way, and as the limo had just pulled out, her only options were to enter the building or stand outside on the cold, dark sidewalk. The latter held no appeal.

Before she had time to change her mind, her feet carried her across the pavement. Orange and red leaves from nearby trees squished under her shoes, still wet from the most recent rain. She took a moment to rub her feet across the red carpet that rolled out of the hotel and under the large awning. Tracking wet leaves into the hotel would surely be frowned upon. A bellhop, dressed in maroon and gold, smiled and held the door open for her, and Gwen stepped inside.

She clamped her lips together to keep her jaw from dropping. The inside of the hotel dripped with opulence, but someone with Carrie's money probably wouldn't have thought twice about it. A vein of gold ran through the marble flooring and carried up the walls and across the ceiling. An enormous chandelier hung from the middle of the room sending rainbows of color cascading across the area, and one wall held a fountain apparatus that made it appear water flowed down the wall. Gwen had never seen such a beautiful room.

"Can I help you?" The deep, velvety voice came from behind her.

Gwen pulled her shoulders back hoping to appear

confident as she turned to the masculine voice. A man wearing a white shirt, black pants, and a cape stared back at her. A large mask hid most of his facial features, but Gwen saw his icy blue eyes and his perfect lips beneath the mask.

Her stomach clenched, and she forced her voice to sound even and not the jittery mess she felt inside. "Um, I'm here for the Masquerade Ball."

His lips turned up at the corners, hinting at the sexy smile that could follow. "Well, as fate would have it, so am I. May I show you the way?"

Gwen's heart raced in her chest. She wanted to go with him, this Adonis, but he was a strange man, and if foster care had taught her anything, it was that she couldn't trust everyone. "I…"

Now his lips pulled into that smile, and it was even more charming than Gwen had pictured. "I understand your hesitation." He leaned in and glanced around. "I'm Drew Devonshire." He paused as if waiting for that to mean something to her, but his name meant nothing. Was she supposed to know him? Was he famous? "This is my hotel."

The light went off in her head. The Devonshire Hotel, of course, but was he really a Devonshire or some con man just pretending so he could lure her off somewhere? Gwen shook her head. She needed to get her morbid ideas in check. Not everyone was out to get her.

He appeared perfectly respectable, and this *was* a public hotel. However, stories of people killed in hotels littered the internet, and she'd read H. H. Holmes built one for that very reason. She took a deep breath and swallowed her inane fears. "I'd be honored to have you lead the way to the ball."

"Wonderful, follow me." He led the way across the marbled foyer to the hallway where four gold plated elevators waited, two on each side of the hallway. A circular button with an up arrow sat in between each door. The man pushed the button, and a moment later when the door of one opened, he stepped inside.

"Are you coming?" His voice held a teasing note, and though she couldn't see it, Gwen imagined his eyebrow was lifted. He probably wasn't used to indecisive rich women.

Gwen paused for just a moment, knowing she was blowing her cover, but unable to help it. Once she stepped into the small box, she would be at his mercy. Surely the ride would be short though, and a hotel this big had video cameras. "Um, yeah, sorry." She joined him inside and tried not to show her apprehension as the doors slid closed. Her hands clenched her shawl tighter to keep from shaking.

"Not a fan of elevators, huh?"

Gwen looked down. "Oh, no, it's not that. It's…." but she couldn't tell him her fear was of strangers. Men, in particular. Fearing strangers was a child's fear, not a grown woman's one and certainly not a fear of a famous designer. So, she said the first thing she could think of. "I don't like small spaces." It wasn't a complete lie. Gwen preferred open areas where the option to run existed.

"Hmm." He stared at her as if trying to gauge if she was telling the truth or not. "Well, that is understandable." A pause ensued as if he wanted to press the subject more, but finally he nodded and then leaned in towards her as if sharing a secret. "So, I understand this is a masquerade ball and sharing our identities is discouraged, but since I told you who I am, can I at least get your name?"

Gwen didn't want to state her actual name in case a guest list existed she wouldn't be on, but it felt wrong telling him Carrie's name as well. What if he tried to look her up later? Perhaps if she just gave a first name, it would be okay. "It's Carrie, but that's all I'm saying." She hoped she sounded coy, but she feared the lie was evident in her voice.

"Well, I'll take what I can get." He nodded and flashed another small smile as the doors opened. With a flourishing gesture, he held out his arm for her to go first, and Gwen stepped out of the elevator.

Her heart sank as she saw a large man with a clipboard standing outside the door. He was obviously checking names off a list, which would be fine as long as he didn't know the real Carrie Bliss. But a stack of cards sat on the table beside him. Invitations? Carrie had said nothing about bringing an invitation, and Gwen didn't have one. Had she gotten all dressed up only to be turned away at the door?

"Invitations?" the man asked as they approached.

"I, um, don't have one, but I should be on the list," Gwen mumbled.

"No invitation, no entry." The man crossed his arms sending the sleeves of his suit bulging with the motion. He might look fancy, but he was obviously a bouncer who wouldn't be afraid to throw a little muscle around if needed.

"Well, I have no invitation either, but I would hate to inform my mother you denied her son, Drew Devonshire, entrance into his own event." He lifted his mask, and the guard's demeanor instantly changed.

"I'm sorry, Mr. Devonshire, sir, I didn't recognize you. Of course, you don't need an invitation."

Drew nodded. "Thank you, and neither does my friend. I'll vouch for her."

Indecision crossed the guard's face. He looked from Drew to Gwen and back again. "All right, sir, if you're sure."

"I am." Drew held out his hand to Gwen. "Carrie? Shall we?"

Suddenly, Gwen grew nervous for a new reason.

Clearly, the man before her was Drew Devonshire which meant he did own the hotel. He wasn't likely to harm her, but what if he realized she wasn't who she said she was? Would he throw her out? Call security? Call the police? She would just have to be careful what she said and did.

She placed her hand in his. A tingling sensation raced up her arm at his touch, and she looked down at their hands. How long had it been since a man had touched her? The answer was ages. Gwen didn't allow most men to touch her, at least not until she knew they were safe and not like the first foster father she'd had. And though she dated, she was cautious and picky in her choices. First dates rarely turned in to second ones.

When she looked back up, Drew was staring at her. "Ready?" he asked.

Gwen nodded, not trusting her voice. She was probably already sending out many signs she wasn't the wealthy elite she was pretending to be, but she knew if she opened her mouth and her voice quivered, he would glean that information for sure. Carrie never seemed unsure of herself though whether that was due to her money or just Carrie's personality Gwen wasn't sure.

Drew opened the door to the ballroom. Just like downstairs, the room was elegant and refined, and Gwen had to force herself not to stare as she took everything in.

Drew watched as Carrie's eyes widened when they entered the room. He was used to such elaborate decor, but her expression revealed that she wasn't. Though she fought to keep her face composed, he could tell the room awed her. And she'd been standing downstairs like a scared rabbit. He wondered if she would have stood in the lobby all night if he hadn't approached her. Plus, she'd had no invitation though she'd claimed to be on the list. Could she be a new millionaire, maybe? Or a relative of someone? Either way, she intrigued him. Perhaps this evening wouldn't be so bad after all.

"Would you care to dance?" he asked her as they stepped farther into the room. Couples already filled the dance floor while others lingered at the tables around the room.

Her eyes dropped to the floor. "I'm not much of a dancer," she said in a soft voice. What was this lack of self-confidence she exuded? It was not typical for people with money.

"Lucky for you, I am." He flashed a smile as he pulled her to the middle of the dance floor. "My mother made me take a year of ballroom dancing lessons. I might as well put them to good use." Drew wrapped an arm around her waist and cinched her closer. Not only did she fit nicely in the crook of his arm, but the sweet smell of vanilla drifted up from her. He wasn't sure if it came from her hair or her skin, but he enjoyed the scent.

She followed his steps but felt stiff in his arms. Had she had no dance training? Not that everyone of wealth did, but it was standard practice among the elite. Perhaps she had only recently become wealthy. One of the rising stars his mother had invited?

"Did you enjoy them?" she asked.

"What? Oh, the lessons?" She nodded. "Not really, but when you are a Devonshire, there are rules you have to follow."

"There are always rules," she said.

"That is true, but our rules are stricter than most. Surely, you must have similar experiences." He fixed his eyes on her as he waited for her answer.

"Oh, um, sure, you know always wear the right outfit and makeup, things like that, but we didn't have to dance." She glanced up at him before her eyes shifted to the side. Clearly, she was hiding something, but what? And, more importantly, why?

"What do you do?" he asked changing the subject and hoping to elicit a little information from her.

Carrie cleared her throat and her eyes flicked around the room. Everywhere but on him. "I um run my own business."

Interesting. Drew had become adept at reading people. It helped when you had money to know if people were lying to you, and he could tell Carrie wasn't telling the truth. She didn't seem confident enough to be a con artist, and a good one would have had an excuse to get in, but something was off about her. "What sort of business?"

She cleared her throat. "Design, but let's not talk about business. Don't you get enough of that during the day?"

He chuckled. She was adept at changing the subject. "Indeed, I do."

"Great, so let's talk about something else."

"All right, what did you have in mind?" This time he would give her the leash and let her run. He needed to know about her, but direct questions obviously would not get him any answers.

"Oh, I don't know." She glanced around and then finally back at him. A tiny sparkle flashed in her eyes. "What do you do for fun?"

That question caught Drew off guard, and he blinked. What did he do for fun? When he was in college, he had enjoyed the weekly bonfires after football games, and though his mother thought it Neanderthal, he liked watching football games on Sundays, but that was about the extent of it. Work consumed most of his days now. Buying hotels, renovating hotels, hiring employees to work in the hotels. Hotels dominated his life. He enjoyed traveling and seeing new places, but even those trips were often for work and rarely for pleasure which took some of the joy away.

"Don't tell me you don't know how to have fun?" Her head tilted to the side as she looked up at him. For the first time, her voice held a teasing note as if she were finally relaxing around him.

"I know how to have fun; I just don't always have the time for it, I suppose. Though I used to." He sighed as he thought back to his college days when life was simpler. People had known he was wealthy, and the friends he had made came from money as well, but they hadn't talked about it. Money hadn't ruled their life as it seemed to do now. "When I attended college, I was 'free' for a bit. I used to enjoy watching football games and attending the bonfires, actually." He smiled as the memories of those evenings filled his head. The smell of the fire, the relaxed company, the food that neither his cook nor his mother would approve of. "I loved S'mores."

Her lips pulled into a smile. "Really? S'mores? I would have taken you for a more refined dessert eater."

He twirled her around as the music changed. "First off, S'mores are refined. It takes a lot of talent to get the marshmallow toasted just right so it's gooey but not black."

She chuckled, and her smile grew. Her top teeth were straight but one tooth on the bottom turned in slightly.

Drew found it endearing. "Granted," she said with a nod. "What's the second reason?"

He pulled her closer and brought his lips to her ear. "I'm not as refined as people think I am."

"Oh, really?"

"Really. I keep my limo stocked with Doritos and beef jerky."

At this she laughed out loud, garnering looks from the people closest. A pink flush claimed her face, and she snapped her mouth closed. Her eyes dropped to the floor and his heart ached as he watched her wilt. She obviously embarrassed easily.

"Don't worry. They've already forgotten you. So, what about you? What do you do for fun?"

Her posture regained some of its strength, and the corners of her lips twitched. "I love to read and attend church. I especially love the days I get to work in the nursery."

Finally, something he was certain was true about Carrie. He could tell by the tone of her voice. Wistful and honest. He wasn't much of a reader himself, and he was more of a holiday attender than a regular attender at church, but he could relate to the desire to be around children. As an only child, he had no siblings with children, but he liked kids. He wanted kids. He had thought he and Marjorie were headed that direction until she.... Drew shook his head slightly. Marjorie was gone.

"Do you have kids of your own?" he asked Carrie. Not that he was against an instant family, but it changed the dating dynamic. Dating? He was getting ahead of himself. He barely knew this woman, but he could not deny he was attracted to her.

She dropped her eyes and her voice fell flat. "No, I have no kids. Maybe someday."

He touched a finger under her chin and tilted her head up, so she was looking in his eyes. "I have no doubt that some man will sweep you off your feet some day and make that wish come true." As the words came out of his mouth, he found himself wanting to be that guy. What was it about this girl? He rarely found himself enamored so quickly, at least not after Marjorie. She had burned him too badly. Since then, he hadn't met a woman who attracted his interest and managed to hold it this long.

Her teeth bit down on her bottom lip as a sigh raised and lowered her shoulders. "I hope so."

A look of resigned defeat danced across her face, and Drew wondered what was in her past to elicit such emotion? He wanted to fix it, to let her know how beautiful and interesting he found her, but the words in his head sounded hollow, trite. The conversation stalled then, but Drew counted it a victory as her eyes stayed on his. When the song changed, he took her hand and led her to the side of the dance floor. "Are you hungry?"

A small gurgling sound answered his question as Carrie threw her hands over her stomach. "I guess I could eat a little." A sheepish grin played across her face which Drew found endearing. Most of the women he associated with had starved themselves so long, their stomachs never rumbled because they didn't remember the taste of food.

"Come with me then. If I know my mother, she hired the best caterer in town and the food will be delicious though not entirely filling."

"Isn't that always the case at expensive restaurants?" she asked with a laugh though it sounded forced. The charade was back on, the wall back up.

He smiled back at her, but he filed the information away. Wealthy people rarely referred to restaurants as expensive because, while they might be, it was an expected expense and often a tax write off if done correctly.

The back table was indeed laden with delicacies - canapes, truffles, and more. They grabbed a plate and loaded it with goodies before finding a place to sit. It pleased Drew to see Carrie's plate overflowing with food. He was so tired of women who ate nothing but salad.

"Does your mother always throw such elaborate parties?" Carrie asked as she lifted a canape to her mouth.

Drew noticed her nails for the first time. Or perhaps it was the lack of her nails. Most of the women he'd dated either had fake nails or at the very least had them trimmed and painted. Carrie's nails were devoid of polish and all different lengths. She hadn't seen a manicurist in quite some time. His interest in her grew. Who was this woman?

"Yes," he said dragging his eyes from her hands back to her face. "She does nothing small. Even before my father died, she would throw elaborate parties. I think they might be even bigger now as if she's trying to make up for him being gone or something."

Carrie's smile faltered. "I'm sorry about your father."

"Me too, but he was a good man. I'm glad I had him around as long as I did."

"Yeah, that must be nice." Carrie's voice was so soft that Drew wasn't sure he'd heard her correctly. Her eyes had dropped to her plate.

"Are you close to your family?" he asked.

"I used to be, but no, not anymore."

He wanted to ask her more, but the tone in her voice led him to believe the subject was off limits.

Suddenly, she stiffened. Her eyes widened, and she stood. "I'm sorry, I have to go."

"Wait." He rose as well and grabbed her hand. "I

want to see you again. Can I at least have your whole name?"

"No, I'm sorry, I have to go. Thank you for a wonderful evening." She wrestled her hand out of his grip and hurried from the room. Drew stared after her wondering what had just happened. He wasn't used to women running out on him. That was usually his move.

Something sparkly caught his attention. He bent down and picked up a diamond tennis bracelet from the floor. Drew was almost certain it belonged to Carrie. He examined it for some clue of who this mysterious woman was, but the bracelet didn't appear out of the ordinary. It contained no engraving, and while he wasn't a jeweler, he wasn't even sure the diamonds were real. He looked again to the direction she had fled. He had a name, a bracelet, and a partial description. Would it be enough to find her again?

❧ 3 ❧

Gwen didn't stop running until she exited the hotel. She paused just long enough to text Carrie and ask her to send the driver, but the limo hadn't arrived yet. Gwen pressed herself against the building in a shadow to wait. She'd been having such a good time. Why did Grant have to show up and ruin it?

Gwen hadn't seen him enter, but she had been a little distracted. Drew Devonshire was charming. Probably a little too charming as she'd let her guard down. At least until Grant caught her eye as he turned from the buffet table. Gwen just knew he had been coming her direction. Not only would he have ruined it for Carrie, but for Gwen as well. Surely Drew Devonshire would have had her thrown out for crashing his party. At the very least, he probably would have been angry that she lied to him even though it was a tiny lie.

Ugh, this was why she hated lying. It never ended well. No, it had been better just to leave. Unfortunately, as much as she told herself that, it didn't stop her heart from pounding in her chest at the thought of his blue eyes. Nor did it stop her mind from replaying every moment he had held her in his arms while they danced. She'd never felt so attracted to anyone, and she had felt none of the usual anxiety she felt around men. She'd felt like she fit. But of course, he had to be someone completely out of her league who thought she was someone else. Gwen had the worst luck.

She pushed herself off the wall and hurried to the limo when it pulled up to the curb. The driver opened the door for her, and Gwen scrambled inside. As he shut the door, she pressed her face against the darkened windows and peered out, but it appeared neither Grant nor Drew had followed her outside. With a sigh, she leaned back against the seat. It was too bad Grant's appearance had cut the evening short. It was fun while it lasted.

"What happened? Are you all right?" Carrie asked when Gwen arrived at her penthouse twenty minutes later.

Gwen shook her head and dropped her handbag on the table. "I'm fine. The evening was great until Grant showed up. He was making a beeline to talk to me, er, you I guess, and I panicked. I knew he'd know I wasn't you, so I ran."

Carrie's face folded in sympathy. "Oh, Gwen, I'm so sorry. I was hoping you would have a good time."

Gwen plopped onto Carrie's settee and removed her shoes. "I did have a good time. I met the most amazing man, and we danced. He had these arresting blue eyes."

Carrie settled on the settee beside her, and her eyes sparkled. "Ooh, do tell. Did you catch his name?"

Gwen chuckled and rolled her eyes. "Yeah, Drew Devonshire." Her eyes fell to her lap and she picked off a piece of lint. "Evidently, his family owns the hotel." Gwen lifted her eyes to gauge Carrie's reaction.

Carrie's eyes widened, and her head fell forward. "Drew Devonshire? You danced with Drew Devonshire?"

"Yeah, why? Is he a big deal? I mean I understand he owns the hotel, but-" Gwen reached up to undo her hair. The pins were digging tiny gauges in her head.

Disbelief filled Carrie's voice. "Gwen, Drew Devonshire is only the most eligible billionaire bachelor in the city."

Gwen's hand froze. "What?" How could she have attracted the attention of the most eligible bachelor in the city? She was a nobody. Except that Drew didn't know he'd danced with Gwen Rodgers, lowly teacher. He thought he'd been dancing with some wealthy woman named Carrie.

Carrie chuckled. "Yeah, he doesn't just own *that* hotel, Gwen. His family owns a whole chain."

A sigh escaped Gwen's lips as her hair tumbled about her shoulders. "Figures. I knew he was rich, but I had no idea he was a billionaire." Ugh, embarrassment flooded her. She should never have gone, but at least it had been only the one night. She would never have to see Drew Devonshire again, and he would never have to know.

"You liked him."

"What's not to like? The man is handsome, wealthy, and displayed manners. He was down-to-earth too." Gwen tried to play off her affection, but her heart ached inside.

"No, I mean you *liked* liked him."

Gwen groaned and dropped her head into her hands. "I did, but that's a fantasy, Carrie. He's a billionaire, and I'm a foster kid turned teacher. He would run the other way if he ever knew."

Carrie touched her shoulder. "You don't know that. I'm wealthy and we're still friends."

Gwen lifted her head to look at her friend. "Yeah, but you aren't dating me. You said yourself that one thing you hated about the money was having to live up to the expectations of others. People expect a billionaire like

Drew Devonshire to date an heiress or a princess or something. Not someone like me."

Carrie opened her mouth to say something but then closed it again. Gwen knew she had no words either. With a sigh, she pushed herself up. "I'm going to change out of your dress. Guess my Cinderella evening is over."

"I'll pour us a glass of wine while you change," Carrie said as she headed toward the kitchen.

Gwen padded down the hallway to Carrie's bedroom. She slipped out of the dress and pulled her clothes back on. As she hung up the dress, a pang of jealousy coursed through her. It wasn't that she wanted Carrie's life, but it had been nice to pretend. If only for one night. Her hand lingered for a minute on the satin, and then she headed out of the closet to return the earrings to Carrie's dresser. As she put the earrings on the top, her breath caught. She looked at her left wrist and then her right, but both were empty. Where was her bracelet?

Gwen scanned the floor then retraced her steps in the closet. Nothing. No, this couldn't be happening. She couldn't lose the last thing her parents had given her. "No, no, no," she mumbled under her breath as she cleared the closet and headed down the hall. Her heart wound tighter as she walked as if squeezed by an invisible vice, and she felt the tears building behind her eyes.

"What's the matter?" Carrie asked as Gwen entered the kitchen.

Gwen looked up, tears blurring her vision. "I can't find my bracelet." With those five words, the dam broke and the tears spilled down her cheeks. "I think I lost it."

Carrie's eyes grew large and she sucked in her breath. "I'll call Antwon and see if it got left in the limo. He's good people, Gwen, he wouldn't have taken it."

"But what if I lost it at the Devonshire Hotel? I'll never find it again."

Carrie wrapped an arm about Gwen's shoulder. "It will be okay. I promise we will find it."

Gwen's knees gave out and she sank to the floor. "It's all I have left of them, Carrie."

"I know, and it will be okay. I promise."

But Gwen wasn't so sure.

"There you are, Drew, I've been looking all over for you."

Drew turned to see his mother, dressed as Queen Elizabeth and wearing a fancy mask, heading his direction.

"Where have you been?"

He ignored her question and posed his own as his hand closed over the bracelet, hiding the contents from sight. "Is there a guest list?"

The question seemed to fluster his mother. "Is there

what? What are you talking about Drew? I asked where you've been."

"I've been here, Mother, dancing with an amazing woman, but she ran off and dropped her bracelet. I'd like to return it to her. So, I'll ask you again. Is there a guest list?"

His mother puffed up. "Of course, there is a guest list. This party was by invitation only, but why don't you just deliver it?"

"Because I didn't get her full name, Mother. It's a masquerade ball, and she was playing coy."

"Well, what about her bracelet? Is it engraved at all?"

Drew unfurled his hand to show his mother the bracelet. "No engraving."

His mother picked up the bracelet and examined it. Her forehead furrowed behind her mask and disdain dripped from her voice when she responded, "This isn't even real, Drew. These are fake diamonds. This woman was probably an imposter."

"Perhaps, but she was intriguing and imposter or not, I want to return her bracelet. It might be nothing to us, but I have the feeling it was to her. Why else would a woman wear a designer dress and a fake bracelet?"

His mother rolled her eyes. "I can think of many reasons. I'll get you the guest list but promise me you won't waste your time chasing after some ghost."

Drew couldn't promise, but he nodded hoping it would satisfy his mother.

She let out a large sigh. "Fine, come with me."

He followed her out the ballroom and down the hall to her office. The namesake hotel was the one she liked to work out of most days. She said she felt the strongest connection to it since his father had purchased it first before Drew even was born.

She pushed open the office door after producing a key from some fold in her dress. After a minute of scanning the papers on the desk, she picked up a large stack and held it out to him. "Here you are." Without another word, she whizzed past him and left the room.

Drew took the stack of papers to the desk and sat down. He grabbed a pen from his mother's container and began scanning the list.

Fifteen minutes later, Drew sighed as he finished the last page of the guest list. It appeared his mother invited everyone in the Tristate area. A dozen Carries filled his list that he would have to check and that was only if she'd given him the right first name. Drew wasn't even sure of that. Finding this woman might be like finding a needle in a haystack, but he would try. He didn't even know why it was so important, other than she was the first woman who had excited him in a long time.

D rew typed in the next name on the list. It had taken him a few days to find the time to search the Carries on the list, but determination pushed him to find the woman from the ball. Carrie Garner. An older brunette woman popped up on the screen. Real estate mogul. Nope, not the right one. That just left one more name. Carrie Bliss. He typed it into the search bar and a dress designer's website pulled up, but there was no picture. Great. He added her to the list of other no picture Carries. At least this list was smaller. Only three names. Down from twelve. Drew glanced over at the diamond tennis bracelet. He wasn't optimistic, but maybe his jeweler could help.

He shut the laptop screen and pocketed the bracelet before pulling out his cell phone. "Manuel? Can you have the limo ready in five? Wonderful, I'll be right down." Drew flicked his wrist to read the time on his Rolex. He had a few hours to spare. Enough time to see his jeweler before the auction tonight if he hurried.

With a hastened step, he crossed to his closet and pulled out his blue dress shirt. Women always told him it made his blue eyes pop, and though he wasn't looking for a woman tonight, he wouldn't mind the confidence booster. His mother had insisted he attend a charity auction with her.

He tucked the shirt into his black slacks and shrugged into an Armani blazer. Tie or no tie? Drew regarded his appearance in the mirror. He hated ties. They always made him feel as if he was choking, but his mother nagged him when he didn't wear one. No. No tie. He might have to attend this event, but at least he could be comfortable during it.

Being the public face had never been Drew's strength. That's where his father had excelled and so when he passed, his mother assumed Drew would too, but he hated it. Maybe if he was married, it would be different, but being single and wealthy, it just made him feel like a piece of meat at the market. Men would eye him like competition and women would scan him from head to toe. It was even worse after Marjorie left as he was never sure if those stares were of interest or pity.

Either way, they made Drew uncomfortable, and one day he hoped to pass the job off to someone else.

He trotted down the grand staircase and out the front door. Manuel was just pulling in front of the house as Drew shut the door behind him. Drew folded himself into the spacious backseat when Manuel held the door open.

"Where to, sir?"

Drew fingered the bracelet in his pocket. "To Barelli's, Manuel."

Joseph Barelli had been his father's jeweler before Drew was even born. He was a wealthy Italian a few years older than Drew's father would have been. Though his hair was grey, the man was still extremely handsome and always immaculately dressed. Drew figured it had to be some magic gene Italians were born with.

"Ah, what can I do for you today, Seignior Devonshire?" Mr. Barelli asked when Drew entered the shop.

"I need to see if you can tell me anything about a bracelet." Drew withdrew the bracelet from his pocket and handed it to the elder gentleman.

"Mm, let me see." Mr. Barelli grabbed a magnifying tool from the counter behind him and perused the bracelet. His brows knitted together in confusion as he turned the bracelet in his hand. "I don't know what you are hoping for, sir, but this is an ordinary tennis bracelet."

Drew sighed. "I figured as much. Are there no distinguishing features?"

Mr. Barelli shook his head. "It is not even high quality. This could have been sold at any discount store in the country. May I ask why you are so curious about it?"

"A woman who attended my mother's masquerade ball the other night dropped it."

Mr. Barelli blinked at Drew. "Why would someone of your mother's status be wearing such a trinket?"

"That seems to be the million-dollar question, my friend," Drew said with a smile. "This woman was intriguing, but very different from Mother's normal guests."

"Well, I wish you the best of luck in finding the owner, and please, let me know how the story ends."

"I will, if I ever find her again." Drew took the bracelet back and stared at it for just a moment before returning it to his pocket. "Thank you again."

"No luck, sir?" Manuel asked as Drew slid into the back of the limo.

"No. Just a trinket as I suspected. The good news is the list is smaller now, so I'll check out the few remaining women tomorrow. Tonight, however, I have to get to the auction."

"I admire what you are doing, sir," Manuel said as he started the limo. "Not everyone would display such commitment."

Drew nodded and leaned back against the seat. It was true. Most people in his position would not have gone searching for the owner of the bracelet. He wasn't even sure why he was doing it, other than some urge compelled him. No, not just an urge. It was something else. Something in the woman's bright green eyes or the way she felt in his arms. It was something different that he hadn't even realized he was missing until it was gone.

Gwen sighed and tried one last time to twist her unruly red curls into some semblance of an up do. Her boss was particular that no tendrils hung down while she was serving food, but the Irish in her blood made pinning them down almost impossible.

She squeezed a tiny bit of gel into her hands and rubbed them together. Then she wiped her hands across her hair. The gel managed to tame the last few locks into place. Of course, Gwen had no idea if it would last all night, but at least it was a start.

After a final look in the mirror, she decided her appearance would suffice, flicked off the light, and wandered into the living room to grab her purse.

Carrie looked up from the couch where she sat playing with Tabby. Tabby was Gwen's kitten - her one financial splurge because she had been so lonely. Carrie had offered to cat sit Tabby while Gwen worked her second job as a caterer. She didn't want the responsibility of a pet full time, but Carrie loved coming over and having play time with Tabby while Gwen catered.

"Where are you off to tonight?" Carrie asked as she tucked a lock of hair behind her ear. Gwen tried not to envy Carrie's hair. Though also a ginger, God had blessed her with hair that followed directions, and it lay on her shoulders like velvety copper.

"Who knows? I never know till I get there." Gwen didn't love catering, but her teaching job was barely earning enough to pay the bills. Every paycheck went directly to her student loan, rent, cell phone, groceries, and her car. It was enough to get by but not enough to start saving, so Gwen had picked up a second job catering on the weekends.

Carrie wrinkled her perfect ski-sloped nose, and Gwen swallowed another tiny seed of jealousy. Carrie was feminine perfection. Small nose, delicate lips, slender hands. Gwen, on the other hand, wasn't. Her nose was too big and dusted with freckles, her lips were too thin, and her feet were a size ten - too large to be considered delicate. In fact, her last boyfriend had called them Hobbit feet. She didn't miss that aspect of him.

"Ugh, I'm sorry. I don't know how you work around food all night. I'd either be eating it all or vomiting from the smells."

Gwen rolled her eyes. Carrie rarely ate more than a salad and chicken breast. There was no way she would put the greasy half-baked half-fried food that Gwen served in her mouth. Of course, that was probably why Carrie was a size six while Gwen struggled to maintain her thicker size eight to ten.

"Well, we don't get to eat the food often, and puking on the job is frowned upon." However, it wasn't always easy. She didn't like most of the food she served, but the London Broil was fabulous. Occasionally, when there was food left over, the caterers could eat after they cleaned up. It wasn't always warm by then, but the London Broil even heated well.

"What do you think it is tonight? A wedding?"

Gwen shook her head as she grabbed her coat and scarf. "No, wrong time of year for a wedding. Birthday party maybe or some work thing." Gwen was generally more upbeat, but the loss of her bracelet plus her landlord raising her rent had her down. People said God never gave you more than you could handle, but Gwen felt at the end of her rope.

"I know it's hard right now, but if you ever need money, all you have to do is ask," Carrie said.

Gwen sighed. "I know, but you know I want to take care of myself as long as I can." She'd had to depend on people too long in foster care, and things hadn't always turned out in her favor. When she reached the age of eighteen, Gwen made a promise to herself that she would be self-sufficient. She hoped she wouldn't have to break it. "Take care of my fur ball," she said as she pulled open the front door and headed into the parking lot.

Ten minutes later, Gwen pulled into the parking lot of the catering company. She grabbed her green apron from the passenger seat and stuffed it in her purse before exiting the car and locking the door. She didn't mind the work, but the uniform left a lot to be desired. Black pants, white shirt, and the ugly forest green apron.

Her co-worker, Rachel, was already hard at work grabbing items from the list and stuffing them in the bins. In addition to the food, they had to bring enough plates, bowls, cups, and silverware along with serving utensils and the Sterno containers to heat the food. Someone cooked most of the food the night before and then wrapped it up and placed in the refrigerator.

"What can I help with?" Gwen asked as she tossed her purse on the table. She grabbed her apron from it and tied it about her waist.

"I'm packing the serving utensils. Do you want to grab the plates and bowls?"

"Sure." Rachel handed over the list and Gwen scanned the numbers. This would not be a large party. Probably not a birthday party then. Small parties meant fewer dishes, but it meant serving people at the table instead of in a buffet line. It was a good thing Gwen had worn her comfortable shoes. She'd be earning her ten thousand steps tonight.

Gwen grabbed a tub and began loading the plates in. They were in the cabinet in sets of tens, so she placed five rows in the tub. Then she filled in the remaining space with the bowls packing them carefully to avoid breakage. By the time she finished, Rachel had packed the utensils and moved on to checking the food.

"Who's working with us today?" Gwen asked. Fifty people wasn't too large for two, but it would be easier with three.

Rachel rolled her eyes. "Martin, but you know how he is. It might as well be just you and me."

Martin was their boss. At only twenty-three, he was younger than them both, but he was the manager because his family owned the catering company. Gwen hated nepotism, especially when it allowed inept people to be in positions of power. Martin was such a person. He didn't think he needed to do the prep work or the clean-up work. He would show up just in time to drive the truck. Then he would disappear when it came time to unload until everything was set up. Even during the serving, he would spend more time chatting with the patrons than serving people.

Gwen sighed. It would be a long night, but at least the pay would be worth it. Hopefully, she would earn enough to sock some away in her savings. Her apartment was fine, but she wanted a home of her own - something she hadn't had since the age of twelve when her parents died. She had been putting a little from every catering job in savings, and she hoped to put a down payment on a little house soon.

Gwen joined Rachel in loading the food, and after a second check, they began carting the tubs out to the van. As the last tub slid in, Martin appeared.

"Oh, good, it looks like you two are ready. Sorry, I was caught in a phone call."

Gwen and Rachel traded looks. Martin was always caught in something. It was called an aversion to work.

"Well, let's load up." As expected, Martin climbed into the driver's side. Gwen slid into the middle, and Rachel followed suit, sitting closest to the door. The ride was quiet and uncomfortable. Gwen couldn't wait until they arrived, and she could focus on work.

A few minutes later, Martin pulled up in front of the back entrance of the hall where the event was being held. "I'll park here while you girls unload, and then I'll be in to help set up."

Rachel let out a soft snort. They both knew that wouldn't happen. She opened her door and held it open for Gwen to scoot out as well. When it was shut, they walked to the back of the van to begin unloading.

"At least we can do it all in one trip," Rachel said with a sigh as she eyed the tubs.

"Just tell yourself it's your workout." Gwen tried to hit the gym a few times a week after work, but she knew she needed to lift more. Her clothes always fit a little better when she did.

"Yeah, if only I liked working out." Rachel was larger than Gwen, short and stocky. Though Gwen didn't know her well, Rachel often spoke of cooking as her hobby. Gwen thought she had mentioned wanting to author a cookbook once.

They pulled down the first cart and hefted one of the tubs onto the bottom shelf. Then they climbed back in the van to grab a second tub for the top shelf.

"You'd think he could help while he's parked here," Rachel hissed under her breath.

Gwen shrugged. She didn't like it either, but she wasn't one to buck authority. She needed the job too much, and she'd never had the courage to stand up to people. When her parents had been killed, she'd gone into the foster system. Some foster kids bucked the system and revolted, but Gwen had gone the other direction - retreating into her shell. Her first home had been awful, but when the CPS worker had finally checked on her and found her locked in a closet, she'd been removed. The next place had been much better. Those foster parents had been nice, but Gwen had never really let them in. Losing people hurt too much, and trust was hard for her to give.

With the first cart full, Gwen helped Rachel load the other cart, and they wheeled them into the building. The kitchen was large and uncluttered which Gwen was thankful for. She hated when there was no kitchen and they had to bring back the dishes to wash them. By then, caked on food made it harder to scrub off, and they invariably had to wash the tub as well.

Rachel checked her watch. "Well, we have about an hour, so I guess we should get set up. We can wait to start the Sterno for another few minutes."

Gwen nodded and opened her tub.

5

The limo stopped in front of the small building. "Here we are, sir," Manuel said from the driver's seat as he turned off the engine.

Drew waited for Manuel to open the door before stepping out. His eyes scanned the building as he stood. Not large, but a nice location nonetheless. The hall sat on the edge of a river, and one wall was entirely glass, granting an astounding view of the area.

"Thank you, Manuel. Keep your phone on in case I can sneak out of here early."

Manuel nodded. "As you wish, sir."

Drew returned the nod and ran a hand down his suit before heading into the building. A man in black pants and a crisp white shirt opened the door. Drew hadn't been expecting a doorman at such a small event. He motioned to the closed doors straight ahead. "Enjoy your night, sir."

If only he could, but Drew had been attending these events for so long that the novelty had worn off. There had been a time he once loved dressing up in a suit and attending the affairs. They had made him feel important, something he didn't always feel knowing his money wasn't his but an inheritance from his father. In addition, he had harbored the notion he would meet his future wife at one of these events.

However, the women were much like the food - they all looked the same after the first few events. Sure, they showed up in their designer dresses looking like a million dollars. They smiled at all the right times and laughed at his jokes, but on the very next date, their true colors emerged. The smile was a little tighter, the questions a little more personal, and he could almost feel their fingers reaching into his bank account to spend his money. He didn't want a woman like that.

Drew took one final deep breath, plastered his fake smile on, and opened the door. The room held ten round tables focused on a podium at the front. Most of the tables were already full. He glanced around for a waiter or a bar but found neither. Drew wasn't much of a drinker, but nights like this he needed one.

His discomfort grew when he heard the shrill voice of his mother beckoning him from across the room.

"Drew, over here, darling." She waved at him from across the room. At nearly sixty, his mother was still in great shape. Of course, she paid good money to have a cook and a personal trainer, but he wished she wouldn't draw such attention to herself or him.

Shaking his head, he made his way across the floor to her table. He gave her the obligatory peck on each cheek before addressing her. "Mother, I wish you wouldn't yell like that across the room. I abhor these things as it is, but I especially detest when you make a scene."

His mother folded her arms and leaned back as she regarded him. "I brought you into this world, Drew Devonshire. Need I remind you of my twelve-hour labor?"

Drew rolled his eyes. This was always the card she played when he brought up anything she disagreed with. As if he controlled how long she was in labor. "No, you needn't, but, Mother, really. I would have made my way over to you, eventually."

"Perhaps," she said, tilting her head, "but I needed you here sooner rather than later."

His heart sank as her eyes twinkled. "Oh, no, Mother, what did you do?" He knew that look in her eye, and he rarely liked it.

She held out her thin, perfectly manicured hands. "I did nothing. I happened to meet a lovely woman earlier.

She's new to these charity events, but it turns out she has a daughter just about your age."

Drew groaned. "Tell me you didn't." His mother was always setting him up with one wealthy debutante after another even though he'd told her they were too vanilla, too boring for him.

"Relax, I just said they should sit with us. The rest is up to you. Oh, here they are now. Camilla, over here, darling." Her arm waved in the air again and Drew stifled his sigh. This was what he hated more than the stuffy event itself, this awkward moment when he met someone his mother was clearly trying to set him up with and had to play nice, no matter what she looked like or what strange habits she had.

The last time his mother had done this, the woman had been obsessed with her weight. Even though she had been tiny, she had tugged on Drew's arm every few minutes asking how many calories were in that canape or would that drink cause her hips to grow? He couldn't get away from her fast enough.

The time before that, the woman had seemed normal enough at first. Then, she had proceeded to pull a tiny compact out of her bag to check her appearance. Not unordinary for women, but the compact had then disappeared and reappeared ten times in the span of five minutes. Who needed to look at themselves that often?

Needless to say, Drew was not a fan of these set ups, so he was pleasantly surprised when he turned around.

"Avery?" Though he hadn't seen her in years, he was sure it was Avery. This woman was small and petite with her brown hair piled on her head. Her silver gown hugged her frame, and her blue eyes sparkled.

"Drew?" There was a hint of laughter in her voice as she answered.

His mother blinked in confusion. "You two know each other?"

Drew chuckled. He and Avery had dated a few years ago. She was one of the few wealthy women he had met who held his interest, but before they grew serious, she had moved away. "Yes, we know each other. You look beautiful, Avery."

"You clean up pretty nice yourself," she said as she placed her hands on her hips and looked him up and down.

"Well, I guess there's no need to introduce the two of you." His mother turned her attention to Avery's mother. "Camilla, I'm so glad you could make it. This is my son Drew."

Camilla was an older version of her daughter. Grey streaks ran through her hair and the lines around her eyes were more pronounced, but she appeared to take good care of herself. "Pleased to meet you, Drew," she said as she extended her hand to him. "Though I'm surprised I haven't met you before if you know Avery."

Drew took the woman's hand. Soft, but slightly leathery. "A pleasure to meet you as well." His eyes shifted to Avery. "Well, Avery and I knew each other a few years ago, but then she moved away. Are you back now?"

Avery returned the smile, but it didn't reach her eyes. "Yes, apparently I am." There was a sadness in her voice that he didn't remember. What had happened to her? When her mother looked away though, Drew caught Avery's eye roll and bit back a smile. Maybe this evening wouldn't be so bad after all.

"It's showtime, ladies," Martin said. "I'll stay back here and get the plates ready as you two serve."

Rachel rolled her eyes, but Gwen spoke up. "Sure, Martin, that sounds good." She picked up two plates and headed for the swinging door that connected the kitchen to the hall. The tables were now full, and a dull hum of conversation filled the air.

Gwen fixed a smile on her face as she approached the first table. Interacting with the guests was her least favorite part of catering, but it came with the territory. At least at events like this, the men and women rarely spoke to her. They were too engaged in their own conversations and conversing with "the help" was beneath them.

She placed a plate in front of the first woman who didn't even bother to look her direction and then one in front of the man next to her. He flicked her a passing glance, but that was all. Gwen returned to the kitchen and grabbed two more plates.

Rachel had taken the other half of the room. Five tables apiece was still a lot, but it was manageable. Gwen placed the next two plates down and returned to the kitchen one more time. She repeated this procedure until only one table remained. As she approached the final table though her eyes widened. No, it couldn't be.

Only two men sat at this table. One was an elderly gentleman with a round face and a receding hairline. The other was a dashing young man with dark hair and blue eyes. He looked remarkably like Drew Devonshire. It was true she had only glimpsed his face that night when he lifted his mask, but those blue eyes were seared in her memory. Her heart sped up in her chest.

Unfortunately, he wasn't alone. A stunning brunette sat to his right, and from the smile on her face, she appeared as smitten as Gwen felt. She looked around for Rachel. Was it too late to trade tables? She wasn't sure she could work this one all night. What if he recognized her? Or maybe worse, what if he didn't?

Rachel was just placing a plate down at her final

table. Too late to switch now. Gwen would just have to hope he ignored her like the others had or that he wouldn't recognize her without the mask. She kept her head turned slightly away from him as she placed her two plates and then made a beeline for the kitchen.

Her face felt flushed as she exited the hall and entered the kitchen. She needed to cool down. If she went back out with a bright red face, she would just draw more attention to herself. Gwen closed her eyes and leaned against the wall trying to calm her heart down.

"Grab a tray and take the last three," Martin ordered when he spotted her. "I'm about ready to start sending out the next course."

Gwen wanted to say no, to come up with some excuse, but she needed this job. She took a deep breath and grabbed the tray. Hoping her face had calmed down, Gwen headed back into the hall. *Please don't look at me. Please don't look at me.* The mantra played over and over in her head as she approached his table.

She placed the plate in front of the older woman first and then turned to Drew. Thankfully, his face was turned toward his brunette friend. She scooted his plate in front of him and then delivered the plate to the brunette. Her heartbeat thundered in her ears. How could they not hear it? Drew's eyes lifted to hers, and Gwen sucked in her breath.

"Thank you," he said and then turned back to his friend.

"You're welcome," Gwen stuttered. She was too shocked to say anything else. He hadn't recognized her. She should be happy, but disbelief was all she could feel right now.

With a sigh, she headed back to the kitchen. One course down and only two more to go.

6

Drew raised his hand to cover his mouth as the second yawn struck him. He'd managed to stifle the first, but the second had snuck up on him.

"Are you as bored as I am?" Avery asked as she leaned in close to him.

"Maybe more." He smiled at her. She was the first wealthy woman he'd met who seemed to hate these events as much as he did. It was one reason they had tried dating years ago. He glanced at his watch. They still had another few hours. They had served the first course along with the main course, but dessert remained, and bidding would probably start during dessert.

"You think we could sneak out during dessert?" he whispered back.

Her blue eyes sparkled. "You mean skip the auction? You bet I do, but only if it isn't a date. No offense, but we tried that once already."

"Yes, but that didn't work out because you left."

"No, that didn't work out because you're exactly what my mother wants me to marry. I don't want to marry what my mother wants. I want to marry what I want, and that does not include billionaires who would drag me to stuffy events like this."

Drew chuckled. He liked Avery, he missed her quick wit, and it was true. Their romance had fizzled before she left though he couldn't really remember why. However, he had enjoyed their friendship, and if she was back in town, he wanted to rekindle it. "Okay, not a date then. I kind of have another woman on my mind anyway."

Avery flashed him a crooked smile and leaned closer. "Ooh, do tell."

"I met her at my mother's masquerade ball the other night. She was beautiful, but she didn't act like she knew it."

Avery chuckled. "How was she at your mother's ball then?"

"I'm not sure she was supposed to be." He moved his arm as the server approached. "She certainly didn't act like the other rich women my mother is always trying to set me up with, but she said she was on the list." The plate clattered against the table and Drew looked up at the woman. Her face was pale, and her eyes were wide, but there was something familiar in them.

"I'm so sorry," she said averting her eyes.

Her voice tickled his ears and triggered a memory, but it couldn't be. She'd said she owned her own business, so why would she be serving at an auction?

Fear flickered in her eyes, and her eyes glanced around for the nearest exit. In that instant he knew. "It is you."

"I'm sorry," she mumbled again and ran for the side door. He wasn't letting her get away this time though.

"What's going on?" his mother asked.

"Nothing. I'll be right back." Drew tossed his napkin on the table and hurried after the woman. He didn't even care that he was causing a scene behind him.

As he pushed open the door, he found her leaning against the wall to his left. When she heard the door open, she looked up and turned to bolt.

"Carrie, wait."

She stopped in her tracks and though her back was to him, he saw her shoulders droop. Slowly, she turned to face him. "My name isn't Carrie."

"What do you mean?" He took a step toward her aware that he should be increasing the distance between them after her admission instead of closing it.

"My friend is Carrie Bliss, the dress designer your

mother invited. She asked me to attend in her place. I'm sorry. I didn't know I would meet you, and I didn't think I was hurting anyone."

"You didn't," he said taking another step. "I'm glad you were there for whatever reason. Those parties generally bore me to no end, but you... you made it interesting."

She stared at him, her green eyes peering into his soul. "Why?"

He blinked, her question catching him off guard. "I don't know why. Maybe because you were genuine."

She raised her eyebrow at him, and he chuckled as the irony of his statement sunk in.

"Okay, other than the fake name part. I felt there were parts of you that were genuine like when you talked about working in the nursery. I'm surrounded by so many people that only say what they think I want to hear. You didn't seem to care about that. It was refreshing."

"Well, I'm glad. Look, I'm probably going to get fired when my boss finds out I caused a scene, but I should really get back to work."

"Wait." He reached into his pocket and pulled out the bracelet. He'd been carrying it with him everywhere since the night of the ball as if he hoped it might help him find her again. As he held it out to her, it surprised him to see her eyes glisten with tears. "It's important to you then?"

She nodded, taking the bracelet from his palm. "It's the last thing my parents gave me before someone killed them. It's all I have left, and I thought I'd lost it for good. Thank you."

"You're welcome." He should leave it at that. Say 'you're welcome' and walk away. His mother would never approve of him seeing someone like this woman, whatever her name was, but he couldn't make his feet move away from her. They were rooted in place, glued to the floor. He'd felt something when he danced with her that he'd never felt, and he wanted to feel it again. "Will you tell me your real name now?"

She chuckled and shook her head. "It's Gwen. Gwen Rodgers."

"Well, Gwen Rodgers, I would really like to see you again. Do you think we could arrange that?"

Her eyes lit up for a moment and then the light flickered and faded. Sadness laced her voice as she answered. "No, I don't think that would be a good idea. We come from two different worlds, Drew. Thank you for returning the bracelet, but I have to be going."

Stunned, he watched her walk away. He should be relieved because she was right of course. They did come from different worlds, and his mother would never approve, but that didn't erase the tug of curiosity he was feeling.

The door behind him opened and Avery's head

appeared. "You better get back here. Your mother is livid, and she wants an explanation."

With a sigh, Drew followed Avery back to the table.

"What is going on, Drew?" his mother asked. "You have caused quite a scene in here. The looks have been downright scandalous, and you know very well there will be talk tomorrow."

"I'm sorry, Mother. That was the woman from the dance the other night. I wanted to give her back her bracelet."

"You carried it around with you?" His mother's forehead wrinkled, and her nose turned up in disgust. "You better not be falling for this girl, Drew."

Gwen waited until she was around the corner and out of sight of Drew to let the tears fall. She was thankful to have her bracelet back, embarrassed at the scene she had caused, and angry or disappointed - she wasn't sure which - that she had turned him down. Gwen knew she had made the right decision - telling him they were too different - but a part of her wished she had said yes. She hadn't felt a connection like that with anyone, ever.

She opened her hand and stared down at the bracelet. It looked so ordinary compared to the jewelry the women were wearing out there, but it meant the world to her.

With a shaky hand, she fastened it around her wrist once more and then continued to the kitchen.

"Where have you been?" Martin asked. "Rachel has already started bringing back her dishes."

"Sorry, I uh had to take a short break. I'll get right back out there."

"No, you stay here and start washing. *I'll* bring your dishes back." Martin emphasized the word to let her know she was causing him extra trouble. Then he shot her an agitated look before exiting through the swinging door.

Gwen bit back a smile. He thought he was punishing her, but she'd rather be holed up back here than face Drew and his party again. She rolled up her sleeves and filled the sink with water.

"You gonna tell me what happened out there?" Rachel asked as she placed another round of dishes on the counter.

Gwen kept her head down and focused on scrubbing. Maybe if she feigned ignorance Rachel would let it go. "I don't know what you mean."

Rachel scoffed. "Yes, you do. Some handsome, wealthy man left his entire table to follow you. The whole room saw it."

Gwen bit her lip and sighed. Nope, ignorance was clearly out of the question. "Okay." She turned off the water and glanced toward the door to make sure Martin wasn't around. "I met Drew Devonshire at a masquerade ball the other night."

"You were invited to a ball that Drew Devonshire attended?" Rachel's words were slow and incredulous.

"No, not me, my friend, Carrie. She didn't want to go, and we look similar, so she asked me to go as her. I didn't know it was an elite ball. Anyway, I lost my bracelet and when Drew recognized me tonight, he followed me out to return it."

Rachel narrowed her eyes. "That's it? He followed you out to return it?"

Gwen shrugged. "And to tell me he wanted to see me again, but I said no," she added quickly.

Rachel's eyes bulged, and her jaw dropped. "You said what? Girl, have you lost your mind? Drew Devonshire wants to see you again and you said no?"

"It would never work out. He's… well, he's Drew Devonshire, and I'm… no one."

"Girl, that's why you say yes. Don't you remember Cinderella? Pretty Woman? They were nobodies too, but rich men fell for them and their whole lives changed." Rachel shook her head as if she couldn't believe Gwen could be so dense.

"Yeah, but those were fairy tales, Rachel. This is reality, and *that* just doesn't happen in reality."

"Guess you'll never know now." Rachel shot her one last disbelieving look before exiting the swinging door.

Gwen stared after her. Was she right? Had Gwen passed up a chance to be a real-life Cinderella? She shook her head. No. She believed in God and she believed in miracles, but that just seemed too farfetched to be true.

7

D rew woke up the next morning determined to learn all he could about Gwen Rodgers. He kicked off the heavy comforter and padded to his desk where his laptop sat. He started with a simple search for her online. It was rare nowadays for people to have no online presence. There was usually a social media page or three, videos and pictures that others had posted, and sometimes even an address. Gwen had none of these. In fact, the only thing he could find was her school picture.

So, she was a teacher as well. A noble profession. And she must not have a lot of money if she was working two jobs. But this wasn't the information he sought. He wanted to determine if she was married and what her interests were. He wanted to know her. It was time to call in a favor.

He picked up the phone next to his computer and rang Manuel. "Can you have the car ready in fifteen? I need to go downtown."

"Of course, sir. It will be waiting for you."

"Thank you." Drew hung up and shut the laptop lid. He needed a quick shower and something to eat and there was no time to waste.

Ten minutes later, clean and dressed, Drew headed down to the kitchen to grab a breakfast on the go. Usually, he let his master chef, Ernesto, whip him up a healthy fare, but there was no time today.

"Good morning, Mr. Devonshire," Ernesto said in greeting as he entered the kitchen. "Egg white omelet today?"

"No time, Ernesto. Must see about a girl. I'll just take a bar with me."

Ernesto's lips pulled into a grimace and his nose rose in the air. "If you had let me know, sir, I could have had breakfast waiting. You needn't have resorted to a processed bar."

Drew smiled. "I suppose that's true. Tell you what, Ernesto, if I'm back in time for lunch, I'll let you serve whatever you feel like making, okay?"

A tiny light of enthusiasm sparked in Ernesto's eyes,

but he was too composed to show much more than that. "I await your word."

Drew nodded, ducked into the pantry and grabbed the forbidden bar, and then headed to the front door. Manuel was indeed waiting for him. He leaned against the limo but straightened as soon as he saw Drew.

"Good morning, sir."

"Morning, Manuel. I need to go to the police station downtown."

If Manuel wondered why, he said nothing, just nodded and opened the door for Drew.

Twenty minutes later, the limo pulled to a stop in front of the police station. Drew waited for Manuel to open the door before stepping out and taking in the short brick building. How Scott worked in this bland building every day was beyond him. He must really love his job.

Scott was the one college friend Drew kept in touch with. It never hurt to have someone on the force in your corner. Drew had never had to ask for a favor, but he hoped that his annual donation would be enough to buy him one today.

"Drew Devonshire?" Scott's voice carried across the small room as Drew entered. Several other heads swiveled his direction as he crossed the room to his friend. "Well, I never thought I'd see you in here." Scott shook Drew's hand and motioned at an empty chair.

Drew cleared his throat. "Actually, is there a private room in which we can converse?"

Scott's eyebrow arched, but he led the way down the hall to a conference room. When the door was shut, he turned to Drew. "Okay, you want to tell me what's going on?"

"I was hoping you could find out some information on someone for me."

"Someone who owes you money?"

Drew chuckled. "Hardly. I doubt this person has much."

"So, someone you are hoping to buy out?" Scott was clearly fishing.

"No, a woman I met. She's like no one I've met before; she won't even let me take her to dinner. I tried to gather information about her online, but she doesn't even have a social media page. Who doesn't have a social media platform nowadays?"

This time Scott smiled. "More people than you'd think but continue."

"She's a teacher at Ryland High. That's all I know, but that means she'll be in the system, right? You can find something out about her?"

"Her fingerprints will be in the system, yes. It doesn't mean I'll be able to find out much about her. If she's a teacher, I doubt she has a record."

"Please, whatever you can find."

Gwen was just finishing prepping for her final lesson of the day when Carol, the school secretary, popped her head in her doorway. "Gwen, you got a second?"

"Sure, Carol, what's up?"

Carol laughed. "How about you tell me? These just came for you." She stepped the rest of the way into the room, and Gwen's eyes widened. In her hands was an enormous bouquet of white carnations and stargazer lilies. "It seems you have an admirer."

A soft heat crawled up Gwen's neck. She assumed they were from Drew, but she didn't want to accept them. After finishing the dishes and packing up the night before, Martin had informed her that she was fired. Evidently, someone at Drew's table had complained about her causing a scene. Rachel had tried to stick up for her, but it was no use. Now, in addition to everything else, she needed to find another part-time job. However, that was way more than she was prepared to share with Carol. She would graciously accept the flowers and get rid of them later when no one would notice.

"Thank you." Gwen took the flowers and looked around for an empty counter to set them on. Her desk was out of the question. She was what most people referred to as "organized chaos." Papers cluttered her desk, and while no one else knew where anything was,

Gwen could always find anything needed. She figured it was an unconscious rebelling from living with her mother.

Gwen and her mother had been polar opposites. Her mother was a complete neat nick while Gwen thrived with a little clutter. She always hated Saturdays when her mother made her dust the furniture, vacuum the house, and clean her room. At least, she hated them until her mother died. Then Gwen regretted ever fighting with her mother, and she had bargained with God to never complain about cleaning if he just brought her parents back. Of course, that hadn't happened, and Gwen had retreated into her shell. But as much as she tried to be like her mother, she just couldn't be as organized as her mother had been.

Her file cabinet was about the only furniture in her room clean enough and large enough to hold the flowers, so she set them there. They filled the space looking more like a small garden in her room than a bouquet. A white card sat nestled in a plastic contraption that looked a little like a tuning fork. Though she wasn't sure she cared what the note said, Gwen plucked it out and opened the card.

"It was such a pleasure to meet you, Gwen. I know you think we are worlds apart, but there is more to me than the money. My hope is you will enjoy these flowers and give me another chance. I have included my number,

so you can reach out to me, and I await your call." -
Drew

His number was indeed at the bottom, but there was no apology. Did he not know she had gotten fired? Gwen bit her lip as she contemplated rushing to her phone and calling him right then though she wasn't sure 'thank you' would be the words out of her mouth.

"So?"

Gwen looked up surprised to still see Carol standing in her room, "Oh, just a thank you for someone I met the other night."

Carol's brow shot up. "Wow, that must've been some meeting."

It really had been, and Gwen wasn't even sure why. They had just danced and talked, but there was something in the way he had held her that made her feel safe and secure. Something she hadn't felt in a long time.

But she didn't want to share this with Carol. For one thing, she really couldn't even explain it. For another, she feared if she talked about it, the night would feel less real, less special somehow. And there was the firing thing. So instead, she feigned nonchalance. "I guess it was."

Carol stood a moment longer as if expecting more, but she finally shrugged. "All right, well, I look forward to the story one day. Enjoy your flowers."

Gwen wasn't certain she could do that. Were these

apology flowers? If so, was he so arrogant he thought he didn't need the actual apology? She hadn't thought he was. So, maybe he didn't know Martin had fired her, and he was interested in seeing her. The question then was who had gotten her fired and what should she do about it?

"Whoa, Ms. Rodgers, who did you get the flowers from?" Rhea, one of her students asked as she entered.

One thing was for sure. Gwen would have to take the flowers home. "Just a friend saying thank you."

"That's some thank you." Rhea's statements were echoed by the other students when they entered, and it took an extra ten minutes to get the class on task.

When the clock read three thirty, Gwen packed up her things and picked up the flowers. They were so large they blocked her vision, and she was forced to turn sideways to see where she was going.

"Whoa, that is an armful. Need some help?"

Gwen's heart dropped when she recognized the voice of Tom Boyer, the PE teacher. He had asked her out several times, but Gwen had always turned him down. Not only was he not her type, but he cursed like a sailor. Gwen couldn't stand the sound of curse words, never used them, and had made a promise she would never be with anyone who did. Unfortunately, Tom hadn't taken her declining his offer well. He'd made it a point to stop by her classroom at least once a week, always with the ruse that he was discussing a student but really, he simply wanted to compliment her.

"No, I'm fine, thank you." She kept her tone friendly, hoping he would get the hint and leave her alone. No such luck.

"Someone die?" He said it like a joke, but Gwen didn't find it funny. She hadn't wanted flowers when her parents were killed. She had simply wanted them back. He had probably never lost anyone close to him if he could joke about death so callously.

"No, they're from a guy I'm seeing." Gwen didn't mean to lie. The words slipped out before she could rein them in, however, they did have the intended effect. A look of disbelief crossed Tom's features followed by one of resignation, but he did drop the pursuit and walk away. Unfortunately, Gwen also knew he wouldn't keep the knowledge to himself. By tomorrow, everyone would want to know about this new mystery man.

With a sigh, she continued to her car but paused when she reached it. Her eyes flicked from the front seat to the flowers. It would be a tight squeeze just to fit them in. She slung her purse in the backseat first and then maneuvered the flowers into the passenger seat. They filled most of the seat, and she debated buckling them in with the seatbelt but decided against it. She looked comical enough as it was.

The drive back to her house was slow though. Every

time she tapped the brakes, she feared the flowers would tumble off the seat and onto the floor, and her arm would shoot across as if protecting a child.

When she reached her apartment, she circled it once to see if any of her nosy neighbors were out. An elderly woman lived a few doors down and made it her mission to know everything that was going on in the apartment. While Gwen didn't normally mind the woman or her curiosity, she had no desire to answer the woman's questions tonight. Thankfully, the woman was nowhere to be seen.

As quickly as she could, Gwen parked the car, grabbed the flowers and her personal items, and high-tailed it into her apartment. Only when the door shut behind her, did she allow her guard to drop.

Gwen placed the flowers on her small bar and pulled out her cell phone. She needed Carrie and her advice.

Half an hour later, Carrie arrived at the front door, bags of Chinese food in her hands.

"I've got fo…. whoa, are those from Drew Devonshire?" she asked as she stepped into the room.

"Who else would they be from? That arrangement had to cost a few hundred dollars."

Carrie set the bags on the table and walked closer to the flowers. A low whistle escaped her lips. "At least. Please tell me you'll see him again now."

Gwen sucked in her breath. She still wasn't sure.

After her last class had left, she had decided to call - she needed to at least find out if he knew about her being fired - and then chickened out. The first time, she had barely touched the phone. The second time, she managed to dial the first number. The last time, she managed to dial all but the last number. But she just couldn't complete the call.

"He didn't have to send flowers, you know," Carrie said. "He had already given back the bracelet. He had no reason to connect with you again."

"Unless it was to apologize for getting me fired. If that's the case, flowers aren't enough."

"Was there a card?"

Gwen sighed. "There was, but he didn't mention an apology. Could he really not know though?"

Carrie folded her arms across her chest and cocked her head. "Well, there's one way to find out."

"I know, but what do I even say to him?"

"I don't know," Carrie said, punctuating her words with an eye roll. "How about thank you for starters?"

Gwen stared down at her cell phone. Could she do it? Could she call him?

"Come on. I'll be right here for moral support."

Her fingers trembled as she punched in the numbers. Then the sound of a ring reached her ears.

Drew read over the paperwork again. Fate had dealt Gwen Rodgers a rough hand. Her parents had died in an auto accident shortly after her twelfth birthday. Drew couldn't even imagine. How did you go to bed one night and wake up the next day with no family? Not surprisingly, the police report stated that Gwen had been almost unresponsive when given the news.

Then, she had been taken into Child Protective Service custody. Drew knew that most of the time, the case workers did great work and found wonderful homes for children who needed a safe place, but he also knew bad people slipped through the cracks. It appeared Gwen's first house had been one of the latter. The father had apparently locked her in a closet and fed her through a small door. She had been deprived of sunlight for nearly a week until the school had finally called the case worker looking for her. Why it had taken a week was beyond Drew, and he could only imagine how traumatized Gwen must have been. In fact, considering all she had been through, it was amazing she was as well-adjusted as she seemed now. What had made that difference?

Beside him the phone rang, and he picked it up without bothering to check the caller ID. Few people had his personal number, so it was probably his mother anyway. "This is Drew."

There was a pause, and then a quiet voice said, "Hi, Drew, this is Gwen Rodgers."

Instantly, he gripped the phone tighter and turned all his attention to the call. "Hello, Gwen. Did you receive the flowers?" He wanted to smack himself as the words left his mouth. Of course, she had gotten the flowers. Otherwise, she wouldn't have his number.

"I did, and um thank you, but I need to ask what they were for."

For? He thought back to what he had written on the note. Hadn't he said what they were for? "They were a thank you for the lovely evening of the masquerade ball and an offering in hopes you would let me take you out."

"So, they weren't an apology?"

Drew's brow knitted together. An apology? Was there something he needed to apologize for? "I'm not sure I know what you mean."

There was a small sigh on the other end. "I was fired last night from my catering job."

"What? Gwen, I didn't do that. I would never have asked them to fire you."

"I believe you," she said, "but someone did. Do you know who might have done that?"

Drew had an idea. His mother had been upset at the scene. If anyone had said anything to her, she might have retaliated. "Gwen, I'm so sorry. It might have been my mother. This is all my fault."

"No, it's my fault. I should never have been at the ball."

"Gwen, let me make it up to you. What do you need?" He didn't think she would take his money, but he was offering it anyway. "Do you want me to speak to your boss?"

Gwen scoffed on the other end. "Don't bother. It won't do any good. I'll find another job somewhere."

He could help with that. From looking over her paperwork, he knew she donated a little money to a foster care charity. "What if I could give you a job?"

Gwen's answer was a nervous chuckle. "I wasn't looking for a pity hire, Drew."

Man, she was perceptive, but maybe he could play it off. "It's not a pity hire. I've been looking for new tax write offs, and I know we don't donate all we are allowed. It wouldn't be a lot of hours, but I could use someone who has a passion for a cause to handle our donations."

There was a pause on the other end. "How do you know I have a passion for a cause?" Her voice was hesitant.

Drew bit the inside of his lip. He wasn't ready to tell her he had been looking into her. "I'm sorry, I just figured since your church seemed so important to you that you might support a cause. Don't church people do that?" he finished lamely.

"Have you ever been to church?" Gwen's voice held a note of disbelief.

"A few times, but I'm certainly not a regular attender. I'm sorry if I assumed incorrectly. If you don't want the job, I'm sure I can find someone else-" As he hoped it would, the reverse psychology spurred Gwen into action.

"No, don't do that. I'd be delighted to take that on for you. I have a few charities very dear to my heart, and I would love the opportunity to send more money their way."

"Wonderful. Can you meet me at the Kingston tomorrow?" The Kingston was another of their hotels. Drew didn't want to meet at the Devonshire for fear of running into his mother, but she rarely visited the Kingston leaving the management of it up to him.

"I work until four, but I could meet you there after?" The hesitation was back in Gwen's voice and made her statement come off like a question. Was it due to his meeting choice?

"How about five? I'll meet you in the lobby, we can discuss business, and then perhaps we can partake of some food." He, on the other hand, phrased his request as a declaration. He had learned long ago that confidence won a lot of battles.

"I can do five. Do I need to bring anything?"

"Your ID and Social. I'm sure it won't be an issue, but we run a background check on all our employees." This was perfect. Hiring her had been a spur-of-the-moment decision, but now he wouldn't have to act like he didn't know about her past.

"Understood. I'll see you then."

As Drew hung up the phone, he couldn't help but feel a little excitement at the prospect of seeing Gwen again. Even better, he was going to have her near him at least once a week. The way he saw it, this was a win-win situation all around.

8

"You feel like getting a coffee?"

Drew looked up from the reports he was studying to see Avery, looking pressed and pristine in the doorway of his office.

"Sure. I need a break from these anyway. Quarterly reports always mire down my day."

"Grab your coat then. There's a place just down the block I've really missed."

Drew nodded, wondering if the place she was referring to was Chez Cafe. It was a trendy, hipster place just around the corner that served specialty coffee and French pastries, and it was one of his favorite places as well.

He shrugged into his Burberry coat and plucked the scarf from the coat rack. The air had turned quite chilly today, almost as if the weather knew it was now

November and therefore it needed to plunge into freezing temperatures to prepare for the first snowfall.

"Won't you need a coat?" he asked as his eyes roamed her frame. Her pantsuit was designer and expensive, but it didn't appear very warm.

"I left it with your doorman," she said with a flick of her hand. "It's too warm in here to wear it. Plus, it makes me look twenty pounds heavier. Perhaps I should design a coat that still shows off a woman's curves."

"You could do that," Drew said biting back a smile. Avery was not one who accepted defeat, and he knew if he told her she wasn't a designer that she would do all she could to prove him wrong.

"No, I couldn't." She rolled her eyes at him. "I'm an artist, not a designer."

"Well, I'm sure you could hire someone who could design it for you." Fitted coats was not a topic of conversation Drew wanted to continue further. He didn't care about a woman's coat. In truth, he rarely noticed them. Eyes were what he focused on. There was so much you could see in someone's eyes, especially someone of depth. Like Gwen's eyes who had haunted his visions since the night of the ball.

"Now that is not a bad idea." With a purposeful stride, Avery led the way into the foyer. Her heels clacked against the marble flooring, and Drew couldn't help but notice the subtle swaying of her hips. Was that for him or had she always walked that way? He couldn't remember, but it had been years since he had seen her. She could have acquired the trait along the way.

She paused just long enough to rescue her coat from the doorman and then she was stepping out into the dreary grey weather. The wind pulled at Drew's coat with icy fingertips as he followed her as if trying to peel away his warmth. Drew loved winter - the snow, the colors, the general feeling of good will, but he wasn't a fan of the biting cold. Not unless he could be home in front of his fireplace with a warm cup of coffee and a good movie.

"So, are you back for good?" he asked quickening his stride to pull even with her.

"For the foreseeable future. I ran out of money in Europe, starving artist and all that. Father wouldn't extend me any more credit. So, now I'm back until I can earn enough money to continue doing what I love."

Drew understood that feeling. It was similar to his situation, and he wasn't sure he'd ever get out of the hotel business now.

Avery pulled open the door to Chez Cafe, and a friendly wave of warmth rolled out to greet them. A low hum of conversation buzzed around the crowded room. "It might be standing room only in here."

"A table will open up," Avery said with a wave of her hand. "It always does."

The line moved quickly and within minutes they were at the front placing their order. "I'll have an Iced, Half Caff, Ristretto, Venti, 4-Pump, Sugar Free, Cinnamon, Dolce Soy Skinny Latte," Avery said.

Drew blinked at her. Her words might have been English, but he had no idea what she had even ordered. Surprisingly though, the barista behind the register just nodded and scribbled something on a cup. As Drew never understood the markings on the cup either, he wondered if the employees had some kind of code for snobby drink orders.

"And for you?" the woman asked as Avery stepped to the side.

"Just an Americano with room for cream please."

The woman raised an eyebrow at him but said nothing. However, a small smile played across her lips.

"See? I told you a table would open up." Avery pointed to a small round table shoved in the far corner. "I'm going to go claim it. You get the drinks, okay?"

Before he could answer, she had walked off. Drew bit the inside of his lip and nodded ever so slightly. Now, he was beginning to remember why they had broken up. Avery might not be as obsessed with status as some other women, but she was independent and just a little bossy.

"Here's your friend's drink," the woman said. "Your Americano will be right up."

"Thank you." Drew took Avery's drink and surreptitiously scanned the barista's writing. A series of letters that looked more like hieroglyphics than English stared back at him. Before he could ponder it further, the woman handed him his drink, and Drew meandered through the tables to Avery.

"So," she said when he sat down, "what happened with the girl from last night?"

"What do you mean?" he asked.

"I was there remember?" She took a sip of her drink. "You made quite the scene, and you were telling me about this woman you met at your mother's ball. Was she the one?"

Drew lifted his own cup and pretended to drink. He wasn't sure how much he should tell Avery. He didn't think she would go running to his mother, but it had been years since they were close. Perhaps she had changed in that time. He opted for a diversion. "Did you know we got that poor woman fired?"

Avery blinked at him. "We did?"

"Well, someone did. I presume it was my mother, but I suppose it could have been anyone in the room."

"And how do you know she was fired?" Avery tilted her head as she regarded him.

Dang it. He was off his game today. Perhaps he could get away with a half-truth. "I spoke with her, and she informed me."

Avery nodded slowly. "Just out of the blue you spoke

with this woman? This woman who wasn't supposed to be at your mother's ball and works as a caterer?"

It was clear Avery would not let this go. With a sigh, Drew filled her in. "All right, I sent her flowers and asked her to call me."

"You proposed a date?" Avery let out a soft whistle. "I don't know your mother well, but I can't imagine she would want you pursuing a caterer."

"She's a full-time teacher." Drew felt the need to point out Gwen's qualities though he wasn't sure why. Avery wouldn't care who he pursued. "She was catering on the side to earn extra money. At least until she got fired."

"Well, that's," Avery paused as if searching for the right word, "noble. Teaching, I mean. The world needs good teachers, right?"

Avery's words sounded stilted and forced. Drew wondered what she had against teachers. Or was this a snobby bias of hers emerging?

"Yes, we need good teachers, and I'm sure she is one."

Avery sighed. "Drew, what do you even know about this woman?"

He wanted to tell her he knew a lot, but something gave him pause. Avery didn't need to know he had dug into Gwen's background. "I know she isn't obsessed with money and status like everyone else around us.

She's funny and genuine, and she made me feel alive again."

Avery's stare burned into him. "I get that you don't want to pursue someone in the elite circle, but I hope you know what you're doing, Drew."

Gwen glanced at the clock. It was four already? She was surprised that the time had seemed to fly by and even more surprised that no one had hounded her asking for details on the new boyfriend. Had Tom not said anything then? That seemed unlike him, but maybe he had kept it to himself out of pride. Most of the staff knew of his interest in her. Admitting she was seeing someone else would be like accepting his defeat, and Gwen doubted he had done that.

With a sigh, she stacked the remaining papers to grade in front of her laptop. She had learned long ago not to take work home because she never graded it. The papers merely received a field trip - into her bag, into her car, sometimes even into her house, but inevitably they never left her bag again until she brought them back to school the next day. No, these could wait for tomorrow. She would just have to focus during her planning time to get them graded.

Gwen grabbed her coat and keys and made her way

to the parking lot. Menacing grey clouds filled the sky, and she wondered if the first snow might come early this year. The temperature certainly had dropped enough. She'd even had to scrape ice off her window this morning, something she didn't usually have to do until after Thanksgiving.

Unlocking the car, she slid in and inserted the key. She was anxious to get the heater on. The heated seats of her car were the one upgrade she had purchased when she bought the used vehicle. Carrie had them in her Range Rover, and Gwen had fallen in love with them. There was something comforting about the warmth against her back and legs.

As they heat seeped through her layers, Gwen pointed the car toward her house. She would have just enough time to duck inside and change into something a little nicer before meeting Drew. She didn't know if she needed to dress up, but it felt enough like a job interview that she wasn't comfortable going in her slacks and cotton shirt.

After a quick stop to change and freshen up, Gwen pulled into the parking lot of the Kingston. She had never been inside this hotel though she thought it was older than the Devonshire. Not that it mattered; Gwen had neither the money nor the reason to stay at a hotel.

An older gentleman with graying hair but kind eyes opened the door as she approached. "Welcome to the

Kingston, Miss," he said with just a hint of a British accent.

"Thank you. Do you know where I can find Mr. Devonshire?" Gwen was sure he had an office somewhere, but she didn't want to wander the hotel looking for it.

"Are you Miss Rodgers?"

Gwen blinked at the man. His knowledge of her name caught her off guard. "I am."

The man's lips pulled into a soft smile. He looked like what Gwen had always imagined a grandfather would look like. She barely remembered her own. Her mother's mother had died when she was four and her mother's father when she was ten. She had never met her father's parents as they had passed on before she was born.

"I am to take you to his office if that's agreeable with you." He offered his arm, clad in a blue jacket. White gloves covered his hands.

Gwen hesitated only a moment. Was she becoming more trusting or did he just not radiate a dangerous vibe? With her hand on his arm, he led the way to the back of the hotel. "Your guest, Mr. Devonshire," the doorman said as they entered Drew's office.

Drew looked up and smiled. "Ah, thank you, Fletcher. Come on in, Gwen."

Fletcher patted her hand once before turning and

walking back down the hallway. Gwen stepped farther into the room and stood awkwardly behind one of the chairs. Should she sit? Was there paperwork?

"Sit, sit," he said as if reading her mind. "I am required to have you fill out some paperwork for legal, and then I'll show you where you can work."

Gwen walked to the front of the chair and sat down. Her heart hammered in her chest, and she wasn't sure if she was nervous about the job or about being near Drew again. Probably, it was a combination of both.

"Let's see." He shuffled through the papers on his desk. His mind must work in a similar way to hers because he looked a little like organized chaos as well. The corners of her lips pulled up as she watched him.

"Ah, here we go." He pulled out a few sheets and slid them across the large desk to her. "Basic application plus a background check. Did you bring your ID?"

It was weird being in the room with him like this. She still felt an attraction to him, but his tone was all business. However, the flowers had suggested he wanted more. Her stomach knotted in confusion and she dropped her face to cover the pink she knew covered it. "Yeah, sure, just a second."

She pulled her wallet out and slipped the ID from its holder. Gwen grimaced at the picture as she handed it across to him. She never took pictures well and IDs were the worst, but she looked like a deer in the headlights in this picture. Her eyes were too wide, and instead of a smile, her lips had formed a slight "oh" shape.

He took the ID from her and perused it. Flames of embarrassment licked up her neck. "Doesn't look much like you," he said. His eyes twinkled, and she knew he was teasing, but it didn't ease her self-consciousness. "But I guess not many people take good ID photos," he continued as if sensing her unease. "Let me go make a copy and I'll return shortly."

Gwen nodded and turned her attention back to the form. It appeared to be a standard application. Name, address, social, job history. She put the pen to the paper and began the tedious task.

"Drew, I forgot to ask you...." A female voice filled the room behind Gwen, and she turned her head to see the woman from the other night behind her. She had assumed when she first glimpsed the woman at the table with Drew that she was a girlfriend, but then he had asked her out when he followed her into the hallway. However, the woman appearing now in Drew's office suggested she knew him well.

"Oh, I'm sorry," the woman said as her eyes roamed over Gwen. "I was looking for Drew. Do you know when he might be back?"

Gwen opened her mouth to answer, but never got the chance.

"He's back now," Drew said, appearing behind the woman. "What can I do for you, Avery?"

Gwen was pleased to hear confusion in his voice. It appeared he had not planned for the woman's arrival.

Avery smiled, revealing perfectly white teeth. "Well, I was going to ask you if you found a solution to the little problem you were telling me about earlier, but perhaps this is it?" She finished the statement like a question, her voice lilting up just slightly at the end, and her raised eyebrow and glance at Gwen emphasizing it.

Drew pushed past her, his face tight as if clenching his jaw. "Avery, I'd like you to meet Gwen Rodgers. I've just hired her to manage donations for the Devonshire hotel." His voice carried a pinched quality, and Gwen wondered why he didn't seem to want Avery to know about his hiring her. Was he ashamed of her? Were they together?

Avery glided across the room like a graceful ballerina. "Gwen, it is so nice to meet you. Any friend of Drew's is a friend of mine." On the outside, her words were friendly as was her gesture to shake hands, but Gwen somehow doubted they would ever be friends.

"Thanks for stopping by, Avery," Drew said, "but I need to finish up with Gwen here and give her the information to get started."

Avery blinked, a sign that she wasn't used to Drew addressing her in such a manner, but she said nothing about it. Instead, her lips stretched into an even wider grin. "Of course, I'll leave you two alone. I'm sure I'll be seeing a lot more of you, Gwen." She held Gwen's gaze a moment, but Gwen wasn't entirely certain if her words were a promise or a threat.

"My apologies," Drew said when Avery had left the room. "I had no idea she would show up here."

"Oh, it's fine. I mean your girlfriend is none of my business."

Drew's brow arched. "Girlfriend? No, no. Avery and I dated once years ago, but we're too alike in too many areas to make it work."

"Oh." Gwen hated the thrill of excitement that raced through her at those words. It didn't matter if Avery wasn't his girlfriend. She wasn't either, and while he and Avery might be too similar, she and Drew were too different to make it work.

"Besides, I thought I made it clear with those flowers that I was interested in pursuing you."

There was no way to stop the heat that consumed her face this time. His gaze was frank and honest as his eyes sought hers.

"Drew, I already told you-"

"And I think you're wrong," he said interrupting her. "Look, just let me take you to dinner. If it doesn't work out, at least we can say we tried."

Gwen ran through her options. She wanted to see him

again. He was asking. It was just dinner. "All right. Dinner, but only if I can pick the place."

"Fine, you pick the place. How about tomorrow night?"

Gwen bit her lip but nodded. "Tomorrow night is fine. Let's meet at Charlie's at seven. Are you familiar with it?"

His brow furrowed as if he was exerting energy running down a mental list. "I'm not, but I'm sure my driver is."

Of course, he wasn't familiar with it. Charlie's was a dive, but it served great food. Gwen wondered what his reaction would be. "That will work then."

Drew returned the smile. "Good. Now that that's taken care of, shall I show you your workspace?"

"Lead the way."

9

Drew stared into his closet the next night. He hadn't dressed casually since college, but his search of this restaurant informed him casual would blend in better. The problem was business suits dominated his wardrobe now. Had the trends changed since college? If he wore jeans and a polo would he blend in or stand out?

"Is there a problem, sir?" Pierre asked from behind him.

"I'm not sure how to dress for this date," Drew said. "I'm meeting a woman who is not wealthy, at a bar downtown, and the website said to dress casual."

Pierre's eyebrow rose only slightly. He had been trained not to react, no matter what he saw or heard. "I see. Well, I believe this blue shirt is still very much in style," - he grabbed it off the rack - "and, though I never wear them myself, I have heard Manuel say jeans never go out of style." Pierre handed the jeans and shirt to Drew who nodded and slipped them on.

"You still look very debonair if I may say so, sir."

Drew thought he would feel more uncomfortable but slipping into the jeans felt like rekindling an old friendship. One he hadn't had since college. "Thank you, Pierre. It's different but not altogether bad."

Pierre nodded, and Drew grabbed his wallet and slipped it in his back pocket. With a final glance in the mirror, Drew headed downstairs. Manuel was waiting outside the front door with the limo.

"I almost didn't recognize you, sir," Manuel said as he straightened when Drew approached.

Drew chuckled as he responded, "Good. Maybe no one else will either." He slid into the backseat surprised to feel his heart beating faster than normal. Was that because he would see Gwen or because he was a little nervous about walking into an unfamiliar restaurant? "You know what, Manuel? Can you drop me off at the end of the block?"

"Sir?" Drew always preferred being dropped off at the door, but this time, he didn't want to show off his money. He wanted to pretend to be a little normal.

"This isn't my usual venue, Manuel. I'd prefer not to draw so much attention."

"Understood, sir."

Half an hour later, the car slowed to a stop. Drew glanced out the window. The restaurant appeared to be half a block ahead on the right if the garish neon light was any indication.

"Here we are, sir."

"Thank you, Manuel. I'll get the door." Drew knew it probably made Manuel uncomfortable, but he stayed in the driver's seat and allowed Drew to open the back door himself. "I'll text when I'm ready," Drew said before shutting the door. He waited for the limo to drive off, then smoothed his shirt, took a deep breath, and continued up the sidewalk to the eating establishment.

Gwen sat at a booth in the corner where she could see the entrance. She had arrived ten minutes early hoping to see Drew when he entered. She wanted to gauge his reaction. This was one of her favorite places to grab a burger and if he couldn't fit in, she would take it as a sign this was not meant to be.

Her eyes flew to the entrance every time the door opened, but she still almost missed Drew when he entered. Gone was the Armani suit. Instead, he wore a blue button-down shirt and jeans. He still held the air of someone with money, but he didn't stand out from the rest of the clientele. She raised her hand as his eyes scanned the room. When he noticed her hand, he smiled and started her direction.

"You found it," she said as he slid in across from her.

"I did, or my driver did."

"Does he drive you everywhere?" Gwen couldn't imagine not driving herself places. On one hand, it would be nice to curl up with a book while getting to the destination but letting someone else drive meant having to trust them. There just weren't many people she trusted that much, especially after a drunk driver killed her parents.

"He does. At least since I returned from college." He rolled his eyes. "My mother's stipulation. If you have money, you need to use the advantages it offers."

"So, you drove yourself in college?"

"Yes, I had to have a friend teach me. My parents never allowed me to get my license. They said I would never use it, but when I went to college, I wanted to live like everyone else, and that meant driving myself. Thankfully, I met someone who didn't mind teaching me. I bought an old car and managed to only hit a few things."

His lips pulled into a smile, and something tugged on Gwen's heart. He had a gorgeous smile with perfectly white teeth - not that she expected any less - but it was the dimple in his left cheek that she most enjoyed.

Somehow it softened his chiseled features and made him even more handsome.

"To be honest, I miss driving sometimes," he continued. "I mean I get work done in the back, but it's nice to feel the wheel beneath your hands and the pedal under your foot at times."

"I'm not sure I could let someone drive for me." Gwen opened her mouth to say more, but then clamped it shut. She didn't know him well enough or trust him enough to tell him about her parents. Not yet anyway.

"It takes some getting used to." He paused as he glanced around the room. "So, this place is nice."

"I'm sure it's not your normal fare," Gwen said with a smile, "but they have amazing burgers here."

"I do enjoy a good burger."

The waitress appeared then with two glasses of water and a plastic-coated menu. Drew's face scrunched slightly as he took the menu. Gwen wondered when he had last held one of these menus. College probably. The restaurants he attended now more than likely had a single sheet of typed menu offerings. Two or three starters, a few main course options, and dessert. Nothing like this three-page menu filled with pictures and corny names. Drew appeared almost overwhelmed as he scanned all the choices, and then he chuckled.

"What's so funny?" Gwen asked.

"This menu just reminded me of college. Some friends and I used to study late in a fast-food restaurant and one night some guy came in and ordered fries. He proceeded to eat almost all of them and then told the manager they were cold, and he needed another. The manager was a softie and he filled the guy's fries again. The guy sat down, ate almost all of them, and then back to the counter he went. This went on another two times before the manager had it and kicked the guy out. A few days later, there was a story in the newspaper about this guy. Evidently, he had been trying the same scam at every Whataburger in the city and when they realized it, they banned him from all of them."

Gwen smiled and shook her head. "I'll never understand some people. Why take advantage of someone's good nature?"

Before Drew could respond, the waitress appeared. "Welcome to Charlie's. The special today is the Blazin' Burger and our soup is a chicken tortilla. Would you care for anything else to drink?"

"Do you have any Chardonnay?" Drew asked. He was flipping the pages back and forth. Probably searching for the drink options.

The woman's face creased in confusion. "Uh, no, we don't serve wine, but we have beers on tap."

"Right." Drew's words were slow, unsure. "Um, I'll just have iced tea then. You have that right?"

"Yeah, tea we have. And for you?" The waitress turned her attention to Gwen.

"I'll take a tea as well."

"You got it; I'll give you a few minutes to look over the menu and be right back with those."

Gwen smiled up at the waitress. "Thank you." She glanced over at Drew. "Does anything look good?"

"I have no idea. Do you have a recommendation?"

"The Blazin' Burger is actually my favorite. It has sriracha sauce and an onion ring. Just the right combination of spicy and sweet."

He cocked his head at her. "Can I tell you how refreshing it is to eat with a woman who eats?"

"I'll never be one of those tiny women if that's what you're looking for." Gwen wanted to take back the words as soon as she said them. It was quite presumptive of her to expect he'd want to date her.

He fixed her with an intense stare. "I'm not looking for those kinds of women. I told you I found you refreshing and I meant it."

Gwen's face flamed. She had no idea what he saw in her, but she was flattered.

"Sorry, just a second," he said as his phone chimed in his pocket. He swiped the screen, rolled his eyes slightly, and placed the phone back in his pocket.

"Everything okay?" Gwen asked.

"Yes, just a friend."

Gwen wondered if the friend was Avery but asking didn't seem to be appropriate. After all, this was technically their first date and she had just met Avery yesterday.

"You two have a chance to look over the menu?" the waitress asked as she returned with their iced teas.

Gwen looked to Drew who nodded. "I'll have the Blazin' Burger with onion rings," Gwen said.

The waitress nodded and scribbled it down before looking to Drew. "Make that two," he said as he handed back the menu.

As the waitress walked away, a long pause fell on the conversation. Then, Drew cleared his throat. "I uh hope you don't mind, but I did some research on you in addition to the background check."

"Research?" Gwen blinked at him, unsure what he meant.

"Yes," he took a sip of his tea before continuing, "in my life, it's important to know who people are before you hang around them. I'm sure you understand that some people don't have the best intentions."

While she could understand that, her heart sped up at the thought of him digging into her past. Did he know about her parents? Her foster father? All her sordid secrets? "I'm sure you found that I wasn't after your money."

"I did, but um, I had a question for you."

She twirled her glass on the table as she thought about whether she wanted to hear his question. If it had to do with her past, chances were she didn't want to hear it. However, if they were going to try dating, then she would have to let him in sometime. Finally, she lifted her eyes back to him, granting him silent permission to ask his question.

"There's a lot of hurt in your past," he began, and Gwen bit her lip. She hoped he wouldn't ask for details as she didn't want to ruin the dinner with her troubled past. "But, you seem to be well-adjusted and content. Can I ask how?"

It was a fair question and one that had been asked of her many times in the past, but she didn't know how he would respond to her answer. She took a deep breath as she formulated her response. "God," she said simply.

He blinked at her. "I'm sorry, what?"

She smiled softly. God was the one part of her story she never minded sharing. "God. My parents had been Christians before they died, but I was only twelve. I hit that rebellious teenage streak and was certain I didn't need God. Every Sunday was a fight to get me to go to church, but they never let me *not* go. When they died, God had new meaning to me. He became my replacement father and gave me the strength to not only deal with my parents' death but also everything that came after."

Drew leaned back and regarded her for a moment, and Gwen wondered what he was thinking. Had she scared him away with her talk of God? It wouldn't be the first time, but she was a firm believer that anyone who wouldn't at least listen to her story was no one she wanted to spend more time dating.

"I've never placed much stock in faith," Drew said finally. "My parents were holiday Christians at best - Christmas and Easter when they deemed it important enough to attend - but I've never met anyone like you. To go through such tragedy and emerge with such strength, well I envy you, and so I'd like to inquire. Would you allow me to attend church with you this Sunday?"

This time Gwen blinked. She hadn't been expecting that. For him to have to go or to decide he no longer wanted to see her - *that* she had been expecting, but attend church with her? It was like a dream come true. "Of course, you can."

The waitress returned then with the food, and the conversation stalled while they ate. Gwen couldn't believe how normal eating with him felt. No one had even seemed to notice him. Did he not get hounded by photographers and the press? Or did that only happen to movie stars?

"I'd like to do this again."

She dragged her focus back to him. "Dinner?"

"Yes, dinner, dessert, dancing, you name it. I want to

spend more time with you. Would you be amenable to that?" Drew pulled a hundred-dollar bill out of his wallet and placed it in the black folder. Gwen hadn't even noticed the waitress drop it off.

Amenable. She enjoyed the way the way he spoke. On some people, it would come across like putting on airs, but Drew's use was so effortless that it must have been part of his upbringing. "Yes, I believe I would be amenable to that," she responded with a smile.

"Good." He stood and held out his hand to her. "What are you doing Saturday?"

Gwen took his hand, enjoying the feel of his skin against hers. He led the way through the crowded restaurant to the door and pushed it open.

"As in a few days from now Saturday?" Gwen asked as they stepped outside.

The dimple re-appeared as a smile stole across his features. "That is the one to which I was referring."

"I don't think I have any plans."

"Wonderful." He dropped her hand for a moment to pull out his cell phone. After tapping out a brief message, he replaced the phone in his pocket and took her hand once again. "I know you have an aversion to being driven, but I promise Manuel is a cautious and distinguished driver. I would like to surprise you, so may we pick you up ten am Saturday morning?"

Gwen hesitated. Could she give control to someone

else? Someone she didn't know? The thought terrified her; however, she would have to do it someday. Now might be a good time to start.

"All right. I guess I must let go sometime. I'll text you my address."

Drew grabbed her other hand and held them both against his chest. "I promise it will be worth it. I had a great time tonight."

Gwen's heart thudded loudly. "Me too." Though only two words, it took great effort to get them out of her mouth. Her lungs felt tight as if they couldn't get enough air. Their gazes held a moment longer and then a black limo pulled up in front of the parking lot.

A sigh billowed out of Drew's lips. "I see my transportation has arrived. Please drive safely." He brought her hand to his lips, and Gwen watched as he placed a kiss on the back of her hand. His lips were soft, almost like the wings of a butterfly brushing her skin. Tiny goosebumps erupted on her arm. Then Drew winked at her and dropped her hand. "I will see you on Saturday."

Gwen nodded and walked to her car. Her whole body tingled. Why did he have such an effect on her?

10

Gwen yawned and stretched as the light peeked in her window. Tiny particles floated in the ray of light creating a shimmery feel in the air. Her lips twitched into a smile as Gwen experienced a similar feeling throughout her body. The events of the week left her with warm and fuzzy thoughts. Though Drew had been too busy to meet up with her, he had called her every night. She hadn't thought she and Drew would have anything in common, but he was much more down-to-earth than she had expected.

She ought to know better. Gwen hated it when people made assumptions about her, especially when they found out about her foster care background. It was odd how quickly people's views shifted with that tidbit of knowledge. Those who couldn't hide their response would do one of two things: they would apologize to her as if the experience had to have been awful or they would look for some excuse to get away from her as if she was contagious. The people who tried to hide their reaction were often worse. They would tense up and shower her with pitying looks and head shakes.

Gwen knew most people didn't even have any first-hand knowledge of the foster care system - they only had what they heard on the news or TV shows which rarely put the system in a good light. Gwen, however, had lived through it, both the good and the bad. And while she wouldn't wish foster care on anyone - a loving biological family was what God intended - it had been there for her at a time when she needed it most. She hoped she could change the perception around foster care which was partly why she accepted Drew's job proposal. The fact that she needed extra income and wanted an excuse to be near him also played a part.

A tremor of excitement raced through her, and she kicked off the comforter. He was picking her up at ten and swore he had a whole day planned. Gwen never had anyone take her on a surprise date, and she had no idea what to expect.

As if he was reading her mind, her phone buzzed on the nightstand beside her. She unplugged the charging cord and tapped the screen.

Good morning. I trust you slept well. I will be

arriving promptly at ten. Please have a robe and dress shoes packed.

A robe and dress shoes? Where exactly was he taking her?

She tossed the phone back on her bed and, shaking her head, walked to the bathroom to shower for the day.

Thirty minutes later, she was clean, dressed, and had her bag packed. Her stomach rumbled as she walked into the kitchen, a reminder that she hadn't eaten yet.

Gwen grabbed the oatmeal from the pantry and poured it into a pot with some almond milk and sugar free hot chocolate. Finding "The Hungry Girl" cookbook had been the highlight of her summer. Having lost her mother so young, Gwen hadn't grown up learning to cook, so a lot of the traditional cookbooks lost her with their fancy ingredients and steps. Lisa Lillian, on the other hand, used everyday ingredients in a lower fat version. And since her recipes were usually only for one or two people, Gwen didn't have to worry about wasting food or having a ton of leftovers.

With the oatmeal heating on the stove, she turned to the coffee pot. Gwen didn't really like the taste of coffee - in fact, she loved green tea - but there was something comforting about one cup of coffee flavored with her favorite creamer. She loved curling up in her recliner with it as she read her devotional. Not only was it the best time of the morning, but it always made her feel closer to God.

As she placed the filter in, Gwen heard a sound at her front door. She paused, fingers just touching the rim of the recycled brown filter, but she heard nothing more. Had it been a knock? Or perhaps the sound had been at her neighbor's door and not her own.

The closeness was one thing Gwen abhorred about apartment life. The lack of lawn management, the pool, the weight room - all great benefits, but the fact that she heard the neighbors above her as they argued or the squeaky bed frame of the neighbors beside her drove her nuts. When she could afford it, she wanted a small house on a piece of land, so her neighbors wouldn't be too close.

Gwen poured the coffee grinds in, added the water, and flipped the switch to start the coffee percolating. Now, she could check out the noise. It had probably been nothing but living alone had taught Gwen to trust her sense of sound.

She peered out the spyhole first, but no one stood on her doorstep. Had she imagined it then? Gwen flipped the locks on the door and slowly opened it. If someone was out there, she didn't want to fling the door wide too quickly and make herself a target.

The community area between the two apartments was also vacant, but as Gwen looked around, a black flower caught her eye. Nestled against her front door frame, it lay as if propped there, and further inspection showed a white envelope as well. Gwen leaned farther out to scan the area, but whoever had left the note was gone.

Her heart thudded in her chest as she grabbed the envelope and the flower. It was a rose. Painted black. Black roses didn't exist naturally, at least not unless the Turkish black rose was real, but Gwen had her doubts. However, the black rose had two meanings - passion or foreboding death. Drew had already sent her flowers - a large colorful display, so this didn't seem his style which meant the sender probably hadn't been intending passion.

She shut and locked the door. Should she open this? Call the police? Calling the cops might be jumping the gun, but what if someone sent her poison in the envelope? That happened, right? Well, not to people like her. Maybe if she were well known, some celebrity or politician or something, but Gwen was a simple school teacher.

Crossing to the kitchen, Gwen set the rose down on her table and then turned the envelope over. It was completely white, not even her name on it. Maybe it wasn't for her after all. Maybe someone had put it at the wrong door. It was easy to do that in an apartment complex.

The envelope wasn't sealed however, so Gwen lifted the flap and pulled out the note. It was white card stock with typed black lettering. 'Cinderella wasn't real' was all the note said. Not that threatening in and of itself but combined with the black rose, Gwen didn't have warm fuzzies. And though there was no name, the note had to be for her. While Drew wasn't a prince, he certainly represented the wealthy elite and she the poor parentless girl.

The question was.... Who would send this? It could have been Tom. Though he had said nothing the rest of the week, she was sure his ego was still suffering, and he could have easily found out where she lived. But the black rose didn't seem his style. Neither did the simple, elegant card. Tom was much more literal. Saying it to her face or spreading rumors was more like him.

So, Avery? Gwen didn't know her well, but she had been dressed stylishly. Elegant would certainly describe her, and Gwen had sensed some tension from the woman. Perhaps she still harbored feelings for Drew? But how would she know where Gwen lived? Had she returned while Drew had been showing Gwen around and gotten her address off the paperwork? Gwen would have to ask Drew if he thought Avery capable of such a thing.

A bubbling sound reached her ears, and Gwen dropped the envelope. Her oatmeal. She hurried over to the stove and turned the heat off. She was lucky her pot was copper or else she would have a sticky disaster on her hands. Gwen scraped the oatmeal into a bowl and poured her coffee into a mug.

She would come back to the envelope later, but for now it was time to eat and do her devotional. Gwen felt like she needed it more than ever this morning. She needed clarity on what to do with this whole situation. Did she continue seeing Drew? End it now?

Drew whistled as he dressed Saturday morning. He couldn't wait to spend the day with Gwen. He had spent much of yesterday planning it. He and Manuel would pick her up at ten. Manuel would drive them to the airport, and they would take the jet to Martha's Vineyard. Once there, he had even more planned: a massage, an afternoon wine and cheese pairing, and dinner at the finest restaurant.

A knock sounded at the door and then Pierre stepped into the room. "I have your wallet, sir. The tickets are there as well."

"Thank you, Pierre." Even when he hated the requirements that came with money, he never hated Pierre. The man helped him stay organized, and most days, he seemed to read Drew's mind and know what he needed before Drew did.

Drew grabbed the wallet off the tray and slid it into

the back pocket of his tan Gucci pants. The tickets he inserted into the breast pocket of his jacket before nodding at Pierre and making his way downstairs.

Manuel was waiting out front with the limo, and half an hour later, they were pulling to a stop in an apartment parking lot. Drew stared up at the buildings scrunched so close together. He hadn't been near buildings like these since college. Wanting to experience the college life, he had lived in a dorm for one semester. That had been all he could handle. After that semester, he had rented a large house near campus.

"I'm sorry, sir, this is as close as I can get," Manuel said from the front seat. "Would you like me to park and get the door?"

"No, keep the engine running. I can manage the door." Drew pulled the handle and stepped out of the limo. A man in flannel pajamas carrying a trash bag stopped and stared as Drew scanned the buildings for identification. He must look as out of place as he felt.

Relief filled Drew when he spotted the G on the closest building. Gwen lived in 4G. With purposeful steps, he strode that direction and rapped on her door. It swung open a moment later, and a smile pulled at his lips. Gwen looked simple and radiant in her jeans and hunter green sweater, but there was a pinched look to her face.

"What is the matter?" he asked.

"Can you come inside a minute?"

"Of course. One moment." He tapped out a message to Manuel to let him know they'd be another few minutes and then stepped into her apartment. Though small, it was decorated simply and neatly.

"You know Avery well, right?" Gwen asked as she walked toward the kitchen.

Why would she be asking about Avery? Hadn't he assured her there was nothing going on there? "I do, or at least I did. She left for a few years after we parted ways, but why are you inquiring about Avery?"

"I received something this morning and I want to know if you think she sent it." Gwen picked up an elegant black rose and note and handed them to him.

'Cinderella wasn't real.' He read the typed script and looked up at her. "How did you receive them?"

"Someone left them on my doorstep this morning. Would she do this?"

Drew didn't think so. Avery stated she wasn't interested in him, and she had appeared friendly to Gwen when they had met. "Was there anything else?"

"Just a plain white envelope." She picked it up and held it out to him.

He examined the envelope and turned it over. No distinct markings. "Are you sure it's even for you? There's no name on it."

She cocked her head at him. "Really? You think Cinderella applies to someone else?"

Drew nodded. While it could apply to someone else, it was more likely directed at Gwen, but he still didn't think it was Avery. His mother, perhaps? But how would she even know about Gwen? Perhaps Avery had mentioned Gwen to his mother or maybe she had seen the paperwork. "I'm sorry. It might have been Avery, or it might have been my mother though I'm not sure why they would do it this way. Telling me would be more their cup of tea. Could it be anyone you know?"

Gwen shrugged. "There's a man at my work who's asked me out several times even though I keep turning him down. He saw me with the flowers you sent the other day, but this seems too abstract for him."

"I don't want this to ruin our day. How about I take it with us and have someone investigate it? I have a friend on the force who could run it for fingerprints." Though the note and the flower bothered him, he was more worried the incident would cause Gwen to run again.

"Maybe this is a sign, Drew-" Gwen began.

He dropped the items to take her hands. "Gwen, this is not a sign. It's someone's sick idea of a joke, but it is not a sign. Please, don't give up on this yet."

Gwen bit her lip and her green eyes shifted back and forth. "All right, Drew, if you think your friend can help, then I'll let you try."

"Good." He squeezed her hands before dropping them. "Did you pack what I asked you to?"

She narrowed her eyes at him and pursed her lips in an adorable pout. "Yes, though I would like to know why I need a robe and a pair of dress shoes. Those don't normally get paired together. You aren't taking me to some weird artsy thing, are you?"

Drew chuckled and shook his head. Gwen was a breath of fresh air. "No, nothing like that. I promise."

"Okay, then, I guess I'm ready." She said the words, but she didn't move. Drew picked up the items with one hand and held out the other to her. After a glance down and a deep breath, she placed her hand in his. "I need to get my bag by the front door."

"Let's go then." He tugged gently to lead her back to the front door, and after she grabbed her bag and shut the door behind her, he led the way to the limo.

He opened the back limo door for her and helped her slide in. Then he opened the front door. Manuel looked over at him in surprise. Drew placed the items on the seat beside him. "Please don't touch these. I need to have them dusted for prints later." Manuel said nothing. He simply nodded. Drew closed the front door and joined Gwen in the back, pulling the door shut behind him. "To the airport please, Manuel."

"The airport? Where are we going, Drew? I have to

be back tonight. I have church in the morning, remember?"

The corners of Drew's mouth pulled into a smile. "Don't worry. You'll be back in plenty of time. We're taking a private jet."

"A private jet? Just how wealthy are you?"

Drew smiled, but he didn't want to talk about his money. He wanted to know more about Gwen. "May I ask you something?" he asked instead of answering her question.

"Maybe." Her eyes held his a moment and then fell to her lap.

"I wanted to inquire why you work in the nursery at your church. You seemed excited by it and I was curious to know more."

As he hoped they would, her eyes lit up, and her shoulders relaxed. "I've always loved kids. In fact, I wanted more siblings, but there were complications with my birth, and my mother couldn't have any more after me. We were discussing adoption as a family, but my parents died before the process was complete. So, I guess I've just always had kids on my heart. It's partly why I became a teacher."

"And the other part?" he asked gently. Now that she was opening up, he didn't want her retreating into her shell again.

Her eyes dropped to her lap, and her volume

decreased. "I wanted to help kids like myself. Those in foster care. The ones who think no one cares about them."

She paused for a moment and Drew wanted to tell her that people cared, that he cared, but he knew it would sound trite. Though he couldn't explain his connection to her, he expected she would think it was too early or too fast if he mentioned he cared for her.

"Someday, I think I'd like to foster a few kids. I'm sure you know my story." Her gaze shifted up and she fixed him with a penetrating stare.

"A little," he admitted, "but I'd enjoy hearing more about it from you."

She shook her head. "The past is just that. Past. But I had a not so good family and then a good family. If I can help keep kids from falling in with families like my first, then I want to do it. I can't solve the foster care problem, but I can help. That's what I hope to do with your money. Thank you for the opportunity."

"I'm happy to help. You said people would help if they knew how. I didn't know there was such a need, but now that I do, I'm glad I can do something."

"Well, thank you."

G wen studied Drew for a moment. He was not how she pictured billionaires at all. Yes, he rode around in a limo which was unnecessary and wore designer clothing, but he also seemed genuinely interested in helping others. And he appeared interested in her though she had nothing to offer him.

As they pulled into the airport, Gwen tried not to show her awe when the private jet came into view. She had never been on a plane, much less a private jet. "How often do you fly?"

"Not as often as you'd think," Drew said with a small chuckle. "Most of the time, I drive, but occasionally I have to check out a hotel on the other side of the states. I prefer to avoid the airport hassle if you know what I mean." The door opened, and Drew stepped out and then held out his hand to her.

Gwen didn't. She'd heard stories, but she'd never experienced it firsthand having neither the money nor the reason to fly anywhere. Gwen took his hand and stepped out as well.

A woman in a smart blue skirt and jacket stood at the top of the stairs leading into the plane. "Good morning, Mr. Devonshire," she said as they approached.

"Good morning, Margaret. This is my friend, Gwen."

Margaret turned warm brown eyes on Gwen and smiled. "Good morning, Gwen. Welcome aboard."

Gwen smiled back as she reached the top step, surprised and pleased that the woman didn't seem to care about her social status or lack thereof. She stepped into the plane, and her jaw dropped.

Though she'd never been on one, Gwen had seen pictures and Carrie spoke of how the rows were squished together and the chairs were uncomfortable, but the space before her didn't look like that at all.

Only eight seats existed in this plane. Two rows of two on one side and two rows of two on the other. The seats themselves were wide and luxurious, covered in cream leather and they appeared to recline.

"Take your pick," Drew said behind her. His breath tickled her ear and set her heart stampeding in her chest again. Why did he have such an effect on her? She barely knew him. Was it the money or could there be something real to her feelings?

She chose a seat by the window, wanting to have a view as they took off, and sat down. The seat was as comfortable as it looked, soft and smooth beneath her fingertips, and, after trying all the buttons, Gwen found it did recline.

Drew sat beside her, a small smile twitching at his lips. Did he find her amusing? She must look like a kid in a candy store.

"Would you care for your normal fare?" Margaret asked a moment later.

"I'm not starving," Drew replied. "Perhaps some champagne and strawberries?"

"Yes, sir."

"Champagne?" Gwen asked. "Are we celebrating something?"

"You saying yes to this date." Drew picked up her hand and laced his fingers through hers. "I'm pleased you agreed."

"I am too," Gwen said. Her eyes flew to the window when she felt the plane move. It was just the faintest sensation as the movement was so smooth, but she could see the landscape flying by outside.

"Is this your first time on a plane?" Drew asked.

Gwen nodded. "I've never had anywhere to go nor could I afford it if I did."

"Oh dear, I'm afraid I will spoil you then. Traditional flights aren't as nice."

A soft snort escaped her lips and she pulled her eyes from the window long enough to glance at him. "I figured."

Drew's phone rang, and he slipped it from his pocket. After a glance at the screen, he silenced it and returned it to his pocket.

"Something important?" Gwen asked.

"No, just a friend. I'll call her back later."

She had no right to be jealous, but that didn't stop the small seed from sprouting in her stomach. Was it Avery or some other woman from Drew's past? He was sure to have many, but she would not press the issue. The last thing she wanted to do was come across as insecure though she felt it in every inch of her body.

Margaret returned a moment later with two flutes of champagne and a bowl of red, ripe strawberries. Gwen had never tasted champagne and she wasn't sure if she liked the way it tickled her nose or not. However, the strawberries delighted her. They had long been her favorite fruit and their emergence into the stores was one of her favorite things about summer. The frozen ones just didn't have the same flavor.

They flew in silence for a time until Drew leaned

over her and pointed out the window. "There it is. Martha's Vineyard."

Gwen's eyes widened at the beautiful island below them. Lush and green, it was surrounded by crystal blue water on all sides. "It's breathtaking," she whispered.

Drew enjoyed watching Gwen's amazement as they stepped off the plane. He grew up spending a few weeks out of every year at Martha's Vineyard, so the novelty wore off a long time ago for him, but Gwen's features danced with excitement.

"Are you hungry or would you like to visit the spa first?"

"Spa?"

"Yes, I hope you don't mind, but I figured you might enjoy some pampering, so I purchased a spa package for you. It includes a massage and a treatment of your choice."

"I wouldn't even know what to choose," Gwen said with a laugh. "I guess today will be a day of firsts for me as I've never had a massage either, but what about you? What are you going to do while I'm getting pampered?"

"I'll be getting my own. You didn't think I'd let you have all the fun, did you?" In fact, Drew enjoyed a weekly massage. He held a lot of tension in his shoulders. At least that's what his masseuse told him.

Gwen smiled up at him. It was a sweet smile and one he could get used to seeing every day. "All right, the spa it is then."

He took her hand and led her to the limo he had waiting. It wasn't that far into town, but he wanted to spoil her today.

"Did you think of everything?" she asked as the driver held the door open for them.

"I tried." Even as he climbed in, Drew went over the mental list of the rest of the day in his mind. It was just past noon and he expected they would spend two hours at the spa. That left them a few hours to sight see and do the wine and cheese pairing before their dinner reservation at six. And, of course, he needed to get her a dress for dinner.

He settled in next to Gwen and watched as she peered out the window. She was like a kid at Christmas. Her eyes sparkled with awe, and her lips seemed fixed in a permanent smile.

Soon the scenery became filled with colorful gingerbread cottages. "They're all so pretty."

Drew had never paid much attention to the houses, but they were indeed a sight. Reds, pinks, blues, and greens. Each one had a small balcony on the second story and a sitting porch. The railings were also painted. Mostly white but some were yellow and orange.

The limo stopped in front of a bright blue cottage with white trim. A white sign that read Le Chateau hung near the sidewalk and swayed in the breeze. Drew stepped out first when the back door opened and then leaned in to help Gwen out. Hand in hand, they made their way to the front door.

Inside, the house was warm and inviting. A soft yellow light illuminated the area. While decorated nicely, Drew hardly noticed the decor. It was no different from many other spas he had been in.

"Welcome to Le Chateau. My name is Margarite. Have you visited us before?" The woman behind the counter had just the hint of a French accent. Probably born in France but here long enough to lose most of the lilt.

"I have," Drew said, "but it's my friends first time."

Margarite grinned. "I love it when we have new guests." She reached under the counter and pulled out a sheet of paper. As she slid it across, Drew could see it was filled with the services offered. "Did you want a package or the à la carte?"

"Actually, I purchased a package already. Drew Devonshire. I believe it was two options."

She clicked a few buttons on the computer next to

her and nodded. "Indeed. Welcome, Mr. Devonshire. Please let me know which two options you would like."

Drew scanned the offerings. The massage was a definite. He had been too busy to make his weekly appointment this last week, but his second option would depend on what Gwen picked. He wanted to be sure he was done before she was.

Drew gave her another few minutes to scan the sheet as this was her first time before turning to her and asking, "What looks good?"

"They all look good," she said with a laugh, "but I think in addition to the massage I'll get the manicure and pedicure. I've never had a pedicure, and they always look so nice."

Drew figured a manicure and pedicure would run an additional hour, so for his second choice he chose an acupuncture session.

"Wonderful," Margarite said. She handed them over release forms. "Please fill these out, and I'll take you back."

"What are the release forms for?" Gwen asked as they took a seat.

"Standard procedure," Drew whispered back. "Too many lawsuits today, so they have to cover their back."

"But is it dangerous? I thought a massage was supposed to be relaxing." Worry furrowed her brow and her bottom lip folded under her teeth.

Drew smiled. "It is. I promise you that two hours from now you will feel like a million dollars."

Drew had been right. The massage had been wonderful. Gwen wasn't sure how she'd feel letting another person touch her, but the woman they had assigned her had been understanding and waited until Gwen felt comfortable. About halfway through, she had finally relaxed and enjoyed feeling the stress melt out of her muscles.

But the manicure and pedicure had been even better. The woman had rubbed hot stones over her calves and arms, almost like a second massage. And while Gwen had giggled and squirmed a little when the woman scrubbed the bottom of her feet, she had managed to stay still the rest of the time and now sported a lovely reddish orange color on her hands and feet. It was almost the exact shade of her hair. Gwen had loved it so much, she had even written the name down on a business card. She had hoped to buy a bottle, but the twenty-five-dollar price discouraged her. That money could be spent better elsewhere.

"So, how do you feel?" Drew asked as she emerged from the salon room. He must have finished before she did as he rose from a chair in the lobby.

"Like a million dollars," she said with a sly grin.

Maybe it was the polish or maybe the relaxation, but she felt freer, less timid.

"You look like a million dollars too," he said. "Ready for the next adventure?"

"There's more?" Gwen asked. Secretly, she was glad. While she had enjoyed the pampering, she found it odd their date was spent mostly apart instead of together.

"Much more." He held out his arm and she placed her hand on the crook. Gwen savored the feeling coursing through her. He treated her like such an elegant lady even holding the door open for her. They turned left away from the limo.

"We're not driving?" she asked.

"The next stop isn't far, and I thought you might enjoy seeing more of the town up close."

Gwen sneaked a glance at him. Was he reading her mind? As they walked, he told her of his summers spent on the island as a boy. She could almost see him running up and down this sidewalk or flying a kite at the nearby beach they had driven past.

Drew stopped in front of a quaint bistro. "Here we are." He held the door open for her and Gwen stepped inside. The room had a large wine bar at the back and several tables for sitting throughout the room. Most were filled with other patrons and a low buzz of conversation filled the air.

"Grab a seat. We'll be right with you," a man hollered from behind the bar.

Gwen followed Drew to a table for two near the window. She was delighted the table had been free, so she could watch the people outside. Studying people had long fascinated her, probably because she'd retreated into her shell for so long. "So, what are we doing here?" she asked. "Is this lunch?" Gwen hadn't noticed it before but now she could feel a slight rumbling in her stomach.

"Well, they don't serve a full lunch here, but I've ordered us a wine and cheese tasting."

"Wine and champagne? Are you trying to ply me with liquor, Drew Devonshire?"

Though she said the words in a teasing tone, his eyes widened, and he shook his head. "No, that wasn't my intention at all. It never even crossed my mind. If you'd rather not drink the wine-"

Gwen smiled and placed a hand on his. "Relax, Drew. First, I was kidding. Second, it's been two hours since the champagne. I think I'm fine." She hadn't had much champagne on the flight anyway. The bubbly sensation had just been too odd.

Drew sighed. "I'm sorry. I planned out this wonderful day for you, and I didn't want you to think I had ulterior motives."

For some reason, Gwen found this side of him even more endearing. People today were so willing to jump into bed with anyone and everyone they met that it was nice to find someone who wasn't looking for that, at least not on the first date. She wasn't sure where intimacy fit on his timeline, and before they got too serious, she would have to let him know that it wasn't on hers until after marriage. But that could wait. Gwen wasn't even sure he would want to see her again though he appeared to be enjoying himself as well.

"I'm glad to hear it, and I didn't think that of you. You've been nothing but a gentleman, and I thank you."

Relief flooded Drew's face, and his posture relaxed.

"Sorry about the wait," the man from behind the bar said as he approached their table. "It's been busy this afternoon. What can I do for you?"

"I ordered a wine and cheese tasting," Drew said as he pulled the tickets from his pocket. "Under the name Devonshire."

The man's eyes widened as if he knew who Drew Devonshire was. He scanned the tickets before handing them back. "Of course, Mr. Devonshire. I'll be right back."

"Do you ever get used to that?" Gwen asked as the man hurried away.

"What?" Drew asked.

"People changing the way they act around you when they find out who you are. It feels so disingenuous."

A deep laugh escaped Drew's lips. "Yes, I guess it is,

and that is why you are refreshing, Gwen Rodgers. You didn't change when you knew who I was."

"Well, to be fair, you told me who you were within the first few minutes, so you can't really say I didn't change."

"Touché," Drew said. Laughter danced in his blue eyes. "But I'm not sure you believed me when I first told you who I was."

This time it was Gwen's turn to smile. "I didn't. Truthfully, the only reason I went with you is because I doubted you could abduct me or attack me in such a public place."

The laughter faded from Drew's eyes as her words sank in. He stared at her a moment before speaking. "Gwen, I'm so sorry your past has you thinking things like that about strangers. That's no way to go through life."

Gwen bit her lip to keep her emotions at bay. She couldn't believe she had said that. She hadn't meant to put a damper on the mood. When she trusted her voice not to crack, she opened her mouth to respond. "I wouldn't wish my past on anyone, but it made me have to rely on God and for that I'm thankful."

The server appeared then with their wine and cheese and Gwen was grateful for the distraction. The topic had gotten too heavy for a second date, and she hoped the food would lighten the mood and bring them back to their playful banter from before.

"What's next?" Gwen asked when their cheese and wine was gone.

Drew stood and held out his hand. "Next, you let me treat you like a princess."

Gwen shook her head as she took his hand and stood. "You already have been treating me like a princess. What more could you possibly do?"

Drew's lips split in a wide smile. "My dear, you have seen nothing yet." Generally, the very thought of taking a woman shopping reduced him to yawns and tears of boredom, but he could tell it would be an adventure with Gwen.

He pushed the door open and led the way to a clothing shop down the street.

"Drew, I don't need any clothes," she said as he pulled open the door.

"I'm not purchasing you a whole wardrobe, Gwen, but you do need a dress for tonight. Remember, robe and dress shoes?"

A soft pink color spread across her cheeks like water-color on a painting. He adored the look of the blush on her skin. Even more, he enjoyed putting it there. It wasn't often he could get reactions like this from women in his circle. They expected this treatment, and if they ever sported a color on their face, it was generally more often from anger when they didn't get what they wanted.

The shop, while small, housed a myriad of upscale clothing and before they had stepped very far in, a blond woman in a smart tailored suit approached them.

"Welcome, my name is Claire. How may I assist you today?"

"We need a dress. Something simple and elegant for dinner tonight."

The woman nodded, and her eyes traveled up and down Gwen's form. "I'm sure I have something that will suffice. About an eight, is that right?"

"Yes, or ten sometimes." Gwen's voice was soft and aimed at the floor. Was she embarrassed? Drew couldn't care less what size she was, but he knew body image was something most women struggled with.

"Follow me," Claire said and led the way toward the back corner of the store. Drew followed until he noticed the fitting room area. Two large armchairs sat facing an open area with three long mirrors that he assumed was where the woman could model the clothing. He parked himself in one of the chairs and waited.

A few minutes later, Claire opened a dressing room for Gwen and hung up several dresses. "There's a small mirror inside, but if you like the way they look, you can step out and view it in the longer mirrors." She pointed to the open area.

"Thank you." Gwen closed the dressing room door and Drew waited. When she emerged, his breath caught in his throat. The black dress hugged her in all the right places and flared out at the hips. The neckline was black lace. "What do you think?" she asked twirling for him.

"It's beautiful," Drew said. In fact, he wasn't sure he had ever seen such a beautiful vision before.

"Shall I even try the others?"

Though he couldn't imagine one looking any better, Drew encouraged her to model the rest. He was not only curious to see how they would look, but he was taking mental notes on dresses he could buy her in the future. The other four dresses looked stunning as well, but nothing compared to the first one.

"Do you have any jewelry to complement the dress?" Claire asked.

"I didn't bring any," Gwen said shaking her head.

"Do you have any here?" Drew asked.

"Drew, I couldn't-"

"You can," Drew said, grabbing her hand. "The outfit needs it." He lowered his voice and leaned closer to her ear. "Princess, remember?" Gwen nodded, but Drew wondered if he was pushing it. He didn't want to scare her off by pushing his money on her either. "Just a pair of earrings though, I think."

Claire nodded and motioned them to follow her to the other side of the store. The jewelry collection wasn't large, but the pieces were extraordinary. Claire scanned the offerings before plucking off a dainty pair of onyx earrings. "These would look lovely."

"We'll take them," Drew said.

Gwen was quiet as Claire rang up the purchases. She gripped her bag tightly which now held her casual clothes and tennis shoes along with her robe, and her eyes remained on the floor. Drew handed over his platinum card, signed the slip without a second thought, and thanked Claire before taking Gwen's hand again.

As they stepped outside, he turned to her. "I'm sorry. I wanted to spoil you, but I have the feeling I've made you uncomfortable."

Gwen smiled up at him. "A little I suppose. It's wonderful that you have so much money, but I don't live like this. I live paycheck to paycheck and work two jobs. This dress and earrings costs a month's pay if not more. I just...."

Drew pulled her hands to his chest. "Gwen, I'm so sorry. You are amazing, and I wanted to show you that."

"You don't have to spend so much money to show me that. Money is important, Drew, but it's not everything, and it could help so many people who need it." She took a deep breath and looked down.

Drew moved a hand to push her chin back up. "I've

lived a privileged life, Gwen, but I'd like to be the man you're looking for. Help me learn."

Her gaze penetrated his, and he poured his emotion into his gaze. If the eyes were windows to the soul, he wanted her to read his honesty.

"Okay." Her voice was soft and breathy and though he wasn't sure she would be receptive, Drew couldn't fight the magnetic pull that lowered his head until his lips touched hers.

Heat flared between them and raced down his spine warming his body from the inside. His heartbeat doubled as if shot with amphetamine. When the kiss ended, he could tell it had affected Gwen just as much. Her breath was labored, and she blinked rapidly at him. "Sorry, I've wanted to do that since the masquerade ball."

"Me too."

As they rode back in the jet that evening, Drew stole glances at Gwen from the corner of his eye. After the kiss, they had walked around town for a time before their reservation for dinner. While he had wanted to buy more for her, he had refrained. It would be challenging, but he was determined to be the man she needed.

She was so unlike any woman he had ever dated. Even Avery, who claimed she didn't want a billionaire boyfriend, had wanted him to buy things for her. But Gwen truly acted as if money meant nothing to her. It gave Drew pause. Perhaps he was putting too much emphasis on money as well.

"So, tell me about your church," he said turning to her. "I mean what should I expect?"

Gwen's eyes lit up. "Well, it's very welcoming. Someone will greet you at the front door with a smile. Probably shake your hand too. Then they'll hand you a bulletin which details events happening during the week, and we will go in and have a seat."

"That doesn't sound bad so far," he said though meeting new people always set him a little on edge. It came with having money. He constantly had to decide if they liked him for him or for what they hoped to get from him.

"Then there's music," Gwen continued. "It's mostly contemporary though somehow I doubt you listen to Christian radio."

He interrupted her with a smile, "No? What kind of music do you think I listen to?"

She cocked her head as she studied him. "Hmm, I think I'd take you more for a rock 'n' roll kind of guy."

"Guilty." Drew was more a fan of rock music but the oldies like AC/DC or Kiss.

"And then the preacher will speak. His sermon usually lasts thirty to forty-five minutes and then he'll close in prayer. Sometimes we sing a closing song before he releases us. All in all, it's only about an hour of your life, but if you come with an open heart, I can pretty much guarantee it'll be the best hour of your week."

Drew wasn't sure about that. But Gwen had something he found he was missing, and if that something was God, he was willing to take a chance to see.

"I'm looking forward to it," he said.

12

Gwen woke the next morning before her alarm clock. Drew would attend her church today, and she hoped he enjoyed it. As much fun as she had last night, Gwen knew Drew would have to be a believer before she could become serious with him. She wanted to get married and have a family but only with someone who would love and serve the Lord as much as she did.

Gwen kicked back the covers and padded to the bathroom for a shower. Ten minutes later, she stood in her closet surveying her wardrobe. There was nothing wrong with any of it, but she felt more pressure to look nice today knowing Drew would be there. After debating back and forth, she decided on a simple skirt and sweater. The hunter green color brought out the sparkle in her eyes and the copper in her hair.

Satisfied with her appearance, Gwen headed to the kitchen to make breakfast and coffee. Drew would pick her up in half an hour, and she didn't want to still be shoveling food in when he arrived.

The knock at her door arrived just as she was getting the bacon out of the fridge. This time she didn't wait; she hurried to the door in case it was another threat. It was too early to be Drew, and she wasn't expecting anyone else.

She flung the door open and stared in surprise when Drew's face greeted her from the other side. "You're early." Gwen hadn't meant the words to come out like an accusation, but it was clear from his raised brow that they had landed that way.

"Should I go then?" He turned to walk away, but Gwen caught the smile on his face. He was teasing her.

"No." She grabbed his arm to stop him and a tingle shot up her arm. "I just haven't eaten yet is all."

"Good, I was hoping to catch you before you did. I have breakfast waiting in the car, and I was hoping you would join me."

"Eat in the limo?"

"Why not? It's not pancakes or waffles, so you won't have to worry about syrup." His blue eyes danced.

"All right, let me put the bacon away. Lucky for you,

I hadn't started the coffee yet." She couldn't believe how easy it was to joke around with him.

"You wouldn't have come with me if you had?" His face pulled into a forlorn expression. "I see how I rate."

Gwen just laughed. She loved how he made her feel lighter. "Just let me grab my Bible and purse." *And a stick of gum* she thought to herself as she wouldn't get to brush her teeth after breakfast now.

She dashed into the kitchen and stashed the bacon back in the fridge. Then she rummaged in her drawers until she found a pack of gum. She didn't chew it often, but she tried to keep some around just for moments like these.

Gum in hand, she grabbed her purse, slipping it in, and then her Bible and journal off the table where she had been about to do her devotional. "Okay, I'm ready."

Drew held out his arm, and Gwen slipped her hand through it enjoying the strong essence of masculinity and security from him.

As they climbed into the limo, she was surprised by the smell of eggs and bacon. Drew had said it wasn't pancakes or waffles but trying to eat eggs in the car might be just as messy at least if they landed on her outfit. "Eggs?" she asked as he shut the door.

A crooked smile alighted on his lips. "Egg burritos. The best in the city." He opened a compartment near the fridge and pulled out two large tin foil cylinders.

"This is enormous," Gwen said with a laugh as he passed one to her.

"And delicious. My mother hates that I eat these, but I'm addicted."

Gwen glanced at him as she unwrapped one side of her monstrosity. The comment about his mother had caught her attention as it wasn't the first time he had said something about her disapproval. "Your mother isn't a fan of some of your habits?"

Drew snorted. "Not at all. My mother is the epitome of the wealthy elite. One must always eat healthy, dress appropriately, and never cause a scene."

Gwen's heart ached for him. It was clear from his words that he and his mother had a rocky relationship and while that was better than no relationship at all like she had, it was still challenging. "That must be difficult."

"That's one word for it, but let's not discuss my mother. Let's enjoy the wonderful food, the company," he winked at her, "and the ride."

Gwen wanted to say more, but it was clear from his words that he was finished with the conversation, so she finished unwrapping her burrito and took a bite. It was delicious. Eggs, bacon, and cheese mixed together to create an explosion of flavors in her mouth. It was the best egg burrito she had ever eaten. Drew was full of surprises.

Drew's bravado faded as they pulled into the parking lot of the church. He disliked situations where he didn't feel in control, and this qualified. There were too many unknown variables. He didn't know the people, the procedure, or the layout. All things he versed himself in before attending new venues.

"You ready?" Gwen's voice was soft and encouraging beside him.

He flashed what he hoped was a confident smile. "As I'll ever be, I suppose."

Manuel opened the door, and Drew stepped out first then held his hand to Gwen. He hoped she wouldn't mind, but he laced his fingers through hers. This was her place and she exuded a feeling of confidence that he needed.

As she had said, a friendly couple greeted them at the door and handed them a bulletin. Drew smiled and nodded but made no attempt at small talk. It wasn't his forte anyway and certainly not when he felt less than confident.

He let Gwen lead the way into the sanctuary and sat beside her. Three large screens hung behind the stage which was filled with instruments. The large room could probably seat three hundred though Drew doubted even half that amount was there currently. "Does it usually fill up?" he asked her quietly as his eyes scoped the area for exits. Not that he expected a scene, but it was always nice to know the quickest way out of a building in case.

She shook her head. "There are two services. The first one is larger, maybe two hundred most weeks. I'd say this one is half that. Maybe a little more."

That made him feel better. At least there wouldn't be a huge crowd if something did unfold. A minute later, several people stepped onto the stage and the music began. It wasn't rock, but Drew could appreciate the talent of the people playing. He had never heard the songs, but he enjoyed listening to Gwen sing beside him. Her voice was soft but clear, and occasionally, her eyes would close as she sang. She looked peaceful as if the rest of the world didn't matter.

"This next song is new," the worship leader said, "and it has powerful words. If you'll let me, I'd like to personalize the words and read them over you. If you're comfortable with it, please close your eyes and listen."

The woman began to read in a clear voice, but the words meant little to Drew. At least until she reached the chorus. "... The love of God chases you down, fights till you're found, leaves the ninety-nine. You didn't earn it, and you don't deserve it, but still He gives Himself away..." The woman continued but Drew's ears stopped listening. He didn't know what the ninety-nine were, and he was having trouble grappling with him not deserving it. While not a believer, Drew felt he was a decent person. He donated to charities, he hired those he could, and he had done nothing truly terrible. Why wasn't that enough for God?

The pastor's message didn't seem to address the lyrics, and Drew knew he would have to ask Gwen about them after the service.

"What did you think?" Gwen asked him when the final song ended, and people began exiting the church.

"I have questions," he said. "Do you have time for lunch?"

Gwen squeezed his hand and offered a smile. "Of course."

Half an hour later, they parked at a viewpoint in the city. Drew had opted to grab fast food and eat in the car, so they wouldn't be interrupted.

"So, what's your question?" Gwen asked as she opened the Styrofoam container. The salty smell of soy sauce reached Drew's nose, and his stomach rumbled.

"It's about that song the woman read. She said 'you don't deserve it' but I'm a good person, Gwen. How could I not deserve it?" He took a bite of his noodles as he waited for her response.

"It isn't about being a good person, Drew. God says that 'by Grace are you saved through faith, and that not of yourself, it is the gift of God, not of good works lest any man should boast'. It's not about doing good things. It's about letting God into your life."

"So, the only way to receive God's love is by letting him into my life?" That sounded like a piece of control that Drew wasn't sure he could relinquish.

"You already have God's love, Drew. There's nothing you could do to make Him love you more than he loves you right now. He's just waiting for you to want a relationship with Him."

"But a relationship with Him requires changing my life, right?"

Gwen smiled. "Well, when you accept Jesus into your life, you want to live differently. I don't feel like I'm missing out on anything, and I couldn't imagine living any other way."

Drew let that sink in. Gwen had something he was missing in his life, but he wasn't sure he was ready to give up control.

13

"How come you have returned none of my calls, Drew?"

Drew glanced up at Avery who stood leaning in his doorway. "I was on a date, Avery. It would have been rude to answer your calls on a date." Suddenly, he remembered the flowers and the note in his car. He needed to stop by and see Scott this afternoon.

Avery sashayed into the room. "With Gwen?"

"Yes, with Gwen. Who else would it be with?"

Avery tilted her head and crossed her slender arms. "You should be careful, Drew. You will only break her heart."

Drew blinked at her. This was a new side of Avery and one he didn't like very much. "And why is that?"

"Because you're from two different worlds. It will never work out."

"That's ridiculous and antiquated thinking. There have been plenty of relationships where one party was poorer than the other that worked."

Avery shrugged. "It didn't work for me. I'm just trying to save you both some heartbreak."

"What do you mean?" Drew asked. "I thought you came back because you were broke."

With an exaggerated sigh, Avery plopped down in the chair across from him. "I did, but I became broke because of this guy I met. He was amazing, or so I thought. Poor, but charming. Turned out he was a con artist and was siphoning my money away right under my nose."

"Avery, I'm sorry that happened, but Gwen isn't like that. I ran a background check on her. She might be poor, but she's no thief."

"You're probably right." Avery flicked her hair off her shoulders. "Have you told your mother yet?"

"No, I'm still working on that, but I will soon. I'd appreciate it if you didn't tell her either."

Avery held up her hands. "I'm not going to say anything. So, how about lunch?"

"I'd love to, but I've got an errand to run. Maybe we can do lunch another time."

"All right, I'll try to find a hole in your schedule, so we can meet up."

Drew did not miss the hint of hurt in her voice. He felt bad, but he needed to go see Scott before he was off work. When he was sure Avery was gone, he texted Manuel, grabbed his coat, and headed out of the building.

"Back so soon?" Scott asked as Drew crossed the room.

"I know I'm out of favors, but I need one anyway."

Scott raised a brow. "Okay, but it's going cost you a bigger donation this year."

"Understood, and I'll be happy to."

Scott's eyes dropped to the bundle in Drew's hands. "Fine, follow me." He led the way to the office again and pulled the door shut. "What is it this time?"

"It's these." Drew set the flowers and the note on the coffee table. "The girl, the one I asked you to run the background check on, she got them delivered to her apartment before our date yesterday. It's not much, probably a prank, but I was hoping you could dust them for prints. Mine will be on there and hers too."

"What does the card say?" Scott asked.

"Cinderella wasn't real. I know it seems silly," Drew continued when Scott raised a brow, "but she's had a hard life and she spooks easily. I just don't want to ignore this, and have it turn out to be something bigger."

"All right, I'll see what I can do, but I wasn't kidding about that check, my friend."

"It will be in the mail, I promise. Just let me know when you have anything."

Gwen sighed as she stared at the mountain of papers in front of her. She was trying to stay focused, but memories of the last few evenings with Drew kept flooding her vision. It had been less than two weeks since she'd met him, but she already felt herself falling for this guy and that scared her. The only thing that gave her pause was his faith. He hadn't committed his heart to God, but he had agreed to come to church with her again.

A glance at the clock revealed she was out of time. Drew was taking her to some benefit tonight and she needed to get to Carrie's to find a dress and get her hair done. Drew had offered to buy her a dress, but Gwen didn't feel right about taking his money until they were more serious. The last thing she needed was to have him buy her a ton of gifts and then they break up for some reason. She would never get over the guilt.

With a final look at her papers - she'd have to come in early tomorrow - she packed up her things and headed out.

"How are things with your Prince Charming?"

Gwen sighed as Tom's voice reached her. It had been a quiet week with no hounding from him, and she had hoped it would stay that way. Then his words sank in. She whirled to face him. "What did you say?"

"I asked how things are with your Prince Charming."

Fear flooded Gwen and her knees began to shake. Had she been wrong about the sender of the flowers? Or was it just a coincidence he had called Drew Prince Charming? She didn't want to stay to find out. "I have to go." She turned and sprinted to her car.

When she was safely in the car with her doors locked, she allowed herself a moment to close her eyes and calm her breathing. She wouldn't be able to concentrate with her heart pounding like a snare drum out of her chest, and she didn't want to risk getting in an accident. Thankfully, Tom hadn't followed her and a few minutes later, she was able to turn the ignition.

"What happened to you?" Carrie asked as Gwen stepped inside.

"You remember the flowers and the note I told you about?"

Carrie's nose wrinkled. "The creepy black ones?"

"Yeah, well Tom, this guy at work who keeps asking me out, asked me how my Prince Charming was."

"Maybe it was just a coincidence," Carrie said, "but I

agree that sounds creepy. Try to put it out of your mind though. You've got a benefit to get ready for."

"You're right." But it was easier said than done. If her stalker turned out to be Tom, what was she going to do about it?

14

Drew smiled when Gwen opened the door. Her emerald green gown showed off her porcelain skin, and her red hair was pulled up on her head in an artistic up do. "You look beautiful," he said.

"Thanks. It's a little tight, but I think I'll be okay. Just don't let me eat too much." She patted her stomach in a self-conscious gesture.

"Gwen, I would have bought you a dress that fits."

"I know, Drew, but I don't feel right accepting such extravagant gifts until-"

"Until you're sure about us?" he supplied.

A sheepish grin stole across her face. "I'm sorry-"

"Don't be. I understand. Thank you, Carrie, for the dress," he said to Carrie as she entered the living room.

"My pleasure anytime, Drew."

"You sure you don't want to go with us? I'm sure I could get you in."

Carrie flicked her hand. "Thanks for the invite, Drew, but I have a date with Raphael tonight."

Gwen chuckled and rolled her eyes. "Come on, let's go."

"All right. Have fun then." Drew took Gwen's hand and led her outside. "Is Raphael the one she skipped the ball for?" he asked as the front door closed behind them.

Gwen smiled. "No, that was Lorenzo, but I honestly couldn't tell you who Raphael is. Carrie's what I like to call a serial dater. I love her, but I don't always understand her."

"Well, I'm glad you don't take after her." He held the limo door open and helped her slide in.

"Me too."

His phone chimed as the limo door shut. It was Scott. While he normally wouldn't answer the phone on a date, this one concerned Gwen too, so he flashed an apologetic smile and tapped the button. "Hey Scott, you find anything out?"

"I'm afraid not, Drew. There were prints but only yours and Gwen's. I'm sure it's nothing to worry about, but if she gets anything else, let me know."

"Thanks, Scott." Drew swallowed his frustration and ended the call. "Sorry about that. It was my friend, the police officer. I was hoping he had information about your flowers, but he couldn't find any usable fingerprints."

"That's all right. I think it might be the guy at my work after all. He asked about my Prince Charming today."

A knot formed in Drew's stomach. He didn't like anyone threatening Gwen and certainly not at her job where he had little control. "Would you like me to speak to him?"

"No, that would probably make it worse. I think he'll let it go, eventually."

Drew wasn't sure about that - he'd had his fair share of stalkers and they rarely stopped of their own accord - but he let it go. He didn't want to ruin the evening.

Gwen grabbed Drew's hand as she stepped out of the limo. Even though she was here with him, attending this gala still terrified her. What if they didn't let her in? What if she made a fool of herself or him? A camera flashed, and Gwen jumped and curled closer to Drew.

"Drew, who's the new girl?" the man behind the camera asked.

"Don't worry about them," Drew whispered in her ear. "Just ignore and keep walking."

"Oh, come on, Drew, just a name?"

The man was relentless, and Gwen sighed with relief when they were safely in the building and away from the man with the camera. "Will that be printed?"

"It's hard to say. We never know when they take pictures which ones they are going to use, but it's a possibility. Don't worry, you look beautiful though."

Gwen wasn't worried about her appearance. What she was worried about was her privacy. She couldn't imagine her school would be too excited if reporters showed up there looking for her. And what if they looked her up? She didn't need her past being splashed across the headlines. What had she been thinking? "Drew, I don't know-"

Before she could finish, a woman's voice called out to them. "Drew, Gwen, over here." Avery waved to them from the doorway of a large room.

Beside her, she felt Drew stiffen, and Gwen wondered why. She had thought he and Avery were friends.

"I was hoping you two would come." Avery was stunning in her low cut floor-length gown. It sparkled as the light caught it. "Gwen, you look absolutely radiant."

Gwen didn't know Avery well enough to discern if she was telling the truth or just being nice, so she gave her the benefit of the doubt. "Thank you, Avery. You do as well."

"Oh pish," Avery said with a wave of her hand. "Come on, we're seated at the same table." She turned and led the way to the table. Gwen didn't miss the slight swinging of her hips, and she glanced at Drew to see if he was watching, but his facial features were pulled tight and his eyes stared straight ahead.

Avery sat down at the table and pointed to the seats next to her. Drew's name was on a card directly on Avery 's left, and Gwen's name was on a card next to Drew. On Gwen's left was a woman's name. "Who's Jacqueline?" she asked.

"My mother," Drew said with a pinched smile.

Gwen's heart dropped like a lead weight. She had never met the woman and now she would have to sit next to her all evening? As if the very thought had summoned her, a thin woman with graying hair strode their direction.

"Avery, it's so good to see you again," the woman said as she picked up and squeezed Avery's hands. "And you got Drew to say yes? Good for you."

"Actually, Mother, I'm here with Gwen." Drew spoke up. His arm slipped around Gwen's waist, and he pulled her closer to him.

Gwen was thankful for the support as Jacqueline's eyes raked over her in a disapproving glance.

"And just who is Gwen?"

"She's the woman from the masquerade ball, Mother."

"I thought you said her name was Carrie."

"It was a simple misunderstanding," Drew said. "This is Gwen Rodgers."

"I see. And what do you do, Gwen?"

Gwen swallowed. Drew's mother was terrifying. Though beautiful, her eyes flashed daggers into Gwen, and her posture was so straight Gwen wondered if a rod had been attached to her spine. "Um, I'm a teacher."

Jacqueline's eyes shifted to Drew as her brow arched. "And just how did a teacher get invited to my ball?"

"Gwen also manages charitable donations for some rather large companies," Drew said. "Perhaps that is how she was invited." That wasn't the truth - she only managed donations for his company - but Gwen knew better than to contradict him.

"I see." Her eyes bore holes into Gwen, and she licked her lips as if she was going to say something else. "Well, I look forward to getting to know you, Gwen."

Gwen doubted that, but she flashed a tight-lipped smile at the woman. Nice. She could be nice. She might have to remind herself that this woman was a child of God as well. A lot. But she could be nice.

Drew squeezed her waist and leaned in close. His breath tickled her ear as he whispered. "Don't let her get to you."

Gwen appreciated the encouraging words, but she had no doubt his mother was out to make her night miserable. Drew pulled out her chair, and she took her seat thankful that a glass of water was in front of her. Her throat was already parched. As she reached for the glass though, her hand slipped, and she sent the glass crashing against the table. Water spilled out across the table pooling towards Avery and Jacqueline as if it knew exactly who would hate it the most.

"Oh my gosh, I'm so sorry." Gwen stood to search for a napkin and her sudden ascent knocked her chair over. Her chair crashed to the ground causing Gwen to jump. And of course, she couldn't jump Drew's direction. No, she had to jump Jacqueline's direction. Jacqueline had just picked up her own water glass and Gwen just barely bumped her arm, but it was enough to send the water spraying out of the top and all over Jacqueline.

"Well, I never."

Gwen's eyes widened, and her heart exploded into a trillion tiny pieces. His mother would never like her now. Recovering slightly, she grabbed a napkin off the table behind them and tried to dab at Jacqueline's dress.

"Young lady, stop. You have done quite enough, and I am capable of drying myself off."

Gwen dropped the napkin and stepped back. "Of course, ma'am, I'm so sorry." She looked to Drew who had managed to keep his wits about him and was sopping up the table. "I'm so sorry." Then she fled for the door before the hot tears building up behind her eyes could spill down her cheeks. She had let Carrie help with her makeup and she didn't need to add insult to injury by staying as tears created black trails of mascara down her cheeks.

She didn't stop running until she burst through the front door. Too late she remembered the photographer. Camera bulbs flashed in her face and his voice carried to her. "Excuse me, are you the woman with Drew Devonshire? Did he break up with you? Hit you?"

Oh crud, she had leaped right out of the frying pan and into the fire. They might not have used her picture before, but she had just given them interesting fodder. She pulled the door open behind her and stepped back into the building. It was safer inside right now though that wasn't saying much. She turned, hoping to find a corner to hide in, but found herself against a solid chest instead. Gwen knew it was Drew before her eyes reached his face.

"Why did you run?" His hands clasped her arms, not tightly but with enough force that she couldn't bolt again.

"Are you kidding me?" She sniffed. "I made a mess in there."

"Yeah, you did."

She gaped at him wondering how he could be so

cruel, and then his lip twitched. Merriment flickered in his eyes. "It was great."

"How can you say that? It was mortifying."

He pursed his lips together, but she could see his shoulders moving just slightly. He was laughing. At her. "It's not funny, Drew."

"Actually, it is, Gwen. These benefits are always so stuffy. I hate coming to them, but this one...this one will go down in the books."

"Yeah, but not in a good way." Gwen had known it would be hard to win over his mother, but now she was fairly certain that door was closed for good. And though she wasn't dating his mother, having the woman hate her would put a strain on any kind of relationship they might have. "And why did you invite me if you hate these things?"

Drew shrugged. "Because I'm supposed to be here and coming with you at least made the thought of the night bearable."

"Drew, maybe you need a woman like Avery. I'm not cut out for events like this. I'll only keep embarrassing you."

"Hey." He let go of her left arm to place a finger under her chin. "I don't need a woman like Avery. I needed a reason not to go to these stuffy events and now I have one. In fact, let's get out of here."

"Have you lost your mind? Your mother will kill you

if you leave, and that reporter outside already saw me and thinks we broke up or you hit me or something."

A mischievous gleam appeared in Drew's eyes. "Then let's really give him something to talk about."

Before she could say anything more, he opened the door and pulled her out with him. As expected, the cameras flashed, but Drew said nothing. Instead, he turned to her, circled his arms around her waist, and pulled her in for a kiss.

Gwen was so shocked that she stood as still as a statue for a moment, but the heat from his lips traveled through her body, and with a mind of their own, her arms wound around his neck. She could hear clicks, but she was no longer sure they were from the cameras because it felt like fireworks were exploding all around her.

Too soon he pulled back. "Come on, let's go get some S'mores."

"What?" She looked up at him still dazed from the kiss, but he didn't answer. He tightened his grip on her hand and pulled. With his other hand, he retrieved his phone and hollered for Manuel to meet them at the corner.

He must have been close by because the limo pulled up just as they reached the end of the block. Without waiting for Manuel to open the door, Drew yanked it open and piled in after her. "Drive," he shouted to Manuel and the limo sped off.

"This is where you live?" Gwen asked. Her eyes widened like saucers as the limo pulled up to a palatial estate. The mansion looked as if it took up an entire city block. She could count at least three chimneys and a four-car garage.

Drew's lips twitched into a smile, and his dimple popped out. "Yes, this is home. It's a little much for just me."

"I'll say." The words tumbled out of Gwen's mouth before she could stop them. "I'm sorry. That was rude."

"Perhaps, but it's the truth. I didn't want such a large place, but my mother insisted I take it over when my father died. She moved to a smaller place in the city thinking I would fill it with a family, but I haven't accomplished that yet."

"Do you want to? Fill it with a family?" Why was she asking such personal questions? Except she knew the answer. She wanted to know everything about him.

His eyes caught hers and Gwen's breath stilled as the flood of emotion emanating from him hit her.

"Yes, I hope one day to marry and have kids."

"Have you ever been close?" Gwen wasn't sure why she cared, but a part of her felt compelled to know. How many women had been in his past? How many close enough to marry?

Drew nodded, "I was close once. Her name was Marjorie, and I thought she was attracted to me rather than my money. However, shortly after I proposed, she ran away with my chauffeur."

Gwen's eyes widened, and her hand flew to her mouth. "I'm so sorry. That's awful."

"It was, but I'm glad I found out who she was before I married her. What about you? Were you ever close?"

Gwen's smile was wistful. "I was once. I'm sure you understand that with my past, it's hard for me to let people in, but Adam made it past all my walls. He was charming and said all the right things to a girl who needed to hear them. I'm not sure why he even proposed to me because it turned out he was having an affair with his secretary."

Drew's blue eyes softened in sympathy. "Gwen, I'm sorry. I'm sure that didn't help your trust issues."

She sniffed and bit the inside of her lip. Her head shook slightly. Help them? It made them nearly insurmountable. "I should have known better though. Adam attended church with me, but I could tell he wasn't a believer. He was just going through the motions, but I kept telling myself he just needed a little longer." Gwen stopped as she realized she could be talking about Drew as well.

Drew opened his mouth as if he were about to say something, but before he could, the limo pulled to a stop. "Hungry?" He asked with a lopsided smile.

Gwen's stomach rumbled in answer, and a sheepish grin stole across her face as her hands covered her traitorous belly. "I guess so."

"Let's go then." He grabbed the grocery bag full of marshmallows, chocolate, and graham crackers they had stopped at the store to get and stepped out of the limo.

His backyard was expansive. Not that she would have expected any less. A gazebo sat near the house and overlooked both a pond and a swimming pool. Near it was a fire pit with several chairs and beyond that was a grassy area and a tennis court.

"Are you cold?" he asked. "I could send Manuel to get a coat while I start the fire."

A shiver raced across her shoulders and Gwen nodded. She hadn't realized she was cold, but that was because the limo had been so toasty.

"Manuel, can you fetch a jacket for Gwen?"

Manuel issued a nod and raced off toward the house. Gwen followed Drew over to the fire pit. There were already logs in the fire pit and near it, a small chest. Drew opened it to reveal matches, lighter fluid, and metal rods. A few minutes later, he had a roaring fire going.

Gwen inhaled the smoky air. Her foster parents had taken her camping once, and it was one of her favorite memories. There was something about watching the flames of the fire dance. Beautiful and deadly.

"Ready for S'mores?" Drew asked. He had already set out the graham crackers and broken up the chocolate on a nearby table.

"I've never had them," Gwen said with a shrug.

Drew's eyes bulged. "What? How could you have never had S'mores? They're like an American staple."

"I've only been camping once and unlike you, my friends at college didn't hang out at bonfires." That was because she hadn't had many friends at college. And even after she and Carrie had become friends that hadn't been Carrie's idea of a fun Friday night.

"Well, then I'm glad I get to be here for your first experience."

Manuel arrived then with a jacket, and Gwen slipped her arms in thankful for the extra heat.

"Now, the trick is that you warm the marshmallow

before you blacken it, so that the inside is nice and gooey." Drew held a silver rod out to her with a marshmallow shoved on the end of it. Gwen took the rod and turned to the fire.

"Like this?"

Drew filled the space behind her and his hand guided her arm to a slightly higher position. "Here," he said. His lips were close to her ear and Gwen had to focus to keep her arm from shaking. Just the nearness of his body was sending tremors through hers.

They stood that way for a minute, then he dipped her arm down. "Now, we blacken it just slightly." The marshmallow caught fire and Gwen gasped, but Drew simply pulled back on her arm and blew the flame out like a candle on a cake. "Now, sandwich it between the crackers and chocolate."

Gwen hurried to the table and placed the marshmallow on a graham cracker with chocolate. Then she used the top graham cracker to hold it in place while she pulled the rod out. When the rod was clear, the marshmallow squished, and white goo trickled out the sides of the miniature sandwich. She brought it to her mouth and took a bite.

"Mm, this is delicious," she said, her mouth full of the concoction.

The corners of Drew's lips curled up and his eyes crinkled. "You're enjoying that, huh?"

Gwen nodded and took another bite. How had she never had these before? They were like the perfect little dessert. Delicious and handheld.

"I can see that," he said taking a step closer to her. "Want to know how I know?"

Gwen swallowed her bite. His tone had changed from playful to a deep, sexy tone. His hand reached out and touched the corner of her lip. "I can see the evidence on your face."

He wiped slightly and showed Gwen the white residue on his finger, but she couldn't speak. Her eyes were fixed on him. He took another step toward her, and before she could say a word, his lips found hers. They were sweet and hungry at the same time. The remainder of her cracker fell to the ground as her arms wound around his neck, and Gwen felt herself falling. Oh boy was she in trouble.

16

"Why do you smell like smoke?" Carrie asked as Gwen floated past her into the living room. "No, not just smoke, you smell like a campfire. Why do you smell like a campfire?"

"Because we had S'mores." Gwen couldn't wipe the goofy smile from her face. Her cheeks felt glued in a perpetual grin.

"S'mores? I thought you were going to a benefit." Carrie crossed her arms and leaned against her counter. "All right, spill it."

"It was amazing," Gwen said with a sigh and then blinked to focus. "I mean not at first. The benefit was scary. Everyone was perfect and important, and I spilled water on the table. Then I spilled water on his mother."

"Wait, you met his mother?"

"Yeah, and she hates me. I tried to mop up the water I spilled on her. Then I ran out, but Drew followed me, and he kissed me for the cameras."

"What cameras?" Carrie asked.

Gwen shrugged. "I don't know. Some reporter. Then we ran. We ran to the limo and drove to the grocery store."

"The grocery store? Gwen, did you have special brownies or something?"

Gwen laughed. "No, we bought marshmallows, graham crackers, and chocolate. Then he took me back to his place. It's huge, Carrie, and he made a fire and we roasted S'mores."

"I think toasted is the proper word."

"It was amazing."

"You made S'mores instead of going to the benefit? Who is this guy?"

Gwen had an answer for that. He was her idea of a perfect man, but she would not say that out loud yet. She didn't want to jinx it, so she changed the subject. "I'm sorry about your dress. It might be a little dirty, but I'll pay for the dry cleaning."

Carrie smiled. "I don't care about the dress. I'm just glad to see you smiling."

Gwen was glad too. She hadn't known how lonely she was until tonight. Over S'mores and a crackling fire, she and Drew had opened up to each other. She'd told him about her past and her insecurities with men. He'd told her about his desire to do something more noble than run hotels.

"What are you going to do?" she asked.

"I will tell her I'm leaving. I'll stay until I can train someone else, probably until the end of the year, but then I'm leaving. Tonight made me realize that life is too short to do something you hate. You made me realize that." He pulled her closer to him and wrapped his arm around her shoulder.

"Drew, I don't want to the be the cause for you leaving the family business."

"You aren't. I haven't been happy for a while, but I couldn't place my finger on why. Until tonight. I miss this. I miss relaxing with friends and chatting by the fire. My life is meetings and hotels now, and that's not a life."

"Okay, Cheshire cat, you're staying here tonight."

"What? No, I'm okay," Gwen said. "I need to get back to Tabby."

"Tabby will be fine. I've been trying to get your attention for three minutes. You cannot drive. You're a risk. I've never seen anyone so high on life they couldn't drive, but that is definitely you."

Gwen wanted to protest, but Carrie was right. She hadn't heard her friend and her focus was on the last few hours and nothing more. "Okay, you win, but I don't have any pajamas."

Carrie smiled. "I've got you covered as long as you promise not to smoke them out too."

Drew was just about to retire for the evening when Pierre appeared at his door. "I'm sorry to bother you, sir, but your mother is downstairs, and she will not take no for an answer."

Drew sighed. He had known his mother would want to talk to him, but he hadn't been expecting her so soon. "Tell her I'll be right there, Pierre."

He grabbed his robe as Pierre left the room and flung it about his shoulders. There was no way he wanted to have a conversation with his mother in his sleepwear. The robe wasn't much better, but it was something.

"Are you happy?" She accosted him before he made it to the bottom of the stairs. "You've made us the laughingstock of the town!" His mother shoved a phone in his face and Drew glanced at the headline. *Billionaire Blows off Charitable Event.* Underneath was a picture of Gwen and him running toward the limo. Well, at least they hadn't used the one of her crying. He had been worried about that headline. This? This was manageable.

"Wow, that was fast."

"Of course it was, Drew. This is the information age. They don't have to wait to print it when they can throw it up on the internet where it lives forever."

"Mother, you are being dramatic. I didn't blow off the benefit. I attended. I just left early."

"You left before it began with that hooligan you brought."

A spark of anger flared in Drew and he folded his arms across his chest. "She is not a hooligan, Mother. She is a perfectly nice girl who got nervous. Perhaps if you had been nicer to her, she might not have been so skittish."

"It is not my job to placate your playthings-"

"She is not a plaything, Mother. She is a hardworking, honest teacher, and I care for her."

"You've only been seeing her a few weeks," his mother said in a dismissive tone as if the conversation was finished.

"Those few weeks have been long enough. She's real, Mother, and she made me realize what I was missing. I hate those benefits and galas and balls. I'm not Father. I'm not cut out to be the face of the Devonshire hotel chain, and I've decided I'm not going to do it anymore."

"What?" Her eyes narrowed to tiny slits.

"I'll stay until the new year. That will give me plenty

of time to train someone else, but then I'm stepping down. I don't want to keep doing this."

"You would turn your back on family?"

"I'm not turning my back on you, Mother. I'm simply following my heart."

"Well, hopefully your heart doesn't bankrupt our family." With a final pointed look, she whirled and strode out of his house.

Drew sighed. He had known his mother would take it hard, but he hadn't quite expected that reaction.

17

D rew was surprised to find his mother in his office when he returned from his errand. It had been three weeks since their discussion at his house and she hadn't spoken to him once in that time. What could she want now?

"Hello, Mother. To what do I owe this pleasure?"

His mother rose from his chair and walked around the desk. "I've been thinking, Drew, that perhaps I've been too hard on you. You should do what you want with your life and spend it with whom you want."

Drew cocked his head but said nothing. He didn't know where this was going yet.

"I'm going to hate losing you from the family business, but I am pleased with the man you've hired to replace you."

"Thank you." Drew didn't dare say more until he could discern her motive for being here.

"But I have one favor to ask of you."

And there it was.

"There's a charity benefit tonight. I'd like you to attend. It will be your last one."

Drew shook his head. "Sorry, Mother, I have a date with Gwen tonight."

His mother's lips pulled into a tight smile. "I don't think I was clear, Drew. If you want to keep your fortune, you will attend this last benefit tonight. Alone."

"I can't cancel on such short notice, Mother. It would be rude, and haven't you always prided yourself on not being rude?"

Her smile widened, but it didn't reach her eyes. "Of course, I wouldn't want you to be rude. That's why I purchased two spa packages. Avery is going to take her out tonight. She can get all relaxed for your date tomorrow."

Drew's eyes narrowed. Was it possible his mother was being nice to Gwen? Somehow, he doubted it. "Why is it so important she isn't at the benefit tonight, Mother? I could just tell her we had to change our plans and bring her."

"No offense, dear, but I remember the way she behaved last time. This is an important benefit. One that could set us up with some new investors, but only if everything goes smoothly, if you get my drift."

Drew got her insinuation all right. Gwen wasn't welcome because she might screw things up. He didn't want to be there either, but he had been spending the last few days trying to figure out how he'd live if his mother cut him off. He knew he had a little in a trust his father had left him, but it wouldn't be enough to pay for the house and all the help. And while Drew didn't care if he had to downsize, he didn't want to put his employees out of a job. If he just did this, this one favor, then he wouldn't have to worry. He could keep his share of the money and his employees. Everyone won. He wished he felt better about it.

"All right, Mother. Just let me text her to let her know what's going on."

"Oh, don't worry about it, dear. She's already with Avery probably relaxing in some tub full of mud. Call her afterward and you can share stories. Besides, the benefit starts in half an hour, so we need to get going."

Her words rubbed Drew wrong. Why wouldn't she want him to text Gwen? He glanced at his watch. It was five thirty. He was supposed to be picking up Gwen at six. Even if she was away from her phone, he wanted his text to be there. Gwen had shared too much about men lying and letting her down. He didn't want to be one of those men.

Wrangled into doing a benefit with my mother tonight. I'll fill you in later. Sorry, I must cancel.

"See, that took no time at all," Drew said with a triumphant smile at his mother. Now, even if she had some sinister plot planned, Gwen would know he'd had nothing to do with it.

"Very well. Shall we go?" His mother strode out of the room and Drew followed though he felt a little like a lamb being led to a slaughter.

"Avery, what are you doing here?" Gwen asked as she opened the door. She had been expecting Drew even though he'd said he wasn't picking her up for another hour.

"Drew got called into a late meeting tonight. He sent me over and asked if I could entertain you for a bit until he was free. I thought maybe we could do a makeover and then go to dinner." She held up a bag that Gwen assumed contained hair and makeup items.

"Um, all right, sure." It wasn't that she and Avery never spoke, but this would be their first time hanging out as friends though Gwen wasn't sure she would call Avery a friend. She was nice to talk to, and she'd been very helpful whenever Gwen had questions about the donations, but that was about the extent of their relationship.

"Wonderful." Avery stepped into Gwen's living room and scanned the area. "Your place is lovely."

"Uh, thank you." It was nothing grand, but Gwen had decorated the place as nicely as she could. She'd been fortunate enough to find matching furniture for sale on Craig's list shortly after she moved in, and her decorations came from Ross.

"Let's sit at your dining room table. The light there looks good." Without waiting for an answer, Avery crossed the room and began removing things from the bag. A straightener, a curling iron, hair spray, gel, makeup.

Gwen shook her head, afraid of what she was getting herself into, but she followed Avery and sat down in the chair she had pulled out.

"So, how are things going with Drew?" Avery asked as she picked up a brush and began running it through Gwen's hair. "It seems like you two are pretty happy."

"We are," Gwen said. In fact, things had been great with Drew lately. They had spent Thanksgiving just the two of them as Gwen didn't have family and Jacqueline hadn't invited either of them to dine with her. Drew didn't seem too upset his mother was giving him the silent treatment though it weighed on Gwen. She couldn't help feeling responsible for ruining their relationship.

"Except?" Avery asked.

Gwen bit her lip. She wasn't sure she trusted Avery, but she did need to talk to someone. "I just feel awful for driving a wedge between Drew and his mother. I've been praying every day they'll talk to each other, but-"

"Praying? You're a believer?" Avery set the brush down and sprayed Gwen's hair with some fruity smelling mist.

"Yes." Why did Gwen have the feeling Avery would use that against her?

"And Drew knows this?"

"Yes, he's been attending church with me." Unfortunately, he still hadn't given his life to God. It was the one thing keeping Gwen from giving him her whole heart. She wanted to be with a believer, and though she thought he was close, she'd assumed the same thing about Adam.

"Wow, that is surprising. I figured he would have turned his back on all that after Sarah."

Gwen blinked. "Sarah? Who's Sarah?"

"Sarah was a girl he was seeing when we met. She was the religious kind always dragging him to church. They were going to get married, but then she left to go do mission work. Broke his heart." Avery picked up the curling iron and twisted Gwen's hair around the metal rod.

"He never mentioned a Sarah." Nor had he mentioned attending church. He'd told her he was a holiday Christian. So, who wasn't telling the truth? Her gut told her not to trust Avery, but her insecurities and her past had her questioning Drew as well.

"I'm not surprised. He was rather embarrassed by the incident. He'd bought the ring and everything. He loved Sarah and decided he'd never date a believer after that, so I'm surprised you got him to a church again is all."

"Hmm." Gwen didn't know what else to say. She wanted to talk to Drew about this and get his side of the story. Avery had known him longer, but her story just didn't ring true for Gwen.

"But maybe he's over it now. He looks at you much the same way he used to look at Sarah." Avery finished with the curling iron and moved to applying makeup on Gwen. "Wow, you have great skin. I'm not going to do much, just a little shadow, some liner, and a hint of blush."

This was not much? Gwen felt as if her face had at least three extra layers on as Avery moved from one area to the next.

"I think I'm done. Why don't you go change into something a little dressier and I'll pack up?"

"Sure." Gwen headed to her room, hoping her face didn't look as awful as it felt. She made a beeline for the bathroom and flicked on the light. It was more makeup

than she normally wore, but Avery had applied it taste-
fully. Gwen supposed she could leave it on for the
evening.

She turned to her closet and flipped hangers until she
landed on a simple black dress. With a long necklace, she
would look...well, not elegant, but not dowdy either.
Gwen slipped the dress on and grabbed an appropriate
necklace from her jewelry box before heading back to
the dining room.

"Perfect," Avery said. "I packed your bag for you to
save time. We have reservations for dinner at six."

Gwen found that pushy but said nothing. Maybe
Avery was just like that. She took the bag and motioned
for Avery to lead the way, so she could lock the door
behind her.

"Oh, do you mind if we take your car? I gave my
driver the night off knowing you prefer to drive
yourself."

"Uh sure." Had she told Avery she had an aversion to
being driven? She thought back over their conversations
but couldn't recall. Maybe Drew had mentioned it. It
wasn't a big deal; it just unnerved her a little that Avery
knew. As she unlocked the car door, she pushed the
thought from her mind. She was determined to have a
good time tonight and get to know Avery better.

Drew tugged at his neckline as he followed his mother into the ballroom. She had insisted he wear a tie and brandished one from her purse when he explained he didn't have one with him. He hated ties. They felt like a noose, and this one even more so as it represented the leash his mother held on him. He would be so glad when this night was over, and he didn't have to attend any more of these events.

He still wasn't sure what he planned to do after, but he had enough money that he could take a few months to decide. A part of him wanted to return to the teaching degree he had never finished. Another part of him was considering something to help foster kids. Gwen was rubbing off on him. In fact, he'd been planning to tell her tonight that he had made the leap of faith and accepted Jesus as his savior, but he didn't want to do it over a text.

"Ah, here's our table," his mother said as she stopped in front of a table near the back.

"*This* is your table?" His mother hated sitting near the back. She felt her place was front and center and everyone should know it.

"Ah, well, it was a last-minute thing. I didn't think you would attend, and then when I decided on the offer to extend to you, the front tables were all full."

"Uh huh." Drew wasn't sure he was buying what his mother was selling. She was too chipper, and her eyes darted around the room as if she were looking for something or someone.

"Shall we sit?" She pulled out her chair and perched on the edge. Drew followed suit and sat beside her.

"I wonder if we know our other table guests." She leaned to her right. "I have an Emily S. here. How about you?"

Drew didn't care who was sitting to his left, but he leaned over to oblige his mother. "An Alexandra K." He rolled his eyes, certain he would be surrounded by women. Had this been an attempt by his mother to set him up with some rich woman so he'd forget Gwen? Well, it would not work.

"Oh, I think I know Alexandra K. Her mother used to

attend my gardening club. She's a lovely thing. Just about your age. Blond and beautiful."

"Mother, I'm seeing Gwen, remember? Have been for over a month."

His mother puffed up like a peacock. "Well, that doesn't mean you can't be nice to the girl. I wonder if her mother will attend as well. Oh, there she is. Katarina, over here." His mother waved her arm back and forth and hollered again to a woman across the room.

The woman, a stunning older blonde, smiled as she saw his mother's hand and headed their direction. Behind her trailed a younger version of herself. Blonde and beautiful was an understatement. Her daughter was easily one of the most striking women Drew had ever laid eyes on. *Is this a test Lord?* He prayed silently. *If it is, please don't let me fail.*

"Jacqueline, it is so good to see you again." Beside him, his mother stood to greet the woman who had a thick Russian accent. "You remember my daughter, Alexandra."

"Yes, of course, how nice to see you again. This is my son, Drew. I believe he was off at boarding school when you attended garden club, so I'm not sure you ever met."

Katarina's eyes shifted to Drew, who had stood when his mother had and now felt awkward and like a piece of meat at a market next to her. If this wasn't a set up, he would be surprised.

"I must say, Drew, that you are a very handsome young man, but then look at your mother. The apple does not fall far from the tree, no?"

Drew smiled politely and discreetly checked his watch. Ten more minutes. Just ten more minutes of small talk and the benefit would start. He could survive ten minutes.

"Alexandra, don't you think Drew has the most amazing eyes?" Katarina continued.

Alexandra stepped forward and looked at Drew. Her perfectly plucked brow arched just the tiniest bit before the corners of her lips pulled into a smile. Drew forced himself to stare into her eyes because he could see in his peripheral vision that she had a brilliant smile. One that could suck men in and ensnare them, and he didn't want to be a victim.

"They are a beautiful shade of blue," she said, her words lilting softly with her accent.

"Thank you," Drew said. "Yours are stunning as well, but might I suggest we all sit down? I'm sure our other table mates will arrive shortly."

As if summoned, a waitress came by and snatched the two remaining names off the table. "Sorry, they were unable to make it," she said before walking away.

"Well, that will give us more time to catch up and get

to know one another," his mother said as they took their seats around the table.

Drew stifled a sigh as he folded his napkin in his lap. That was the last thing he wanted.

"Oh, dear," Alexandra said. "I think I have lost an earring. Drew, will you help me look? It must be on the ground."

Drew had no desire to crawl around on the ground for this woman he barely knew, but it would have been rude for him to decline. He scooted his chair back and dropped to his knees, scanning the area.

"I don't understand," Gwen said as they entered the expensive hotel. "What are we doing here? I thought we had dinner reservations."

"We do, but I couldn't find my card in the car and I believe I dropped it here when I was working earlier. We'll just take a quick look in the ballroom and be on our way."

"All right." Gwen followed Avery down the elaborate hallway. As Avery pulled open the ballroom doors though, her heart stopped. She blinked, not believing her eyes. Drew was on his knees in front of some beautiful woman and holding something out to her. Was he proposing?

"What's the matter?" Avery asked. She followed Gwen's gaze and exhaled. "Oh dear. That's Sarah. She must have come back. I guess he's not over her after all."

Hot tears exploded in Gwen's vision, and she didn't wait to see more. With an anguished cry, she ran from the room. Her low heels pounded against the floor as she raced for the entry. This could not be happening. Not again. She'd told him about Adam. Why in the world would he do the same thing to her? Maybe he had never been into her. Maybe him taking her out had been part of some sick joke to poke fun at the poor, lower class.

She pushed the door of the hotel open and raced into the cold. Tiny white flakes pelted her in the face and chilled her tear-stained cheeks, but she didn't care. She just had to get away. As far away as she could from this place, from Drew. How could she have been so stupid?

Her keys nearly fell from her grip as she pulled them from her pocket with cold fingers. The temperature was dropping quickly. She needed to get home before the worst of the storm hit. There she could curl up with Tabby, flannel pajamas, and a big bowl of ice cream and drown her sorrows.

She shoved the key into the ignition, wiped her eyes, and started the car. The snow fell harder now, exploding against her windshield in tiny white balls. Gwen turned the wipers up as she pulled out of the parking lot. All she wanted to do was get home, but the snow and her tears were forcing her to drive slower than normal.

"Come on." She pounded the wheel in frustration as a car in front of her slowed to a near stop. She tapped her brakes, so as not to plow into the back of him and took the opportunity to wipe her eyes again. Her tears were falling freely now, racing each other down her cheeks.

The car ahead of her turned off, and Gwen pressed the accelerator. It had been wet enough earlier that she knew the streets would freeze soon and she wanted to be safely home before that happened.

She turned her wipers up another notch. The snow was coming in thick sheets now, obscuring the road almost completely. Gwen let her foot off the accelerator to slow her speed. Her turn was coming up somewhere, but she couldn't see the sign. Suddenly, something ran across the road. Gwen slammed on her brakes out of instinct and they locked up, sending the car into a spin. She yanked the wheel to the left and then to the right, but nothing helped.

The car veered to the left and Gwen sucked in her breath. She was on House hill - a street named for its extreme descent. As her car picked up speed, Gwen sent a prayer heavenward. *Please, Lord, don't let this be the end.*

19

"Thank you, Drew, you are such a gentleman," Alexandra exclaimed as he handed the earring to her.

"No problem." As he stood, he caught sight of a familiar face in the doorway. Avery? What was she doing here? And why did she look so smug? "Excuse me, I'll be right back." He strode over to her. "What are you doing here, Avery?"

"Just delivering on a promise to your mother."

"My mother? What are you talking about?"

"That was lovely by the way. It looked just like a proposal. I couldn't have timed it better had I tried."

"Avery, are you okay?"

"It's so nice to see you've forgiven Sarah and you two are getting back together."

"Sarah?" Drew looked back at his table. "The woman's name is Alexandra and we're not together. I only met her tonight. She dropped her earring and I was giving it back to her."

A wicked smile flitted across Avery's features. "Yes, but that's not how Gwen saw it."

Drew's eyes widened. "Gwen was here? Where is she?"

Avery shrugged. "Gone. I doubt she'll be back. See, I told her all about Sarah, your ex-fiancée, who left to go do mission work, but it looks like she's back and you still have feelings for her."

White hot anger flared within Drew, and he clenched his fists to his side to keep from choking the woman in front of him. "What did you do?"

"What I had to do," she snapped at him. "I came back hoping we could pick up where we left off, but you had some gold digger on your mind."

"Avery, we would never have worked anyway. You said so yourself. Neither of us enjoy these snooty events..." he trailed off as realization dawned on him. "Except you do, but then why would you need me?" He exhaled and crossed his arms. "You need my money."

Avery's lips pulled into an unattractive sneer. "I lost mine in Europe and when I came home, I found that my father had gambled all of our family money away. I figured I could charm you again, we could marry, and then I'd take what was mine and keep painting, but there was Gwen. Sweet, little, innocent Gwen whom you needed to save." She rolled her eyes. "I figured she'd be easy to get rid of, but my note and flowers evidently didn't work, so I had to try something else."

Drew's head was spinning. How had he been so wrong about Avery? Had she always been this way or had her greed consumed her after she'd left?

"I went to your mother. She wanted Gwen out of your life as much as I did, and she paid me handsomely to get rid of her. Not as much as I would have gotten if I'd married you, but enough that I can probably invest it and rebuild."

"My mother paid you?" He glanced to his mother who stared back at them. At least she had the decency to look chagrined.

"She did, and this little setup," she waved her hand toward the ballroom, "was her idea. She took care of the invitation and your beautiful blond friend over there. I took care of Gwen. Made sure she was here to see what she needed to see to think you were a lying cheat."

Drew had never hit a woman, and he didn't want to start now, but it took all his energy to keep from ripping her to pieces. Instead, he lowered his voice and leaned in as if he were going to whisper in her ear. "I'm going to find Gwen. If you ever show your face around her again,

I'll make sure your reputation is ruined forever. Do you understand me?"

She kept a brave face, but he saw a flicker of fear dance in her eyes. "Now, take your money and get out of my sight, Judas."

Avery stared at him a moment longer. Her eyes shifted to his mother and back to him. She opened her mouth to speak but then must have thought better of it. With a final angry stare, she spun on her heel and disappeared down the hallway.

Drew took a deep breath to calm his nerves before turning to his mother. His heart beat an insane rhythm in his chest, and he forced his feet to walk slowly and deliberately to give it time to slow down. "How could you, Mother?"

"I don't know what you're talking about," she said, tilting her nose up in the air.

"Avery told me everything. You paid her? Why? What's so horrible about Gwen that you had to pay someone to get her out of my life?"

"She's poor," his mother spat at him. "You are a Devonshire. You deserve more than some poor school teacher and keeping poor company would ruin our image."

Drew narrowed his eyes at his mother. "Well, you won't have to worry about our image any longer, Mother."

"There, see? I knew you would see it my way if you had a chance."

"You won't have to worry about our image because I will destroy it. I'm going to make sure everyone in this town knows what you did to Gwen."

"But, but, you can't," his mother stuttered. "We'll lose everything."

"We'll lose some things," he said. "You might have to downsize, but I'll keep what really matters. Honesty and integrity. The rest are just idols, and if you haven't figured it out by now, I no longer care about idols." With that, he turned and walked out of the room, leaving his mother and the other two women at his table gaping at him.

He pulled his phone from his pocket and dialed Gwen's number. It rang four times before her voicemail picked it up. "Gwen? It's Drew. I know what you think you saw tonight, but it was staged. Please let me explain. I'm coming over to talk."

He ended that call and dialed another number. "Manuel, get the car ready," he said as he hit the hallway. He had a woman he needed to find and offer an apology.

20

"Can't we go any faster, Manuel?" Drew was sitting beside him in the driver's seat instead of in his usual seat in the back.

"I'm sorry, sir. The snow is bad. I'm going as fast as I can." Manuel's hands gripped the steering wheel tightly in a perfect three and nine formation.

"I know, I don't mean to pressure you. I'm just worried about her." He closed his eyes and leaned his head back against the rest, sending a prayer up to his newfound savior. *Lord, help me find her. I can't lose her like this.*

"Mr. Devonshire, we are here, sir." Manuel was shaking his arm. Drew opened his eyes. Had he fallen asleep?

"Do you see her car?"

"No, but it is hard to see anything. The snow is getting worse. The news station said it is near blizzard conditions and that we should stay off the streets."

"All right, Manuel, let me see if she's in there. I'll be quick if I must, but I have to explain."

Manuel nodded, and Drew pulled the door open. A wall of white greeted him, and the snow whipped and tugged at his coat. He shut the door behind him and carefully made his way up the walk to Gwen's apartment. "Gwen?" He pounded on the door. "Gwen, if you're there, please let me in."

Behind him, the door of the apartment across the way opened. "Yo, man, I don't think she's there. She left like an hour ago and ain't been back since."

"Thank you," Drew said. If Gwen wasn't in her apartment where would she have gone? Carrie. Drew hurried back to the limo and pulled out his cell phone when he was back in the warmth. He hadn't thought he would ever call her, but he was glad he had gotten her number.

"Hello?"

"Carrie? It's Drew. Is Gwen there?"

"No, I thought she was with you. Didn't the two of you have a date?"

"We did, but there was a miscommunication. If she calls you, will you let me know?"

"Of course. Should I be worried, Drew?" He could

tell by the sound of her voice that she already was worried.

"I don't know yet, Carrie, but pray. I'll call you if I find anything out."

He hung up the phone and stared at it. Now what did he do?

"Sir?"

"Hang on, Manuel, I'm thinking." Drew closed his eyes again. He needed help of the omniscient kind. His lips moved slightly as he prayed for wisdom and guidance to find Gwen. Then his eyes snapped open. "Go back."

"Back where, sir? To the hotel?"

"Yes, like you're going back to the hotel, but we won't go that far. Just go slowly."

Manuel nodded and eased the limo out of the parking lot. They started back the way they had come with Drew hollering out a turn now and then. "Right here." "Left at the next street." Drew had no idea where they were going, but he could feel the words in his bones.

Suddenly, he sat up straighter and pointed. "There." Ahead of them, they could just make out the flicker of something in the snow. Drew noticed the darkened houses on either side of the road. Someone had hit a power line, and he knew, he just knew it was Gwen.

Sure enough, a few minutes later, her car came into sight. The car was pinned underneath the fallen power pole. "Call 911," he said to Manuel before sprinting out of the car toward Gwen.

A live wire flashed and jumped on the street and Drew gave it a wide berth. He was relieved to see the pole had missed Gwen when he reached the car, but they would still need the jaws of life to get her out. The pole had crushed the passenger side around her and mushed the dash, so it was pinning her thighs.

He yanked on her door, but it was no use. Her window was a spiderweb of cracks, so Drew jammed his elbow into the upper right corner. The glass shattered inward, falling on Gwen like iridescent drops. He hoped none of them would cut her, but he needed to know she was still alive.

"Gwen?" He reached in and felt for a pulse. There, but just barely. "Gwen? Can you hear me? Help is on the way, okay? Stay with me. Help is on the way."

Her eyes opened the tiniest bit. "Drew, what are you doing here?"

"Shh." He patted her hair. "Don't talk. I came to apologize. What you saw wasn't truth. It was staged to make you run."

"How did you find me?"

Drew shook his head. "I don't know. I followed a feeling."

The corners of her lips twitched as if she were trying

to smile. "I think that might have been God talking to you, Drew. Now do you believe he exists?"

Drew chuckled. "I do, Gwen. I accepted him earlier today. I was going to tell you tonight."

"That's good," she said and then her eyes closed again.

"Gwen?" He didn't want to shake her. He had no idea if she'd injured her neck. "Stay with me, Gwen."

The blessed sound of sirens reached his ears, but they could not come fast enough for Drew.

21

"How is she?" Carrie cried as she rushed toward Drew. Knowing she would be worried, he had called her as soon as the ambulance took Gwen away.

He shook his head. "I don't know yet. The doctor hasn't said."

"What was she doing driving in the snow? Didn't she know the storm was hitting tonight?"

"I don't think anyone knew it would hit that quickly," Drew said, avoiding her original question. He didn't want to tell her Gwen had been trying to get away from him even if what she had seen had been a lie.

"Mr. Devonshire?" Drew and Carrie both turned to the approaching doctor.

"Yes, I'm Drew Devonshire. Is… is she all right?"

"Physically, yes. She was very lucky the pole missed her. She'll have some bruising on her chest and legs from the impact, but that's not our main concern. Does Gwen have family we should notify?"

"Gwen's parents are dead," Carrie said in a small voice, "and she hasn't seen her foster parents in years. We're her family."

The doctor looked from Carrie to Drew. "Well, our bigger concern is that she isn't waking up. It could be that her body is just in shock, and she'll come out of it soon, but we don't know for sure."

Carrie sobbed and buried her face in Drew's chest. Instinctually, his arm wrapped around her shoulders. "Thank you, doctor. Please keep us informed if anything changes."

"I will." The doctor nodded before turning and walking back down the hallway.

"Drew, what are we going to do? I can't lose my best friend." Carrie's voice was muffled as she cried into his chest.

He led her to the seating area and pulled her down next to him. He took her hands in his and squeezed them. "Carrie, I don't believe God brought Gwen and I together only to have this end in tragedy. She has had too much sorrow in her life, and she deserves some happiness."

Carrie sniffed. "Yes, she does."

"So, we pray, and we sit with her. Why don't I take

the first shift? You should go and check on Tabby, especially since Gwen might be here for a few days."

Carrie nodded and wiped her cheeks. "Right. I can do that, and I'll close the shop tomorrow, so I can sit with Gwen."

"That sounds like a good plan." Drew stood and pulled her up beside him. "Drive home safely please."

"I will, but Drew, you better call me if she wakes up."

"I promise," Drew said. He watched Carrie exit the hospital into the blinding snow before collapsing back into the chair. He did believe God had plans for them, but it sure was hard to trust that right now.

"Drew Devonshire, I want a word with you."

His head popped up at his mother's voice. What was she doing here? How had she known where he was? Knowing his mother, she had pinged his cell phone. He certainly wouldn't put it past her. "Mother, what are you doing here? Haven't you done enough?"

"Done enough?" she asked. "What exactly have I done besides look out for you?"

He glared at her. "Do you not know, Mother? Gwen was in an accident after she fled the hotel. She's in a coma now, so I hope you're happy."

His mother reeled back as if punched in the stomach. "She's… but she's going to wake up, right?"

"They don't know, Mother. They have no idea if

she'll wake up again. Do you know the life this woman has had? No, you don't because you never bothered to get to know her. She lost her parents when she was twelve. She had a foster father who locked her in a closet. The one man she let get close to her proposed and then she found out he was cheating on her, and still this woman wears a smile. She became a teacher to help children like herself. She donates time and money to local foster care charities. She may not be wealthy monetarily, but she is rich in so many other ways, Mother, and you could never be bothered to see that."

His mother's hand covered her mouth and she sank down in a chair. For a moment she sat there, as if letting the words sink in. "Drew, I am so sorry. You're right. I judged her without knowing her, and I can see now how very wrong I was." She looked up at him with tear-filled eyes. "Please, tell me that you'll forgive me."

Drew wanted to snap at her, to tell her that he would never forgive her, especially if something happened to Gwen, but the sermons the pastor had been preaching on forgiveness resounded in his mind. He knew he had to forgive his mother. It was what God said, and it was right, but it wasn't easy. "I'm trying to, Mother. With the help of God, I'm trying to, but when Gwen wakes up, you will apologize to her as well. And if, after that, you don't want to be around her, that's your choice. But I am choosing Gwen, and you will either accept this relationship or we will part ways."

She wiped a tear from the corner of her eye. Drew couldn't remember the last time he had seen her cry, but he wasn't going to let that affect his decision. "I will, Drew. I haven't been the best example, but I'm going to change, and I will make this up to both you and Gwen." She stood and pulled her shoulders back. "I promise."

Drew hoped his mother would make good on that promise, but he didn't care right now. Right now, he just wanted to see Gwen, to hold her hand, and to pray.

22

Gwen tried to open her eyes, but they felt glued shut. And her body ached everywhere. What had happened?

"Hey, don't move too much."

Was that Drew's voice? Drew. Suddenly, the memories came flooding back. Drew proposing to his ex, her running out, and the car spinning out of control. She must have crashed.

It took all her energy, but she forced her eyelids open. The room was hazy, and she found it hard to focus. Then a face appeared in her vision. "Drew, what are you doing here?" Her voice came out soft and raspy. How long had it been since she had spoken out loud?

His face was still mostly a blur, but she could make

out his smile. "Are you kidding? I'm never leaving your side again."

"But Sarah-"

He shook his head. "Sarah was never real. Avery made her up to scare you away. She also sent the flowers and the note."

"Why?"

"She needed you out of the way, so she could try to entice me to marry her. She wanted my money. Evidently, she lost all of hers when she went to Europe. We had dated briefly before she left, and I guess she thought we could pick up where we left off. I don't know what happened to her while she was gone, but she is certainly not the same woman she was when she left."

Gwen let all of this sink in. She had left the hotel thinking that yet another man had betrayed her when it was really him who had been betrayed. Still that didn't explain why he was at the hotel to begin with. "Avery said you were working late. Why were you at the hotel?"

Drew's face fell. "I'm afraid my mother was in on some of this scheme too. She didn't want me falling for a girl with no money, so she hired Avery to get rid of you. She came to me the night of the benefit and told me I could keep my half of the fortune if I attended one final benefit. I was trying to save the jobs of my employees, so I went." He grabbed her hand. "I called you though and left a message. Did you never get it?"

Gwen shook her head slightly. Pain still pounded in her head like an orchestra of hammers. "No, but Avery came over that night and did a makeover on me. I was in my room for a few minutes. She could have done something to my phone. Then she packed my bag. I thought that was odd at the time, but I never bothered to check it. Was my bag in the car?"

Drew's eyes dropped to the floor for a moment. "Gwen, a power pole hit the car. It barely missed you. Shortly after they got you out, a spark from a downed line touched the gas that must have been leaking and the car went up in flames. They couldn't get anything else out. I'm sorry."

Gwen closed her eyes. She didn't care about the car. Not really. It was old - a 1993 Mitsubishi Mirage - but it had been paid for, and she couldn't afford to take out a loan on a new one, especially as she was missing work. Work. Her eyes popped open. "Drew, how long have I been here?"

Another side glance and his hand raked across his stubbled chin. Two sure signs it was longer than she hoped. "A week. You hit your head pretty hard and were in a coma."

"A week?" The words came out barely more than a squeak. "Do I even still have a job?"

"Of course, you do. I went there myself and explained the situation. That Carol in your office is a big fan of yours."

Gwen managed a small chuckle. "She's just glad she finally knows who the flowers were from."

At that, Drew let out a deep laugh. The chocolate tones of it tickled Gwen's ears. She could get used to that laugh. "I feel like you told me, Drew, but how did they find me? It sounds like it was close."

Two lines of concern creased Drew's brow. "You don't remember?"

"Guess not."

"I found you, Gwen. You spoke to me in the car. I thought you'd remember."

"Wait, you found me? How?"

Drew's smile widened, and a light danced behind his eyes. "I think God told me. I accepted him that morning and was going to tell you that night. When I found out what my mother and Avery had done, I had Manuel drive me to your place, but you weren't there. I called Carrie, but she didn't know where you were either, so I prayed. On the way back to the hotel, I heard- no, I felt directions in my head. Those directions led us straight to you."

"That's amazing, Drew." Gwen had thought he seemed different. Lighter, more smiley. This news explained it. "Tabby. Did someone take care of Tabby?"

"Don't worry. Carrie's been cat sitting dutifully. Now, if you feel up to it, you have another visitor."

Gwen wasn't sure she felt like more visitors. She still

didn't know the extent of her injuries, but he seemed so excited that she couldn't say no.

"Promise you'll hear her out," Drew said as he headed for the hallway.

Gwen didn't like the sound of that. Surely, he hadn't brought Avery here. She knew the Bible preached forgiveness, but she was going to need a little time. But it wasn't Avery who walked in. It was Jacqueline, and contrite didn't begin to describe her appearance. The haughty expression was gone from her face, replaced with what appeared to be genuine concern.

"Hello, Gwen."

"Jacqueline." She better have something good to say because as far as Gwen was concerned, she wasn't much better than Avery. Who hired someone to get rid of their son's girlfriend?

"I'm glad you agreed to see me."

"Well, in all fairness, I didn't know it was you." Stop it. Ephesians 4:32 filled her mind, and Gwen knew she needed to forgive Jacqueline as God had forgiven her.

"Yes, I suppose that's true. I came here today for a few reasons. The first is to tell you how truly sorry I am. Money and my place in society had become my idol. Drew's been helping me see the error of those ways." She flashed a tight smile Drew's direction. "I should never have tried to separate you. He cares for you a great deal."

She paused as if waiting for an acceptance of her apology, so Gwen gave what she could. "Thank you, Jacqueline. That means a lot."

The woman twisted her hands together in a nervous gesture and then reached into her bag. She withdrew a small green box with a bright red bow. "I know Christmas is still a few days away, but I wanted to give this to you now. I hope you'll accept it."

Gwen took the present. Curiosity outweighed her dislike of the woman, and she opened the lid. Inside was a key. She looked up to Jacqueline. "I don't understand."

"Drew told me the accident totaled your car, and I feel responsible for you crashing that night. I've already taken care of all your hospital bills, but I knew you'd need new transportation. This is a key to your new car. I wasn't sure what you would like, but Drew mentioned something about a Mini Cooper."

Gwen smiled as she touched the key. That conversation had happened over lunch one day. They had ventured into a topic of their love for all things British, and Gwen had told him of her secret desire to own a Mini Cooper one day.

"If you don't like it, I can have it returned, but-"

"I'm sure I'll love it, Jacqueline."

"Oh, good." Her hands twisted together again. "I have one more thing then. I'd like you to spend Christmas with us. I know I messed up Thanksgiving, but Drew and I have bonded over the last week, and I'd like to make it up to you."

Gwen nodded, her heart warming. If Jacqueline was acting, she was putting on quite the show. Gwen was much more inclined to believe the woman was changing or trying to at least. "I would like that."

Jacqueline's eyes brightened and the somber expression on her face lifted. "Yes? Oh, that's wonderful. Thank you, Gwen. I believe you might be as amazing as Drew claims you are."

"All right, Mother," Drew said, "I think you've propped me up enough. Don't put me too high on that pedestal or I might fall off."

"He's a keeper," Jacqueline whispered to Gwen before patting her arm. "It's time I let you rest anyway. I've got a Christmas party to plan." She flashed a small wave and then walked out of the room.

"I missed a lot in a week," Gwen said with a smile. She felt a little like Alice in Wonderland. Everything seemed different.

Drew issued another one of those deep laughs. "You did. God works in mysterious ways, and though I wouldn't wish your accident on anyone, I'm thankful it made my mother see the error of her ways. Oh, and I checked with the doctor. He will come examine you, but as long as he finds nothing out of the ordinary, he said you could go home today."

Home. She could think of no place she'd rather be.

23

"You look beautiful," Carrie said as she batted Gwen's hand down. "Stop messing with it."

"I'm sorry. It itches." Gwen had agreed to let Carrie take her for a full day of pampering before the Christmas dinner party. Her hands and feet were neatly painted, her skin was scrubbed fresh, and her hair was pulled up, but the woman had put a few too many pins in her hair and they were digging into Gwen's scalp. She tried one more time to scratch, but Carrie shot her a disapproving look. "Okay, fine. Thank you for coming with me by the way."

"Are you kidding? My pleasure. I want to live in a place like this someday. Who would have thought that you would live in a mansion before I did?"

Gwen scoffed and ducked her head as they walked up the ornate path. "I'm not living in one yet."

"You will be. I've seen the way Drew looks at you. He may not propose tonight, but if I were a betting woman, I'd wager he pops the question within six months, and you're married before next Christmas." Carrie pressed the doorbell.

Gwen hoped Carrie was right. Ever since she had returned from the hospital, her apartment had seemed lonelier. And even when Drew came over to bring her food or do a devotional with her, the stillness only abated while he was there. As soon as he left, it creeped in again with a quiet ferocity. Gwen knew it was because she had finally found the man she was supposed to be with. She could feel it in her soul every time they were together.

The door opened, and Pierre smiled at them. "Good evening, Miss Gwen and friend. Please come inside and join the festivities." He stepped back to allow them entrance, and Gwen gasped.

The room had been transformed into a magical wonderland. Christmas lights hung from the ceilings, tinsel draped across every surface, and at least three trees sat around the room.

"It's beautiful," she said in a hushed voice.

"Not nearly as beautiful as you." Drew had come up behind her and his arm circled her waist. His voice was quiet in her ear. He spun her around and stared into her eyes. "I'm afraid, Miss Gwen, that you are standing under mistletoe and that I am forced to supply you with a kiss."

Gwen giggled and glanced up to see Drew holding a sprig over their heads. "Well, we don't want to mess with tradition, now do we?"

"We do not," he said as his lips found hers.

Now this was home. In Drew's arms, in a warm house, with Christmas music playing in the background. This was the relationship Gwen had hoped for.

"All right, you two love birds," Carrie said breaking into the kiss. "You can resume that later. I, for one, would love some eggnog."

With a smile, Drew laced his fingers through Gwen's and led her into the kitchen. Jacqueline stood at the island icing cookies.

"Oh good, you made it. I just finished this batch. What do you think?" She turned the plate around and Gwen bit her lip to keep from smiling. The santas looked more like clouds and the colors on the trees clumped together, but she knew Jacqueline had worked hard on them.

"They look beautiful, and I'm sure they taste just as good."

"They better," Ernesto said stepping into the kitchen. "I worked hard on them all day." His eyes fell to the iced disasters. "Oh, no, what have you done to my cookies?"

"Come on," Drew tugged on Gwen's hand. "I have something for you." He pulled her out of the kitchen and over to one of the trees where he picked up a small gift and handed it to her.

"It's not present time yet," she said.

"Think of it as a gift to enhance your outfit," he said with a smile.

Gwen glanced down at her outfit. It was a hunter green dress with a red sash. She wasn't sure what else it needed, but she humored him and took the small package. As she lifted the lid, her lips parted, and emotion welled up in her throat. Inside was a dainty gold locket.

"Do you like it?"

"I love it," Gwen answered. She flicked the clasp and tears flooded her eyes. Somehow Drew had found a picture of her mother and father and they stared back at her now.

"This way you can always have them close to your heart." Drew picked the locket up and fastened it around her neck. Gwen stared at it one more time. She had never had a more thoughtful gift.

"Thank you, Drew Devonshire. This means the world to me."

His hands slid to her shoulders. "You mean the world to me, Gwen Rodgers. You've turned my world completely upside down in the short time that I've known you, but in a good way. You brought my mother and I closer together. You've pushed me to follow my dreams, and you've made me a better man. You are my Christmas miracle, and I love you."

"I love you too." Gwen wrapped her arms around his neck and let herself melt in his embrace. This would be a Christmas she would remember for a long time to come.

The End!

If you want to follow Carrie's story, be sure to check out The Billionaire's Cowboy Groom.

If you liked this storyplease leave a review at your retailer. Just a few words really helps!

IT'S NOT QUITE THE END!

Thank you so much for reading *The Billionaire's Christmas Miracle*. The Billionaire's Christmas Miracle was a fun book to write. I loved the idea of Drew, a wealthy good guy looking for something real, and Gwen, being the down-to-earth teacher (not unlike myself).

It was fun to do a Cinderella take. Perhaps I'll dabble in some more fairy tales in the future, but before I could even do that, readers wanted Gwen's and Drew's wedding, so of course I had to do that and decided giving Carrie her own book would be the perfect way. Keep reading for a sneak peek.

I hope you enjoyed the story as well. If you did, would you do me a favor? If you did, please leave a review at your retailer. It really helps. It doesn't have to be long - just a few words to help other readers know what they're getting.

I'd love to hear from you, not only about this story, but about the characters or stories you'd like read in the future. I'm always looking for new ideas and if I use one of your characters or stories, I'll send you a free ebook and paperback of the book with a special dedication. Write to me at loranahoopes@gmail.com. And if you'd like to see what's coming next, be sure to stop by authorloranahoopes.com

I also have a weekly newsletter that contains many wonderful things like pictures of my adorable children, chances to win awesome prizes, new releases and sales I might be holding, great books from other authors, and anything else that strikes my fancy and that I think you would enjoy. I'll even send you the first chapter of my newest (maybe not even released yet) book if you'd like to sign up.

Even better, I solemnly swear to only send out one news-letter a week (usually on Tuesday unless life gets in the way which with three kids it usually does). I will not spam you, sell your email address to solicitors or anyone else, or any of those other terrible things.

And if you're interested in meeting the rest of the billionaires in the series, be sure to check out The Billionaire's Cowboy Groom. Turn the page for a sneak peek.

LORANA HOOPES

The Billionaire's
COWBOY
Groom

A SWEET BILLIONAIRE'S ROMANCE

NOTE FROM THE AUTHOR

Thank you so much for picking up this book. After readers read The Billionaire's Christmas Miracle, I got a ton of emails wanting Drew and Gwen's wedding, so I obliged and decided to give Carrie her own story as well.

In addition, you'll see Max and Alyssa again from The Billionaire's Secret. If you haven't read it, be sure to pick it up to hear their story, and you'll get a glimpse of Sam and Brent from Brush with a Billionaire.

I hope you enjoy the story and the characters as they are dear to my heart. If you do, please leave a review at your retailer. It really does make a difference because it lets people make an informed decision about books.

Sign up for Lorana Hoopes's newsletter and get her book, The Billionaire's Impromptu Bet, as a welcome gift. Get Started Now!

C arrie zipped up the back of her best friend's dress and stepped back to admire it.

"Oh my goodness, Carrie, this is more beautiful than I even imagined." Gwen fingered the white satin, her hand trailing across the lace and bead detail. She turned and studied the image in the full-length mirror. With her red hair pulled up, her slender shoulders were even more defined in the strapless dress.

"Well, you deserve it. Besides, if you are going to marry Drew Devonshire and become a Devonshire, then you must dress like one." Carrie smiled at the vision that was Gwen. The white pearls and lace accentuated her creamy skin, and her green eyes sparkled. Happiness filled Carrie that she was able to make Gwen feel so good about herself.

"You are the best friend a girl could ask for." Gwen turned from the mirror and enveloped Carrie in a hug. "Now, let's get you dressed. Alyssa should be back soon."

Gwen had met Alyssa a few months after Drew proposed. Evidently, Drew had gone to college with Maxwell Banks, and they had reconnected when Drew searched for friends to make his groomsmen. It hadn't been too hard to find him considering they were both billionaires.

Max and Alyssa had visited, and Gwen and Alyssa had hit it off. They became close enough friends that Gwen had asked her to be a bridesmaid. Carrie didn't mind. Gwen needed more friends, and she liked Alyssa too. And of course, Peyton was a doll.

The door opened then and Alyssa and Peyton rushed in. Well, Peyton rushed in, Alyssa's entry was more of a waddle seeing as how she was eight and a half months pregnant. "Sorry, Gwen, when you gotta go, you gotta go."

"Wow, Miss Gwen, you look so pretty," Peyton stared up at Gwen with wide eyes. "Almost as pretty as Mommy looked when she married Daddy." Peyton looked back to Alyssa, her eyes full of admiration.

The girls all laughed. "Well, I wouldn't expect to look prettier than your mommy." Gwen smiled at Alyssa over Peyton's head. "And don't worry about the time.

Your dress is here. Carrie was just about to get dressed as well."

"I realize it's not my wedding, but I feel like a chicken with its head cut off." Alyssa patted her pregnant belly. "How do you two keep up here?"

"I hire help." Carrie laughed as she slipped out of her clothes and into her bridesmaid dress. The emerald green satin hugged her figure like a second skin. She was glad she had been so strict with her diet lately, or the dress might not have fit her. "I've had to hire another designer to help me."

"It's because you are so amazing," Gwen said. "I mean this dress is stunning." She twirled in front of the mirror again.

"I'd say she's a fan." Alyssa chuckled as she stepped into her own emerald green dress. Gwen had chosen emerald green because she thought both Carrie and Alyssa would look good in it. Alyssa's hair was a dark brown unlike Carrie's red locks, but the emerald green was a color that brought out the best in both of them. "I wish I had known you when I got married. I would have loved to have worn a dress you designed."

Carrie stepped over to the mirror to check her reflection. "I saw your wedding picture. Your dress was beautiful."

"Did you see my dress at Mommy's wedding too?"

Peyton asked. She was already in her flower girl dress and practicing throwing fake petals from her basket.

Carrie turned, smiled, and squatted down to the little girl's level. "As a matter of fact, I did. You looked just as pretty then as you do now." She tapped the end of the girl's nose earning a giggle in reply.

"Yes, it was beautiful," Alyssa said picking up the original thread of conversation again, "but there's something about having a friend make your dress that makes it extra special. I mean if you hadn't made this one, I doubt I would have found one that fit. I am as big as a house."

"You're welcome and you still look radiant," Carrie said. "When is the baby due?"

"A month. Can you believe that? It's a good thing you didn't plan this wedding any later, Gwen or they might not have let me fly."

"I'm sure Max would have found a way to get you here," Carrie said with a laugh. "I don't know him well, but he seems like a take charge kind of guy."

"Oh, he is that all right." Alyssa smoothed her dress and turned in front of the mirror. "What about you, Carrie? When are you going to marry that handsome French man I met? What was his name?"

"Philippe." Carrie shrugged her shoulders. "I'm not sure. He hasn't asked yet, but we've only been dating a few months." Of course, that was forever in Carrie's dating history. For as long as memory served her, she had flitted from one man to the next. Obviously, she was looking for something, but she wasn't sure what yet. She hoped she it would smack her in the face when she found it so she didn't miss it.

"Well, I'm sure it will be beautiful whenever it happens." Alyssa rubbed her belly again.

"And I'm sure this baby will be beautiful," Gwen said. "You better send pictures."

"Of course I will. Chances are he'll resemble this one though." She hugged Peyton to her. "Max's genes seem to run strong. Thank you, Gwen, for letting her be your flower girl."

"Yes, thank you, Miss Gwen. I promise to do a good job." Peyton's innocent face held the sincerest expression Carrie had ever seen on a person so young.

"I know you will, sweetie. Your mom said you are a natural at throwing flowers. And I have no younger sisters or nieces, so you are doing me the big favor." Gwen picked up the bag of flower petals and filled Peyton's basket.

Suddenly music carried into the room. "I think that might be our cue," Carrie said. "Everybody ready?"

"I can't believe it's finally time." Gwen's voice dripped with happiness and awe. Her face shone, and her smile stretched from one ear to the other.

As Carrie opened the door and led the way to the sanctuary, she wondered if she would ever have the same expression on her face. When would it be her turn?

Cal Roper looked down into the basket of baked goods as he tried to come up with the right words. Though everything looked and probably was delicious, he needed to find some way to make Ginny understand he wasn't interested in her romantically. She was as sweet as cherry pie, but he preferred apple.

"Thanks, Ginny, this was real nice of you," Cal said as he looked back up at the perky blond.

"Oh, you know me, Cal, always baking more than I need." She dropped her eyes to the ground and her toe dug a circle in the soft dirt. "So, I thought to myself - who could use some homemade goodies? And you popped right into my head." She glanced up and flashed him a megawatt smile revealing nearly every one of her teeth as she batted her eyes at him.

Cal supposed she was waiting for more than a thank-you. An invitation to dinner maybe or a ride on the mares, but he couldn't do it. He wouldn't lead the poor girl on.

"Well, I do appreciate it, and I'm sure Stacy will as well, right, sis?" He flashed his sister a help-me-out-will-you glance as he spoke.

Stacy opened her mouth to reply, but Ginny beat her to it. "Not that I'm sure you're not a good cook, Stacy," she added as if just realizing how insulting her words might have sounded to his sister.

Stacy held up her hands. "I take no offense. Cal does his own cooking. I just work here, but I'm sure we both will enjoy these muffins. It was real sweet of you to think of Cal."

Ginny smiled again and turned her eyes back to Cal. Her smile faltered when she realized he wasn't going to extend any sort of invitation. "All right, well I better be getting my own dinner going, so I guess I'll see you both at church on Sunday."

"We'll be there," Cal said, "and thanks again." He lifted the basket and forced a small smile.

"She likes you," Stacy said as Ginny walked away.

Cal sighed and dropped the basket onto the porch. "I suspected." Ginny was a nice girl. Cute with a bubbly personality and a believer, but his heart belonged to someone else.

"But?" Stacy pressed.

Cal shrugged. "But I'm not interested."

"You haven't been interested in the last three women who have shown an interest in you. You didn't have enough in common with Gabriella, you had too much in common with Heather, and Sophie lived too far away."

"Well, she did," Cal said. "I don't want a long-distance relationship."

Stacy fixed her steely gray eyes on him. She might be a year younger than him, but she could turn a heart to ice with her fierce expression. He would want her watching his back in a fight any day. "Cal, it's been six years. When are you going to let that woman go?"

"When God tells me it's time." He took his Stetson off and wiped the light sheen of sweat from his forehead though he wasn't sure if the sweat was from his recently finished chores or this conversation. "I know you think I'm crazy, but I married her and that means something to me. God hasn't told me it's time to move on yet, so I'm going to follow His will until He does."

Stacy's eyes softened. "Cal, I understand you want to do God's will, but you married this woman on a whim in Vegas. That's not what God had planned when He created marriage."

Cal nodded. While Stacy didn't have the whole story, she was right that he shouldn't have married the woman. Cal hadn't even believed in love at first sight, but when he'd seen the fiery red head in the casino, his heart had jumped. It spun. It danced the tango in his chest, and he just knew he couldn't lose her. After spending hours talking with her, he'd proposed to her, and she'd said yes. An all-night wedding chapel had been delighted to take their money, and Cal had spent an amazing night with the woman. Unfortunately, she hadn't been quite as excited about the marriage the next morning. She had begged him for an annulment and when he'd refused, she had thrown her ring at him and left.

"I know you write her every year." Stacy continued breaking into his walk down memory lane. "Has she ever responded?"

"Not yet, but she will." Every year on their anniversary, Cal sent her a card requesting a rekindling of their relationship. Every year, he heard nothing from her - he honestly wasn't even sure if his letters were even getting to her. Still, Cal felt deep down in his bones that someday he would hear from her. He might not have waited on God's timing to marry her, but now that they were married, he was determined to wait on God's timing to make it right. And God kept telling him to wait. So, he would. He would wait as long as he had to.

Carrie linked arms with Scott as Alyssa and Max reached the front. She had hoped to be able to walk the aisle with Philippe, but Scott was Drew's best friend. It only made sense he would be the best man. Besides, she would have plenty of time with Philippe at the reception, and he would be sitting in the first few rows on Gwen's side. She would have a great view of him.

"Ready?" Scott asked.

"Absolutely." In step, they walked up the aisle parting ways at the stage. Carrie stepped to her left to stand beside Alyssa and Scott went to his right to stand between Max and Drew. Carrie turned to face the congregation as the music changed. Her eyes scanned for Philippe first who flashed her a charming smile. She returned it and then shifted her gaze to the back of the church to watch Gwen enter.

The lights hit the pearls and sequins on the dress as she entered, and Carrie smiled as gasps of delight echoed around the room. She had never been prouder of one of her designs.

Gwen handed her the bouquet as she stepped on the platform and took Drew's hands.

"Dearly beloved, we are gathered here today to celebrate the marriage of Gwen Rodgers and Drew Devonshire. On the outside, they may seem like opposites - a teacher and a billionaire - but they have learned one of the most important lessons in life. They have learned to see past money and outside appearance and into the heart. It's what's in the heart that matters most, and in that respect, they are two of a kind. They love each other, and they love the Lord."

Carrie glanced at Philippe as the minister spoke. "You look beautiful," Philippe mouthed to her, and a blush stole across her cheeks. Could he be the one for her? She hadn't seen any red flags that sent her running yet, but she had expected to feel something different if he was the one. Some tug on her heart, the sound of fireworks, something.

"Do you Drew, take this woman as your wife to have and to hold through sickness and in health, forsaking all others until death do you part?"

Carrie shook her head to clear the thoughts. She had a job to do, and she needed to pay attention.

Drew's smile lit up his whole face as he said, "I do."

"And do you Gwen take this man as your husband to have and to hold through sickness and in health forsaking all others until death do you part?"

"I do."

"Then by the power vested to me by the great state of New York, I now pronounce you husband and wife. You may kiss the bride."

Carrie cheered along with the rest of the congregation as Drew leaned forward and kissed Gwen. Then they faced the church and held their hands up before running out the aisle. Carrie took Scott's arm and followed suit. They burst out the doors and joined Gwen and Drew in the foyer. Max, Alyssa, and Peyton joined them a moment later.

"Congratulations, Gwen," Carrie said enveloping her in another hug. "You looked so beautiful."

"I'll second that," Drew said. "Carrie, that dress is perfection."

"Well, I had a good model." She handed the bridal bouquet back to Gwen. "You might need these."

"I might, but I have a sneaking suspicion it'll be finding its way back to you soon enough." Gwen took the flowers and flashed a knowing glance at Carrie.

"I'm not sure about that," Carrie said with a shake of her head. "Philippe doesn't seem in any hurry to propose."

"He will," Alyssa said joining the conversation. "I predict a wedding in your near future."

Carrie appreciated the sentiments of her friends, but she wasn't so sure. Philippe may have been her longest relationship in years, but they were only going on four months. It was way too early for him to propose, and she was still sorting out her feelings. "Come on, we better get to the reception area before the stampede hits," Carrie said changing the subject.

"Just not too fast." Alyssa placed her hands on her large belly. "This pregnant woman can only go so quickly."

"We'll see you there in a minute," Gwen said as Drew pulled her toward the holding room where they would wait a few minutes to give the rest of the congregation time to get to the reception area.

Carrie led the way down the hallway and opened the

doors to the reception area. It was decorated with white lights and tulle. White roses nestled in green foliage covered every tabletop and large windows granted expansive views of the city. The elegance, though understated, permeated the room. Gwen's personality shone through in every simple touch.

"Wow," Peyton said beside Carrie. "It looks like a princess lives here."

Carrie nodded. "Her wedding planner was pretty amazing, but I think most of this was Gwen's idea. I'm guessing that's our table up there on the stage. Shall we go find a seat?"

"Yes, please," Alyssa said. "I would love to get out of these shoes."

By the time they sat down, the rest of the guests were making their way in. Philippe joined Carrie at the head table. "That was a nice ceremony."

"It was." Carrie stared at him a moment wondering if he ever imagined what their wedding might look like.

"Ladies and gentlemen." The DJ's voice interrupted her moment, "please welcome for the first time Mr. and Mrs. Devonshire."

The room erupted in clapping and cheers as Gwen and Drew walked over to their table. As soon as they sat down, the waiters began bringing out the dishes. Carrie only picked at the delicious food, afraid if she ate too much that she would bust the seams on her dress. It was already getting uncomfortable just from sitting.

When the bride and groom finished eating, Scott and Carrie each gave their toast, and then Gwen and Drew danced their first dance.

"Come on." Carrie grabbed Philippe's hand when other couples were invited to the floor. This was the moment she had waited for. Carrie loved dancing and Philippe would never indulge her, but surely, he wouldn't say no at a wedding. It was expected guests would dance at a wedding.

"I don't dance," he said with a shake of his head. "I've told you that before."

"I understand, but it's my best friend's wedding. I want to dance at her wedding."

"Two left feet." He pointed to the floor. "Don't like making a fool of myself."

"But what about our-" Carrie snapped her mouth shut. She had been about to ask him about their wedding and he hadn't even proposed yet. She must be caught up in the wedding fever.

"Our what?" he asked.

"Nothing, I'm going to grab some punch." She turned away before the hurt expression on her face displayed her true feelings. If they did marry, would he not dance with her? Surely, he would make an exception for his own wedding.

"May I have this dance?"

Carrie looked to her left to see Max staring at her with his hand outstretched. "No, it's fine, really."

"Come on, Alyssa sent me over here. She's too pregnant to dance. Besides, it might help your man see what he's missing."

Carrie glanced over at Alyssa who smiled and shot her a thumb up sign. "Okay," she said with a laugh. "If it's all right with Alyssa. She's a pretty amazing woman."

Max situated her in his arms when they reached the dance floor. "Don't I know it. She's way too good for me. You know, I never expected I'd marry. I was rather like you - a serial dater, though I wasn't as nice about it. I was pretty awful to the women I dated." He spun her around. "My point is that if I can find love, you can too."

"Thank you." Carrie smiled up at him. He might not have started out a kind man, but he certainly was now.

After Max, she danced with Scott, then Drew, then random guests who came and asked her. It almost seemed as if they were keeping her busy to distract her from remembering her own date's refusal to dance, but Carrie didn't mind. Before she knew it, it was time for the bouquet toss. She lined up with the other women, and Gwen's aim was as true as her word. The bundle of flowers landed squarely in her hands.

"I told you," Gwen said before she was whisked away.

Carrie smiled and then turned to Philippe. She almost laughed at the pained expression on his face as she held up the bouquet. It was a silly tradition, but she couldn't help hoping that maybe catching the bouquet would turn things around for her. With all her friends married or getting married, she was starting to long for that solid foundation as well.

2

"Carrie, you are not going to believe this." Excitement filled Gwen's voice as she burst through Carrie's boutique door.

Both Sierra's and Carrie's head shot up at the outburst. Carrie dropped the paper she was sketching on and rushed to her friend throwing her arms around her. "Gwen, you're back. I've missed you so much."

Gwen laughed as she returned the embrace. "It's only been two weeks, Carrie."

"I know, but I've been so bored without you here."

"Hey," Sierra piped up from the back of the store where she was working on an alteration. "What am I? Chopped liver?"

Carrie flashed an apologetic glance toward her assistant. "Sorry. I've just missed my best friend."

"Well, I doubt boredom will plague much longer. Did you see this?" Gwen held up the paper clasped in her hand.

Carrie took it and scanned the page. Her eyes widened as she read the headline. "The wealthy elite may have found their next Vera Wang in Carrie Bliss?" She sped through the rest of the article which highlighted Gwen's and Drew's wedding and included a large picture of Gwen's dress. Underneath it was an entire paragraph dedicated to Carrie and her business. She looked up at Gwen. "When did this run?"

"A few days ago. Are you telling me you really hadn't seen it?"

Carrie shook her head. She rarely read newspapers or even watched the news. "No, but my phone has been ringing off the hook with orders since yesterday. I guess this explains it. I'm going to need to hire another few seamstresses to help me sew all these dresses."

"Yes, please," Sierra's voice carried from the back.

"Carrie that's amazing. I bet you'll hit billionaire status before the end of the month."

Carrie hadn't even made that connection. It was what she wanted more than anything in the world, but she thought it would still be a few more years in the future. She'd only been a multi-millionaire for a few years. However, with Gwen's wedding dress splashed all over the page and her name listed as the designer, perhaps she would hit it sooner than she thought.

"We should celebrate," Carrie said. "Do you think Drew will let me pry you away from him for dinner tonight?"

Gwen smiled. "I'm sure he could use a break from me, but what about Philippe? How are things on that front?"

"Same as ever." Carrie shrugged. "I finally find a man I might want to commit to and he has no desire. Always the way, right?"

"I'm sure he'll get there. Sometimes, it takes men a little longer to realize what they have." Gwen squeezed her arm and offered a sympathetic smile.

"Yeah, you're probably right," Carrie said. The phone began ringing again behind her, and she sighed. "You know what? Let's start the celebration early."

"What about your orders?" Gwen asked indicating the ringing phone.

"Let Sierra get it. It's partly what I hired her for." In truth, she had hired Sierra to help her sew, but answering phones had been a small part of her job description. Today, it would just be a larger part. She would need to get more help started soon.

"Okay, if you're sure. I would love to catch up."

"And tell me all about the honeymoon." Carrie

ducked behind the counter to grab her purse. "Sierra, I'm heading out for the day. Don't forget to lock up."

Sierra, phone to her ear, shot Carrie a look of frustration but waved. Carrie would have to do something nice for Sierra after leaving her with all the work today, but she so wanted to catch up with Gwen.

"Well, I'll tell you some of the honeymoon, but I'm keeping some parts to myself," Gwen teased as they exited Carrie's boutique.

Cal sighed and raked a hand through his hair as he stared down at the bill. Even if he sold half his cattle, he would only buy himself a few months. He needed a miracle and he needed it soon.

"Not good news, huh?" Stacy's voice carried across the room and he turned to see her leaning in the doorway.

"No, it's not. That sickness last year hit us hard. We don't have nearly the herd we would have had this year if half of them hadn't been wiped out."

"So, what are you going to do?"

Cal let out his breath and shook his head. "I have no idea. I'll sell half of what I have, see if I can get an extension on the loan, and pray."

"Cal, I know you don't want to think about it, but Ginny's family is wealthy. Maybe if you-"

Cal cut her off before she finished. "I'm not doing it, Stacy. I will not court a woman just for her money. Besides, I'm still married, and I'm not giving up on her yet."

Concern filled Stacy's eyes. Cal knew she worried about him. She was already married and had a wonderful family, and he... he was still waiting. Waiting for a woman who might never come around. But right now that was a good thing. He didn't need any added distractions while he thought about how to save his ranch.

"All right, Cal. Well, will you come to dinner? Annie and Trevor miss their uncle."

"I'll try, Stacy. I've got a lot to do today." He needed to check on the cattle and the fence to make sure there were no weak spots. Cal certainly couldn't afford to lose any more cattle. Then perhaps he would ride over to The Morrison ranch to see if the fellow rancher might be interested in a trade. If he could save on the price of hay, another month of payment might be possible. It wasn't much but it might give him time to come up with another plan.

The concern on Stacy's face deepened. "Don't work too hard, Cal. There's more to life than the ranch."

Maybe for her - she had the general store to fall back on - but Cal was born to ranch. He was happiest when he was on his horse with the sun shining down on him. Yes, he could probably find another job where he rode, but it wouldn't be the same. There was something about owning your own piece of land that he would miss if he was forced to sell it.

"I'll come by soon. I promise." He grabbed his hat off the desk and gave her a hug before continuing to the back door.

The warm air kissed his face. Cal scanned the horizon, but the sky was clear. There would be no rain today. With a sigh, Cal continued to the barn and saddled up his favorite horse, Ginger. Her coat was the color of chocolate - more brown than red, but he couldn't bring himself to name her Chocolate when he bought her six years ago, so he'd picked Ginger. She had been his first purchase when he took over the ranch, and he probably shouldn't have bought her. Buying her sent him upside down the first year, and he had yet to recover fully, but she was worth the cost as far as he was concerned.

"All right, girl, let's go for a little ride, shall we?" He walked her out of the barn and shut the door. Then with a graceful ease, he swung himself onto the saddle. The hard leather of the saddle didn't mold, not really, but he felt like it did. In the saddle was where he belonged and there was always a sense of coming home when he mounted up.

He led Ginger along the north side of the property

first. The Morrison ranch was to the south, so he might as well save it for last. His eyes scanned the fence as he continued down the line. It appeared to be in decent shape, but it ought to - the snow the previous winter had buckled several pieces of wood and he'd had to replace a good portion of the fence. That had been another unseen expense especially as Soda Spurs didn't get snow that often.

Satisfied the fence was in good condition, he turned his attention to the herd. There were too many to count individually, but he had learned a long time ago to scan the herd and visually identify ten to twenty at a time. It wasn't a perfect count, but it was one he could do daily and be fairly accurate. He did a more thorough count once a week.

When he was confident no cattle were missing, he scanned the grass. It was looking a little thin on this side. He'd have to move the herd soon and hope for rain. If he could just catch a break, he might be able to start turning a little profit.

Cal urged Ginger toward the south fence. He'd worry about the grass tomorrow. Right now, he needed to finish checking the fence. The wood on this side also appeared in good shape, so he led Ginger off his property and over to Don Morrison's ranch.

Cal found Don working with a new colt in his corral. Frustration creased the older man's face, and a stiffness filled his posture.

"Hey, Don, you got a minute?" Cal asked as he pulled Ginger to a halt.

Don looked up and smiled. "Sure, Cal, I need a break from this guy anyway." He led the colt back to the barn and Cal dismounted. A few minutes later, Don returned. "So, what can I do for you?"

"That illness last year hit my herd pretty hard. I was hoping perhaps you might be interested in a little trade to save money. I could break that colt for you if you have extra hay or grass."

Don rubbed his chin as he considered the offer. "This one is being more difficult than normal. I could save some time if I wasn't having to break him. All right, Cal, you got yourself a deal."

"Thank you, Don." The two men shook hands and exchanged small talk for a little longer before Cal bid him goodbye and returned to his ranch. It wasn't a permanent solution, but he would take all the time he could get.

3

Carrie stared at the paper in her hand. Wow, that happened quickly. The story on Gwen's dress ran only a week ago, and while orders had quadrupled, Carrie hadn't expected her wealth to increase with such speed. Still, it pleased her. She felt... secure for the first time in a long time.

It was stupid really. She had always been wealthy; her father had been a millionaire. He even gave her a trust fund to get her shop started, but shortly after college, her father had been diagnosed with cancer. The resulting medical bills wiped out his money and as her mother was a homemaker, there was no income coming in to offset them.

Carrie offered to sell her boutique to help out, but her father refused. He hadn't beaten the cancer, but his life insurance policy had at least allowed her mother to keep the house she'd lived in for the last thirty years. Carrie promised herself then though that she would be richer than her father. She wasn't sure a billion dollars would protect her from facing the same fate, but it made her feel better.

The bell above the door jingled and she looked up and smiled. Philippe stood in the doorway. He flashed her a wicked, sexy smile and strode her direction.

"Are you ready for dinner, Chéri?" She loved his French accent and the fact he called her Chéri. It didn't hurt that he was devastatingly handsome either.

"Yes, just let me grab my purse." Carrie folded the paper and shoved it in the drawer under her register. She would have to show Gwen later and thank her.

After ducking into the back room to grab her bag and coat, she stopped by the sewing room to inform Sierra and the new hires she was leaving for the night. Then she returned and linked her arm through Philippe's.

"Where are we going tonight?" Carrie asked as they stepped out into the crisp evening air. Winter seemed to be hanging around a lot longer this year though no more snow was predicted. Carrie longed for spring. She detested winter, except for Christmas of course. Maybe it was because she got cold too easily or perhaps it was her love of wearing short sleeves and skirts - neither of which were practical in the cold New England winters.

"Someplace special." He opened the door of his silver BMW for her and she slid in relishing the feel of the leather seats. While she enjoyed having a driver, she liked that Philippe drove his own car. Sometimes it was nice to do things for yourself. She hoped that wouldn't change now that she was officially a billionaire. Though they were trying to break the stereotypes, Gwen often shared some of the crazy requirements that Drew faced as a billionaire.

"Oh, yeah? What's the occasion?" Carrie didn't dare to hope that he would be proposing - it was probably still too soon - but that would be a nice occasion. Philippe seemed to fit the bill of the perfect man in her head, and while most of her relationships lasted a month or less, she could envision herself with Philippe. He was driven, nice, and he attended church with her.

"You'll see," he said and flashed her a wink as he started the car.

A few minutes later, they pulled into an upscale Italian restaurant. Carrie bit her lip as disappointment surged through her. While she loved Italian food, she avoided it most of the time to keep her trim figure. Philippe knew that, or she thought he did. Plus, he was French. Why wouldn't he take her to a French restaurant? Well, she supposed the restaurant would have a salad.

"Come on," he said as he turned off the ignition and opened his door.

Carrie's lips pulled into a tight smile as she unbuckled her seatbelt. She pushed open her side and took his hand when he offered it.

Philippe held the restaurant door open, and they stepped into the quaint building. The sweet smell of tomatoes and garlic and bread floated on the air. Carrie tried not to inhale too deeply. Just sniffing bread always seemed to put five pounds on her. Instead, she focused on the intricate artwork on the wall that displayed a vineyard and an Italian chateau. The designer had even added lines to make it appear cracked and faded giving it a charming vintage look.

"Hello, we have reservations under Caron," Philippe said as he approached the hostess, a smart looking blond in black pants and a pressed white shirt.

"Very good, sir. Follow me." She led the way toward the back of the restaurant to a small booth lit by candlelight and a small lamp attached to the wall. Curtains hung around the booth giving it an extra measure of privacy.

"This is nice," Carrie said as they sat. The hostess handed them menus and then as if sensing they wanted to be alone, she turned and walked away.

"Only the best for my girl." He took her hand and stared into her eyes.

"Ah, that's sweet."

"I hope it's enough. It's my first time dating a billionaire." He flashed her a crooked smile as if he were teasing, but there was a seriousness behind his words like he believed she required different treatment.

More than that though were the words themselves. She had just found out her net worth today and had told no one. So how did he know? "Who said I'm a billionaire?" Carrie asked as she pulled her hand back and took a sip of her water.

For a moment, his face held the expression of a child caught with his hand in the cookie jar. Then it shifted and a genuine smile lit his features. "Well, I understand business has picked up since the article on you ran, and you are such an amazing designer that I can't believe you aren't there already. I presume you will be soon."

Relief flooded Carrie. Would it always be like this? Would she second guess everyone's intentions? "That's very nice of you to say, but I owe my success mostly to Gwen. It was her wearing my designs that got me noticed."

He took a sip of his water. "Yes, it's good to have wealthy friends, but you were on your way there before Gwen."

Philippe couldn't know that since he entered her life after Gwen had started wearing her designs, but it was sweet of him to say. And she probably would have gotten there herself, but having Gwen wear her wedding dress had shot her up the ladder faster than she had imagined. Still, she didn't want to talk money with Philippe. Perhaps it was a baseless fear, but Carrie needed to know he wanted to be with her for her and not for her money.

"Thank you, but let's talk of something else. How is business for you going?"

Philippe ran a computer consulting firm. They helped businesses choose the best computers for their needs, aided in setting up their systems, and repaired them when needed. Philippe wasn't hurting for money either which was another thing Carrie liked about him. The fact that he made his own money made her less wary of him being after hers. But, she believed her worth was higher than his, and she knew that bothered some men. He never said anything, but she'd known many men in the past who hid their feelings behind calm exteriors until they finally exploded.

"Can't complain. Business is going well."

The waitress appeared then and placed a basket of bread in the middle of the table. "Are you ready to order?"

Carrie opened her mouth to ask for more time - she hadn't even surveyed the menu - but Philippe spoke before her words formed.

"We'll both have the Tour of Italy and two glasses of red wine," Philippe said.

Carrie stared at him incredulously. He had never ordered for her before and she didn't appreciate it now. "Um, I don't feel like pasta tonight. I'll just have whatever salad you recommend." She locked eyes with the waitress to convey her seriousness.

The waitress's eyebrow rose as she scratched the order out on her pad. "Okay. Anything else?"

"Sorry, I thought since it was a special occasion-" Philippe began.

"It's fine," Carrie said interrupting him. Although it wasn't fine. She probably wouldn't mind his ordering for her if he took her dietary needs into consideration, but he hadn't even consulted her or asked what she wanted. "I'm simply craving salad is all."

"All right, a salad for the lady and the Tour of Italy for me. Also a bottle of your best red wine."

"Of course, sir." The waitress hightailed it from their table as if she couldn't wait to escape the tension.

A silence fell. Philippe grabbed a piece of bread from the basket. Carrie was tempted to as well, but she'd just put her foot down about pasta; she'd feel like a hypocrite if she did. Still, she wished she had something to chew on to fill the heavy silence.

Philippe finished his bite and then looked at her. He cleared his throat. "I was going to wait for dessert, but perhaps this is the right time." His hand reached into his pocket, and he pulled out a box. "I know we haven't been seeing each other that long, Carrie, but I love you. And my heart tells me you are the woman for me. Would you do me the honor of being my wife?" Philippe flicked open the box, and Carrie stared at the ring.

A thousand different things ran through her mind: they hadn't been dating long enough, the ring was beautiful, why hadn't he gotten down on one knee, did she love him? But none of them were the real reason that gave her pause. That was a secret she had told no one. Yet.

Cal stared at the piece of wood in his hands. Usually, inspiration hit him as soon as he held the block of wood, but this time it was slow in coming. It was probably the stress from the lack of money. He'd managed to get an extension with the bank, but it was simply plugging a hole to slow the leak and not stopping it entirely.

"You know, you could sell some of your carvings as a side job." Stacy set a mug of coffee on the table next to him.

"That's what I told him," Jim, Stacy's husband, said from across the room. "I'm sure I would sell a ton of them at the store." Jim and Stacy owned the general store in Soda Spurs. She did the books for both the store and his ranching business while Jim ran the day-to-day operations.

"Plus, I bet you could make an online store and sell them there too." Stacy sat on the other side of the couch Cal occupied. "Isn't that what everyone does nowadays? Set up stores and sell things online?"

"Maybe some do, but I wouldn't even know where to begin." Cal turned the wood over in his hand again. Maybe a horse. He could whittle a horse like Ginger or perhaps a dog like Dexter.

"I bet Ginny would help you with that," Stacy pushed, "I've heard she's pretty computer savvy. Just another reason you guys would complement each other so perfectly."

Cal glared at his sister. "Stacy, we've been over this. I'm not interested in Ginny, and I'm not going to use her for her money or her computer skills."

Stacy's shoulders pulled back in a defensive posture. "I'm only trying to help."

"I know, but I'm not ready yet." Cal brought the knife to the wood and scraped off a sliver of wood. He wished he was. He wanted to start a family soon, but right now his heart still belonged to the fiery red head who had stolen it six years ago. It wouldn't be fair to date any other woman seriously until he could give her his whole heart. Cal just wondered when he would ever be able to do that.

With a sigh, Stacy turned her attention to her husband and they caught up on the rest of the day's events. This time, after dinner and after the kids had gone to bed was their best time to share about their day and Cal often felt like he was intruding. His knife continued to scrape against the wood, and he wasn't surprised when the image that began to appear was the heart- shaped face of the woman he could never seem to get out of his head.

4

"Philippe proposed?" Gwen's eyes shot to Carrie's hand. Disbelief filled her voice.

Carrie glanced down at the large diamond ring on her left hand. It still felt foreign and not completely right. "Yeah."

Gwen's brow furrowed sending tiny crinkle lines across her forehead. "You don't seem excited."

"No, I am, it's just that..." Carrie bit her lip. She had shared most of her past with Gwen, but there was one tidbit she had never told her - never told anyone.

"What?" Gwen asked. Concern replaced the shock and Gwen leaned across the table to give Carrie her full attention. Carrie loved that about Gwen, how effortlessly her emotions shifted.

Carrie's eyes fell to the floor and she studied the

speckled flooring of her kitchen as she tried to formulate the words in her mind, "There's something I never told you. It happened before we met, and it… well it's embarrassing."

Gwen chuckled and leaned back in the chair. "Embarrassing? This is me you're talking to, remember? I'm the one who spilled water on my future mother-in-law at a high brow gala. I should have a degree in embarrassing."

Carrie was glad that money hadn't changed Gwen. She was still the same warm, caring person she had always been. "Yeah, but that was water. Nothing permanent. Trust me, this is much worse."

An impish expression stole across Gwen's face, and she wiggled her eyebrows. "What? Do you have some criminal past I am unaware of? Let me guess. You got caught streaking across campus your freshman year."

"No, nothing like that," Carrie said with a laugh. "At least I hope not. There were a few parties before I met you that are a little hazy, but I would remember that, right?"

Gwen's eyebrow arched, and Carrie chuckled. "I'm kidding."

"Okay," Gwen shrugged, "so if you're not a closet streaker, I doubt you have anything to worry about."

Carrie sighed. She didn't know about that, but she did need her best friend's advice. She took a deep breath and spilled it out. "So, on my twenty-first birthday, some friends and I flew out to Vegas. We got drunk, of course, I mean that's what you do in Vegas when you're twenty-one, right?"

"I wouldn't know," Gwen said softly.

Carrie blinked at her. Had the girl never had a wild side? She realized Gwen had lived a simpler life, but had she never let loose? Carrie shook her head to clear the rabbit trail thoughts. "Right, well anyway, I guess I was so out of it that I sort of... got married." Carrie's gaze dropped to the tabletop as the heat crawled up her neck.

"Wait, you sort of did what?" Gwen's eyes grew to the size of quarters, and she leaned farther across the table.

"I know," Carrie moaned as she dropped her head onto her hand. "It was crazy and wrong and and I barely even knew the man, but I guess I thought I felt something there. I agreed to marry him, and the next morning when I woke up, he was there."

Gwen's eyes softened. "Okay, I mean mistakes happen, but are you sure it was even legal? A lot of people think they get legally married in Vegas, but they really don't."

"No, I remember getting the marriage certificate before we went to the chapel. They still require a certificate, but you can get it within an hour. No three-day waiting period in Vegas." Carrie raised her head. "Why is there no three-day waiting period in Vegas?"

A soft chuckle escaped Gwen's lips. "Well, probably because people want to get married quickly. But, why didn't you get it annulled? You could have done that the next morning. Claimed insanity or something."

Carrie shook her head. "I... I don't know. I've asked myself that same question many times over the years. I do remember asking him that first morning, but he said we belonged together, and he wouldn't agree. I couldn't convince him, so I think I just convinced myself it hadn't happened, and then I guess I forgot about it for a while, but now it's an issue. I won't be able to get a marriage license as long as I'm still married."

"Do you remember his name? Anything else?" Gwen crossed to the stove and set the kettle boiling. Evidently, she felt this conversation needed tea.

"His name is Cal Roper. He lives in a small town in Texas - Soda Pop or something like that."

A small smile played across Gwen's lips as she crossed to the pantry. "That seems like a lot to remember from one night six years ago. Just how do you know where he lives?"

Busted. Carrie cleared her throat. "Hang on."

Gwen turned from the pantry, an inquisitive look on her face and the box of green tea in her hand.

Carrie rose from the table and walked down the hall

to her room. On the top shelf of her closet was an innocuous red shoe box. Any person who looked in her closet would simply think it was a pair of shoes she hadn't unpacked. Goodness knew she had enough of them, but that wasn't what the box contained. She pulled the box down and took a deep breath before opening the lid. Inside were six plump envelopes. One for every year she and Cal had been married.

She wasn't even sure why she had kept the letters. Maybe it was to reminisce. Every once in a while, she would pull them down and read over them. Maybe it was to remind her not to be so spontaneous in the future. Whatever the reason, she had them and she was about to share them with another person for the first time.

Carrie took a deep breath and returned to the kitchen. She set the box on the table and glanced at Gwen whose face still held a quizzical expression. "I know all that information because he writes me every year on our anniversary."

"Is that why you get so weird around your birthday?" Gwen opened the cupboard that held the mugs. She grabbed two and placed them on the counter near the stove.

Carrie nodded and picked up a letter. "Every year, I get a card from him a few days before my birthday. He tells me it wasn't a mistake, and he asks me to come see him." She slipped the letter out of the envelope and scanned the slanted writing.

"Carrie," Gwen's voice was soft, like a gentle caress, "Do you think maybe Cal is why you can't settle down with anyone?" She dropped a tea bag in each mug and leaned against the counter.

"What?" Carrie's jaw dropped open, and she shook her head. "No way. I don't belong with Cal. He's…. he's a cowboy on a ranch somewhere. He's probably dirty all the time. Can you imagine me on a ranch with animals?"

"Well, I've never thought about it, but love can change people. I would never have imagined myself marrying a billionaire, but it happened."

"Yeah, but that's totally different, Gwen. You're in love with Drew. You two belong together. I was young and stupid and-"

"And you've never done anything about it." Carrie opened her mouth to protest, but Gwen held up her hand. "I'm just saying that maybe there is a reason you never did anything about it. Maybe there's a reason you don't stick with men very long. Maybe there's a reason you've kept every letter he mailed you. Maybe this Cal holds more of your heart than you want to admit."

"But, but it was just one night." Even as she said the words, Carrie wondered if Gwen might be right.

Her longest relationship after that night in Vegas had been two months until Philippe. She always found some reason to stop dating the men. They were too stiff, they were too free-spirited, they didn't make enough, they worked too many hours. But she couldn't really be comparing them to Cal, could she? What did she even remember about Cal?

She remembered twinkling green eyes and a charming smile. She remembered the cutest dimple in his right cheek and the way his arms felt around her as they danced across the floor. Oh, dear. Did she really have unresolved feelings for Cal? No, those were just physical characteristics. He had been handsome, but so what? Philippe was handsome too, and she loved him. Didn't she? She glanced down at the diamond on her left hand, but suddenly she wasn't so sure.

"Sometimes one night is all it takes," Gwen said with a slight shrug of her shoulders. "I knew after one night with Drew that something was there. I was just too stubborn to do anything about it at first." She cocked an eyebrow. "Perhaps stubbornness is a trait we share."

The tea kettle whistled then halting the conversation for a moment as Gwen turned off the kettle and poured the water into the two mugs. She handed one to Carrie and blew softly into her own. "So, when are you going down there?"

"Soon," Carrie said with a small sigh. "I have to remedy the situation. Hopefully Sierra can run the store while I'm gone." Sierra had been her assistant for three months and knew her way around the shop. In addition, Carrie had hired Lilly to answer the phones and take orders and Devyn who was a whiz with the sewing machine and could whip out Carrie's designs in a few days.

"I'm sure she will have no problem doing that," Gwen said. She set her cup down on the table and picked up an envelope.

"Yeah, this just isn't how I thought I'd be celebrating," Carrie said.

"Well, you can still celebrate. Have you told Philippe?"

"No, and I'm not sure I want to." Carrie had been pondering what to tell Philippe since the night before. How did she tell her fiancé that she had to go get divorced before they could marry?

Gwen pulled the letter from the envelope and scanned the contents. "If you don't tell him the truth, what will you say?"

Carrie didn't miss the disapproving tone in Gwen's voice. "I don't know. Maybe just that I have some business to take care of. It certainly wouldn't be a lie."

Gwen set the letter down and fixed Carrie with a knowing stare. "No, but it wouldn't be the whole truth either, and you know how things can spiral out of control when there're secrets."

"I know. I know," Carrie said shaking her head.

She'd figure out what to say to Philippe later. Right now, she just wanted to change the conversation. "The engagement wasn't really what I was talking about celebrating though."

"You have more to celebrate?"

Carrie chuffed softly glad that the letters had been forgotten for now. "I made it into the billionaire's club."

Gwen's mouth fell open. "What? That's terrific, Carrie. I know you've wanted it for ages."

"Well, I have you to thank. That article and the picture of you wearing my wedding dress got me noticed. I didn't think it would happen that quickly, but I got the notice from my accountant yesterday that I'm officially a billionaire."

"That's wonderful, Carrie." Gwen's eyes sparkled as she set her mug down and squeezed Carrie's arm. Then her features shifted. "Did you... did you tell Philippe?"

"Not exactly. The paper came before he picked me up and I didn't say anything about it, but he did mention dating a billionaire at dinner." She narrowed her eyes at Gwen. "Why do you ask?"

Gwen's eyes slid to the ground. "I don't know. I don't want to speak ill about him as I don't know him as well as you do, but I just wonder at the timing of it."

Anger flared within Carrie. "You think he's only asked me to marry him to get my money?"

Gwen shook her head. "I didn't say that, but you two haven't been dating long."

"Drew proposed to you after only a few months." Carrie knew she was being defensive, but she couldn't help it. Gwen had hit on the very insecurity Carrie had been struggling with. She liked Philippe, but she also wondered at his timing and his slip of the tongue the night before. "Besides, Philippe has his own money."

"I'm sure you're right." Gwen picked up her mug again and kept her eyes focused on the liquid. "Dating Drew has made me a little cynical about people's intentions I fear."

"It comes with the territory," Carrie said softening her tone as well. She'd dealt with the fear that people only liked her for her money all her life, and she knew Gwen, because she was new to it, was just looking out for her.

"Did Cal know about your money?" Gwen asked.

"Well, I wasn't as wealthy then," Carrie began, but she thought back to that weekend. Most of it was fuzzy, but she had no memory of telling Cal about her money. "I don't think I told him though."

"Well, that's something then."

"What is?" Carrie asked. She wasn't following Gwen's train of thought.

She picked up the folded piece of paper again. "This is romantic, Carrie, and I imagine the others are similar.

If he didn't know about your money, then I'd wager he has real feelings for you. Why else would he write you every year for six years even though you never write back?"

Carrie bit her lip as Gwen's words sunk in. If she hadn't mentioned the money, why would Cal want to stay married to her? Why would he write her year after year with no reply? Could it be that he had really fallen for her?

5

"What do you mean you have to go to Texas?" Philippe asked as he crossed his arms. This stiff almost angry posture was unlike him.

Carrie bit the inside of her lip. She hated lying, but she didn't think telling Philippe the whole truth right now would be a good thing. So, she'd opted for the lie of omission. "I told you, I have some business to take care of."

"Business in Texas? Have you ever even been to Texas, Carrie?"

He didn't believe her, and she had clearly aroused his suspicion, but there was nothing to do now but carry on the lie. "I have a friend there."

His jaw clenched. "A friend? Carrie, we just got

engaged. Shouldn't we be planning a wedding or something?"

Well, at least he hadn't asked who the friend was. "We have plenty of time for that, Philippe. I promise. Drew's letting me take the charter jet. That will cut back on the time, and I'll be back before you know it. Probably by tomorrow night."

"I don't like the idea of you traveling alone. Why don't I come with you?"

Carrie twitched as the thought ran through her head. That could be the worst idea ever. She had no idea if Cal had changed at all, but the two men in the same room would more than likely just turn into a competition if not a full-fledged fist fight. "You have work," she said shaking her head. "Didn't you just take on a new company?"

Philippe's face twisted and Carrie figured he knew she was right, but he was trying to come up with another option. "Fine," he finally said. The words came out more like a sigh than a statement. "But please keep me informed of your journey and progress."

Another prick pinged Carrie's conscience. She had no intention of telling him her progress, but she could update him on her arrival. "I will."

Though he didn't look entirely satisfied, he accepted her kiss and stepped back. Carrie couldn't help but notice the worry lines still etched in his face as she walked past him to Gwen and Drew who stood at the bottom of the stairs leading into the plane.

"Thank you for letting me take the private plane," Carrie said to Drew. "I suppose I could have chartered my own-"

"Nonsense." He held up a hand cutting her off. "There's no sense chartering a second one when I have this plane and no reason to deal with airport issues when you have a plane at your disposal. Now, there's no airport in Soda Spurs, so you'll be landing about an hour away."

"That's fine," Carrie said. "I'd rather keep a low profile anyway. No sense causing a scene."

"So, do you have a plan?" Gwen asked in a quiet voice. Undoubtedly, she'd told Drew the real story, but Carrie had asked her not to tell Philippe. At least not yet. Gwen hadn't been happy, but she'd agreed it was Carrie's story to tell when she was ready.

A plan. Carrie had thought all night about how best to handle the situation but come up with nothing. Would Cal fight her? She hoped he would change his mind about wanting to marry her when he saw her again, sign the papers, and let her be on her way, but she doubted it would be that easy. Whatever he did, she figured honesty would be the best option. "I'm just going to show up and ask him to sign the papers."

"And what if he doesn't?" Gwen asked.

Carrie understood Gwen was just playing devil's advocate, but it annoyed her nonetheless. "He has to. I'm going to ask nicely. Bribe him if I have to." Gwen shot her an incredulous stare, but Carrie wasn't kidding. "I am not sure what I'll do if he doesn't."

Gwen squeezed her arm and flashed a sympathetic smile, but it didn't lessen Carrie's worries. What would she do if Cal refused?

Dexter's ears perked and his head turned toward the barn entrance. A soft whine escaped his throat. Cal had heard nothing, but Dexter, who possessed much better hearing, obviously had.

"What is it boy?" Cal asked as he led Ginger from the stall.

Dexter's response was a sharp bark and a tail wag. His eyes never wavered from the barn door.

"All right, let's go check it out." Cal tugged on Ginger's reigns to get her moving. As they stepped out of the barn and back into the open air, the crunch of tires on gravel reached Cal's ears. He checked his watch. Stacy usually returned at day's end to check on everything, but it wasn't quite that time yet, and he wasn't expecting anyone else. Surely it wouldn't be the bank wanting payment on the loan yet. He had told them he was working on something and they generally left him alone as long as he delivered.

Dexter barked again and pranced around Cal's legs as if urging him to hurry or give permission to run ahead.

"Go on then," Cal said giving him permission. "I'll secure Ginger and I'll be right there."

Dexter's head bobbed as if agreeing with a nod. People said dogs didn't talk, but Dexter seemed to be an exception to that rule. He gave one final glance at Cal and then bounded toward the front of the house.

Cal shook his head as he tied Ginger's reins to the corral. That dog was sometimes more human than canine. Before he made it around the side of his house, a feminine scream carried through the air, and Cal quickened his pace, wondering what Dexter had done now.

When he rounded the corner, he pulled up short and bit his lips to keep from laughing at the scene in front of him. A mid-sized sedan he didn't recognize sat parked in front of his house. Dexter had pinned the driver to her door and was attempting to sniff or lick her face - it wasn't clear from Cal's position. What he could discern was that the woman was actively trying to avoid Dexter's tongue. Her red mane swished from side to side as her face darted to the left and right. Wait, red hair? Could it be? The lingering sunlight picked up the copper in her hair and Cal thought back to the first time his eyes saw the beautiful color.

"Will someone get this mangy mutt off me?"

Cal's breath caught. Though it had been years, that voice was burned into his memory. Coupled with the coppery red hair, it could be no one else. Carrie Bliss was in his driveway.

"Dexter, down," he called when he found his voice again. The dog whined but dropped to the ground and returned to Cal's side.

"You really should teach that dog some manners," she said as she wiped at her white jacket. The remnants of dusty paw prints remained even after her hands finished.

Cal crossed his arms and leaned against the porch post. "He's just excited. We don't get a lot of visitors and no one we know wears all white to a ranch."

Her posture stiffened a moment at the sound of his voice. Then she turned around and caught his gaze, her emerald eyes fierce and resolute. "Hi, Cal."

Two words. That's all she said, but that was all it took. Immediately he was transported back to Vegas.

He had been there attending a friend's bachelor party and while everyone else pounded enough liquor to become stupid drunk, Cal had only partaken of one beer. He wasn't really a fan of the taste, and he didn't like the feeling of being out of control.

"Dude, go ask some girl to dance," his friend John said with a slur.

"I'm good, really." Cal was honestly hoping the party would end soon. Fatigue covered him, and he just wanted to crawl into bed, but it would be rude to leave this early.

"No, you're not. You're not having any fun. You're barely drinking, so go find a girl. Look, there's a perfect one."

Cal followed John's finger not expecting much. His friend was three sheets to the wind at least, but as the sea of people parted briefly, Cal's heart paused in his chest. A beautiful red headed woman surrounded by a few friends danced freely to the music. Her body swayed in perfect time to the beat, and a smile stretched across her lips as if the dance floor made her feel alive. She was the most exotic, intoxicating woman he had ever seen.

His feet propelled him across the room though he had no idea what he would say to her. When nothing brilliant came to mind, he said the first thing he thought of. "Hi, I'm Cal, and I think you're beautiful."

Her eyes flicked to his and the corners of her mouth pulled into a flirtatious grin. She closed the space between and splayed her hands across his chest. "Hi Cal," she said as she looked up at him with sparkly green eyes.

"Are you just going to stand there all day?"

The harsh tone in Carrie's words drug him back to

the present, and Cal shook his head to clear the cobwebs of the past away. "How you been, Carrie?"

A tight smile played across Carrie's lips. "I've been better, Cal." She walked around the front of the car toward him. Physically, she looked the same, but there was a difference in her. She seemed stiffer, more polished. Her white jacket was tailored perfectly to her form as were her pants, and the emerald shirt that skirted her neckline brought out the same color in her eyes. She was a vision of perfection. "But you can help." She held out a stapled packet to him. "I need you to sign these."

He took the papers though he knew what they were. Only divorce papers would bring her all the way out to him. Cal scanned the papers - he had no plans to sign them, but she didn't need to know that. "Why now?"

Carrie bit her lip and her eyes fell to the ground. "I should have done it ages ago, but I just kept ignoring it. However, I can't ignore it any longer because..." she lifted her left hand, "because I'm getting married. He's a wonderful man and this time I'm ready to be married, but I can't do that until we get divorced."

Cal searched her eyes. She did seem earnest and sincere, but she'd never given their love a chance, and he wasn't ready to give her up without a fight. "I'll make you a deal," he said crossing his arms. "You stay here for a few days and give us a chance. If, at the end of that time, you still want a divorce, I'll sign the papers."

Her eyes flashed, and a spark of the old Carrie reappeared. "No, I'm not dating another man while I'm engaged. That's not right."

"Technically, you already have been." His gaze never wavered. He might still lose, depending on how stubborn she was, but at least this gave him a chance.

"But that's... that's not the same thing. We barely knew each other. We were both inebriated-"

"I wasn't drunk," he said cutting her off. "I was very aware of what I was doing. I knew from the moment I saw you that I felt something and when you said my name and put your hands on my chest, I knew I wanted to marry you. And you can claim intoxication all you want, but you were pretty firm in your decision that night as well."

"I..." Carrie opened her mouth but her words stalled. She held his gaze for a minute before pinching her lips together. A tiny vein throbbed in her clenched jaw, and Cal had to bite back a smile at how cute she looked when she was angry.

Cal raised a brow and tilted his head to the side. "It's either stay the few days or we stay married."

Irritation flared on Carrie's face sending a red flush up her neck. "What do you even hope to get out of this, Cal?"

He locked eyes with her. "You."

6

Carrie blinked as the wave of emotions rolled over her. Flattery hit first. That he would still want her after all this time was ego boosting, but it was followed quickly with disbelief. Why would he still want her after all this time unless he was after her money? Indignation flared soon after. How dare he barter with her life as if it meant nothing! She had a fiancé back home whom she loved or at least thought she loved, and she should not be staying here with this practically perfect stranger. It didn't matter that they were married on paper; she knew almost nothing about him.

Carrie returned his frank stare as she weighed her options. He had her between a rock and a hard place. She couldn't very well leave and stay married so that left staying. "Fine, but I'm not staying here. It wouldn't be proper. This town has a hotel, right?"

A deep, irritating chuckle spilled from Cal's lips. "A hotel? No, but there is an inn, and since there's no festival going on this weekend, you might find a vacancy. I do have plenty of room here though-"

"Not on your life," Carrie seethed. "I'll take my chances on the inn. Do you have an address?"

"Nah, but I can take you there. You could get settled in and then come back here for a bit. I'll make you dinner and show you around."

None of that sounded appealing to Carrie, but as she was at his mercy, at least for the time being, she agreed. "Fine, get in. You can lead the way, but I'm driving."

Cal tipped his hat at her before pushing himself off the railing and sauntering to the sedan. The way he confidently carried himself was sexy and Carrie watched him fold his long frame into the passenger seat before shaking her head and crossing back to the driver's side. This was not what she had planned at all, and she had no business thinking of him as sexy. That was a rabbit trail she should not go down.

"This is nice," Cal said as she started the engine. His hand glided down the leather seat beneath him.

"It's a rental," Carrie said, "but thanks. Now where are we going?"

Cal removed his hat and pointed straight ahead. "You drive, and I'll tell you when to turn."

Carrie swallowed her irritation and shifted into drive. A few minutes later, they pulled up in front of a quaint two-story home. "You sure this is an inn?" Carrie asked. "I mean other than the sign, it looks more like a house."

"Well, that's the charm of Soda Spurs. It's got that home-grown vibe."

The corners of Cal's lips pulled up into an irresistibly charming smile. *Darn it. Why did he have to be hand-some?* This would be so much easier if she felt no attraction to him.

"Right." She pulled her eyes from his face and turned off the ignition. "Let's see if there's any room at the inn then."

"The sign said Vacancy, so I think you're good," Cal said as he opened his car door.

Before she even had her seatbelt off, he was opening the driver's side door for her.

"I can open my own door," she said. Did he think she was incapable or weak?

"I'm sure you can," he took off his cowboy hat and flashed her a wink, "but my momma raised me right, and it's only fitting I open the door for my wife."

"I'm not your-" Carrie trailed off at the teasing glint in his eye. She would not win this particular argument with him, so she might as well stop trying. "Fine, thank you."

He placed the hat back on his head and tapped the brim at her. "You're very welcome. Shall we head inside then?"

"Unless you want to stand outside all day." Carrie poured enough vitriol in her voice to garner an eyebrow raise from Cal.

"Nah, no sense in that. Momma would have my hide if I left you to wilt out here." He glanced toward the trunk. "Do you have bags I can help with?"

"No need," Carrie said. "I hadn't planned on staying long, so I only have one bag. I'm certain I can manage to carry that." She punctuated her words with sharp steps to the trunk of the car. Her heels made a satisfying clacking sound on the pavement. When she reached the back, she punched the button on the remote, staring at Cal as it popped open. Then, she pulled out her bag before shutting the lid.

He was waiting at the side of the car as she shut the trunk, and he nodded at her before leading the way up the pathway. A tiny bell jingled as he pushed open the front door, and a wave of warmth rolled out to greet them.

"Welcome to the Soda Spurs Inn." The bubbly voice belonged to a short, stout woman with curly brown hair. "Oh, hey, Cal. What can I do for you?"

"Hi, Dixie, this is my friend Carrie, and she needs a room for a few nights."

Relief flooded Carrie that he had called her his friend instead of his wife. Though she would probably never see the people in the town again once she left, she didn't want to explain to everyone her situation with Cal.

"Welcome, Carrie," Dixie said turning her friendly gaze on Carrie. "How long will you be staying?"

Carrie raised a brow and turned to Cal. "That's a good question. Cal?"

His lips twisted into a mischievous smile and he shrugged leaving Carrie on her own.

"At least tonight with the option to extend?"

Dixie looked from Cal to Carrie clearly picking up on something. "Lucky for you, this is not a busy time. I can certainly do that for you, and you can tell me each night if you'll be checking out the next morning or not."

"Thank you. That sounds perfect." Carrie would have preferred to be on the jet already heading back, but as that wasn't possible, she would make the best of the situation.

"Great. Well, let me show you to your room." Dixie grabbed a key from the rack behind her.

"I'll wait here." Cal nodded at Dixie and then wandered over to an open chair.

"So, what brought you to Soda Spurs?" Dixie asked as she led the way up the stairs.

"Cal did, actually. We met each other a few years ago, and now I need a favor from him." Carrie hoped that explanation would be enough to satisfy Dixie's curiosity.

"Oh, I'm sure he will do whatever you need. Cal is the sweetest man, but I'm sure I don't have to tell you that." Dixie inserted the key into the door and opened it to reveal a small room decorated in a soft rose color. "It's not huge, but it has a private bath and a closet," Dixie said gesturing to the door on the right side of the room.

"It's fine, thank you," Carrie said. "I didn't bring much anyway."

"All right. Well, don't hesitate to call me if you need anything at all. If I don't have it here, I can tell you where to get it." Dixie flashed a final sweet smile before turning and exiting the room.

When the door closed behind her, Carrie walked to the bed and placed her small bag on top. She had brought little, hoping to only spend a day or two in town, but she should probably unpack what was folded in her overnight bag to keep it from getting too wrinkled.

Before she did that though, she needed to call Philippe and inform him of her arrival, so he wouldn't worry.

The phone rang four times in her ear before going to voicemail. As she listened to his announcement, she wondered what he was doing that kept him from answering the phone. It was nearing eight pm back in New York and he rarely worked that late. "Hey, Philippe, I made it to Texas. It looks like it might take a few days to finish up my business, but I rented a nice room. I guess you are working late, so I'll try you again later. Bye."

Carrie ended the call and then dialed Gwen. At least talking to her might lighten Carrie's mood. Unlike Philippe, Gwen picked up on the first ring.

"Hey, Carrie, how is it going?"

"Not well," Carrie said. "Cal is still refusing to sign. He wants me to spend a few days here and then he said he'll sign if I haven't changed my mind. He has some nerve." Carrie shoved clothes in the dresser drawer as she seethed and then turned to the closet to hang the few items that needed it. She shouldn't care about wrinkles. Cal and Dixie both wore jeans and plaid shirts, so they probably didn't care about her wrinkles, and maybe if she came across as a slob, Cal would decide he didn't want her and sign the stupid papers. No, she wouldn't do that. Even if it might work, Carrie could never handle looking like a slob.

"I think it's kind of romantic," Gwen said softly from the other side of the phone.

Carrie stopped unpacking long enough to hold the phone out and stare at the screen. She knew Gwen couldn't see her, but she couldn't believe those words would come out of her mouth. "Whose side are you on anyway?"

"Yours, but you have to admit, Carrie, it's like a Hallmark movie. This guy has held a torch for you for six years and all he wants is one last ditch effort to win you over."

"But I'm engaged to Philippe." Why did no one seem to understand that?

"But should you be?"

Carrie shook her head and placed her toothbrush on the bathroom counter. Had Gwen lost her mind? "Should I be? Of course, I should be. He asked, and I said yes. That's all there is to it."

Gwen sighed in Carrie's ear. "Do you hear yourself, Carrie? You didn't even say you loved him."

Irritation flared inside Carrie. "Yes, I love him. I wouldn't have said yes if I didn't love him." Would she have? All of a sudden, she wasn't so sure. Carrie sank onto the bed and dropped her head onto her hands. "This is such a mess."

"Or a message." Gwen's soft voice held no condemnation. "Sometimes there are reasons we do things. Maybe you never divorced Cal because you had feelings for him even if you didn't realize it. Maybe this is God's way of giving you both a second chance."

"I think you have newlywed brain," Carrie said with a shake of her head. "It was one stupid night six years ago. I'm not supposed to be with him. He's just being stubborn, but two can play at that game." She stood and smoothed her shirt. "In fact, I think I will go have another word with him."

"Okay," Gwen said with a sigh. "I hope you know what you're doing."

"I do know what I'm doing. I'm doing what I came here to do. I'll keep you informed." Carrie hung up the phone, pulled back her shoulders, and yanked open the door. This was crazy. She had married Cal on a whim, not because she cared for him, and she was going to remind him of that.

Cal stood as she entered the foyer, his black Stetson in his hands. "You all good?"

"Yeah, I think so."

"Ready for the tour then?"

Carrie rolled her eyes. As if she had much choice in the matter. "Sure, why not?"

They loaded back up in her car, and Carrie drove back to Cal's ranch. Though the drive was quiet, she couldn't help sneaking sideways glances at him. He'd been handsome six years ago, but the dark stubble on his cheeks added to his look giving him a rugged masculinity which sent her heart thumping. She tightened her grip on the wheel and forced her eyes to stay on the road and off his face.

When they arrived back at his house, Cal again

rushed around to open her door before leading her up the front porch steps. "Welcome to casa Roper," Cal said as he held the door open for her.

Carrie stepped into a warm living room decorated simply in blue and browns. The furniture was wooden and appeared handmade, but the cushions had obviously been given to Cal as they didn't match. Still, though the room was clearly decorated by a bachelor, it had a homey feel to it.

A large fireplace filled the left wall and above the mantle was a portrait of a beautiful sunset. Carrie's eyes scanned the room, but no television hung on any wall or sat on any surface. Instead, there was the portrait, a cross, and some pictures. Interesting, but she assumed he had a television in his bedroom or in another room of the house. Philippe had three - one in his living room, one in his bedroom, and one in his kitchen. In fact, Carrie couldn't name a man who didn't have at least one.

"The living room is simple, and it could use a woman's decorating hand, but it's home." Cal flashed a wink at her and Carrie bristled. He was acting as if this was some elaborate game, but it wasn't to her. This was her future.

Cal continued into his modest kitchen. "Here's the kitchen," he said pointing. "Again, not much, but I'll rustle us up some grub after the ride."

She narrowed her eyes and placed her hands on her slim hips. "So, a drive? To where? No offense, but I didn't see much to experience in this town."

Cal mashed his lips together to keep from smiling. "Well, there's more than you think, but I wasn't talking about a drive. I said a ride."

Carrie waved her hand. Her fingers were long and slender, feminine. He wondered what they would feel like clasped in his own. "What's the difference?"

A deep chuckle bubbled in his chest, but he didn't feel like sharing just yet. "A lot. You'll see. Come on." He led the way through the kitchen and out the back door.

Dexter looked up from where he had been laying on the porch and rose to his feet, his tail wagging like a metronome.

Carrie stepped back in a cowering gesture. "He won't jump on me again, will he? I'll probably never get all the dirt out of this white as it is."

"Well, you'll learn that wearing white at a ranch isn't the brightest idea, but I'll keep him from jumping on you. At ease, Dexter," Cal said. "Give the lady a chance to warm up to you."

Obediently, Dexter sat back down and stared expectantly at them.

"I think you'll be fine now. Come on."

She flashed the dog another withering stare before straightening and taking a step forward. Her eyes widened as she took in the expansive grounds. "Is all this land yours?" There was a hint of awe in her voice as her eyes scanned the area.

"Everything inside the fences you see. It takes a little land to raise cattle."

"Is that what you do? Raise cattle?"

"Yes ma'am." He offered his hand to help her off the porch as her feet seemed rooted to the spot. Cal wasn't sure if she feared the step or the dirt that would greet her at the bottom.

She stared at his hand a moment before placing hers in his. Though a simple touch, Cal relished the softness of her skin. His own hands were rough from years of hard work outside. Carrie held his hand just until her foot touched the ground and then she dropped it as if a searing flame had erupted from it.

Cal chuckled to himself as he continued to the barn. Ginger was still tied up at the corral, but Carrie would need a horse too, and Mabel would be perfect for her. Dexter joined him but was careful to stay out of the way and farther from Carrie.

"Wait, did you mean ride horses?" Her eyes rounded like half dollars and her mouth fell open.

"Well, I certainly didn't mean ride pigs though Stacy tried that one time. Didn't last too long and by the end of it, she ended up dirtier than the pigs." He laughed at the memory, but Carrie didn't seem to find it quite as funny.

"Who's Stacy?"

"My sister. I've talked about her - both that night in Vegas and in the letters I've written. You have received them, right?" He kept his tone light, but inside he was bursting to find out what she did with those letters. Obviously, she had at least gotten them or else she wouldn't have his address, but had she read them? Thrown them away? Kept them twined with a ribbon in a drawer somewhere? He opened the barn door and stepped in toward Mabel's stall.

"Yes, but Cal I don't ride horses or any animal for that matter."

She had brushed over the information he really wanted, but he didn't press the issue. It would surface later. "Nonsense. You only say that because you never have. This here is Mabel and she's as gentle as they come." He touched the dark mane of hair that flowed down Mabel's neck before turning to grab her saddle.

"I would have no idea how to control her," Carrie said holding up in her hands as if warding off evil.

"You don't have to do much." He placed the saddle pad on Mabel's back and then hoisted the saddle up. Then he reached under her to cinch the front and back girth. Finally, he checked to make sure none of her skin had gotten folded into the cinch. When he was sure she was comfortable and the saddle was secure, he led her out of the stall and toward the barn door. "Mabel here is a good girl. She'll follow whatever Ginger does, and I promise I won't go galloping off on you."

"I'd rather not. The only animal I really like is Gwen's cat and even then, it's only because I don't have to take care of her. I just cat sit sometimes."

Cal stopped and turned to her. "You cat sit?"

Her face flushed, and her eyes fell to her hands. "It sounds corny I know, but Gwen's my best friend and before she met Drew, she had to work two jobs. I would go to her place and take care of her cat, Tabby."

"Hmm, I've never owned a cat, but I always thought they rather took care of themselves. I mean you put food and water out and change a litter box, right?"

"Well, yes, but Tabby also climbs on my lap and we watch movies together." She glanced up at him, and he couldn't help but chuckle at the serious expression on her face.

"Okay, so why don't you get your own cat?"

"I can't," she said shaking her head and hands at him. "I kill everything. Even houseplants. Gwen once got me a cactus to try to make me feel better, but I killed the cactus. It took a little longer, but I assure you it is dead."

His grin stretched further, and he turned away from her to keep from laughing as he continued toward the corral "I see the problem, but I promise you can't hurt Mabel."

"I'd still rather not take the chance."

He turned back to her, his best hang dog expression on his face. "Come on, Carrie. Let me show you my land and brag a little. You told me back in Vegas that you wanted to see it when I finally did it."

Carrie's brow furrowed. "I did? I have no memory of that conversation."

Cal chuckled to hide the hurt from her words. "Well, it happened. We were talking about what we wanted out of life. You told me your dream of becoming a famous designer, and I told you I wanted to own a large plot of land and ranch. Then you told me that maybe you could design blankets for the cattle to keep them warm." His lips parted in a smile and he shook his head as he replayed the memory. She had been so cute talking about cattle blankets that he hadn't the heart to tell her they wouldn't wear them.

Indecision flooded Carrie's eyes as she looked from Cal to the horse and back again. "Are you sure it's safe?"

"Cross my heart." He signed the X across his chest for good measure.

"All right," she said, "but if I get hurt-"

"I won't let that happen." The teasing lilt dropped from his voice as he spoke the serious words. He would never allow anything to hurt her if he could help it.

Their gazes locked for a moment, and electricity crackled between them. He wanted to kiss her to show her how much he had missed her and how serious he was, but he knew she wouldn't be receptive. Yet. So, he cleared his throat and broke the moment.

"Just put your foot here in the stirrup, and I'll help you up."

She gave him an unsure look but approached the horse. "Like this?" she asked as she lifted her right leg.

"No, left leg in the stirrup. Then you throw your right leg over."

"Cal, I'm not sure-"

"Carrie, it's okay. I've got you." He placed his hands lightly on her hips to reassure her and she stiffened beneath his touch.

"Okay." She lifted her left leg high and managed to get it in the stirrup, but then she lost her balance and fell right into his arms.

Thankfully, Cal had planted his feet, or they might have both ended up in the dirt. He certainly didn't mind Carrie in his embrace, but she was flustered. Her eyes flicked to his and a rose color flooded her cheeks.

"I'm sorry," she said untangling herself from his arms in a hasty effort to escape his touch. "I'll try again."

He applied a little more pressure to her hips to steady her and lifted as she pushed up. After another precarious moment, she swung her right leg around.

"Oh my gosh, did I do it?" A timid smile played on her lips.

"You did. Now hold still so I can adjust your stirrups." He bent down and cinched the stirrups up slightly. Stacy generally rode Mabel and it appeared she was a smidge taller than Carrie.

"What are the stirrups for?" Carrie asked as she wiggled her feet.

"Stability and control. You won't really need them much today other than mounting and dismounting, but if you were galloping, they would be useful to help you stay on the saddle and control Mabel."

He held onto Mabel's reins as he untied Ginger and then mounted as well.

"You make that look so easy," Carrie said.

Cal smiled. "Well, to be fair, I have been doing it a lot longer than you have. I grew up around horses."

"Did your parents own this ranch before you?" Carrie asked as Cal clicked to Ginger and led them in a slow walk toward the field.

"No, this I purchased a few years ago, but my father worked at a stable, so I got to take care of the horses and occasionally ride them. I knew when I was about ten that I wanted to be a rancher. I love being out on a horse, and I can't imagine doing anything else."

"It is pretty out here, but Cal, that's one reason we should end this charade. I'm a city girl. I own a dress shop, and I can't imagine doing anything else either."

Cal glanced at her out of the corner of his eye. He'd had similar thoughts over the years, but God still hadn't given him peace about a divorce. "Where there's an open heart, God will find a way."

Carrie sighed but said nothing more as they continued slowly toward the edge of his property. Cal scanned the area as they rode. The grass was looking thin on this side too. He'd have to look into herding the cattle to the outer field soon to keep them fed. It made his job of monitoring them harder, but at least they would be fed.

"Cal, where do you see me fitting in with all this?" Carrie asked as they turned back to the house.

"Wherever you want to fit in," he said. "Do you have to be in New York to design your clothes?"

"It certainly helps. That is where the high paying customers are. Who would I even sell to out here?"

Her question gave Cal pause. He hadn't really thought about her side. Still, he knew that God could make anything work if people trusted in him, and Cal wasn't willing to give up yet.

7

It surprised Carrie to see a woman standing on Cal's back porch as they returned. Was she an employee? A friend? She was a nice-looking woman with long brown hair pulled into a ponytail, a red and black flannel shirt, and jeans. A tiny seed of discomfort sprouted in Carrie's stomach. Was that jealousy? Surely not. She didn't want Cal; she was trying to divorce him.

"Well, there you are," she called out when they were close enough. She spoke to Cal, but her eyes were on Carrie. "I was beginning to wonder if I needed to send out a search party."

"And who would head such a party, Sis?" Cal asked as he pulled up on Ginger's reins.

Ah, the sister. Carrie should have known. She could

see a little of the resemblance now. The same brown hair and strong nose. His sister didn't have the chiseled features of Cal, but it was clear they shared genes.

"You got me there. I certainly wasn't going to come looking. I was, however, going to ask you if you wanted to come to dinner, but it appears you have a date, so we can do it another time." Was that surprise Carrie heard in the woman's voice?

"Well, not really a date. This is Carrie. She's come to visit." Cal dismounted his horse and turned towards Carrie.

"Not really a visit," Carrie said at the same time his sister said, "Oh."

"Hold on to the horn here," Cal said ignoring Carrie's comment. "Then swing your right leg over. I'll help you down."

Carrie followed his directions and tensed slightly when his hands landed on her waist to steady her descent. She figured it was necessary, and she appreciated the gesture; she simply wished she didn't get tingles from it.

"Carrie? Really?" His sister's expression matched the tone in her voice. "Well, nice to meet you, Carrie." She extended a hand as Carrie approached. "I'm Stacy, Cal's sister."

"Nice to meet you," Carrie said and shook the woman's hand.

"I'll pass on dinner tonight," Cal said coming up behind Carrie. "I was planning to make chili for Carrie and me."

"You can go have dinner with your family if you want," Carrie said. "I can eat at the inn or somewhere in town and come back tomorrow. You do have restaurants, right?"

"We do. A few, but I'm not leaving you in this town all alone. However, I need to brush down the horses so perhaps Stacy can help start the dinner while I do that?" His voice held a hopeful tone and Carrie recognized the same dogged expression he used on her earlier. He certainly understood how to play to his attributes.

Stacy rolled her eyes, but a smile played across her lips. "I guess if I have to, but you'll owe me."

"Whatever you say, sis." He turned to Carrie. "Go ahead and make yourself at home inside. I'll be there as soon as I finish out here."

Carrie nodded and followed Stacy into the house. "Can you tell me where the bathroom is? I'd like to clean up?"

"Sure, it's right down the hall." Stacy pointed down the hallway before opening the door of the fridge.

Carrie started down the hallway before realizing all the doors were shut. With a pause, she glanced back toward the kitchen knowing she should turn back and ask Stacy which door the bathroom was, but not asking gave her deniability. She probably shouldn't, but curiosity filled Carrie. What was in the other rooms?

She opened the first one to find a home office. A desk, chair, and bookshelf were the only pieces in the room and it held few decorations. In fact, she only saw one picture frame in the whole room and it sat next to a wood carving on the clutter-free desk. Who was so important to him to be the only pictures in the room? Curious, she crossed to the desk and turned the frame around.

It was one of those folding frames that held two pictures. On one side was a picture of his sister, a man, and two children. Carrie assumed that was her husband and children, but it was the other side that grabbed her attention.

She stared at it trying to figure out when he could have gotten it. It was a picture of the two of them at the chapel in Vegas. A broad smile lit up his features and her head leaned against his chest. She certainly didn't look unhappy. Had she held feelings for him then? Carrie returned the frame to the desk and picked up the wood carving. It was beautiful and eerie. Whoever carved it had created a woman's face. A very familiar woman's face. She traced the curve of the face, and her eyes widened. Was that her face staring back at her? She replaced the carving and backed out of the room closing the door behind her. She needed time to process what she had seen.

The next door opened to a small bathroom. Carrie could tell a bachelor decorated it as nothing matched and the simple decor held no woman's touch. Blue towel, black shower curtain, and a plastic soap dispenser that looked like the kind you bought at general stores. Still, it was clean and clutter free like the rest of the house. He took care of his place. That she could appreciate, but the lack of necessities in the house unnerved her. What did he do for fun?

Next was a simple guest room. It held a bed, dresser, and a nightstand with a lamp. She wondered if anyone ever used it.

The last door opened to the master bedroom. Carrie paused and bit her lip. She shouldn't go in his bedroom without asking. She would hate it if someone did that to her, but she couldn't seem to stop her feet from entering.

The neatly made queen bed filled most of the room, a blue comforter spread across it. The empty nightstand on the right side led her to believe he slept on the left as that nightstand held an alarm clock, a lamp, and a Bible. His dresser was also neat. Only a small box sat on top which Carrie assumed held tie tacks or some other things. Above the dresser hung a beautiful photograph of a sun setting on a barn. The reds, oranges, and pinks in the picture came to life making Carrie feel almost as if she were there.

The only other thing in the room was a door which Carrie assumed led to the closet and maybe another bathroom. She forced herself not to open it and look. She had invaded his privacy enough.

"Did you find something you like?"

Carrie froze at the sound of his masculine voice behind her, and a heated flush clawed up her neck. She scrambled for an excuse as she turned to face him. "Sorry, I was looking for the bathroom. You forgot to give me the complete tour earlier."

His eyebrow arched in a sexy, teasing expression as his hand raked across his stubbled cheek. "So I did. You'll find one through there," he nodded at the closed door, "but it's the one I use so I make no guarantees on the state of it." Cal flashed her a wink before stepping back and gesturing toward the hallway. "Or there's a guest bathroom down the hall."

"I um guess I'd prefer that one." Carrie felt tongue tied, like a schoolgirl with her first crush, and embarrassment flooded her that he had caught her snooping in his room.

"Well then, let me lead the way." Cal exited the room and Carrie meekly followed. How had he sneaked up on her?

Cal swallowed his laughter as Carrie ducked into the bathroom. He'd caught her snooping, but he let her think he believed her story of getting lost. He didn't want to embarrass her any further and it gave him hope that she had gone looking. If she truly felt nothing, she wouldn't have bothered to explore his life. Besides, he had nothing to hide.

The sound of the faucet carried through the closed door, and Cal smiled. Maybe she really had wanted to clean up. If not, she was certainly playing it up. He leaned against the wall as he waited for her to open the door.

"Oh." Her startled voice matched her face as it swung open. "I didn't think you'd still be waiting out here."

"Well, I wanted to escort you to dinner, and I didn't want you getting lost again." He bit his lips to keep from laughing at the indignant look on her face.

"Ha-ha. You're quite the comedian."

"So I've been told." He flashed his most charming smile and wiggled his eyebrows at her delighted when he got a return smirk. "Shall we get some grub then?"

Carrie's response was an eye roll, but as a smile accompanied it, Cal counted it as a win in his favor.

"Stacy started the food, but I have to add the

finishing touches," Cal said as they entered the kitchen. He picked up his apron and tied it around his waist before tasting the chili. "Mm, needs a little more salt." Grabbing the shaker from the counter, he poured a little more in before turning back to Carrie.

"Do you always wear that when you cook?" Her voice was muffled behind the hand she held to her mouth and her eyes twinkled.

He looked down at his 'Kiss the Cook' apron and grinned. "It was a gift from my sister."

"And yet you still wear it." Her left eyebrow rose giving her a quizzical expression.

"Well, I wouldn't want to hurt her feelings and it keeps my shirt from getting dirty."

At that Carrie laughed out loud. "Doesn't your job as a rancher already get your shirts dirty?"

"Touché, but I promise I washed my hands before I touched any food." He smiled at her and his insides tangled. What was he going to do if she insisted on the divorce? Over the years he imagined what it would be like if she returned but having her here was way better than his imagination ever conjured.

Her face shifted, and she shrugged. "I probably won't eat much anyway. I doubt it's on my diet."

Cal raised a brow, but he wasn't offended. This wasn't the real her. In fact, it gave him hope. If she were throwing up emotional walls that meant she was feeling something for him. "Actually, I considered that. The chili is homemade, just meat and vegetables. I made cornbread too, but I'll understand if you aren't eating starches."

Her mouth fell open, but no sound came out for a minute. Then her face shifted. "How can you be sure? Didn't your sister start the chili?"

"She did, but it was my recipe, so I think I know what's in it. Do you want to grab two bowls?" He nodded at a cabinet on his right.

"Uh sure." Carrie crossed to the cabinet and pulled out two bowls. "So, your recipe, huh?"

"Yeah, it was learning to cook or starve. Turns out I'm rather good at it. This chili has won the blue ribbon at town festivals three times."

"Oh really? Well, then I look forward to judging for myself then."

"Good because it's ready."

He brought the pot to the table and dished them each up a bowl. Then he returned to the stove to retrieve the cornbread. She might not be eating any, but his mouth was watering just from the smell.

Cal set the cornbread on the table and then scooted his chair in. "I hope you're still a believer because we pray in this house over our food."

"I am," Carrie said before closing her eyes.

Cal nodded and bowed his head. "Thank you, Lord,

for this day, for this food, and for bringing Carrie and me back together for however long it may be. In your name, amen."

Cal opened his eyes and tried to gauge Carrie's reaction, but she said nothing. She merely dipped her spoon into the chili, blew on it, and brought it to her mouth. He continued to glance at her as they ate. Since her arrival, he had seen two different Carries. There was the haughty one who pretended she was too good for him and this town and there was the Carrie he had taken on a tour of his land. The relaxed one who smiled and showed delight. He figured, unless she had changed drastically in six years, that she was the real Carrie and the other was an act, but he wished he knew how to get her true side to stay.

"So, I have to do a little work tomorrow morning, but would you like to see the rest of the town?"

She looked up at him briefly before dropping her eyes back to her bowl. "I don't suppose I can convince you to sign the papers tonight and let me get back to New York?"

"Nope."

"Then I'm kind of at your mercy, so let's see the town."

Cal caught the insinuation in Carrie's words. He was messing up her plans, but he couldn't lose her without a fight. The fact that she hadn't filed for divorce in all these years had to mean something. "I know you think it's a podunk town, but we have a rather interesting history."

"Can I ask you something?" Carrie's voice was direct, and her green eyes stared into his.

"Sure."

"Why do you still want me? It's been six years, so why haven't you moved on?"

Cal set his spoon down and smiled. "Before my dad decided he wanted a simpler life, he was in the Air Force. My mom's dad was too. My grandfather introduced my father to Christ and when he was a Christian, he introduced my father to my mother - through the mail. They wrote letters back and forth for months. He proposed through the mail, she accepted through the mail, and they met face to face a week before their wedding."

"That's a sweet story," Carrie said. "How long have they been together?"

"Fifty years, and while that's amazing," he shook his head, "it's not the most amazing part."

The corners of Carrie's lips pulled into a grin. "Okay, I'll bite. What's the most amazing part?"

"My father had recently broken up with a woman he thought he would marry. When my grandfather introduced him to Christ, he prayed for God to bring his Elaine back to him." Cal paused for dramatic effect and took a drink of his tea. "My mother's name is Elaine. God answered his prayer. Just not in the way Dad figured He would."

"That is amazing, but you haven't answered my question yet."

Cal smiled at Carrie. She would keep him on his toes, but he wouldn't want it any other way. "I was getting to that. You needed the background on my parents to understand me. See, I wanted what my parents had. That real, long lasting love, but I kept not finding it. I dated before I met you, but none of them felt right. There was no feeling that 'she's the one.'

"But all that changed when I saw you. When you smiled at me with that beautiful smile, I felt something I had never felt before. I had never believed in love at first sight, but the night I saw you, I just knew. Then we spent the evening talking. I probably don't have to tell you, but you have this amazing personality. We laughed and shared stories of our past and our hopes for the future, and every time you looked at me with those green eyes, I knew I wanted to gaze into them forever.

"I should have prayed about it longer than I did, but I didn't want you to get away. The next morning when you told me you regretted the marriage, it killed me, but I took those marriage vows seriously, and I didn't feel at peace with the idea of a divorce. I prayed. No," he shook his head, "I pray every day for God's guidance on this. I trust, like my father did, that God is watching out for me and has the best planned."

Carrie sat back in her chair and her eyes studied him. "I appreciate your wanting to follow God's will, but what if His will isn't for us to stay together? I've moved on with my life, and I'm not getting the same feelings you are."

Cal matched her position, leaning back a little himself. "You seem like a knowledgeable Christian, and no doubt you've heard the phrase 'let no man separate what God has joined,' but I understand your question. You and I seem worlds apart, and you're wondering if I'll hold on to you out of spite or some misguided notion."

Carrie raised her brow but said nothing. However, her steady gaze told him he had hit the nail on the head.

"If God gives me peace about letting you go, I'll do it. I'll hate it, but I'll do it."

"Okay, as long as we're on the same page."

"We're in the same book anyway." He flashed a wide smile as he stood and gathered the dishes from the table. She took his lead and picked up the few remaining pieces handing them to him at the sink. "Will you do me a favor?" Cal plugged the sink and filled it with hot water before setting the dishes in. They could soak until Carrie left. There'd be plenty of time to wash them later.

Carrie's brow lifted, and she folded her arms across

her chest. "You mean in addition to changing my plans to spend the weekend with you?"

Cal smirked as he wiped his hands on the nearby plaid towel. "Touché, but this is a small favor. I wanted to see if you would join me in my devotion tonight." He hung the towel back on the rack.

"You want to read the Bible with me?" Carrie asked.

"I do. It's something I always hoped to do with my wife, and even though you may not be here long, I would enjoy sharing that with you."

She blinked at him. "Um, okay, I guess."

Her hesitation surprised Cal. "Do you not do devotionals with your fiancé?" Cal crossed to the living room grabbing his Bible from the coffee table as he did.

Carrie's eyes shifted to the side. "Well, we haven't yet, but I'm sure we will when we marry. We're both busy professionals, but he attends church with me." She pushed her nose up in the air as if that settled the discussion.

"If you're too busy now, how are you going to make the time when you're married?" He meant it as an innocent question, but Carrie bristled as if he'd attacked her.

"We just will. I'll make sure it's a priority." Her defensive tone told Cal he had hit a nerve, and he backed off. He wanted to win her over not push her away.

"I hope you do." He sat on the edge of the couch. "I think it's the most important time a couple can spend together. I'm in Isaiah. Join me?" Cal patted the couch beside him.

Carrie hesitated a moment but sat down next to him. Far enough away, he noticed, that she didn't have to touch him. Cal smiled to himself as he flipped the pages to the right chapter. Baby steps, he reminded himself. He would need to take baby steps to win her over.

Carrie entered the hotel room in a fog of confusion that night. Dinner with Cal had been amazing. Even though she knew he needed to cook to eat, she couldn't remember the last time a man had cooked for her. Philippe always took her out to restaurants or ordered food in. While that was nice, she wondered if he would ever cook for her. With her money, she could hire a cook - he could as well - but there was something about a man cooking a meal for her that warmed her heart. Perhaps it stemmed back to memories of her father.

He had worked several years on Wall Street and when she was growing up, she rarely saw him. He left before she woke in the morning and arrived home after she'd gone to bed for the night most nights, but when he finally made his million, well several of them actually, he quit Wall Street and lived off the amazing investments he had made until the cancer got him. Carrie had been eight or ten when that happened, and she had loved waking to the smell of bacon in the skillet or pancakes on the grill.

Then there was the devotional. While Philippe attended church with her, he had never offered to read a devotional with her, but she had also never asked. Would he if she asked? Carrie wasn't sure, but she had enjoyed the time with Cal. Listening to his deep, velvety voice was enjoyable in and of itself, but discussing the reading with him was even better. He was much more knowledgeable than Carrie was, and she found herself hanging on his every word.

The whole experience left her confused to say the least, and she needed to talk to Gwen about it. Carrie was glad Gwen's number was on speed dial because she wasn't sure she would have been able to recall the number in her current condition.

The phone rang twice before Gwen answered. "How did it go?"

"It was interesting." Carrie sat on the bed, her mind a jumble of emotions. "Cal took me riding."

"Riding?" Gwen's voice held the same disbelief Carrie had felt. "Riding what? Horses?"

Carrie chuckled. "Yeah. I think he thought putting me on a horse and showing me his land would just magically change my mind about staying married to him. He even asked if I had to be in New York to design. Can you believe that? Like who would I design for out here?" Carrie hated the tone of her voice, but she was so confused.

She had come here expecting a quick conversation, maybe even a laugh as they traversed memory lane, and then departing and returning to her life with a signature on the papers. What she hadn't expected was this. This jumble of feelings colliding within her. She hadn't expected Cal to be so handsome or her heart to flip whenever he got near her. She hadn't expected the story he told her at dinner or to be questioning her engagement, her job, or her life. But she was.

"Did you tell him how you felt?" Gwen asked.

Carrie snorted. "Yeah, and he said God could find a way to make it all work. I mean I believe in God, but that just sounds like Cal using God as an excuse to make me stay."

Gwen was silent on the other line. Carrie could tell there was something was on her mind, but she didn't dare ask. At least not right now. She was still battling her own thoughts, and she didn't need Gwen's confusing her even more.

"Then he made me dinner."

"He made you dinner?" Surprise laced Gwen's voice.

"Yeah, nothing big. It was chili, but it was superb." Carrie traced the flower pattern on the bedspread with her finger.

"I'd say it's something. He didn't have to cook for you."

"Well, he had to eat. Anyway, he wants to show me the town tomorrow, so we'll see how that goes."

"Okay, I'll keep praying for you over here. Just remember to be open to God's words."

"I'll try. I just wish He would speak a little louder."

Carrie hung up the phone and plugged it into her charger. Then she wandered into the bathroom to brush her teeth and get ready for bed. She stared at her reflection in the mirror as she brushed her teeth. Open to God's words. She thought she was open to His words, but He didn't seem to be speaking into her ear. Carrie wished, as she had often in the past, that God would yell in her ear. She wanted to be sure she was doing the right thing.

With a sigh, she rinsed her mouth, brushed her hair, and then flicked the bathroom light off. As she changed into her pajamas, she sent up a silent prayer for wisdom.

8

Carrie woke to the beeping alarm of her cell phone the next morning. She turned it off and, out of habit, checked her messages for one from Philippe, but the mailbox icon on her phone remained empty. That was odd. He almost always texted her before going to work. Perhaps he had been working late and simply slept in this morning. But it was Saturday, and he usually worked on Saturdays at least in the morning. He should be getting ready for work, or with the time difference already be at work. Maybe he was with clients and had just turned his phone off.

Figuring that was why he hadn't answered, Carrie kicked off the covers and padded to the bathroom to shower. Cal had said he would pick her up late morning, whatever time that was, and she wanted to eat before he arrived. The warm water erased the last lingering bit of sleep and Carrie stepped out of the shower feeling refreshed and ready to take on the day. And Cal. She needed to keep her feelings in check today and not get sucked into his dreamy eyes and sweet smile.

Carrie wiped the fog off the mirror and leaned in to regard her appearance. Was it her imagination or did her skin look better than normal? She didn't have bad skin, but she always needed to add some tinted base to her face in New York to give her skin a little color, but she didn't need it today. Her skin shone, and her eyes sparkled back at her. Was it the Texas weather or was it Cal?

Irritated that thoughts of Cal kept invading her mind, she quickly brushed her hair and teeth before flicking off the light and heading to the closet to get dressed.

Her options were limited as she had brought little with her, but not knowing what Cal had in store for her, Carrie changed into the most functional outfit she had - a pair of flared pants and matching shirt she designed last summer. If she ended up staying much longer, she would have to see about finding a laundromat or a store.

The tempting aroma of bacon drifted in the air as Carrie neared the kitchen, and her stomach rumbled. She hadn't thought she was hungry, but her stomach begged to differ. Carrie entered the homey dining room and grabbed a seat by the window. Only a few other tables filled the room and currently she was the only diner. Dixie, however, appeared a moment later.

"Well, good morning, Carrie. Did you sleep okay?"

"I did, thank you." Surprisingly, the bed had been quite comfortable. Not her own bed by any means but more comfortable than many hotel beds she had stayed in.

Dixie smiled and clasped her hands together. "Wonderful, well I've made eggs and bacon and pancakes. What would you like?"

The tiny spontaneous part of Carrie almost said pancakes - one of her guilty pleasures - but she had been low carb for weeks. "Mm, the bacon smells delicious, so I think I'll take the eggs and bacon."

"Coming right up. Help yourself to coffee or juice at the counter there." Dixie pointed to a little table on the other side of the room. It held a coffee carafe, a pitcher of orange juice, a basket of creamer and cups and mugs.

"Thank you." Carrie smiled up at the woman as she stood. "I will certainly partake in a little of that."

Dixie smiled back and nodded before disappearing through a swinging door near the back of the room. Carrie continued to the table and picked up a ceramic mug. Each one held a different saying or picture, and the one she held currently had the words "Chocolate solves everything" emblazoned across it. Carrie smiled at the apt description of her - interesting that she would choose that mug. She poured a little cream and sugar into the mug and then filled the rest with coffee enjoying the way the dark liquid swirled with the cream to create a satisfying tan color. She had never been able to drink her coffee black.

Dixie reached the table at the same time Carrie was returning. "Bacon and eggs," she said placing the plate down.

"Thank you." Carrie set her mug down and then pulled the chair out to sit down again.

"Can I ask you something?" Dixie asked.

"Uh, sure, I guess." Carrie had no idea what she could want to ask a perfect stranger.

Dixie pulled out the opposite chair and sat down. Then she leaned forward as if sharing a juicy secret. "Where did you get your outfit? It's so beautiful and stylish."

Carrie blinked, caught off guard by the question. "I made it. I'm a designer."

Dixie's eyes grew wide. "You made it?"

"Yeah, that's kind of what I do." Carrie took a sip of the coffee and appraised Dixie. Though older, it was clear the woman took care of herself, but her style did leave a lot to be desired. Today, she wore a basic pair of black pants, a solid red shirt, and a black-and-white checkered vest.

Dixie folded her hands and leaned her chin upon

them. "I wish we had clothes like that in our general store, but supplies are limited. Of course, you can order online, but then there's the hassle of returns if it doesn't fit."

"That is a hassle." Carrie had always loved designing but one reason she stuck with it was for that very reason. She wanted to help women look their best and outfits online rarely fit correctly unless you had the perfect body type. "Maybe one day a designer will move to town." She had hoped to pray before eating, but as it appeared Dixie was in no hurry to leave, Carrie threw up a silent thank you and took a bite of the eggs.

"Yes, maybe," Dixie's eyes twinkled, "So, you and Cal-"

"Are just friends," Carrie finished before Dixie probed any further. She should have known that question would come up.

Dixie's face fell in a portrait of disappointment. "Oh, that's too bad. He's such a nice guy, but he won't date anyone around here though many have tried. Rumor is that he's pining for a woman from his past."

"Sorry, I wouldn't know," Carrie said with a shrug, careful to keep her face stoic.

"Well, I guess I'll keep praying she comes back then. I was sure hoping with the way he looks at you that he had finally moved on. He will be an amazing husband to some woman one day." Dixie pushed back her chair and stood up.

"I'm sure he will." Dixie nodded before returning to the kitchen and allowing Carrie to return to her breakfast. Her thoughts no longer remained on the eggs and bacon though. They now firmly lingered on Cal. *Did* he really gaze at her differently? More importantly, did it matter to her? Her life was back in New York with Philippe, so she shouldn't care how Cal looked at her, but if she were honest with herself, she did.

Cal pulled up in front of the inn and took a deep breath. He wasn't sure how much longer he had, but he imagined Carrie wouldn't stick around much longer. Today would be important, and he needed everything to be perfect. He stepped out of the truck and ran a hand down his green plaid shirt. It was his favorite and Ginny often made it a point to tell him how handsome he looked in it more than once. Cal hoped Carrie might feel the same.

He opened the door of the inn and smiled at the remaining smell of breakfast. Dixie was a good cook, but he hoped to convince Carrie to join him for breakfast tomorrow. He made a mean skillet.

"Morning, Cal," Dixie said as she entered the foyer. "Carrie's in the dining room."

"Thank you." Cal nodded. "I figured that's where I'd find her. Breakfast sure smells delicious."

"You want me to grab you some bacon?"

Cal shook his head. "No, I already ate, and I'm planning to show Carrie the town today, but perhaps we'll come back for dinner."

Dixie's eyes lit up. "Oh, you should. Dan and I were planning a little impromptu party with music and dancing, maybe a movie."

"Oh, yeah, what's the occasion?" Cal racked his brain, but he couldn't place any nearby holiday. Easter had just passed, and Cinco de Mayo remained over a week away.

Dixie's wide eyes shifted to the left. "Oh, um, it's the anniversary of the inn. Been open for over one hundred years this year." Dixie's parents had run the inn before her and evidently her parents had run it before them. Cal knew Dixie's family was one of the first residents, but he'd had no idea they had been in business that long.

"Well, that's amazing, but why aren't we making a bigger deal of it? The whole town should be in on something like that." The festivals were one thing Cal loved about a small town. There was a festival nearly every month of the year, but the apple festival and the cowboy roundup were their two biggest - both of which happened in the summer months.

"I thought it would be nice to have a smaller affair on

the actual day and then we can plan something bigger for next month. You'll come, won't you?"

"Sure." Cal shrugged. He wanted to show Carrie the town, but what better way to show her the small-town lure but a party. "Wouldn't miss it for the world."

"Great, well, I have to get planning, I mean, decorating and cooking. We'll start at 6pm. See you then." And then without another word, Dixie disappeared into the kitchen.

Cal shook his head and continued into the dining room to find Carrie. She sat at a table by the window sipping on a mug. As her eyes were focused out the window, he took a moment to study her. Her green pantsuit made the red and gold in her hair stand out even more than usual. He wondered if she had any idea how beautiful she was.

As if she sensed his eyes, Carrie turned his direction. A slight smile stole across her lips as Cal crossed the room to her. "Hey, Carrie."

"Hey Cal. You look nice."

"As do you. Are you ready?"

She glanced into her mug and sighed. "Yep, coffee's gone, so I guess I am."

"Big coffee fan, huh?" he asked. He hadn't taken her for a caffeine junkie.

"Not really. I like to have one maybe two cups a day but any more than that makes my stomach feel weird."

She stood and pushed her chair in. "If I need something warm after that, I usually opt for green tea."

Cal didn't tell her he generally drank an entire pot by himself, but he guessed he was also up much earlier than she was.

"Should I take the dishes somewhere?" Carrie asked uncertainly as she looked around.

"No, Dixie will take care of them. Part of the guest experience."

"All right, if you're sure," she said.

Cal wanted to hold out his hand, but he wasn't sure she would take it and he didn't want to make her uncomfortable. She smiled as he held the door open for her.

"We're going to walk?" Carrie asked as he turned away from the truck.

"Are you opposed to a little exercise?"

"No, it's just… it looks like it's about to rain." Her nose wrinkled as she stared up at the dark sky, but Cal wasn't sure if it was from disgust or fear.

The clouds looked a little menacing, but a little rain never hurt anyone. "Are you afraid of rain?" He bit the inside of his lip to keep from laughing out loud at her. The woman he married six years ago would have danced in a fountain with him if he'd asked her, but now she appeared hesitant. Again, he wondered what had made her change so drastically.

Her eyes narrowed, and he knew he had pushed a

button. "No, I'm not afraid of the rain." She tossed him a haughty glare. "Come on."

This time Cal did chuckle. Here was a glimpse of the girl from six years ago - feisty and unwilling to appear weak.

"Well, where do we start?" she asked as she scanned the area.

"Right here. I just found out today that the inn is one of the oldest buildings in town. Evidently, they've been open over one hundred years."

Her eyebrow formed a pointed arch. "You just found out today?"

Cal shrugged. "So, I'm not a town history buff, but Dixie said they are having a small party tonight to celebrate. Anyway, the post office over there was another of the first buildings in Soda Spurs."

"Why is it named Soda Spurs?" Carrie asked as they walked up the street.

Cal blinked at her. He had never looked up why the town was named what it was. He simply accepted it. "You got me there," he said with another shrug. "I have no idea."

"If you're going to be a tour guide and tell people the town has an interesting history, you really should learn a few of its facts." Her words could have sounded harsh, but her teasing tone and impish smile softened them.

"I've missed this side of you." Cal sneaked a sideways glance at her. "This spunky personality is the one I fell in love with. Why have you been hiding her?"

"I haven't been hiding anything." There was a defensive hint in her words, and her nose lifted into the air. "She comes out back home."

"Does she?" Cal didn't believe her. Something had changed her over the last six years.

"Why won't you sign the papers?" Carrie asked abruptly switching the topic.

"We exchanged vows, Carrie. That means something to me. Doesn't it to you?"

"We rushed into it, Cal. That doesn't mean we have to force it to work."

He shook his head. How would he get her to understand? "We may have rushed into it, Carrie, but that doesn't make it wrong. I've asked God often if I should let you go, and He's never told me yes."

Carrie looked as if she wanted to argue more, but before she could, a large drop of rain smacked her nose. A yelp escaped her lips and her hand swiped the bridge of her nose. "I think we better head back."

"It's just a drop of rain. You're not going to melt." But before the sentence completely left his mouth, the dark skies opened up and poured down buckets of rain. Within seconds, Carrie's red hair was plastered to her face, and her eyes were wide with shock.

She looked as if she was about to bolt back to the inn,

but Cal seized the moment and her hand. He had to make her remember. "Come on."

"Cal, we'll catch pneumonia," she said.

He flashed her his best grin and squeezed her hand. "First, that's an old wives' tale, and second, so what? We can be sick together." That thought held great appeal for him. He wouldn't mind caring for Carrie while she snuggled under a blanket. "Have a little fun, Carrie."

Her eyes narrowed to thin slits. She might have looked fierce if it weren't for the black trails of mascara snaking down her cheeks. "I have fun."

"Then prove it. Come run in the rain with me." He let go of her hand and took off running for the elementary school a block away, hoping he had goaded her enough that she would follow. It didn't take long before he heard her footsteps behind him, but he'd had a head start and his legs were longer, so he still reached the school first. He touched the brick wall before turning to face her.

"You cheated," she said with labored breath when she reached him. Her finger reached out to poke him in the chest and he grabbed it and pulled her closer to him.

"I gave you a chance." Cal had been a track star in high school. He could have easily outdistanced her had he wanted to, but this wasn't about winning. It was about getting her to relax and drop the emotional wall she had built some time since he'd last seen her.

Their gazes locked, and her lips parted. Cal took that

as his sign and leaned forward. How perfect would a kiss in the pouring rain be? Movie perfect, that was how perfect. Time seemed to slow down as he inched closer, and the heat between them grew. Her lips were inches from his when he closed his eyes. The beating of his heart sped up in anticipation of the moment he had only dreamed of for years, but when he reached the place he thought her lips would be, there was nothing but air.

Then her hand escaped his grasp and pushed against his chest. "Cal, I can't. Not while I'm engaged to someone else."

Cal wanted to protest, to remind her that they were married, but he didn't want to push her back into her shell. And she had said not while she was engaged to someone else which gave him hope that she was reconsidering their divorce. He could wait a little longer if it meant he could be with her forever.

"You're right. I'm sorry. I got caught up in the moment."

"Me too." Her voice was soft as her eyes sought his. They still brimmed with a hunger, and it was clear she was fighting the urge to kiss him as well.

Though desire still clouded his vision, he would respect her words. "We could have more moments like these," Cal said. His hand twitched at his side. He wanted so badly to touch her face, to feel her cheek in his hand.

Carrie's eyes slid to the side and Cal wondered if he had stepped too far. He wished he could rewind time and take the words back.

"This was dumb," Carrie began, and Cal's heart dropped, but then her lips curled into a small smile, "we should have run toward the inn. Now, we just have farther to walk back in the rain."

Though she tried for a teasing tone again, he could hear the difference in her voice. The moment was gone, and all Cal could do was hope he would have another chance.

❧ 9 ❧

When they reached the truck, Cal opened the door for her and she slid in feeling a little like a drowned rat. He entered the other side a moment later and started the truck, turning on the heater to warm them up and dry them off a little.

"Okay, that was more than a little rain," he said with a smile, "but I can give you most of the rest of the tour from here anyway. Over there is the town hall and Marnie's, a sit down but casual eatery." He shifted in his seat to point out her window. "Down that street is the flower shop, the general store, and Ernesto's, a more upscale restaurant, though I'm confident it's nothing like you have in New York."

"Can we stop at the general store?" Carrie asked. She wasn't sure why but she wanted to see what they offered.

Dixie's comments were still rattling around in her brain, and she hated that such a nice woman couldn't get the kind of clothes she wanted.

"Uh sure," Cal said putting the truck in drive, "Any particular reason why?"

"I want to see their clothing section."

His lips twitched at the corners. "Feeling the desire to dress a little more casually?"

"Something like that."

The general store was much smaller than Carrie had expected, about double the size of her apartment back home. They made a mad dash for the inside as the rain still poured down.

"Perhaps we should get an umbrella," Carrie said with a laugh as she shook the water out of her hair.

"Hey, watch where you're flinging that mane." Cal held up his hands and turned away from her.

"Oh, sorry, did that get you wet?" Carrie grinned and shook her hands at him sending a few more droplets his way.

"What's going on here?" A deep voice asked from behind her. Carrie's smile faded, and she lowered her hands.

Cal's smile, on the other hand, deepened. "Sorry, Jim. It's a little wet outside. I guess we got a little carried away. If you'll point me toward a towel, I'll clean it up for you."

"Nah, I'll get one of the employees to clean it up, but you can introduce me to your friend."

Carrie turned around to face the man and stuck out her hand. "I'm Carrie Bliss." As she regarded him, she had the distinct feeling she had seen him before though she couldn't place where.

Jim took her hand but flashed wide eyes Cal's direction as if for confirmation. Cal nodded. "Jim, Carrie. Carrie this is my brother-in-law, Jim."

Brother-in-law. Now, Carrie understood why he seemed familiar. This must be Stacy's husband and she had recognized him from the picture on Cal's desk. "Nice to meet you, Jim. I'm sorry about the water. It was my fault."

"Ah, well in that case, I'm certain Cal deserved it," Jim said with a smile.

"Hey," Cal protested but his smile told Carrie that he knew Jim was teasing him.

"Anyway, don't worry about it. I'll get one of the guys to lay out some extra mats. I'm positive you two won't be the last wet customers we have today."

"Thanks, Jim. See you guys at church tomorrow?"

"You bet. It was nice to meet you Carrie." Though he said the words to her, Carrie didn't miss the expression he flashed Cal's direction. He must know who she was.

"So, clothing section?" Cal asked as Jim walked away.

Carrie nodded and followed him to the right. The general store was set up much like a Walmart only on a much smaller scale. Groceries were to the left and everything else was to the right. The whole clothing department was about the size of Carrie's bedroom, and the selection was dismal to say the least. Two racks of dresses in sizes six to fourteen, two racks of shirts, and one rack each of pants and skirts. Nearly everything was either monochromatic or plaid flannel and all of it lacked imagination.

"Are you looking for something in particular?" Cal asked as Carrie flicked through the offerings.

"No, I just wanted to see the offerings." It was clear now why Dixie wished more was available. It would be hard to have an individual style with what was here. She wondered how profitable a shop would be out here? Maybe she could hire someone to run a small branch. Surely rent wouldn't be expensive in such a small town, but would it make enough to be profitable?

Carrie shook her head. She was getting ahead of herself. The first thing she needed to do was find out what kind of clothing Dixie wanted and if she had an idea on what might sell. Then she could figure out the cost and see if what the people could afford would be profitable to her.

"You're not going to buy anything?" Cal asked.

A laugh escaped Carrie's mouth before she registered how rude it must sound. She composed herself and thought about her words carefully. "Uh, not yet. Nothing here is really my style, but I do want an umbrella. Plus, I rather think I owe your brother-in-law."

"You don't, but all right, let's get you an umbrella." Cal led the way to a small sporting good section and Carrie chose a simple black one.

After paying, they headed back to the truck, but the rain had stopped, and Carrie had no need to open the umbrella. The air had cooled though, and she found herself wishing she had brought a coat.

"I'd be happy to finish the tour, but do you mind if we stop by the ranch, so I can check on Dexter and the herd?"

"Sure." Carrie shrugged. "I'm at your mercy today."

Cal pulled into the ranch and Carrie opened her door and stepped out. Involuntarily, a shiver raced down her spine. The air had certainly cooled with the rain.

Cal's eyes filled with concern, and he closed the space between them. "Are you cold? Come inside with me, and I'll get you a jacket."

"No, I'm fine," Carrie protested, but even as she did, another gust of wind hit her, and she shook again.

"You are not." His hands twitched at his side causing her to wonder if he was fighting the urge to wrap them around her. "Look, it's going to take a bit for me to check on the herd, and I don't want you freezing. Please, just humor me?"

His emerald eyes pleaded with her, and a flicker of déjà vu surfaced in Carrie's mind.

"I'm not drunk, Cal," Carrie said as she wrapped her arms around his neck. She knew this was crazy, but she'd felt a connection from the first moment he approached her on the dance floor. The gaze he sent her way made her feel something she had never felt before, something she hadn't even known she was even craving, and she didn't want to let go.

He tucked a strand of hair behind her ear, and his hand traced a trail down her face to cup her chin. "You say that now, but I want you to be certain. This is marriage we're talking about, so please just humor me and drink the coffee?"

"If it will make you feel better," she said with a wink. She dropped one arm to the table and picked up the mug of tan liquid. She took a sip and then downed the rest of the coffee. He watched her with a bemused smile and twinkling eyes. When she was finished, she placed the mug back on the counter and turned to him with a challenging stare. "Done, now can we go get married?"

Oh gracious. She hadn't been drunk. She had felt something for him then. No wonder he had been so shocked when she performed a one eighty the next morning.

"Are you okay?"

This time his hand did touch her arm, and Carrie started at the heat that seared up her arm. The image from the past shattered in her mind. "Yeah, fine, I'll take you up on that coat."

"Good, come on."

Carrie followed Cal into the house expecting him to turn down the hallway to the bedrooms, but he stopped just inside the door and pulled a leather jacket off the coat tree.

A masculine scent washed over her as she took the jacket from him and another memory flooded her mind. The woodsy cologne rising from the leather was the same one that had filled her nose the night they married.

"Are you two sure you want to get married?" The *minister, an Elvis impersonator in a sparkly white jump-suit, regarded them as he posed the question.*

Carrie looked around the wedding chapel. She wasn't certain getting married in an Elvis chapel had been her dream but marrying Cal would be worth it. "We're sure," Carrie said as she took Cal's hands.

He squeezed them and flashed a return smile. "Never been surer of anything in my life."

"All right, well then let's get this hunk a hunk of burning love legal." He took the marriage certificate from Cal and scanned over the names. "Dearly beloved," he began in an Elvis drawl. "We are gathered

here today to join this man and this woman in holy matrimony."

"You coming?"

"Huh?" Carrie blinked the memory away and focused on Cal who stood staring at her. He had on another leather jacket, black to match his hat.

"I asked if you wanted to come. You could ride on the back of Ginger with me."

"Um, okay all right." Carrie wasn't positive she should be getting up on a horse behind Cal. She was even less sure she should wrap her arms around him and breathe in his scent, but the words were already out, and her feet carried her his direction anyway.

Cal led the way outside and to the barn. Carrie watched as he saddled up his horse and then led her out of the barn. He swung up first and then held his hand out to her. "Just put your foot in the stirrup like last time, and I'll help pull you up."

"Okay." Carrie followed his directions and before she knew it, she was up and behind him. Her arms wrapped around his waist and she held on for dear life as he urged the horse to speed up. Even through her fear, the heat radiating off Cal reached Carrie. Her heart thudded in her chest at being so close to him and inhaling the woodsy scent coming off him. For the first time since she'd arrived, Carrie knew that if she didn't leave soon, she might never want to go, and it terrified her.

Cal finished checking on the herd and then urged Ginger back to the house. He didn't want to return as he was relishing the presence of Carrie's body pressed against his back, but he had promised to show her the rest of the town, and the weather had him a little worried. The air had shifted again, and the dark clouds looked as though they might pour more rain down any moment.

"Why don't you head inside while I take care of Ginger?" Cal suggested. Carrie's face was flushed though whether it was from the cold or the proximity they had shared, he wasn't sure. He hoped it was the latter.

"Are you sure?" she asked. Her eyes found his for a moment before glancing away, but in that small moment, he read the desire and confusion in her gaze.

"Yeah, I'm sure. Make yourself at home. I'll just be a minute." He smiled as he walked Ginger to the barn. Carrie was remembering. He was almost sure of it. Twice he had caught her staring off into space. If he could get her to remember that night - well, he had to. It would change everything.

He removed the saddle and brushed Ginger down quickly before returning to the house. He found Carrie staring at the photo above the fireplace.

"Ready?" he asked as he entered.

She turned to him, an unreadable expression on her face. "Do you have a television?"

"What?" He hadn't been expecting that question.

"A television. You know. TV." She turned back toward the fireplace. "The black box you watch entertainment on."

Cal's lips twitched. "I am aware of what a TV is. Yes, there's one in my bedroom though I don't watch it much. Why do you ask?"

Carrie's thin shoulders rose slightly and fell back down. "Everyone in my circle has multiple TVs. I found it odd that you didn't have one in here."

Would that be a deal breaker for her or was she comparing him to the men in her life? "I've never been much for TV. Too many other things to occupy my time."

She turned back to him, her forehead wrinkled in confusion. "In this town?"

"There's so much to a small town. There's community and nearly every month we have a festival. Almost everyone comes out and pitches in with food or decorations or music. I bet you don't even know your neighbors' names, am I right?"

Carrie sucked in a breath, opened her mouth as if to answer, and then sighed. "Guilty. I can recall the doorman's name and that's about it."

"See here everyone knows everyone else in town. There's an army to help if you're sick or down on your luck. People pray for you, say hello in the grocery store. You learn about your neighbors and friends, so yeah there are too many other things to do besides watch other people live on a black box."

Carrie held his gaze for a minute as if taking in his words. "Where did this picture come from?" She pointed to the landscape shot above the fireplace.

"Stacy took it."

Her eyes widened. "Stacy took it?"

Cal shrugged. "Yeah, she always had a photo bug growing up. I remember when she first got a camera. I think she was six. Most girls that age wanted dolls or stuffed animals, but not Stacy. She wanted a camera, and she was really careful with it. It took her awhile, but by the next Christmas, she was taking amazing pictures. She learned how to develop her own in high school."

"Why didn't she become a photographer then? She's talented."

"She met Jim and wanted to raise a family. Now she takes pictures in her free time kind of like my whittling."

"You whittle?" Her eyes shifted to the side as if puzzle pieces were falling into place.

"I do." He said the words slowly wondering if she would elaborate on why she was asking. "Ranching can be a little lonely in the evenings without someone to share them with. I whittle to pass the time."

Her eyes caught his, and his breath stilled. The desire

to kiss her flooded through his veins creating a pounding sensation in his head. Electricity crackled in the air, and he leaned forward.

"It's beautiful, the picture I mean." Her voice was soft, but she had pulled back. The moment was broken.

"Thank you." Cal swallowed his disappointment and motioned to the kitchen. "Shall we get some lunch? I don't want to eat anything too big because if I know Dixie, she'll have a feast planned."

Carrie nodded and followed him into the kitchen.

10

When the sandwiches were gone, and the paper plates thrown away, Cal held out his hand to Carrie. "Can I show you something?"

She nodded and took his hand, but as he led her down the hallway to the guest room, she protested, "Cal, what are you doing?"

"Just wait." The simple guest room didn't contain much, but it held one large secret. He opened the door to the closet and stepped back. Inside he had installed a few shelves and they were lined with his carvings.

She gasped as she stepped forward. Her hand touched a few of the carvings, delicately as if she were afraid they would crumble under her fingers. "Cal, these are beautiful. Why do you keep them hidden?"

"They're nothing special, only a hobby."

She turned to face him, her beautiful green eyes shining with intensity. "These are not nothing, Cal Roper. They are amazing, and people would pay big money for these."

This was the moment. He felt it. "What changed you, Carrie?" He held his breath hoping she would answer and he hadn't misread her.

Her eyes held his, bored into his soul as if searching his intentions. Then she sighed. "My dad got sick. Shortly after I graduated from college."

Cal could tell there was more to this story, so he crossed to the bed and sat down. Then he patted the space next to him. Carrie hesitated but finally joined him.

"I told you in Vegas I wanted to be a designer. When I graduated, my dad gave me money to start my boutique, but then he was diagnosed with cancer. My mom was a stay at home mother, and my dad's money was consumed pretty quickly with the treatments. I tried to sell the boutique to help out, but he wouldn't let me. He died a few months later, and I swore that I would be successful to make my dad proud."

Cal placed his hand on Carrie's. "Carrie, I'm sure your dad is proud of you. You are an amazing woman." His other hand stroked her face, and she leaned into it. Oh, how Cal wanted to kiss her. He wanted to hold her in his arms and kiss all the hurt and pain away. It made sense now, this drastic change from the carefree girl he had married to the focused woman in front of him now.

As if Carrie sensed his desire, she pulled away from his touch and stood up. "Anyway, enough of my past. We should head back to the inn. Maybe we can help Dixie out."

Disappointment flooded Cal, but he nodded and stood. He would continue trying. Whatever it took, he would keep trying.

The ride back into town was quiet, but Cal pointed out a few of the more memorable places on the outskirts of town, like Norma's and Fannie's place before continuing to the inn. Carrie hoped Dixie would need some help. She needed a break from Cal and his magnetism.

She'd almost kissed him back there when he'd asked about her father. The moment had been perfect with his hand on her cheek, but then she'd thought of Philippe. Philippe had never inquired about her father. Of course, to be fair Philippe hadn't known her before her father passed away, but he had never asked about any of her family.

A touch on her elbow brought her back to the present. "We're here. You ready?"

"Yeah." Carrie tucked her hair behind her ears and

pulled back her shoulders. She could do this. She could get through the evening without thinking about kissing Cal.

Inside, the inn was a flurry of activity. Carrie almost didn't even recognize the place. The furniture in the living room had been pushed to the walls to open up the floor and beautiful flower arrangements filled the room.

"I can see Rose has been here," Cal said with a slight chuckle as he scanned the room.

"Who's Rose?"

"She runs the local flower shop. Ironic, right?"

Carrie grinned at him. "Um, that's not really irony, but it is interesting."

Tiny creases erupted at the top of Cal's nose. "What's irony then?"

"Well, there's three types but the one you mean is situational irony. That's when an event is contrary to what one expects and is often amusing because of it."

The creases deepened. "And that's not the same thing as Rose running the flower shop?"

"Not quite." Carrie smiled and swatted his arm playfully. "Let's go see if Dixie needs any more help."

They found Dixie in the kitchen surrounded by piles of goodies. "Oh good," she said when she spotted them, "I'm not sure where the rest of my helpers went. Can you two bring all this to the dining room? We're going to set it up on tables and let guests grab what they want."

"Sure, Dixie, we'd be happy to." Cal picked up a few of the trays and Carrie followed suit. They passed through the swinging door and into the dining room where a woman was hanging a sign that read 'Happy 100 Years!'

"Hey, Rose," Cal said as he placed a tray down on one of the tables. "The living room looks great."

"Thanks." She finished attaching the last corner of the sign and turned to them. "Next time, I hope Dixie gives me more notice though. I had to freehand the sign." She glanced at Carrie. "I don't think we've met. I'm Rose."

"Carrie." Carrie shook her hand. "I'm a friend of Cal's."

Rose shot Cal a look but to Carrie she said, "Nice to meet you. Why don't you two go into the living room? I can help Dixie finish in here."

"No one was in the living room," Cal began but the sound of music cut him off. "I stand corrected. Apparently, there is now. Shall we, Carrie?"

"Sure." Carrie followed him out of the dining room and back toward the living room where an older couple now danced slowly around the floor. Other guests?

"I'd love to fill your dance card. What do you say?" Cal's eyes sparkled in the light, and tiny gold flecks appeared that reminded Carrie of fireflies though it had been ages since she had seen one.

Fireflies rarely appeared in New York, but Carrie remembered one summer when her parents took her camping. Out in the dark, they had zipped back and forth amazing and delighting her with their color.

Carrie blinked to shake the pull of Cal's gaze. She should say no. It probably wasn't right for her to be dancing with Cal, especially with the crazy feelings that kept popping up randomly - feelings that perhaps she should be with Cal instead of Philippe. But they were simply that, crazy, impetuous feelings that meant nothing. Those feelings had gotten her married to a stranger in the first place, and she wasn't that spur-of-the-moment impetuous girl any more.

"I doubt it is in danger of filling up," Carrie said with a teasing smile as she glanced around the room, "but sure."

Cal chuckled, and Carrie smiled at the sound. It was rich and velvety and relaxed, not at all like Philippe's laugh which always sounded tight and forced to Carrie. She shook her head as Cal took her hand and led her to the middle of the floor. She had no business comparing Philippe to Cal. Cal was her past and Philippe was her future, wasn't he?

As his arms wound around her waist, her thoughts drifted back to Gwen's wedding. Philippe wouldn't even dance with her there, but Cal spun her around the small wooden floor as if there was no place he'd rather be. Her mind flashed back even further, and she remembered dancing in Cal's arms in Vegas. He hadn't been self-conscious then either. He had twirled her effortlessly around that floor as well. No two left feet for him.

Her eyes glanced furtively to his face. The dark stubble on his cheeks called to her and before she could stop it, her hand was on his cheek. His feet slowed and then stopped. Time seemed to stand still as his eyes bore into hers. The gold flecks in his eyes danced, and Carrie found herself getting lost in them before her own eyes closed.

When his lips touched hers, a spark erupted in her soul. Was this what she had been missing the last six years? The reason she had run from every other man? Suddenly, the realization of what she was doing sunk in and she pushed back from Cal. "I'm sorry. We shouldn't have done that. I need.... I need some time." The pained expression on his face gave her pause, but she couldn't focus on that right now. She needed to sort through her feelings or distance herself from Cal, so she could at least think.

"Wait," Cal called out. "Can I at least pick you up for church in the morning?"

Church. Yes, that's what she needed. Church would ground her and remind her of what was important in her life. Her job, her friends, Philippe. "Sure. See you then." Then she dashed up the stairs to her room.

"Oh, dear, I certainly wasn't expecting that reaction," Dixie said as she came over to Cal.

"I was. She's remembering what we had and she's fighting it. I just need more time." He looked at Dixie. "I'll be back in the morning to pick her up for church. Can you make sure she's ready?"

"Of course."

11

Confusion still clouded Carrie's mind when she came down the next morning for breakfast, and she hoped Dixie wouldn't ask what had happened. After leaving Cal, she had prayed about the situation asking for clarity, but none had come. She still felt torn in two different directions.

"Morning, Carrie," Dixie said as Carrie entered the dining room. "What would you like this morning?"

"Actually, I'll take the pancakes today." Comfort food sounded delicious this morning, and she could always work it off later.

"All right, I'll be right back."

Carrie took the opportunity to fill up a mug of coffee and pick a table. When Dixie appeared a moment later with her food, Carrie motioned for her to join her.

"Dixie, I went by the general store yesterday, and you're right. Their selection is lacking. What kind of clothes would you most like to see if there was a store here?"

Dixie's eyes twinkled. "Are you thinking of opening a shop here, Carrie Bliss?"

"Not me personally. I have to stay in New York, but I'm thinking of finding someone who might like to open a shop here."

"Oh." The disappointment was palpable in Dixie's voice, but she quickly mustered a smile. "Well, I guess clothes like you were wearing yesterday. Some flowing shirts, skirts, and pants. And more colors offered. I love plaid, but occasionally I'd like to wear something else."

Carrie chuckled at that. "Their selection didn't give a lot of options in that area to be sure. Well, I'd love to get your measurements later and send you some design sketches. Maybe while I'm working on finding someone to open the shop, I could at least send you some designs to wear to drum up anticipation."

Dixie clasped her hands together and smiled. "That would be lovely, and I would happily wear anything you sent."

"Okay, this afternoon or evening then."

As Dixie scooted back to the kitchen, Carrie took a bite of her pancake enjoying the warm buttery flavor of the fluffy flapjack. She'd have to put in an extra workout when she got home, but it would be worth it.

Cal entered the inn unsure of what to say to Carrie. Did he bring up the kiss? Pretend it hadn't taken place? He didn't want to pretend it hadn't happened; he wanted it to happen again and often. But she was still figuring out her heart and as hard as it was, he needed to give her time to do that.

Carrie, thankfully, saved him the hassle of deciding. She stood in the doorway of the dining room, clearly finished with breakfast and waiting for him. "I hope this will do," she said indicating her pantsuit. "I hadn't planned on attending church while I was here, so I didn't bring my normal attire."

"Well, as you may have figured out, it's a farming and ranching small town community. We're pretty laid back around here, and while most people dress nicer for the Good Lord, I doubt anyone will say anything to you as a guest. Besides, what you're wearing now is nicer than a lot of people around here wear."

"Good. Now about last night. I let myself get carried away by the music and the atmosphere, but I promise it won't happen again."

Cal nodded and forced his disappointment down. "Whatever you say." He held out his arm to her, but she glanced down at it and then shook her head. Right, so she didn't want to touch him. Was that a good thing as it showed he clearly had an effect on her or a bad thing as if she'd reformed her wall and would no longer be persuaded?

They exited the inn and climbed into his truck. It wasn't far to the church, but the cool air still lingered after the recent rains. Cal didn't want to chance Carrie's catching cold or getting drenched again before they reached the small church.

As he drove, Cal hoped the Soda Spurs church would appeal to Carrie. He loved the small-town appeal, and he thought if she gave it a chance that she would as well.

The small parking lot was nearly full when they arrived, and Cal had to circle the lot to find an empty space. It wasn't usually this full, but perhaps more people had driven today instead of walking as they often did.

"Huh, I didn't realize this many people lived in this town," Carrie said as he parked the truck.

Oh no, was the snarky Carrie reappearing? He had thought she had gone away after dinner the first night, but perhaps she had just been taking a break. Cal sneaked a glance at Carrie's face, but the snide expression didn't reside there. Instead, the corners of her mouth twitched as if she was fighting the urge to smile. Was she teasing him?

"There's a lot about this town you don't know," Cal said as they approached the front door. "For example, I bet you were unaware we have a real-life billionaire in this town."

Carrie's head whipped his direction, and she turned accusatory eyes on him. "Who told you?"

"Who told me?" Cal's forehead wrinkled. That was an odd question for her to ask. "I think it's common knowledge around here."

"It is?" Her voice had a frantic edge to it which he didn't understand.

"Yeah, but even if it weren't, I'm fairly certain I'd know because Sam has worked on my truck."

"The billionaire's a mechanic?" Confusion filled Carrie's voice, and her head titled to the side as she regarded him.

"What? No, the mechanic is married to the billionaire. Look, there he is now." Cal nodded discreetly at the couple approaching on the sidewalk. "That's Brent McKasson. He used to be an actor in action movies. Played Derek McCloud."

"Why would a billionaire actor live here?" Carrie asked.

"Because he found love." Though he hadn't said the words at her, he sneaked a glance to gauge her reaction.

Her mouth opened, then closed as if she were trying to formulate the right words. Then her eyes flicked to Brent and Sam before darting back. "What does he do now?"

Cal smiled at the hint of interest he heard in her voice. Maybe if she realized some other city dweller had found a reason to stay here, she might find one as well. "He writes now. Gave up acting and pens novels. And he's happy." He added the last part just to emphasize the point a little more.

Carrie raised an eyebrow at him, but before she said anything more, Tina greeted them at the front door.

"Good morning, Cal, I see you've brought a friend."

She was fishing for answers as to who his pretty friend was, and Cal obliged her - to a point. "Hello, Tina, this is my friend, Carrie."

A twinkle flashed in Tina's eyes, and Cal expected she would want more details soon, but Tina was too poised to say anything to cause a guest discomfort. Instead, she turned her kind eyes and her motherly gaze to Carrie.

"Welcome, Carrie, I hope you'll enjoy your visit with us."

"I'm sure I will."

"Tina is the pastor's wife," Cal whispered as he led Carrie into the sanctuary.

Carrie nodded as two small figures raced toward them. "Uncle Cal," they shouted.

"Hey guys." He dropped to his knees to give his niece and nephew a hug.

"When are you going to come visit us again, Uncle

Cal?" Annie asked. Her light brown hair was pulled into pigtails today, and her bright blue eyes twinkled as she grabbed his hand.

"Soon, Annie, I promise."

"How about for lunch this afternoon after church?" Stacy asked as she approached with Jim right behind her.

"Stacy, I've got company in town." Cal glanced at Carrie who seemed to be watching the scene with amusement.

"So bring her," Jim spoke up. "The more the merrier. Stacy cooks for an army anyway."

Stacy swatted his arm playfully. "I'm afraid you've got that a little backward - you eat like an army - but we would love to have you, Carrie."

"Oh, um." Carrie looked to Cal as if asking what he wanted to do. Cal wasn't sure submitting Carrie to his crazy family was such a good idea but declining the offer now would break Annie's and Tyler's hearts, and they were already staring up at him with puppy dog eyes. Plus, they were charming. Maybe they could help him convince Carrie to stay.

"Fine. We'll come to lunch, but only if Carrie agrees to let me make her breakfast tomorrow."

"Cal, I have to be getting back to New York," Carrie said.

"Well, you have to eat even if you leave tomorrow. So, what's the harm in breakfast?"

Her lips mashed together forming a tight line, and he could tell she was trying to decide how much to say in front of his family. "Fine, breakfast. It will give us a chance to talk." She flashed a pointed look his direction that told him she was ready for a decision.

Cal hoped by tomorrow morning they would be talking about starting a life together, but he would have to step up his game. He couldn't keep her here forever - he knew that.

"Okay, great," Stacy said quickly. She must have sensed the tension in the air. "We have to drop these two munchkins off, but we'll see you this afternoon, okay?"

"We'll be there." Cal watched as his sister and her family walked back toward the Sunday school room hallway before turning to Carrie. "I'm sorry. I've been promising them I would get over to visit them, and I just couldn't break their hearts again."

"You guys are close then?"

"Yeah, Stacy is my account manager and she helps out around the ranch. We've always been fairly close, but after my parents moved away, we became even closer."

"That's nice, but Cal, we do need to talk about the papers."

"Not here though," Cal said continuing into the larger room. "Right now, it's God's time."

❧ 12 ❧

Carrie had thought she would feel uncomfortable and out of place in the little church. After all, the church she attended in New York was much larger and flashier, but she had found the church quaint and friendly. People had greeted her with smiles and warm handshakes and more names than she would ever remember. The music had been nice, the pastor a good speaker, and overall the place had seemed... genuine.

Carrie's mind had even wandered at times, conjuring up images of her attending this church with Cal on a regular basis before she shook herself back to reality. She wasn't staying. She was going home. To Philippe. The need to remind herself of that played over in her head like a broken record. Philippe was her fiancé. New York was her home. Soda Spurs was a momentary bump in her road.

"What did you think?" Cal asked as he held the truck door open for her.

"It was nice. Homey. I can understand why you like it." Though she'd never lived in one, she was beginning to perceive the charm of a small town. At her church, people said hello, perhaps they even gave you their name, but little connection continued beyond that. Here, people knew each other - the good, the bad, and the ugly. Their hellos and handshakes seemed much more genuine and Carrie couldn't deny there was an attraction to that - to friends who knew you as opposed to fellow believers who greeted you and forgot your name ten seconds later.

Carrie tried to sort out her emotions during the short ride to his sister's place, but it was like trying to untangle strands of Christmas lights that had just been thrown in a box and shook up.

On one hand, she had Philippe - handsome, wealthy, and everything she thought she had ever wanted. He attended church with her, supported her career as a designer, and he lived in New York. On paper, he appeared perfect.

And then there was Cal. Also handsome but in a more rugged way. He didn't seem to care about wealth which Carrie found refreshing. Odd but refreshing. He appeared a man of God, maybe even more than Philippe, but he was impulsive and stubborn, and he lived hundreds of miles from New York. On paper, he seemed anything but perfect, but that didn't change the way Carrie felt around him. Her heart did this funny little two step whenever he came close to her, but surely, she had the same feeling with Philippe. She was simply having trouble remembering it because being near Cal was so confusing.

Cal had asked her why she'd changed in the last six years and she supposed she had a little - losing a parent did that to you, but she hadn't thought she had changed as much as he said. But the change was clear now. The New York Carrie would never have raced through the rain like she did yesterday, and the Carrie from six years ago would have tilted her head back and danced in the puddles.

So, what had changed her? Was it simply her father's death? The need to be wealthy and make him proud had driven her daily after his death, and now that she achieved billionaire status, would she still be as driven?

Was it becoming a designer? She'd had to develop a tougher skin for sure. Design, like any "art" seemed subject to people's approvals and disapprovals, and she'd had many more people hate her designs than like her designs when she first started.

Or was it New York? She'd grown up near the city, but not in the city itself. She'd been surprised when she first moved into the city. The people there appeared more closed off, more focused on themselves. Strangers rarely said hi to one another, and it wasn't unheard of to witness a crime at least once a month if not more. Carrie always felt like she had to watch her back there, but she hadn't had that feeling here. She probably could have left the keys to the rental car in the ignition and not have had the car get stolen - something she would never do in New York.

Perhaps it was a combination of all three.

"Penny for your thoughts," Cal said peeking at her from the corner of his eye.

Carrie blew out a breath of air and shook her head. "You couldn't afford my thoughts."

"I'm good for a loan," he said taking his eyes off the road just long enough to flash her a crooked smile.

"Honestly, I'm just trying to sort out my feelings. I was so sure I knew what I wanted. Being a designer has always been my dream - I told you that and being successful in New York quickly became a part of that."

"And now?" he asked glancing at her briefly before turning his eyes back to the road.

She stared at him. How could he even ask that? She had let herself get swept up in the moment last night and kissed him. Even though she had pulled away, he had to perceive her desire. "I don't think I really have to answer that." Nor did she want to. Saying it out loud would only make it more real. "Can I ask you a question though? How are you so confident God wants us to stay together? It's not like He speaks out loud to you."

"Perhaps not out loud, but He speaks in many other ways. Every time I pray about you, He always leads me to Psalm 27:14 which says, 'Wait for the Lord; be strong and let your heart take courage; wait for the Lord!' So, while that isn't words in the way we are used to, it's words to me."

Carrie bit her lip. She wasn't certain God had ever spoken to her the same way, but was it because He wasn't speaking or because she wasn't listening? She had long considered herself a believer but being around Cal made her realize she was going through the motions more than living for Jesus.

"Here we are," he said as he pulled up in front of a small rambler painted yellow and white.

"Oh, good. I'm starving." Carrie's stomach rumbled like a punctuation to her statement, but she didn't mind. A change of conversation would be a welcome reprieve from the intense emotions raging within her.

"Uncle Cal." The two children from earlier ran out as Cal opened his door. Their adoring looks displayed the love they held for their uncle. Carrie wondered if Philippe had any nieces and nephews. She realized she didn't know much about his family either. He had always deflected the questions when she asked.

"Hey guys." Cal opened Carrie's door before bending down to hug his niece and nephew. "Annie, Tyler, you remember my friend Carrie from earlier right?"

"Are you going to marry her?" Annie asked as she looked at Carrie.

Carrie's eyes bulged, and she coughed as she tried to recover from her shock.

Cal smiled at Carrie before returning his attention to Annie. "Well, you never know what God has planned, but for right now, she's just a friend."

"Okay," Annie said. Carrie guessed her age to be four or five from the baby roundness still visible in her face. The boy looked a little older, perhaps seven or eight. "Dad's making hamburgers." She turned her eyes on Carrie. "Do you like hamburgers?"

"Of course, who doesn't?" Carrie usually ate her hamburgers surrounded by lettuce instead of a bun, but that was more than she needed to share with this angel.

"Cool, want to see my dolls?" Annie grabbed Carrie's hand and tugged her toward the house.

"I guess I'm going to see dolls," Carrie said with a laugh as Annie pulled her up the porch.

"Go ahead," Cal flashed a smile, "I'll come rescue you later."

Carrie followed the little girl into the house and down the hall. She tried to take in the surroundings, but all she managed to see was that Stacy was a minimalist much like Cal.

"Annie, don't go far. Lunch is almost ready," Stacy said as they passed the kitchen. "Oh, hi, Carrie."

"Hi, thanks again for inviting me."

"Come on, Carrie." The little girl tugged her a few more feet down the hall to an open door which was clearly her room if the pink walls and purple decorations were any indication. Carrie smiled as she took in the bright room. It reminded her of cotton candy at the fair.

"This is Sherri." Annie held up a cabbage patch doll dressed in a red jumper. "She has red hair just like you."

"So she does." Carrie took the doll remembering her own cabbage patch doll as a kid. She was surprised they were still being made and even more surprised they were still popular. In New York, American Girl Dolls that looked like their owners were all the rage, and while pretty, something about the simplicity of the Cabbage Patch dolls appealed to Carrie more. "She's beautiful."

"So are you," the little girl said.

"Ah, thank you." Carrie felt she should say more after the compliment, but she had no idea what.

"I think you and Uncle Cal should marry," Annie continued. "He always seems a little sad, but he looks happier now that you are here."

"Oh, well, that's good, but I live far away from here, and I'm going to have to get back home soon."

"That's too bad," Annie said as she picked up another doll. "I like playing with you."

"Annie, Carrie, lunch is ready," Stacy's voice carried from down the hall.

Relief flooded Carrie. How could a little person she didn't even know manage to say just the right things to make her uncomfortable? "I guess we better go eat."

Annie shrugged, but she put the doll down and led the way back toward the kitchen.

The rest of the family was already gathered around the table when Carrie and Annie arrived. Carrie took the seat next to Cal as Stacy helped Annie into her booster seat. A plethora of food filled the table top: hamburgers, salad, chips, and fruit. Carrie's stomach rumbled as she looked from one dish to the next.

"Shall we pray?" Jim asked.

Around the table, everyone grabbed hands and Carrie bowed her head and closed her eyes. It was odd how at home she felt. She hadn't even met Philippe's family yet, and the only other people she felt this close to were Gwen and Drew. Still, something comforting and familiar existed with Cal's family. Something she could definitely get used to.

"So, how's it going?" Stacy asked Cal as he helped her clean up after dinner.

He glanced toward the living room where Carrie worked a jigsaw puzzle with Tyler and Jim while Annie played with dolls nearby. "Not as good as I'd hoped, but better than I expected, I guess. She's relaxing, and we kissed last night. It was short, but I think she's starting to remember Vegas."

"And how long are you going to keep this up, Cal? She has a job back home I'm sure. You'll have to let her get back to it."

"I know." He picked up a plate and handed it to her at the sink. "I just keep hoping for a little more time with her."

When the table was cleared, and the dishes filled the sink, Cal joined Carrie in the living room.

"Do you do puzzles?" She grinned up at him, her eyes flashing a challenge.

"I'll have you know jigsaw puzzles are my specialty." He pulled out a chair and sat next to her.

"I thought ranching was your specialty."

"I have many talents." Cal winked at her and picked up a piece. He turned it over in his hand a few times and then placed in the right spot with the first try.

"Hmm, so it seems, but you might have met your match with me." She picked up another piece and placed it next to his piece.

"Yeah, she's pretty good, Uncle Cal," Tyler spoke up. "She put all of that together." He pointed to the right side of the puzzle.

"Well, I'm not surprised." Cal fixed his gaze on Carrie. "I knew she was amazing the moment I met her."

Soft pink flowed up Carrie's cheeks, and her eyes dropped to the puzzle. "I'm not that amazing."

Cal begged to differ, but he didn't want to make her uncomfortable. Silence fell as they raced to finish the puzzle first.

"Hah, I've got the last piece," Carrie teased as she held up the final jigsaw cutout.

He chuckled, enjoying the look of sheer happiness gracing her features. She finally looked relaxed and carefree, the way he remembered her six years ago. "You did a great job."

"No, *we* did a great job."

His heart flipped at the way she said 'we.' "You're right. We make a great team."

Her eyes locked with his and the surrounding sounds faded away for a moment. Just a moment. "We do, but we should head back. I need to check in with my assistant."

Just like that, the carefree look disappeared, replaced with a look of concern that Cal wanted to wipe away. "All right, I should check on Dexter and the herd again as well."

"Ah man, do you have to go?" Tyler asked.

"Yes, but I'll see you again in a few days." Cal ruffled his nephew's hair and gave him a side hug. "You too, Annie."

"Thank you for joining us," Stacy said as she entered the living room.

"Thank you for having me," Carrie said. "Maybe I'll see you again soon."

"We'd like that," Stacy said.

Cal gave her a hug and shook Jim's hand before extending his arm to Carrie. He wasn't sure she would take it, but after a slight hesitation, her skin touched his lighting a fire to his arm that traveled all the way up to his shoulder.

"Thank you for coming with me," Cal said as they reached the truck. He opened the door for her and helped her climb in.

"Of course. Your family is very nice, and it's not like you gave me much choice."

He smiled at her and shut her door before walking to the driver's side.

"I know they'd like to see more of you." He sneaked a glance as he started the truck.

"Mm." Carrie gave him a wistful smile before turning to look out the window.

Cal stifled a sigh as he pulled out of Stacy's drive and headed toward the inn. When they reached it, he turned off the ignition and stepped out to open Carrie's door. As her foot hit the pavement though, a voice carried out to them.

"Carrie? Where have you been?"

Carrie's head whipped toward the sound. "Philippe?" A tall man with dark hair and a hawkish nose stepped out of the shadows. "What are you doing here?"

"What am I doing here? You never called to let me know what was going on, so I felt the need to come check on you."

"I did call you when I arrived," Carrie said. "Your voicemail picked up, but I left a message. I figured you were busy since I didn't hear anything back."

The man's eyes flicked to Cal. "And I see you've been busy since then. Who is this?"

"I'm Cal," Cal said stepping forward. "I'm Carrie's husband." Cal wasn't certain why he said it other than he didn't like the guy, but he regretted the words the instant Carrie turned fiery, accusing eyes on him.

"Husband?" The man's brows inched up his forehead. "What's going on, Carrie?"

Carrie glared at Cal a moment longer before turning back to the man. "Technically, he's right, Philippe. When I was twenty-one, I went to Vegas with some friends. I must have had too much to drink because I married Cal. I came here to get the divorce papers signed. I'm sorry I didn't tell you."

"And it took you two days to get the papers signed?"

"Cal was being a little stubborn." Carrie's voice sounded stiff and forced, but Cal wasn't sure if it was because of what he'd said or because of the man.

"Probably after your money, no doubt." The man turned eyes as cold as ice Cal's direction.

Anger flared in his gut, but Cal took a deep breath to keep from punching the man. "I don't care a thing about Carrie's money."

The man's eyes shot fire at Cal before returning to Carrie. "Hey, what happens in Vegas stays in Vegas, right?"

Cal clenched his hands at his side. The man had completely ignored him - as if he weren't standing just a few feet away. And Cal hated that saying. Too many people used it to do things they wouldn't normally do and count them as okay.

"Yeah, you know how it is." Carrie shrugged her shoulders. "Young and stupid."

Carrie turned to Cal, but the expression in her eyes was unreadable. Still, he knew in that instant that anything they had built was gone. He would have to let her go and sign the papers.

"Carrie, I'll get the papers and bring them over in the morning. Will that be soon enough?" The words pained him, and his stomach clenched.

"I'd rather we go tonight, Carrie. I have work tomorrow." The man grabbed her hand pulling her closer to him.

"No, we can go in the morning. I still need to pack and ready the plane." She turned back to Cal, but her eyes never met his. They appeared locked on the ground at his feet. "Thank you. If you could have those papers here at seven am tomorrow, I would greatly appreciate it."

"Of course." Cal tipped his hat first to Carrie and then to the man - the man he would remember forever as the one who stole Carrie from him. What made it even worse was the man's behavior. It seemed as though he tried to dominate and control Carrie, and it saddened Cal. She possessed such a fiery spirit, but it fizzled around this man. The smile and gaiety he had seen earlier had been erased with one word from the man's mouth. How could she marry him? Didn't she see how wrong they were for each other?

Cal left them there - two people who looked more like strangers than an engaged couple - and continued to his truck. As soon as he got inside, he turned his face upward. "Why God? Why would you bring her in my life only to take her away again? I've waited all these years, and I finally thought you were going to reconcile this relationship, and then this happens. I want to know why!" Cal was surprised at the anger in his voice. He couldn't remember the last time he had raised his voice at anyone, much less at God.

"Trust me." The words filled his head, and Cal's anger softened. Trust. It was hard to do right now, but what other option did he have? He glanced back toward Carrie only to see them entering the inn together. Trust. It wouldn't be easy, but as that was all he could do, Cal took a deep breath and gave the situation over to God.

Carrie woke early the next morning. Truth be told, she wasn't sure she had actually slept. After Cal left, she and Philippe had gone inside to secure him a room. Thankfully Dixie had been able to accommodate them. After that, they spent an hour down in the dining room. Philippe wanted details about the weekend, but Carrie managed to give him just enough information to satisfy him before turning the tables and asking him to tell her about his weekend. One thing Philippe loved was talking about his business. And as long as Cal came through with the papers, Carrie figured she might never have to tell Philippe all the details of the weekend.

After a shower, she finished packing her bag and scanned the room one last time to make sure she hadn't forgotten anything. A bittersweet feeling lay on her. She was glad to be going home, but a part of her knew she would miss this place. Miss Cal and his family even though ire still flowed through her when she thought of him informing Philippe of their marriage.

"Good morning, Carrie." Dixie looked up from the coffee carafe she was filling and greeted Carrie as she entered the dining room.

"Morning Dixie. Philippe and I will be checking out today if you want to get our receipts ready."

Dixie nodded, but her lips hinted at a sad smile. "I'm sorry to hear that. I hoped you might stick around a while, but I'll get right to it. Pancakes this morning again?"

"Sure." Carrie pushed back the sadness she felt at Dixie's words and filled a mug of coffee. Her table from yesterday was open, so she headed that direction. Only one other person sat in the dining room currently, and Carrie wondered how Dixie stayed in business.

"Well, it's quaint. I'll give it that."

Carrie looked up at Philippe as he set his mug down across from her. She smiled up at him as she asked, "How did you sleep?"

"Not as bad as I had expected, but I'm certainly ready for my own bed again. I don't know how you slept here two nights."

She took a sip of the satisfying warm beverage as she

regarded him. "Oh, my bed was fine. I could have stayed longer."

Philippe stared at her, a concerned look on his face. "What happened to you out here?"

Carrie dropped her eyes to the mug. That was a good question, but she didn't have an answer for Philippe. It was probably just the lure of the small town, and she'd be back to her normal self as soon as she returned to New York.

"Here are your pancakes," Dixie said interrupting the uncomfortable silence.

"Thank you."

"Anything for you, sir?" Dixie turned her attention to Philippe.

"Just bacon and eggs for me if you have them."

"I'll be right back with them."

"Pancakes, Carrie? Since when do you eat pancakes?"

"I do on occasion." A movement outside the window caught her attention and she set her fork down. "Oh, I see Cal with the papers. I'll be right back." Before he could argue, she pushed her chair back and raced from the room.

She flung the front door open as he reached the top step. "Hey, Cal."

"Carrie." He tipped his hat, but his voice held none of its usual teasing inflection. "I've got the papers for you." He reached in his pocket and withdrew the familiar bundle of papers. "I hope you'll be very happy."

Carrie took the papers, not even glancing for a signature. She could tell by the expression on his face he had signed them. "Cal," she began, but he shook his head.

"I don't understand why you are marrying him, but perhaps you're a different person in New York. I'm glad I got to see you again, even if only for a weekend."

Carrie's throat choked with tears. She hated that she was hurting him. "I'm glad I got to see you as well. Maybe-" She stopped. There was no use going down that road. She was going back to New York, and he was staying here. The chances they would ever meet again were slim to none. "Tell your family thank you again for everything."

Cal nodded and turned away, but Carrie caught the glistening of his eyes before he turned from her. She watched him get in his truck and fought her own tears, but it was better this way. At least that's what she needed to tell herself.

"Did you get it all taken care of?" Philippe asked as she returned to the table.

"Yep, all good," Carrie said with a tight smile. "I'll get these turned in and it should be finalized soon."

"Good, the sooner the better."

She dropped her eyes to the plate and blinked back the tears threatening to spill over. Crying in front of

Philippe was not an option, and really, she was sure she'd be fine when she returned to New York. Life would pick back up like normal. She would design her wedding dress, plan her wedding, and get back to work. It would definitely keep her busy.

"Are you finished, Carrie? I'd like to get back to New York tonight."

"Sure." Carrie took the last bite of pancake and chewed slowly. She'd doubted many more pancakes would be in her future as she would need to get back to eating clean to fit in the dress she imagined wearing for her wedding.

They checked out with Dixie and then loaded their light luggage into the waiting car out front. Half an hour later, they were situated on the plane and heading home. Only then did Carrie realize she had forgotten to take Dixie's measurements.

Cal pulled into his driveway and turned off the truck. He had firmly believed he would be able to remind Carrie of why they married, that she would change her mind about leaving, and they would have a life together, but instead she was gone. She was gone and the gaping hole in his heart was bigger than before.

"I wasn't expecting to see you today," Stacy said as

Cal entered the hallway. Stacy often came over early to check the books and the orders. "Where's Carrie?"

"On her way back to New York with her fiancé."

Sympathy filled Stacy's eyes as she stood and walked to Cal. "I'm so sorry. I thought the way she looked at you last night that she was changing her mind."

Cal shrugged. He had thought many times over the weekend that he had changed her mind, but it hadn't turned out that way.

"What are you going to do now?" Stacy asked.

"The same thing I've always done. I'm going to work and pray and do my best to serve God."

"Cal-"

"Not now, Stacy. I've got chores to do. Might as well get to them." He continued past her to the backyard barely acknowledging Dexter when he jumped up on him. The world just didn't seem right anymore.

"How long are you going to mope around here?" Stacy put her hands on her hips and fixed him with her best 'snap out of it' expression.

"I'm not moping." Cal cinched the saddle under Ginger and smoothed out her skin to make sure it wasn't folded under the belt.

"What do you call it then? You barely eat. You've lost weight. Even Tyler and Annie have been asking why you never play with them anymore. It's been a month, Cal. When are you going to let her go?" She picked up the brush and ran it through Ginger's mane.

Cal took his hat off and ran his hand through his hair. "I don't know how to, Sis. Every bone in my body still tells me that we belong together."

"You haven't even tried to get over her. Why don't you go out with Ginny and at least see if there's anything there? She's a nice girl, Cal. You could have a decent life with her."

A decent life. Cal didn't want a decent life. He wanted an amazing life, but he was certain that option had left when Carrie did. So, perhaps he should settle. Stacy was right. Ginny was nice and pretty, and she liked him. "Fine, the next time she comes by, I'll take her up on her offer."

"Good. I don't think you'll regret it." She finished the brushing and laid the brush back down.

Cal wasn't so sure about that, but he couldn't keep letting life pass him by. He'd wasted six years on Carrie. If he ever wanted to have a family - and he did - then he needed to move on. "We'll see." Cal walked Ginger out of the barn and then swung up on the saddle before heading out to move the cows. At least when he was riding, he still felt whole. This was where he belonged.

"That was a lovely dinner, Philippe," Carrie said as he opened the door of his BMW for her. It had been delicious, but Carrie couldn't keep her thoughts from straying back to the dinner Cal had cooked for her. Even though she had suggested they try cooking a meal together, Philippe had vetoed that idea insisting they had the money to go out or hire someone to cook for them.

"Yes, it was nice though our server was a little slow on her service. I would have left a much larger tip if she had refilled my glass quicker." He shut her door and walked to the driver's side.

"I'm sure she was doing her best," Carrie said softly. "The restaurant was busy."

"You're probably right." He started the car and backed out of the space. "Hey, let's move the wedding to June."

Carrie blinked at him. Was he joking? "June? That's only two months away, Philippe. That's not enough time to plan a decent wedding."

He glanced at her from the corner of his eye. "What are you talking about Carrie? With our money, we can make it happen as quickly as we want."

Our money. Carrie wondered just how much he was planning to contribute to the wedding. Her mother certainly had no money to give, so the majority would fall on Carrie's shoulders. "Okay, but what's the reason to speed it up?"

"I've been considering the idea since we got back, and I realized after seeing that other man that I don't want to chance losing you. I want to marry you as soon as possible, so we can start our life together."

"Well, I mean I can look around, but June is a busy

wedding month, and I need enough time to make my dress."

"I don't care that much about the venue. Just find a place that can hold five hundred to a thousand people. I'm sure we'll get the same kind of publicity that Drew and Gwen did now that you're a billionaire as well. In fact, you should even get more because you're a female billionaire. Those don't happen every day."

Carrie winced at his sexist comment. Did he have any idea how chauvinistic he sounded? "They didn't ask for the publicity, Philippe. I think it's rather crass if we ask for it."

"Oh sure, sure, I just mean your wedding should be a headline story. Anyway, pick a good place and finish your dress. I can be ready pretty quickly. In fact, I'll have my tailor start on my tux tomorrow."

"Philippe, would you do a devotional with me tonight?" The words surprised even Carrie as they leapt out of her mouth. She had wanted to ask him since they returned from Soda Spurs, but every time she was about to ask, something kept her from it.

"A devotional? What do you mean?" His hands had tightened on the steering wheel and the stiffness in his posture matched the tone of his voice.

"I mean read the Bible and discuss it with me. I've been thinking it would be a good tradition to start."

"Where's this coming from, Carrie? You never wanted to do this before."

"To be honest, Cal did a devotional with me when I was in Soda Spurs, and I really enjoyed it. I want it to be a part of my married life."

"Cal, huh?"

Carrie nodded. She hated mentioning Cal's name as it always made Philippe tense, but the devotional was one thing she had really enjoyed and wanted to continue.

"Sure, if it means that much to you, I'll try. I've never done one before though."

"We'll figure it out together," Carrie said.

CHAPTER 15
JUNE

"Earth to Cal."

Cal shook his head to clear the woman from the past and focus on the woman in front of him. "Sorry, Ginny, what were you saying?" He set down his half-eaten sandwich to give her his full attention.

"I was saying we should try out the new movie theater in town. Sam said they are playing When Harry Met Sally, and that's one of my favorites." Ginny's lips formed a hopeful smile as she picked up her drink.

"Oh, yeah, sure, we could do that." This was his fourth date with Ginny, and while she was not Carrie, she was a nice woman. Still, no desire flamed within Cal for her the way it had with Carrie. He wondered if he would have to settle for a loveless marriage in order to start the family he longed for. He couldn't believe that was what God had planned for him, but he hadn't heard any wisdom from God on the Carrie front since the day she left.

Ginny sighed. "No, Cal, I don't think we can."

"What? What are you talking about, Ginny? I said we could. I can make time."

"It's not that, Cal; it's this." She motioned at the space between them. "We've tried dating for over a month, but I can tell your heart isn't in this. Half the time you're too busy to do something and when you aren't, your mind is a million miles away."

Cal raked a hand across his face. "I'm sorry, Ginny. You are an amazing woman, but you deserve more than I can give you. I'm afraid a woman stole my heart six years ago and I haven't been the same since."

"This is the woman you brought to church that one time, right? The pretty redhead?"

Cal nodded. "Yep, that's the one. Carrie."

"So, where is she now?"

A snort escaped Cal's mouth, and he reached into his pocket. His fingers touched on the envelope he had received in the mail yesterday. He withdrew it and tossed it on the table. "She's in New York about to marry the wrong guy."

Ginny picked up the envelope and peered inside. She withdrew the invitation first. "Carrie Bliss and Philippe

Caron request the honor of your appearance June 15th at six pm?" She raised a brow at him. "She invited you to her wedding?"

Cal scoffed and shook his head. "No, there's more."

Ginny pulled a folded piece of paper out of the envelope and unfolded it. "Dear Cal, you don't know me, but I'm Gwen, Carrie's best friend. I'm not positive exactly what happened with you two in Soda Spurs, but she loves you. Please don't let her marry Philippe. It will be the worst mistake of her life. I've enclosed the invitation, so you know how much time you have. Gwen."

Ginny refolded the letter and tucked it and the invitation back in the envelope. "What are you still doing here, Cal?"

"What do you mean?"

"I mean the woman you love loves you and is about to marry another man. Her best friend is begging you to come and break up the wedding, and you're still here. Why?"

Cal shook his head. "Carrie left. She left me for him. I can't break that up. What if her friend is wrong?"

Ginny leaned back and crossed her arms. "I understand women are hard for men to figure out but let me let you in on a little secret. The best friend always knows best. This Carrie is probably fighting her feelings the same way you tried to and succeeding about as well I'd guess. I guarantee it will not be a wasted trip if you go out there."

Could he do that? Show up and break up a wedding? "I don't know, Ginny. Money is tight; I'm not sure I even have the money to get there. I'm about to have to sell half my herd to make my payments to the bank."

Ginny's eyes lit up. "Actually, you have the money to get there." She leaned down and pulled an envelope out of her purse and handed it to him.

"What is this?" he asked as he took the envelope. He folded back the lip and blinked at the check inside. It was made out to him for a thousand dollars.

A smile stole across Ginny's mouth. "I put up some of your wood carvings online. They sold like hotcakes. People love them, Cal."

Confusion clouded Cal's mind. People liked his carvings? Enough to buy them? "They sold, really?" His carvings were a hobby, not something he had ever considered doing for money.

"Of course they did." Ginny looked at him as if he'd lost his mind. "You are really talented, Cal. Anyway, that should be enough to cover a plane ticket. Then if you can get me some more carvings, I'll upload pictures of them. I bet if you could do a new piece a week then you could pay off your loan in no time."

Cal stared at the amazing woman across from him. A part of him wished he had developed feelings for her because she deserved someone amazing. "Why are you doing this for me, Ginny?"

Ginny shrugged. "While I wish there had been more between us, Cal, you are still my friend. Friends help friends. Now, go home, buy a ticket, pack, and go get your woman."

A surge of adrenaline flooded Cal. Maybe he could do this. He splayed his hands on the table top. "Okay, Ginny, I will."

Carrie zipped up the dress on the mannequin and stepped back to admire it. The dress hung perfectly with the trim barely gracing the floor, and the train pooled out in a perfect circle. It was beautiful to say the least.

"Carrie, it's breathtaking, but are you sure you want to get married so quickly?" Gwen folded her arms across her chest and sent Carrie a narrowed stare.

"Of course I want to get married." Carrie leaned closer and snipped a spare thread.

"Okay, let me rephrase that. I understand you want to get married, but so quickly? Have you forgotten about the misgivings you told me about?" Gwen stepped in front of the dress to capture Carrie's undivided attention.

Carrie bit her lip. Yes, there had been a few misgivings with Philippe since they got back - the first being that he wanted to rush the wedding. Then there had been the devotional disaster. Though he had read them with her, there had been none of the connection she felt when she had done the same thing with Cal. Of course, it probably helped that Cal was much more knowledgeable in the word than Philippe was, so reading with him became a learning experience for her instead of just two people reading the Bible.

"I'm over those. Philippe is a great guy."

"He is." Gwen took Carrie's hand, "but he's not Cal. Are you sure you're over him?"

"What do you mean?" Carrie turned away to avoid Gwen's questioning eyes. "Lace, it needs just a little more lace."

"It doesn't need anything, Carrie," Gwen said coming up beside her. "I know you felt something for Cal when you were down there because you were different when you got back, and I saw that the way you looked at Philippe had changed. Are you sure you don't want to see him one more time before you go through with this marriage just to make sure?"

A giant sigh billowed out of Carrie's lips, and tears burned her eyes. "I already did, Gwen." She crossed to her desk and pulled a letter out of the drawer. It was thick and marked with the words 'Photos! Do Not Bend!'

"What is this?" Gwen asked as she took the envelope.

"It's from Dixie, the lady who ran the inn. I wrote to her saying I was interested if there were any properties for sale-"

"Wait, you're going back?"

Carrie shook her head annoyed at Gwen's interruption. "No, I was thinking about opening a boutique there and finding someone to run it. You should see their clothing selection. It's awful."

"You never told me you were thinking about that."

Was that hurt she heard in Gwen's voice? "I didn't tell anyone. I didn't want anyone to talk me out of it. Anyway, Dixie wrote me back that there's a shop for sale, but then she told me Cal was seeing someone else. She enclosed a few pictures."

Gwen returned her attention to the envelope and opened it. She scanned the letter first and then studied the two pictures. "Okay, so if this Dixie is correct, they haven't been dating long. I mean look at this picture. They aren't even touching." She turned the picture around and Carrie closed her eyes. She had studied the pictures enough when the letter first came in.

"He's with someone else." Carrie wiped a traitorous tear off her cheek. She was not going to cry. She had cried too much already. "I waited too long. He waited six years for me, but I guess when he finally signed the papers, he gave up on me."

"Oh, Carrie, I'm so sorry." Gwen's arms stole around

her, and that was all the tears needed to break the dam. One escaped and trickled down her cheek leaving a cold, wet trail.

"So, you see?" She sniffed against Gwen's shoulder. "Cal is out of the picture and it just makes sense to marry Philippe."

"Carrie, honey, it never makes sense to marry someone just because they are there. You should marry for love, and if you don't love Philippe-"

"I did marry for love once already." Carrie sucked back the rest of her tears and pulled away from Gwen. "I was stupid and wasted it, but I had my chance. Besides, I love Philippe." She stepped back toward the dress and looked at it with a critical eye. "Now, what do you think of this dress?"

Gwen sighed and stepped beside her. "I think it's amazing and you will look beautiful in it."

CHAPTER 16

C al looked at his watch and then out the window as if by looking out the window, he could encourage the plane to move faster or the hands of time to move slower. Why did there have to be a delay today? He was on a tight schedule as it was.

The elderly woman next to him touched his arm grabbing his attention. "You have a hot date?"

"Huh?"

"You've looked at your wristwatch seven times in the last ten minutes. I may be old, but I still have my eyes. Now, as far as I've seen in my life, only two things make a man as antsy as you are. Work and women, so which is it?"

Cal smiled. She must have a been a handful in her prime. "It's a woman. I have to go break up a wedding to win back the bride, and I know little about New York, but I fear I'm going to be too late."

The woman clucked softly. "Breaking up a wedding. Do you know she loves you back?"

"No, but my friend Ginny swears this shows she does." He reached into his pocket and pulled out the wedding invitation. It was crinkled from being in his pocket and starting to show its wear from the many times he had read and reread it.

The woman took the envelope and opened it. She scanned the invitation first and raised a thinned brow at him. Her expression changed, however, when she read the letter. "I find your friend Ginny very wise, but the Manhattan Penthouse is at least twenty minutes from the airport and that's if there's no traffic. Do you have a fall-back plan in case we are late landing?"

Cal's face fell as he took back the invitation. "No, I hadn't expected to be delayed. I don't have Gwen's number and texting or calling Carrie just seems wrong."

"Well, I will pray everything works out for you then. And one more piece of advice."

Cal looked at her expectantly. She seemed knowledgeable about New York, so he would take whatever advice she doled out.

The woman looked to her left and then leaned closer. "Don't be nice getting off this plane. People in New York move quickly and walk over people if they have to.

If you want to make it to the Manhattan Penthouse on time, you'll have to fight for it." She winked at him and patted his arm, and Cal chuckled.

"I'll do my best." The thought of pushing people out of his way to get off the plane first appalled him, but if it meant getting to Carrie on time, he would do it. He was sure his momma would understand and forgive him later.

Cal settled back into the seat, but he couldn't help one more glance at his wrist.

Carrie stared at her reflection in the mirror and tried to find her happiness. She might have convinced Gwen she was in love with Philippe yesterday, but she was having more trouble convincing herself today. Now that the wedding was actually here, the reality of what she was about to do sat on her shoulders like a weighted blanket.

"Another fantastic dress," Alyssa said over her shoulder.

Carrie's eyes flashed to the dark-haired woman behind her. She wore a deep purple empire waisted gown. Her dark hair was pulled up in an elaborate up do with only a few tendrils snaking down around her ears. A wide smile graced her delicate features. Motherhood suited her. Her face held a glow that Carrie only hoped hers would hold one day.

"That's because Carrie is an amazing designer," Gwen said joining Alyssa in the mirror's reflection. Gwen's gown was a match to Alyssa's, her red locks styled similarly. As with Gwen's wedding, Carrie had wanted them not only to look beautiful but to have a gown they might wear again.

Carrie turned to face her friends. "Thank you both. You are the most amazing friends any girl could have asked for."

"What about me?" Peyton spoke up from the couch. She had been playing with her favorite stuffed animal, but obviously didn't want to be forgotten.

"Of course, you are amazing," Carrie said with a laugh. Just like Gwen, she'd had no little sister or young female relative to ask to be her flower girl. Neither, it turned out, did Philippe. He was an only child as well.

"I can't wait until Michael is old enough to be a ring bearer. Then we can both walk down the aisle together." Peyton stood and twirled her dress.

The girls all chuckled, but the lighthearted topic did Carrie's heart good. "Honey, by the time Michael is mature enough to be a ring bearer, you'll probably be too old to be a flower girl," Alyssa said.

Peyton's eyes widened, and her mouth fell open. "There's an age limit on being a flower girl?"

"There is, but don't worry you have several years

left." Alyssa hugged the girl to her side. "I guess I better make more friends, so she can attend more weddings."

"Yes, you better," Gwen said. "I think she might find a way to make being a flower girl an occupation."

"I will." Peyton's head bobbed sending her tendrils shaking. Then her face scrunched up in confusion. "What's an occupation?"

Carrie joined in the laughter, but a little voice whispered in her head that she would never have this with Philippe. She realized she had never even had a discussion about children with him. Well, that wasn't true. She had brought it up once, but he had dismissed the conversation telling her that they would revisit it later. Surely, he would want children once they were married though.

"Well, I think it's about time," Gwen said checking her watch. "Are you ready?"

Carrie took a deep breath and checked the mirror one last time. Every hair was in place, her dress looked perfect, and the beautiful bouquet of purple tulips and stargazer lilies smelled heavenly. By all accounts, she was ready, but the nagging little doubt still tugged at her. Wedding jitters, she told herself, that's all it was. Wedding jitters.

"Yep, let's get me married." Carrie forced bravado in her voice and a smile on her face.

"You can still say no," Gwen whispered as they walked out the door.

"Everybody's here. It's too late."

"It's never too late. You simply say the words."

Carrie shook her head. She had lost Cal, and Philippe was a good man. They worked well together, and happiness would find them. She was sure of it. "They're waiting for us."

Gwen shook her head, a sad expression on her face, but she led the way down the hallway.

If Cal had been a cursing man, he would have let loose a string of expletives as he checked his watch again. It was ten till six. He wouldn't make it before the wedding started. Probably not even by the time they asked if anyone had a reason these two should not be married. All he could hope for was that he would get there before they said 'I do.'

"Welcome to La Guardia airport, ladies and gentlemen. It's been our pleasure to serve you on this flight. The local time is five fifty pm. We'll be taxiing to the gate for the next few minutes, so please stay in your seats with your seatbelts fastened until you see the illumination go off. Bags will be at carousel seven and there will be people to assist you if you need help with a connecting flight. We know you have a choice when you fly, and we thank you for flying United Airlines."

The pilot's announcement did nothing but ramp up the anxiousness in Cal's heart. Another few minutes to taxi? He was going to be so late. At least he didn't have to stop at baggage claim. With the knowledge that his trip would be short, he had only packed an emergency bag with a change of clothes, toothbrush and toothpaste, and deodorant. That way if he did get stuck somewhere, he'd at least be covered for a day.

The elderly woman, who had introduced herself as Ethel earlier, touched his arm. "Remember, this is not the time to be nice. Go get your girl."

One side of his lip pulled into a crooked grin. "I'll try, Ethel." Cal's eyes stayed glued to the overhead display. As soon as the light went off and the ding sounded, Cal grabbed his bag and stood, hunching down from the low ceiling. Ethel scooted over to his side, so he would be even closer to the aisle. The man sitting in the aisle seat glared up at him as he pushed his glasses up his nose. A businessman by the look of his fitted suit.

"Sorry," Cal said to the man, "love waits for no man." Cal was close enough to see the stewardess when she opened the door, and he pushed past the spectacled man into the aisle.

"Thank you for flying with us," the stewardess said, but Cal was already past her and heading up the ramp. By the time it opened into the expansive airport, he was practically jogging. His eyes scanned the large screens in search of ground transportation. When he finally saw the sign he wanted, he hurried that direction. Cal chanced a glance at his watch and shook his head. The only chance he had of stopping this wedding was with a miracle.

Outside the grand doors, Carrie's mother, who was standing in for her father, and Philippe's two friends stood waiting for them. Carrie noticed how much grayer her mother's hair was than the last time she had seen her.

"Wow, Carrie," her mother said taking her free hand, "you did a wonderful job on this dress. It's amazing."

Carrie looked down at her mother's weathered hand. She hadn't had to take up hard labor after Carrie's father passed, but it was clear she had been doing some work as her hands had aged much more than Carrie remembered. Maybe she should send more money to her mother to help her out. "Thanks Mom, I just wish Dad were here to see it."

"Your Dad is watching from Heaven, Carrie, and he's so proud of you. As am I." Her mother pulled Carrie in for a hug and Carrie smiled at the scent of Vanilla and sugar. At least she hadn't given up her love of baking.

The music began then and David, one of the Groomsmen, looked to the rest of the group. "Everybody ready?"

Gwen flashed Carrie one more 'are you sure' look,

but Carrie ignored it and nodded to David. "Let's do this."

David opened the door to the grand ballroom and held out his hand for Alyssa. With a smile, she tucked her arm through his and they stepped into the large room. Peter, the best man, and Gwen went next. Then Peyton followed.

"Are you sure you want to do this?" Her mother fixed her with an intense stare as she squeezed her hand.

"Why does everyone keep asking me that?" Carrie asked. Her heart pounded in her chest and her breath felt short. Nerves, it was just nerves. If everyone would quit asking her if she was sure, then Carrie was sure her heart would return to its normal rhythm and her breath would come normally.

"I saw the look you shared with Gwen. I may not be around you much anymore, but she is. This is marriage, Carrie. You should be sure."

Carrie swallowed her irritation. This was supposed to be the happiest day of her life, and it would be if everyone would support her and stop questioning her. "I'm sure, Mom." The wedding march began to play, and Carrie pulled back her shoulders. "Now, that's our cue, so let's get to it."

Her mother's lips pulled into a tight line as if she didn't believe Carrie, but she followed her lead as they stepped onto the red carpeted train that led into the grand ballroom. The ballroom looked amazing lighted up with the white Christmas lights, the large windows held fantastic views of the city lights, and Philippe looked as handsome as ever standing up front with the wedding party.

Hundreds of guests filled both sides of the aisle and camera bulbs flashed with each step she took. Carrie hadn't expected this many photographers, but this had to be Philippe's doing. He had wanted the wedding to be everywhere. Carrie's cheeks hurt from her plastered smile, but there was no way she would be caught on camera with anything less than a smile.

Her feet carried her forward even though the voice in her head urged louder for her to turn around, to bolt for the door. Before she knew it, she had handed off the bouquet and was taking Philippe's hands in front of the minister.

Cal stepped out of the airport and on to the busy ground transportation area. Though still warm, the air had cooled when the sun set and evening hit. Cal's eyes widened at the number of cars lined up and darting in and out of traffic, but he had no time to linger on the immensity of it.

He hurried to a waiting cab and slid into the back seat. "Can you take me to the Manhattan Penthouse?"

"Of course." The cab driver punched a button and then pulled into the stream of traffic. Cal scrambled to buckle his seat belt as the car weaved in and out. How in the world did Carrie live here? The traffic alone would drive him crazy. His insides were coiled tighter than Dick's hatband.

As the cab left the airport, Cal was assaulted with the visual imagery of all the lights. Now, this he understood someone being intoxicated by. The lights competed for his attention at every turn. Focus, he said to himself sparing another glance at his watch. "Please, can you hurry," Cal urged the cab driver. The wedding had already started, and with every ticking second, he felt Carrie slipping further from his grasp.

Philippe's smile appeared off, forced. Or was it Carrie's imagination? Had the misgivings of her friend and mother started to rub off on her?

"Dear friends," the minister began, "we are gathered here today in the sight of God, and the presence of friends and loved ones, to celebrate one of life's greatest moments. We are here to give recognition to the beauty of love that is shared between Philippe and Carrie as they complete their family in holy matrimony."

No, it was not her imagination. His face had tightened at the word love. Was he having second thoughts as well?

The minister continued his speech. "Marriage is a contract that is not to be entered into lightly but thoughtfully and seriously. There needs to be a deep realization of the obligations and responsibilities it carries. Marriage is the moment where two hearts and souls are joined together for eternity."

This time Carrie's face twitched. A contract. Binding. Obligations. Responsibilities. The words assaulted her and sent her mind swirling back to this moment six years ago. She remembered no hesitation then even though she'd been in an all-night wedding chapel with a man she barely knew. So, why was there such hesitation now?

As if far away, Carrie heard the minister pray, but her mind refused to focus on the words. The presence of slick sweat grabbed her attention, and she glanced down at her hand joined with Philippe's. Was that his sweat or hers?

"The joining of two hearts as husband and wife is a commitment like no other. It offers opportunities for sharing and for personal growth that no other human relationship can equal. A husband and wife are each other's best friends, confidants, lovers, teachers, listeners and critics."

Teachers? Was that why she felt much more of a bond with Cal when they read the devotional? Because in that area, he was her teacher? In fact, in all things religious, she presumed Cal would be a teacher. Carrie forced her mind away from Cal. Surely, Philippe could be a teacher too, but Carrie had no idea what he could teach her. Her eyes rose from their clasped hands to his face, but his eyes weren't focused on her. They were focused on something to his left. Carrie turned to follow his gaze.

He was staring at the clock. Was he so bored that he couldn't wait to leave his own wedding? Could she marry a man who was so impatient? She thought of Cal and his cool ease. He never seemed impatient for anything.

"The bond between a husband and wife deepens and enriches every fact of life. Happiness is fuller, and commitments are stronger. Marriage also encourages new life and new experiences and finds new ways of expressing love through the ups and downs of life. Philippe and Carrie as your journey begins as husband and wife, I would ask you both remember to always treat each other with respect and remind yourself often of what brought you here today."

"I object."

A collective gasp erupted in the room, and all eyes turned to the voice who had broken the solemnity of the ceremony.

CHAPTER 17

"Young lady, I didn't ask for objections." The minister's stern voice surprised Carrie as he regarded the perpetrator.

"I am aware of that," Gwen said stepping forward, "but I can't let this continue." She glanced briefly at the gathered guests, her face as red as her hair. "Carrie, I know you think it's not a big deal and that you don't deserve love or something, but I can't let you marry Philippe." She turned to Philippe. "Sorry, she does care for you, but she loves someone even more."

Philippe's eyes widened, and his mouth fell open, but no words escaped.

"Carrie, you belong with Cal. Perhaps you weren't supposed to be together six years ago when you first married, but I saw you when you came back. You were different, happier. You belong with him."

Carrie blinked. How was this possible? Her best friend was ruining her ceremony. "Gwen, I told you he's with someone else."

"He's only with her because he thinks he lost you," Gwen pushed.

"You can't know that," Carrie said. "You haven't even met him."

"He sent you a letter every year on your anniversary. That's not the actions of a man who would jump into another relationship. Those pictures prove nothing-"

"Wait, what pictures?" Philippe had found his voice and it was filled with confusion and maybe a hint of anger.

"I-" Carrie glared at Gwen before turning to Philippe. What should she say? Opening a branch there had made sense at the time, but Carrie realized how awful it would look now. She decided on the truth. Gwen was right. Lies of omission were just as bad as outright lies. They had created quite a mess. "A few days ago, I wrote to Dixie, the inn owner, about opening a shop there. I wasn't planning to run it, just find someone who would. In the letter, I also asked her about Cal. I suppose I was having reservations, Philippe." She shook her head unable to believe these words were coming out of her mouth. "I was certain

I didn't care for Cal, but when I saw pictures of him with someone else, feelings surfaced or resurfaced, I guess. My brain wanted to convince my heart I hadn't cared for him all these years, but the truth was that I loved him and that's why I ran from commitment before."

Philippe opened his mouth to speak, but he was interrupted by a voice from the guests. "I object too."

Carrie turned to see Sierra standing and making her way to the stage. "I can't let this marriage happen either."

"Why not?" Carrie had no idea if the words issued from her mouth, Gwen's, or Phillips's as they all seemed to speak at the same time.

"Carrie, you can't marry him. He's only marrying you for your money."

"What?" This time the word clearly came from Philippe, and he was indignant.

Sierra glanced nervously at Philippe before continuing. "Don't get me wrong, he might really care for you, but I overheard him outside the shop one day talking about how he was pushing up the wedding date to gain access to your money. Evidently his company isn't doing so good."

Carrie turned to face Philippe. "Is that true?"

His face paled and his Adam's Apple bobbed several times as he swallowed. His eyes shifted to the left and right before finally landing on Carrie's. "It's true that my company is having some financial issues, and I do care for you, but I proposed after I got wind of your net worth increasing."

"You proposed the very night I found out, how could you have known?" Carrie's mind reeled with this knowledge. Philippe didn't love her. She had divorced a man who loved her and almost married a man who didn't. What was wrong with her?

"I had someone keeping tabs on your business. You had more orders coming in and your stock was rising, so I figured it was a good time to propose. I wasn't positive until I found the letter you stashed under the register."

Carrie's mouth dropped open. "You snooped in my shop?"

He shrugged. "I wasn't snooping. I was confirming suspicions. You shoved something under the register that night when I entered your shop. Figured I'd take a look at what you didn't want to show me. I hoped as a billionaire you wouldn't mind helping your husband's company out, but to tell you the truth, I'm glad your assistant said something. I really don't want to be shackled in a marriage."

Shackled? Who was this man in front of her? She opened her mouth to retort, but before she could, another voice spoke up.

"I object to this marriage."

"Oh, good grief," the minister said throwing up his hands. "What now?"

Cal blinked up at the expansive white building looming in front of him. He hoped it had an elevator because even in his good condition, it would take him way too long to get to the top if he had to take the stairs.

He opened the door and scanned for the elevator sign. Thankfully, he found it near the back of the room. With wide and purposeful steps, he strode that direction, his boots echoing on the marble flooring. He pressed the button, surprised to find his finger shaking.

As the door opened and he stepped inside, he practiced the words he would say in his head. Nothing sounded right, and by the time the doors opened, he had decided simple would be best.

A small sign announced the Bliss Caron wedding outside a room with large oak doors. Praying he wasn't too late, Cal pulled the doors open. "I object to this wedding."

As the silence fell, Cal took in the enormous room for the first time. There had to be hundreds of people in the room and every eye focused on him.

"Cal?" Carrie's voice carried from the stage and Cal focused on it. She wasn't holding hands with the groom, so perhaps he wasn't too late. Camera bulbs flashed as he made his way up the red carpeted aisle, but he ignored them. He was nobody, so he imagined they wouldn't care about him nor did he care if they ran an article about him.

"Carrie, I hope I'm not too late, but you can't marry him. I may have signed the divorce papers, but I never should have. Without you, I'm lost. Even more so now that I got to have you back in my life for a few days. I'll do whatever it takes to show you that we belong together."

Carrie's lips twitched and then broke out into a full grin. "I feared I had lost you, Cal."

"Lost me? What are you talking about?"

"I wrote Dixie asking about you. She sent me pictures of you with some blond."

Cal's lips twitched into a sideways smile. "That was Ginny. She's a sweet girl and Stacy convinced me to give her a chance after you left, but there was nothing there. My heart belongs to you. It has since that night in Vegas."

Carrie's eyes filled with moisture. "My heart belongs with you too. I was stubborn and didn't want to believe it, but I see it now."

"Great, is someone going to get married today?" the minister asked.

"We don't have a marriage license," Carrie began.

"But we could have a ceremony and make it official later," Cal continued.

"I was thinking the same thing." Carrie flashed a conspiratorial wink at him.

"Fine, can we do the ceremony then? I do have another engagement to attend."

"Philippe, would you mind taking a seat?" The words came from the redheaded woman next to Carrie, and Cal figured it had to be Gwen. He had never met the woman, but he liked her spunk.

"Gwen!" Carrie was clearly shocked at her friend's behavior.

Gwen simply shrugged. "You aren't marrying him. Cal needs a place to stand."

Cal ducked his head as a laugh bubbled up inside of him. Though Carrie had spoken of Gwen, she had failed to mention the spunk of her friend. Philippe turned a shade of red, but he took a seat in the congregation along with his two groomsmen.

"Drew and Max, why don't you come stand up here for Cal?"

Cal turned to see who Gwen was talking to. Two men from the front row stood up. One held a baby in a pack on his chest. Both were dressed nicely in designer suits.

"Hey, Cal, nice to meet you. I'm Drew Devonshire. I belong to the feisty one." He flashed a wink at Gwen before shaking Cal's hand.

"You have your hands full," Cal said softly.

Drew chuckled. "You're telling me."

The man with the baby stepped forward next. "I'm Maxwell Banks. I'm married to Alyssa there." He pointed at the beautiful brunette standing beside Gwen.

Cal shook his hand. "Thank you both for standing in."

"Our pleasure. These three are thick as thieves now. If you're marrying into this den, then we'll see a lot more of each other."

A brief moment of hesitation flashed through Cal. These men were a different class than he was. He couldn't imagine much commonality existed between them, but Carrie was his focus. If these men came with her, then so be it. He would acclimate to whatever he had to.

The men shuffled into place and Gwen stepped back behind Carrie. Cal took the newly vacated spot next to Carrie and grasped her hands. The minister raised his eyebrow as if asking if they were ready. Cal and Carrie nodded and then shared a smile.

"Okay, so even though this won't be a legally binding ceremony, we are gathered here today to witness a wedding between Carrie Bliss and-" he paused before leaning toward Cal - "I didn't catch your name."

"Cal Roper."

The minister nodded and leaned back again.

"Between Carrie Bliss and Cal Roper. I don't know these two well, but it appears they have a history and are not entering this union lightly. May God bless this union and may no one else object."

A titter of laughter spread through the guests. Though probably not the wedding Carrie had dreamed of, Cal could think of nothing better. It was real and imperfect, just like the two of them.

"Carrie, do you take Cal to be your lawfully wedded husband to have and to hold, to honor and cherish, forsaking all others until death do you part?"

"I do." Carrie accented her words with a light squeeze on his hands.

"Cal, do you take Carrie to be your lawfully wedded wife to have and to hold, to honor and cherish, forsaking all others until death do you part?"

"I do."

"Do you have the rings?"

Carrie's eyes widened. "Oh no, the rings."

Cal grinned as he held up a finger. He reached into his shirt pocket and pulled out the simple silver bands they had gotten married with in Vegas six years ago. "I know it's not much, and I promise I'll get you a better ring soon, but these hold a lot of promise." He handed his ring to her.

"You kept them all this time?" Her eyes sparkled with the wet sheen filling them.

"I told you I knew then, and I hoped one day you would wear it again."

"Take notes kid," he heard Max say softly behind him, "that's how you win a girl's heart."

"Carrie, please place the ring on Cal's hand and say, with this ring I thee wed."

Carrie slid the band on Cal's finger. "With this ring I thee wed." Her voice was choked with emotion and so soft that Cal doubted many in the audience heard it.

"Cal, will you do the same?"

Cal slipped the silver ring on Carrie's finger and repeated the phrase.

"Well, without a marriage certificate, I have no authority here, but I believe that soon this union will be legal, so I pronounce you man and wife to be."

Another chuckle circulated through the crowd and Cal felt laughter bubble up inside him as well.

"You may kiss the bride."

Cal wasted no time in pulling Carrie to him, circling her waist and claiming her lips.

CHAPTER 18

"I was thinking it would be amazing if we flew back to Vegas to get married legally," Carrie said as they danced across the hardwood floor.

After the ceremony, they had walked across the hall to the reception area. The room was set up with a full bar and tables with elegant white cloths and fine china. They enjoyed a dinner of prime rib and vegetables before stepping onto the dance floor for their first dance.

Cal bit his lip as he turned Carrie around. He had been hoping to avoid this conversation as long as possible, but as she brought it up, he figured it was time to come clean. "Carrie, there's something I need to tell you. It was a rough year last year. It forced me to take an extra loan out from the bank. I don't have the money to repay it much less take a trip to Vegas." He looked down at her surprised to see her smiling. "What? Why are you smiling?"

Carrie chuckled. "Cal, look around." He scanned the room wondering what he was looking for. "I paid for this, Cal. The room, the food, the flowers."

"You mean your mother paid for it." Cal's brow wrinkled in confusion.

"No, Cal, I mean I paid for it. I'm a billionaire. So is Max and so is Drew."

Billionaire? The word did not compute in his rancher brain. How much money formed a billion anyway? "A billionaire? I knew you had money, but I had no idea."

Carrie nodded. "Yep, I have more than enough money to pay off your loan and fly us to Vegas."

The chivalrous need to take care of his wife flared within Cal. "But, I can't let you pay off my loan. That was my own fault."

"Technically, we were married when you accrued that debt, so what's yours is mine. Besides, you're not letting me do anything." Carrie placed a hand on his cheek. "My money is your money. You know two become one and everything."

Cal still didn't feel right taking her money, but he also knew he wouldn't win this argument. She had a stubborn streak, and he was man enough not to let money ruin their relationship. "I still plan on working," he said with a smile.

"I wouldn't have it any other way. You are quite sexy on the back of the horse, and I'd like to keep seeing that image."

His face clouded. "That reminds me, Carrie. We do need to talk about living arrangements." They'd been so caught up in the wedding that they had forgotten some of the real details that could pose a problem. Like the fact that she lived hundreds of miles away, and he didn't want to give up his ranch.

She smiled and shook her head. "No, we don't. I told you I wrote Dixie to ask about you, but that was only part of why I wrote her. I asked her to search around for a shop I could purchase so I could open a branch in Soda Spurs."

Cal blinked at her as he let the information sink in. "You planned to come back?"

"No, I planned to hire someone to run it, but I think the women of Soda Spurs need someone who knows the beauty of the town."

Cal didn't know what to say. His heart felt like it was going to burst. He had only dreamed of this day for six years, and the reality was so much better. He pulled Carrie closer to him. "I love you, Carrie Bliss."

"I love you too, but I believe the name is Carrie Roper now though I may have to keep Carrie Bliss on my designs."

Cal chuckled as he lowered his lips to Carrie's.

Always the business head with her, but he didn't care what name was on her designs as long as he got to call her his wife.

"Is everybody in?" Carrie asked as she looked around the limo. After the wedding, she had decided she didn't want to wait to marry Cal again and had asked the wedding party to join her on a quick trip to Vegas. What better way to remarry the man of her dreams than recreating their first marriage?

After a quick stop in Soda Spurs to pick up Stacy and her family, they had re-boarded the jet and landed in Vegas a few hours later. Their first stop had been to get the marriage license which thankfully went off without a hitch. Now, they were on their way to the strip. Though Carrie wasn't sure the original minister who married them was still practicing, she was certain the chapel would still be open.

"Where to?" the driver asked.

"Chapel of the Heart," Cal and Carrie said together and shared a smile.

"I've never seen so many lights," Annie said her face pressed to the window.

"Yeah, this is pretty cool." Peyton's face was also pressed to the window right next to Annie's. The two had become fast friends on the plane ride over and Carrie was fairly certain a reunion existed in their future.

"There it is," Trevor shouted as a large neon red heart with a white cross through it came into view.

Carrie squeezed Cal's hand as the limo pulled to a stop. "You ready to do this?"

"I've never been readier for anything in my life."

The doors opened, and the group piled out. Carrie laughed at the sheer size of their party. She doubted the chapel was used to having this many people there.

"Can I help-" the woman's voice stalled as she looked up from the book she had been writing in. "My, there's an awful lot of you."

"But just two of us to get married," Cal said stepping forward. "Can you tell me if Dave Nichols is still a minister here?"

"You remember his name?" Carrie asked quietly.

Cal smiled at her. "I remember everything."

"Yes, Dave Nichols is still here and working tonight as it turns out," the woman said.

"Great. We'd like him to marry us as soon as possible."

The woman smiled and consulted her book. "Well, how about right now? Give me five minutes and I'll ready the chapel."

She disappeared into the room and a few minutes later the door swung open. The chapel was almost exactly as Carrie remembered though the carpets looked newer like they had been replaced recently. She took her place next to Cal at the front and clasped his hands.

"I may be getting older, but I tend to remember the names of the couples I have married, and I seem to remember that I already married you two once. Is that right?"

Cal laughed, and Carrie dropped her eyes to the floor as a heat crawled up her neck. She hadn't expected the minister to remember them. "You are correct, Sir. We were serious the first time, but life kind of got in the way. However, we have straightened out the life part, and we'd like you to marry us again."

The minister smiled. His face looked exactly the same under his Elvis wig though his jumpsuit seemed to fit a little tighter. "Well, I am not one to stand in the Big Guy's way. How about we get this remedied?"

The wedding party circled around Cal and Carrie as the minister began the ceremony. What a stark contrast from The Manhattan Penthouse she had been at just hours before, but Carrie wouldn't change it for the world. Somehow, this seemed right - the perfect place for her marriage with Cal to begin. Again.

"By the power vested to me by Elvis, God, and the great state of Nevada, I now pronounce you husband and wife. You may kiss your bride. Thank you very much."

Carrie smiled as she leaned forward and met Cal's

lips. She wasn't sure exactly what the future would hold, but she was ready for whatever lay ahead in the next chapter as long as it included Cal.

The End!

If you enjoyed this story, please leave a review at your retailer. Just a few words really helps!

IT'S NOT QUITE THE END!

Thank you so much for reading *The Billionaire's Cowboy Groom*. So Carrie and Cal had their wedding, and we got to see all the other billionaires again. I thought this would be the end of the billionaire series, but as I was working on my new series, The Blushing Brides, my cover designer messed up and used the template from the Billionaires series. I was in a time crunch, so instead of having her redo everything, I decided there was at least one more billionaire story in me, and I just had her change the title. I think this one will be fun, and I'm planning a little sass!

I hope you enjoyed the story as well. If you did, would you do me a favor? Please leave a review at your retailer. It really helps. It doesn't have to be long - just a few words to help other readers know what they're getting.

I'd love to hear from you, not only about this story, but about the characters or stories you'd like read in the future. I'm always looking for new ideas and if I use one of your characters or stories, I'll send you a free ebook and paperback of the book with a special dedication. Write to me at loranahoopes@gmail.com. And if you'd like to see what's coming next, be sure to stop by authorloranahoopes.com

I also have a weekly newsletter that contains many wonderful things like pictures of my adorable children, chances to win awesome prizes, new releases and sales I might be holding, great books from other authors, and anything else that strikes my fancy and that I think you would enjoy. I'll even send you the first chapter of my newest (maybe not even released yet) book if you'd like to sign up.

Even better, I solemnly swear to only send out one newsletter a week (usually on Tuesday unless life gets in the way which with three kids it usually does). I will not spam you, sell your email address to solicitors or anyone else, or any of those other terrible things.

This series will be continued, but for now, would you like to meet some characters for a new series.

❧ 14 ❧
NOT READY TO SAY GOODBYE YET?

Have we seen the last of Carrie and Cal? I doubt it, but be sure to preorder your copy of The Cowboy Billionaire to meet Hunter Garrison and Daisy Keller. Two opposites forced to team up to help each other. Sparks will fly, but will love bloom?

And while you're waiting on that story, why not take a chance on The Cowboy's Reality Bride.

The Cowboy's Reality Bride

He just wants to marry and settle down...

But all the women he's dated want more than a small town and a simple ranch life which is why he allows himself to be talked into auditioning for a reality dating show. He never thought he'd actually get picked.

She is trying to run from her past...

When Laney gets fired from her job, she is free to help her friend out, but she thought she was just doing makeup.

Who wants to play by the rules....

Laney is instantly attracted to Tyler, and he might

feel the same, but there's just one problem. She's not a contestant!

Read on for a taste of The Cowboy's Reality Bride....

THE COWBOY'S REALITY BRIDE
PREVIEW

Laney Swann clutched her designer bag tighter as she weaved in and out of the crowded sidewalk. Why did the crowd have to be so thick today, on the one day she overslept? Normally, she was out the door by six am giving her plenty of time to get uptown, stop at the coffee shop, and make it to work by eight, but sleep had eluded her last night, and she'd slept through her alarm. Now, she was paying the price.

She flipped her delicate silver watch around to read the face and quickened her pace. Time was not on her side today. She was going to be so late, and Victoria Bonavich detested tardiness. It was a fireable offense in her book if you stepped in the office even a minute late, and Laney couldn't afford to lose this job. She'd moved to the city with big dreams but a small savings after college. Without this job, there would be no paying her rent, and she'd have to go home. A nervous spring coiled in her stomach. She couldn't lose this job.

"Watch it," a man's voice cried out as she squeezed between him and another man with a cell phone glued to his ear.

"Sorry," she called back, but her head never turned. Turning around would cost her precious seconds and she had none to spare. Her heart was thudding a constant drum of the precious seconds slipping away.

A tendril of blond hair appeared in her vision and she blew it off her forehead. Great. Now, not only was she late, but her hair was eking out of its sprayed mold, another issue she would have to remedy before seeing Madame Bonavich or The Man-eater as they called her in the office.

The woman was fearsome. With short grey hair, hawkish eyes, and thin lips which rarely smiled, she exuded a no-nonsense air wherever she went, but Laney enjoyed working for her. Mostly. She learned so much in the six months she had been at this agency even though she was still just an unknown assistant to Madame Bonavich. Actually, she had learned so much more from Myra, the makeup artist she assisted before photo shoots, but Laney still hoped to become Madame Bonavich's assistant one day. Then she would have a chance at becoming a well-known makeup artist herself.

At least she had received the promotion to coffee gopher the last month. It gave her a chance to interact with The Man-eater if only for a minute.

However, today, it could be her downfall. Only fifteen minutes remained to obtain the coffee and return to the office, and it wasn't looking good. Laney stepped up her pace a little more. Not too fast though. The last thing she wanted to do was trip, and sadly, she was a bit of a klutz.

"Excuse me," she said as she pushed through another clump of pedestrians. Why did it seem as if people walked slower and in impenetrable groups whenever she was in a hurry? The busy city was always like this, she knew that, but her need to move at a faster pace exaggerated the normal bustling bog and edged her anxiety up another notch.

At last the coffee shop came into view. Sweet relief flowed over her even though her feet ached already from the rigorous pace she had set the moment she stepped out of her door. The four-inch heels were a requirement in the agency - something that had taken Laney months to get used to - and though she agreed they added style to her outfit, her feet were not fans. They screamed for a nightly soak, and she had purchased so much Epsom Salt in the last few months she should buy stock in the company.

A sigh billowed out of her lips as she pulled open the

door, and the spring coiled tighter. At least four other people stood in line. Laney bit her lip and checked her watch again. Thirteen minutes remained. Her foot began a rhythmic cadence on the floor, the impatient tapping garnering a few irritated stares, but Laney didn't care. She didn't have time to care.

The man in front of her turned around. "You appear to be in an awful hurry. Would you like to take my spot?"

"Could I? That would be amazing." Laney stepped in front of the man but remained facing him. He had the most arresting eyes. "My boss is a bit of a time manager, if you know what I mean. If I don't get her coffee and get back to her in just over ten minutes," she blew out a puff of air, "I don't even know what will happen, but it won't be good."

The man said nothing, just raised an eyebrow at her, but Laney couldn't shut her mouth. Perhaps it was his beautiful blue eyes - she had always been a sucker for blue eyes.

"Normally, it's not an issue, but last night sleep evaded me. I just tossed and turned, so when my alarm clock rang, I guess I didn't hear it. Though I must have turned it off because it wasn't still going off when I did finally wake up. Sadly, by then, I was running late, and now I'm in danger of incurring her wrath." Laney paused as the man's lips pulled into a smirk. "What?"

He pointed behind her toward the register. "I believe it's your turn to order."

"Oh, right, thank you." A heated flush crawled up her face as she turned to face the woman behind the counter. She had made a fool of herself with the handsome man behind her. Why did her mouth always seem to run unchecked whenever she was nervous?

"Can I help you?"

"Yes, I uh..." Laney cleared her throat and forced her mind to focus. She could berate herself later. "I need a tall caramel macchiato and-" she shook her head. Even after a month, she didn't have Madame Bonavich's order memorized, but who could blame her? It had to be the longest order she had ever seen. "Sorry, just a second." Her fingers rifled in her purse until they touched a folded piece of paper. She pulled it out and unfolded it. "A double ristretto venti half soy nonfat organic chocolate brownie iced vanilla double shot gingerbread Frappuccino extra hot with foam upside down double blended, one Sweet N Low and one NutraSweet."

The cashier blinked, and a momentary shell-shocked expression covered her face. Then composure set in and she rang up the order and picked up two cups. Laney felt sorry for the woman. She merely had to read off an order, but this woman had to put that nonsense on a cup in a way that the barista making the coffee would understand. Not for the first time, Laney wondered if Madame

Bonavich ordered this drink because she enjoyed it or because she relished putting others through the ringer.

With the bill paid, Laney continued down the line to stand at the other end where the barista placed completed drinks. She kept her eyes on the floor to avoid seeking the nice man again. He didn't need another verbal diatribe from her.

Nine more minutes. She was cutting it so close. The office was just around the corner, but her high heels kept her from running, so she'd have to opt for long strides and hope for the best.

"Caramel Macchiato and gingerbread frap," the barista called as she placed the two drinks down.

"Thank you." Laney flashed the woman an apologetic smile as she grabbed the drinks.

As she pushed open the door, she realized she should have asked for a tray. A cup in each hand made it nearly impossible to adjust her purse strap which kept threatening to slip off her shoulder with every step. Unable to stop, Laney adjusted her body by throwing her right shoulder as high into the air as possible in hopes gravity would keep the purse strap there.

She must look a sight, hunched over to one side. Madame Bonavich would blow her lid if she saw Laney, but it was this or arrive late with the woman's coffee, and Laney honestly didn't know which would be worse.

A sigh of relief spilled from her mouth as the office

came into view. She would not chance looking at her watch, but she figured she had a few minutes to spare. However, she also had a conundrum. How was she going to open the door? She hated taking the chance but stacking one cup on top of the other appeared to be the quickest option.

Before her mind changed, she set the venti on top of her cup and secured it with her chin. Then she reached for the door handle, but as her fingertips brushed the cold metal, the door swung open.

The force knocked her backwards. Her chin lifted from the lid of the cup, and without something to secure it, it teetered. Laney observed in slow-motion horror as the cup not only fell off its perch but onto her chest. The lid popped off and flew through the air as the contents of the drink spilled down Laney's front.

Her body finally unfroze when the searing hot liquid broached her skin. Laney jumped farther back sending the venti cup crashing to the pavement.

"I'm so sorry. Can I help?"

Anger flared in her stomach, and Laney flicked her eyes up to take in the perpetrator before she let loose her vitriol on him. However, the flame fizzled at the sight of the young man with glasses who stood gaping at her. His wide eyes held an apology and his baby face placed his age in his early twenties - probably a college intern. She swallowed the harsh words she wanted to bark at him. If she'd had Madame Bonavich's coffee order written anywhere else, she would give him the paper and tell him to go replace the coffee. It would be late, but perhaps late was better than never, but she didn't.

"No, it's fine. I'll take care of it." She didn't know how exactly. The only option she had was giving Madame Bonavich her drink which probably wouldn't sit well with the woman. She could only hope she was in a good mood.

"Again, I'm so sorry." The man ducked his head and scurried away looking like a scolded puppy with its tail between its legs.

Laney spared one glance at her formerly white shirt now stained brown and sighed. She was late; she didn't have the woman's coffee; and she looked like a slob. These were not the makings of a good day.

Continue reading The Cowboy's Reality Bride...

❧ 16 ❧

A FREE STORY FOR YOU

Enjoyed this story? Not ready to quit reading yet? If you sign up for my newsletter, you will receive The Billionaire's Impromptu Bet right away as my thank you gift for choosing to hang out with me.

The Billionaire's Impromptu Bet

A SWAT officer. A bored billionaire heiress. A bet that could change everything....

Read on for a taste of The Billionaire's Impromptu Bet....

THE BILLIONAIRE'S IMPROMPTU BET PREVIEW

Brie Carter fell back spread eagle on her queen-sized canopy bed sending her blond hair fanning out behind her. With a large sigh, she uttered, "I'm bored."

"How can you be bored? You have like millions of dollars." Her friend, Ariel, plopped down in a seated position on the bed beside her and flicked her raven hair off her shoulder. "You want to go shopping? I hear Tiffany's is having a special right now."

Brie rolled her eyes. Shopping? Where was the excitement in that? With her three platinum cards, she could go shopping whenever she wanted. "No, I'm bored with shopping too. I have everything. I want to do something exciting. Something we don't normally do."

Brie enjoyed being rich. She loved the unlimited

credit cards at her disposal, the constant apparel of new clothes, and of course the penthouse apartment her father paid for, but lately, she longed for something more fulfilling.

Ariel's hazel eyes widened. "I know. There's a new bar down on Franklin Street. Why don't we go play a little game?"

Brie sat up, intrigued at the secrecy and the twinkle in Ariel's eyes. "What kind of game?"

"A betting game. You let me pick out any man in the place. Then you try to get him to propose to you."

Brie wrinkled her nose. "But I don't want to get married." She loved her freedom and didn't want to share her penthouse with anyone, especially some man.

"You don't marry him, silly. You just get him to propose."

Brie bit her lip as she thought. It had been awhile since her last relationship and having a man dote on her for a month might be interesting, but.... "I don't know. It doesn't seem very nice."

"How about I sweeten the pot? If you win, I'll set you up on a date with my brother."

Brie cocked her head. Was she serious? The only thing Brie couldn't seem to buy in the world was the affection of Ariel's very handsome, very wealthy, brother. He was a movie star, just the kind of person Brie could consider marrying in the future. She'd had a crush on him as long as she and Ariel had been friends, but he'd always seen her as just that, his little sister's friend. "I thought you didn't want me dating your brother."

"I don't." Ariel shrugged. "But he's between girlfriends right now, and I know you've wanted it for ages. If you win this bet, I'll set you up. I can't guarantee any more than one date though. The rest will be up to you."

Brie wasn't worried about that. Charm she possessed in abundance. She simply needed some alone time with him, and she was certain she'd be able to convince him they were meant to be together. "All right. You've got a deal."

Ariel smiled. "Perfect. Let's get you changed then and see who the lucky man will be.

A tiny tug pulled on Brie's heart that this still wasn't right, but she dismissed it. This was simply a means to an end, and he'd never have to know.

Jesse Calhoun relaxed as the rhythmic thudding of the speed bag reached his ears. Though he loved his job, it was stressful being the SWAT sniper. He hated having to take human lives and today had been especially rough. The team had been called out to a drug bust, and Jesse was forced to return fire at three hostiles. He didn't care that they fired at his team and himself first. Taking a life was always hard, and every one of them haunted his dreams.

"You gonna bust that one too?" His co-worker Brendan appeared by his side. Brendan was the opposite of Jesse in nearly every way. Where Jesse's hair was a dark copper, Brendan's was nearly black. Jesse sported paler skin and a dusting of freckles across his nose, but Brendan's skin was naturally dark and freckle free.

Jesse flashed a crooked grin, but kept his eyes on the small, swinging black bag. The speed bag was his way to release, but a few times he had started hitting while still too keyed up and he had ruptured the bag. Okay, five times, but who was counting really? Besides, it was a better way to calm his nerves than other things he could choose. Drinking, fights, gambling, women.

"Nah, I think this one will last a little longer." His shoulders began to burn, and he gave the bag another few punches for good measure before dropping his arms and letting it swing to a stop. "See? It lives to be hit at least another day." Every once in a while, Jesse missed training the way he used to. Before he joined the force, he had been an amateur boxer, on his way to being a pro, but a shoulder injury had delayed his training and forced him to consider something else. It had eventually healed, but by then he had lost his edge.

"Hey, why don't you come drink with us?" Brendan

clapped a hand on Jesse's shoulder as they headed into the locker room.

"You know I don't drink." Jesse often felt like the outsider of the team. While half of the six-man team was married, the other half found solace in empty bottles and meaningless relationships. Jesse understood that - their job was such that they never knew if they would come home night after night - but he still couldn't partake.

Brendan opened his locker and pulled out a clean shirt. He peeled off his current one and added deodorant before tugging on the new one. "You don't have to drink. Look, I won't drink either. Just come and hang out with us. You have no one waiting for you at home."

That wasn't entirely true. Jesse had Bugsy, his Boston Terrier, but he understood Brendan's point. Most days, Jesse went home, fed Bugsy, made dinner, and fell asleep watching TV on the couch. It wasn't much of a life. "All right, I'll go, but I'm not drinking."

Brendan's lips pulled back to reveal his perfectly white teeth. He bragged about them, but Jesse knew they were veneers. "That's the spirit. Hurry up and change. We don't want to leave the rest of the team waiting."

"Is everyone coming?" Jesse pulled out his shower necessities. Brendan might feel comfortable going out with just a new application of deodorant, but Jesse needed to wash more than just dirt and sweat off. He needed to wash the sound of the bullets and the sight of lifeless bodies from his mind.

"Yeah, Pat's wife is pregnant again and demanding some crazy food concoctions. Pat agreed to pick them up if she let him have an hour. Cam and Jared's wives are having a girls' night, so the whole gang can be together. It will be nice to hang out when we aren't worried about being shot at."

"Fine. Give me ten minutes. Unlike you, I like to clean up before I go out."

Brendan smirked. "I've never had any complaints. Besides, do you know how long it takes me to get my hair like this?"

Jesse shook his head as he walked into the shower, but he knew it was true. Brendan had rugged good looks and muscles to match. He rarely had a hard time finding a woman. Jesse on the other hand hadn't dated anyone in the last few months. It wasn't that he hadn't been looking, but he was quieter than his teammates. And he wasn't looking for right now. He was looking for forever. He just hadn't found it yet.

Click here to continue reading The Billionaire's Impromptu Bet.

THE STORY DOESN'T END!

You've met a few people and fallen in love....

I bet you're wondering how you can meet everyone else.

Star Lake Series:

Sealed with a Kiss: Meet the quirky cast of Star Lake and find out if Max and Layla will ever find love.

When Love Returns: Return to Star Lake to hear Presley's story and find out if she gets the second chance with her first love.

Once Upon a Star: Continue the journey when aspiring actress Audrey returns home with a baby. Will Blake finally get the nerve to share his feelings with her?

Love Conquers All: Meet Lanie Perkins Hall who never imagined being divorced at thirty or falling for an old friend, but will his secrets keep them apart?

The Star Lake Collection: Get the latter three stories in one place. Series will include book 1 when it releases around November 2020.

The Heartbeats Series:

Where It All Began: Sandra Baker finds forgiveness and healing even after making a horrible choice.

The Power of Prayer: Will Callie Green find true love or be defined by her mistake?

When Hearts Collide: When Amanda Adams goes to college, she finds a world she was not ready for. But will she also find true love?

A Past Forgiven: Jess Peterson has lived a life of abuse and lost her self worth, but when she finds herself pregnant, will she find new hope?

The Heartbeats Collection: Grab all four Heartbeats novels in one collection

Sweet Billionaires Series:

The Billionaire's Impromptu Bet: Can a spoiled rich girl change when a bet turns to love?

The Billionaire's Secret: Can a playboy settle down when he finds out he has a daughter who needs him?

A Brush with a Billionaire: What happens when a stuck up actor lands in a small town and needs help from a female mechanic?

The Billionaire's Christmas Miracle: A twist on a Cinderella story when a billionaire meets a woman who doesn't belong at the ball.

The Billionaire's Cowboy Groom: Will one night six years ago keep Carrie from finding true love?

The Cowboy Billionaire: Coming Soon!

The Billionaire's Bliss: This collection contains The Billionaire's Secret, The Billionaire's Christmas Miracle, and The Billionaire's Cowboy Groom

The Lawkeeper Series:

Lawfully Matched: When the man she agreed to marry turns out to have a dark past, will Kate have to return home or will she find love with her rescuer in this historical fiction?

Lawfully Justified: Can a bounty hunter and a widow find love together in this historical fiction?

The Scarlet Wedding: William and Emma are planning their wedding, but an outbreak and a return from his past force them to change their plans. Is a happily ever after still in their future in this historical fiction?

Lawfully Redeemed: What happens when a K9 cop falls for the brother of her suspect? Contemporary romance.

The Lawkeeper Collection: Get all four books in one collection

The Are You Listening Series:

The Still Small Voice: Will Jordan listen to God's prompting in this speculative fiction?

A Spark in the Darkness Will Jordan be able to help Raven before the rapture occurs?

Blushing Brides Series:

The Cowboy's Reality Bride: He's agreed to be the bachelor on a reality dating show, but what happens when he falls for a woman who's not one of the contestants?

The Reality Bride's Baby: Laney wants nothing more than a baby, but when she starts feeling dizzy is it pregnancy or something more serious?

The Producer's Unlikely Bride: What happens when a producer and an author agree to a fake relationship?

Ava's Blessing in Disguise: Five years after marriage, Ava faces a mysterious illness that threatens to ruin her career. Will she find out what it is?

The Soldier's Steadfast Bride: coming soon

The Men of Fire Beach

Fire Games: Cassidy returns home from Who Wants to Marry a Cowboy to find obsessive letters from a fan. The cop assigned to help her wants to get back to his case, but what she sees at a fire may just be the key he's looking for.

Lost Memories and New Beginnings: A doctor, a patient with no memory, the men out to get her. Can he keep her safe when he doesn't know who he's looking for?

When Questions Abound: A Companion story to

Lost Memories. Told from Detective Graves' point of view.

Never Forget the Past: Fireman Bubba must confront his past in order to clear his name and save lives.

Love on the Run: Graham is forced into lockdown with one of his employees. Will he be able to save her from her ex and will she steal his heart?

Secrets and Suspense: Cara Hunter is hiding something about her military past. When she's suspected of murder, will she be able to convince Cole she's the victim?

The Men of Fire Beach Collection: Books 1-3

Texas Tornadoes

Defending My Heart: Forced to confront his past, Emmitt finds news that will change his life.

Run With My Heart: Sentenced to community service, Tucker finds himself falling for the manager.

Love on the Line: Blaine has hired Kenzi to redo his cabin, but what happens when she finds his darkest secret?

Touchdown on Love: When Mason's injury throws him together with ex-girlfriend, will sparks fly again?

Second Chance Reception: Jefferson is hiding something. When he falls for the team cook, will he let her in?

Small Town Short Stories

Small Town Dreams

Small Town Second Chances

Small Town Rivals

Small Town Life

Life in a Small Town: All four stories in one collection

Stand Alones:

Love Renewed: This books is part of the multi author second chance series. When fate reunites high school sweethearts separated by life's choices, can they find a second chance at love at a snowy lodge amid a little mystery?

Her children's early reader chapter book series:

The Wishing Stone #1: Dangerous Dinosaur

The Wishing Stone #2: Dragon Dilemma

The Wishing Stone #3: Mesmerizing Mermaids

The Wishing Stone #4: Pyramid Puzzle

The Wishing Stone: Mary's Miracle

The Wishing Stone Collection

To see a list of all her books

authorloranahoopes.com

loranahoopes@gmail.com

ABOUT THE AUTHOR

Lorana Hoopes is an inspirational author originally from Texas but now living in the PNW with her husband and three children. When not writing, she can be seen kick-boxing at the gym, singing, or acting on stage. One day, she hopes to retire from teaching and write full time.

www.ingramcontent.com/pod-product-compliance
Lightning Source LLC
Chambersburg PA
CBHW030918020726
47498CB00001B/21